THE WATCHMAN

THE WATCHMAN

by

Chris Ryan

Century · London

Published by Century in 2001

1 3 5 7 9 10 8 6 4 2

First published in the United Kingdom in 2001 by Century
The Random House Group Limited
20 Vauxhall Bridge Road, London SW1V 2SA

Random House Australia (Pty) Limited
20 Alfred Street, Milsons Point, Sydney
New South Wales 2061, Australia

Random House New Zealand Limited
18 Poland Road, Glenfield
Auckland 10, New Zealand

Random House South Africa (Pty) Limited
Endulini, 11a Jubilee Road, Parktown 2193, South Africa

The Random House Group Limited Reg. No. 954009
www.randomhouse.co.uk

A CIP catalogue record for this book
is available from the British Library

Papers used by Random House UK Limited are natural, recyclable products made
from wood grown in sustainable forests. The manufacturing processes conform to the
environmental regulations of the country of origin

ISBN 0 7126 84166 – Hardback
ISBN 0 7126 79529 – Paperback

Typeset by SX Composing DTP, Rayleigh, Essex
Printed in Great Britain by
Clays Limited, St Ives plc

Elizabeth
(Here's to a dance so many years ago)

He kitenga kanohi,
He hokinga whakaaro.
[To see a face is to stir the memory.]

ACKNOWLEDGEMENTS

To my agent Barbara Levy, editor Mark Booth,
assistant editor Hannah Black and the rest of the team at Century.

PROLOGUE

Northern Ireland

There was a moment when Ray Bledsoe might have escaped with his life. If he had trusted his instincts at that moment – if he had reached for the Walther PPK and emptied the magazine through the side windows of the black taxi as it pulled into the parking bay alongside him – he might just have made it. He'd been an undercover soldier for three and a half years now, quite long enough to know bad trouble when he saw it, and a glance at the skinheads in the taxi had told him that this was the worst trouble of all. As he looked away he could feel their eyes lock on to him in icy, murderous anticipation.

But he had done nothing. The voice that whispered danger was drowned out by the voice screaming Yellow Card. If he opened fire on these men pre-emptively and without delivering the warnings specified on the Yellow Card he could find himself pensionless, dishonourably discharged and on trial for murder. The Rules of Engagement were bollocks, of course, and dangerous bollocks at that, but seventeen years in the Royal Military Police and a couple of well-publicised trials of British servicemen had instilled in Ray Bledsoe a deep-seated anxiety concerning the procedures of contact.

And so he had done nothing. Instead of reducing the taxi's interior to a horror show of shattered glass, jetting blood and brain-sprayed upholstery he had sat tight and reached for the packet of Embassy and the lighter on the passenger seat. Then, lighting up, he had wound down his window an inch or two

1

and allowed the cold February air to draw out the smoke. Played it innocent. You don't gun down carloads of total strangers for no reason, Ray Bledsoe told himself, whatever your instincts. Whatever your misgivings.

But as the sharp air lanced at his face and the Embassy smoke hit his lungs he knew that emptying his Walther into the taxi was exactly what he should have done and that the moment in which he might have acted had passed. He sensed the purposeful exit of bodies from the taxi, saw his side window implode in a terrifying shower of sledgehammered glass, felt a gun barrel jammed cold to his head, smelt vinegared breath and knew himself as good as dead.

'Out, soldier.' The voice low, a Fermanagh accent, smooth as the cocking of a heavy automatic. 'And don't even think about . . .'

Talk, Bledsoe ordered himself, conscious that fear was freezing him, locking down his thought processes. *Blag. Use your bloody gob.* He turned to the glassless window but didn't know what words he used. Might have shouted, might have whispered. Couldn't hear himself.

'I said *out*, yer focker. *Now!*'

The door opening, the honeycombed sheet of safety glass sagging inwards, a blur of shaved heads and tattooed arms, and the gulls screaming and wheeling above them. For all the chance of Bledsoe's reaching the Walther PPK at that moment it might as well have been back in the armoury at Lisburn.

Think. Think SOPs. Think yourself past the fear. Think.

And then, as he indecisively half rose, came the smashing blow to the forehead – a 9mm Browning butt, full magazine – and the blood in his eyes and the cold air and the arms dragging him and what must have been the carpeted floor of the taxi's boot rising to meet his face. He never saw the weapon's second chopping descent.

After an hour he began to come to. He did not immediately understand that he was in a moving car, and did not at once connect the pain at the front and back of his head with a dimly remembered sequence of events involving a PIRA snatch squad.

2

Then he did remember and prayed hard for unconsciousness to return, and when it wouldn't return he lay there for the best part – or the worst part – of another hour. His hands were cuffed, he discovered, and he had been stripped naked. There was a smell of vomit, rubberised carpet and lubricating oil.

Please God, he thought, *don't let them take me over the border and out of the Crown jurisdiction. If they get me past the roadblocks and the border posts I'm a dead man.*

At the time of his kidnap Ray Bledsoe had been preparing to drop off payment for a tout named Proinsas Deavey in a car park. It was a standard dead-letter drop – the routine being that Bledsoe stuffed £200 in used notes in the Embassy packet and dropped it into the left-hand of the two bins by the parking bays, and Deavey swung by a short time later with a soft-drink can to dispose of, surreptitiously pocketed the Embassy packet and made himself scarce. It wasn't an arrangement that either party actively enjoyed, but it had worked well enough up to now.

Deavey was an associate of known Republican players, but a self-destructive mixture of greed and stupidity had put him in the pay of the British security services. Things had started going wrong for Deavey when he set up a small-scale business selling pills and blow in Central Belfast's 'Holy Lands'. Named after its principal arteries – Damascus Street, Jerusalem Street and Canterbury Street – the Holy Lands was the bedsitter enclave serving Queen's University, and students from both sides of the political divide washed their socks, heated their beans and drank their beer there. It was Deavey's bad fortune to have approached a group of ultra-nationalist eighteen-year-olds, who had shopped him the moment he left the bar. Later that evening he had been given a severe beating behind a Falls Road betting office. The punishment squad had identified themselves as members of Direct Action Against Drugs, a known cover organisation for the IRA.

Resentful, half-crippled and robbed of a useful source of income, Deavey had been a comparatively easy touch for the

FRU, or Forces Research Unit. The FRU was a small and highly secretive unit set up by the British army for the purpose of cultivating and running touts. It was staffed by soldiers who didn't look like soldiers. Most of them were middle-aged men like Bledsoe – long-serving ex-NCOs with pub bellies, thinning hair and anonymous faces.

Proinsas Deavey was one of half a dozen small-time players that Bledsoe and his colleagues were handling. The former dope dealer had never made contact with any really important players, but the scraps he provided – meeting places, unfaithful husbands, who drank with whom – all assisted in the piecing together of the Intelligence jigsaw. Deavey had sold his Republican soul to Ray Bledsoe in a fish and chip shop outside Carrickfergus for a down payment of £175.

Touts were the bane of the PIRA's existence and their work with touts made FRU members highly desirable to terrorist snatch squads. When it came to his interrogation, Bledsoe knew, the first thing they would demand would be the identity of the touts he was running. The second would be the identity of the special forces personnel he was in contact with – the other FRU members, the Det (or Detachment) soldiers who made up the undercover surveillance teams, the Box (or MI5) teams and, of course, the SAS. Then they would want the radio codes and the rest of the intelligence baggage that he carried in his head.

The PIRA, Bledsoe thought, had almost certainly had him marked down as an FRU member for months. Lifting him now was partly expediency – they badly needed to know the answers he could give them – and partly the desire to raise two fingers to the British government. The larger symbol of that contempt had been the bombing, two days earlier, of South Quay in the Docklands area of London. Like everyone else at the barracks, Bledsoe had seen the pictures on TV, had stared open-mouthed at the devastated City landscape, at shattered office blocks, at streets inches deep in a glittering slush of broken glass. The lorry bomb had killed two people, injured many more and caused millions of pounds' worth of damage. A statement had been issued by the IRA an hour before the explosion revoking the official ceasefire that had lasted for seventeen months and nine days.

It hadn't felt like a ceasefire to Ray Bledsoe. More like business as usual and some of his colleagues said a fucking sight worse. But the bomb signalled a change. The bomb meant that the gloves were off publicly as well as privately. The FRU and the other special forces had been warned to exercise extra caution, to double-check sources, to watch their backs.

But there was only so much, finally, that you could do. Bledsoe's reaction to the warnings had been to request back-up for his drop-off. At his previous meeting with Deavey, Bledsoe had found the tout so jumpy that he had begun to wonder if the little bastard was playing a double game. It wasn't impossible that he'd decided despite everything that he was safer in PIRA's pockets than the army's and had bought his life by promising them an FRU agent on a plate. Or perhaps, even more extremely, Deavey had been PIRA's man all along and had been feeding them false information from the start.

Bledsoe had considered both scenarios highly unlikely – the tout seemed just too solid between the ears to run a sophisticated intelligence scam – but just in case of any funny business he had requested that a second FRU member attend the drop-off in a separate car. Connor Wheen, Bledsoe knew, had parked his Mondeo three hundred yards away near the car park entrance and with any luck he would have witnessed the snatch.

Assuming that he had done so, Wheen would have put out an alert. Perhaps even now there was an SAS pursuit vehicle a mile behind them, showing no lights.

As he bumped and rolled on the floor of the taxi, however, Bledsoe found it difficult to think coherently. He had never thought of himself as a courageous man. If the car he was in broke through the cordon and escaped over the border there would be . . . what? The interrogation, the stomping kicks to the teeth and balls, the burning cigarettes to the eyeballs and . . . *Stop it*, he ordered himself. *Get a fucking grip. You're a soldier. Act like one. And, more importantly, think like one.*

Think of the details. Think of the SAS team bomb-bursting out of

5

the camp at Lisburn within seconds of the alert, all with kit and weapons packed for action. Think of them hammering out on to the roads in their big Beamers and Quattros.

The ground grew steadily rougher, severely testing the big vehicle's suspension, and Bledsoe prayed for the grinding, rubber-flapping lurch that would signal that the car had punctured itself on an army spike chain. But there was no such lurch and then suddenly there was no movement at all. From far away came the heavy, squealing scrape of a sliding door. The car rumbled forward for a further few seconds and the sliding door rasped once more. A moment's stillness, then the boot sprang open to reveal the hard white glare of strip lights and Bledsoe was hauled, blinking, on to a flattened earth floor. The floor was cold and damp beneath his bare feet, the cuffs cut into his wrists and he could feel his hair stiff with blood. There were voices all around him.

Things took shape before his dark-accustomed eyes. He was in a large, iron-sided rectangular barn, surrounded by expectant-looking men in dark-blue boiler suits. Vapour rose from their mouths, and the excited, contemptuous sound of their voices. In the corner to his left, mockingly normal, stood a John Deere tractor and an ordered pile of plastic fertiliser sacks. At the centre of the wall was a workshop area with pulleys and chains, and at the far end a stud-partitioned office. Ahead of him, parked along the right-hand wall, was an unloaded trailer.

He half-turned, still blinking. The entrance through which the car had come was barred by a pair of tall corrugated-iron doors hung from greased rails, in front of which waited two boiler-suited guards. One was fingering an automatic handgun, the other was pissing a steaming puddle on to the ground. Both were smirking at him with hate-filled, delinquent eyes.

Bledsoe stood there for a moment, swaying. Two thoughts hit him immediately. Where were the Regiment lads going to hit the place from? This was bad, but the other realisation was worse, so much worse that his chest began heaving

6

involuntarily and he thought for a moment that he was going to pass out.

They were going to kill him and probably to blood some of the younger foot soldiers in the process. They were going to make it messy, to see who could do the business without flinching and who couldn't.

The nearest man, a burly red-haired figure, sniggered.

Fuck you, Bledsoe thought, shaking badly now but attempting to rally himself. *PIRA cunt. When the Regiment lads get here – and get here they will, blowing the doors off if they have to – I hope they blow your fucking head from your shoulders.*

For a moment things seemed to coalesce in the icy air. Bledsoe was in pain, concussed and very frightened indeed, but he knew what he was going to do. *Breathe*, he told himself. *Clear your head. Ignore the pain. Think.*

And then a dark-blue figure came from one side, slammed a fist into Bledsoe's stomach and brought his knee up hard into the FRU agent's nose, splintering the bone. Blinded by the flash of his breaking nose, gagging for air, Bledsoe went down. *They're going to hit me again*, he thought absently.

He was right. A steel toecap to the balls that froze his mouth into a silent scream followed by a crunching boot to the lower ribs. At least two of the ribs fractured now. His grasp on consciousness wavering, Bledsoe closed his eyes.

Hands took him under the arm, dragged him across to the trailer, slammed him against the iron tailgate and cuffed him to it, arms spread. His legs gave way for a moment and they let him hang there, drooling and half-suffocated, blood pouring down his face from his nose.

Finally he found his feet. Dragged icy farmyard air through his mouth. Opened his eyes a crack. Counted eight of them. Nine – there was one he hadn't seen before, a pale-faced figure with depthless eyes who could have been any age between twenty-five and forty, and unlike the rest was not smiling.

'Name?' The speaker was the one who'd kicked him, a thin, broken-nosed guy.

Bledsoe dragged his head up. Spat blood. Cleared his throat.

'I don't know who the hell you think I am,' he began blearily, 'but . . .'

'I'll tell ye who ye are,' the thin man said. 'Ye're Sergeant Raymond Bledsoe, formerly of the Royal Military Police, presently seconded to the so-called Forces Research Unit. There's not a deal we don't know about ye, cuntie, ye can thank yer Regimental magazine for that, sae don't go gi'in us any crap.'

Silence. The older man from the car regarded him levelly.

'Ye know what we want,' the older man said, zipping himself into a pair of overalls with fastidious and terrifying care. 'Radio codes, SAS names, tout names – everything. We can start with yer man Deavey if you like, though as ye've probably guessed by now he's not quite the t'ick Paddy you took him for.'

Bledsoe said nothing. Stared up at the strip light, tried to distance himself from the pain of his nose and ribs.

The other man smiled. 'Ye see, unlike yer occupying army, we'll always be here. Deavey had the wit to realise that.'

Bledsoe struggled to keep his expression neutral, not to rise to the bait. Here we go, he thought. As rehearsed. 'I'll talk,' he said. 'But not to you. I'll talk to Adams or McGuinness or any of the executive-level officers of Sinn Fein and I'll give them everything they want to know. Or Padraig Byrne.'

Byrne, ostensibly a Sinn Fein councillor, was known to the security services as the chief of the PIRA's Belfast Brigade. There was purpose and calculation in Bledsoe's insistence on talking face to face with senior players: they were watched round the clock and in the event of a British agent being lifted, as Bledsoe had been lifted, this surveillance would be doubled. His trust in Connor Wheen was Bledsoe's only hope of survival. One or other would come through for him. The alternative was quite literally unthinkable.

'Ye'll talk to Byrne?'

'I will.'

His interrogator looked round the room. Everyone smiled.

'Yer word on that, then, ye'll talk to Byrne?'

Bledsoe hesitated, sensing a trap. Was it really going to be this easy?

8

The interrogator took a step closer. 'Well?'

He nodded. 'I'll talk to Byrne. No one junior to him.'

The other man nodded and glanced round the assembled faces. The smiles were wider now, displaying contempt, amusement and bad dentistry in equal measure. The man from the car shook his head, pulled a cellophane pouch of Drum tobacco from his trouser pocket and began to roll a cigarette. As he licked the paper the thin, broken-nosed man turned away, took a 9mm Browning automatic from the pocket of his boiler suit, considered it for a moment, then swung the butt back-handed and with full force into Bledsoe's broken ribs.

The pain was indescribable, an explosion of liquid fire in his chest that seemed, once again, to drain the FRU man of all coherent thought. He fell forward, hanging from the tailgate by his cuffed wrists, and for a moment saw himself as the young Provos surrounding him saw him – a pallid, bloody-faced, flabby-arsed forty-fags-a-day chancer, close to his pension and closer to tears. As an agent handler Bledsoe's world had become that of his informers – a world of beer and bar-stools and clapped-out cars. He had fitted in well, but at the cost of his health and fitness. 'There's no disguise like a fat gut!' the instructors had told them at Tregaron, and Bledsoe had laughed along with the others.

Now look at him. Pathetic.

Something still beat in his chest, however, even as he hung there wheezing and gagging. Some ghost of the bloody-minded squaddie he'd once been still hung grimly on. *There'll be a fuck of a bang when the lads blow that door. A fuck of a bang. And the killing spree of all time. None of these Provie cunts would live to . . .*

A hand grabbed Bledsoe's hair and pulled his head level. Through a film of pain he saw a short, square figure walking out of the office area, a figure whose reddened and bony features, slicked-back hair and carefully buttoned Aran cardigan he recognised instantly.

'Would ye be knowing this gentleman?' It was the gun-butt man again.

'Yeah,' said Bledsoe, attempting to sneer. 'Val Doonican.'

That earned him another kick in the balls and this time, as a lurching despair became one with the pain, Bledsoe kept his eyes shut.

The man in the Aran cardigan was Padraig Byrne. No Det unit was about to follow the fucker anywhere. He was already here – wherever here was – and he had probably been here for days. When Bledsoe finally reopened his eyes it was to see Byrne pulling on a boiler suit.

'Pleased to see me, Sergeant Bledsoe? You will be, that I promise.' The voice was light and cultured, and somehow horribly at odds with the raw-boned features. The considered view in Lisburn barracks, Bledsoe remembered, was that Padraig Byrne took it up the arse.

'You see, Sergeant, we've got something for you.'

A book hit the ground with a thump next to the FRU man's feet. *What the fuck?*

'Raymond John Bledsoe,' Byrne continued in his soft wheedling brogue, 'this is your Death!'

There was snigger of sycophantic laughter from the young Provo foot soldiers. Opening his eyes a fraction, Bledsoe saw that the book was a Yellow Pages directory for the Newry and Mourne area. *He hadn't crossed the border, then. There was still hope.*

Please God, he thought, *let Wheen have hooked a follow car on to that taxi. Let there be a Regiment team out there right now, taking out the sentries.*

He hung on desperately to that hope. He suspected that the interrogation was about to start and he didn't know if he had any courage left to bullshit them with. It was going to be very bad – he was certain of that from the number of young guys they'd assembled, and from the hunger and expectancy on their faces.

And then, with a blast of cold air, the sliding doors opened again and a mud-spattered white van drove into the barn, shuddered for a moment in a haze of exhaust and was still. The barn doors were quickly dragged shut, then a terrible high-pitched screaming issued from inside the van. The screaming seemed to go on and on, and ended in a sound that was halfway between a retch and a whimper.

'Do you recognise that voice, Bledsoe?' asked Byrne, continuing his Eamonn Andrews impersonation. 'Yes, all the way from Lisburn barracks, Belfast, it's your old friend . . .'

A second naked and plasticuffed figure was dragged from the back of the van by two more boiler-suited Provo foot soldiers. He had been severely beaten around the head and upper body, dirt and vomit smeared his chest and legs, and his face was a shapeless blood-smeared mask. In the middle of the room the foot soldiers kicked the new arrival's feet from under him and he fell heavily to the ground.

Byrne looked on, enjoying the moment. 'Good evening,' he addressed the man on the ground. 'And thank you for joining us on this special occasion.'

'Fuck you!' said the fallen man. At least that's what Bledsoe guessed that he was trying to say, but something horrible had happened to his mouth and teeth, and all that came out was a bubbling, gutteral rasp.

Bledsoe stared. Tried to beat back the worst of the fear.

With an immense effort the battered figure squinted around him, found Bledsoe, and winked one blackened and swollen eyelid. As he did so his face took momentary shape and with a sullen jolt of recognition all hope died in Ray Bledsoe.

'That's right,' crowed Byrne exultantly, resuming. 'It's your old mate Connor Wheen!'

I'm dead, Bledsoe thought dully. *We're both dead.*

Byrne watched them, delighted with his coup. A chair was brought from the office and the two men hauled Wheen into it, forcing his cuffed hands behind the backrest.

'I know what you're wondering,' said Byrne to Bledsoe with vast good humour. 'You're wondering if you're still north of the border, so that your SAS pals can drop in on us. Well, you know something . . .' Byrne shook his head at the sheer hilariousness of the situation. '*You're not!*'

Bledsoe felt his sanity slipping away. All that remained now was terror, pain and death. His unhinged gaze found the pale-faced man, who stared back at him with ageless, unsmiling intensity. You are in hell, that gaze told him. Welcome.

Byrne turned to the pale-faced man. 'Joseph, as we agreed earlier, I'd like it to be you that does the killing.' His tone was casual, conversational.

'Please,' whispered Bledsoe. 'I'll tell you everything.' His lips were papery and his voice was a submissive monotone. 'You can have the Det list, the SAS list, the tout list, the codes . . .'

Padraig Byrne frowned and looked at him intently for a moment or two as if wrestling with some complex moral or intellectual issue. Then he smiled again and turned back to the pale-faced man he called Joseph.

ONE

Sierra Leone

After an hour's march, Captain Alex Temple held up his hand and the patrol came to a cautious halt. Above them the waning moon was obscured by lurid bruise-coloured rain clouds. In the forest to either side of them insects drilled and screamed. It was fifteen minutes after midnight and all six men were soaked to the skin. They were sweating too, as their dark-accustomed eyes scanned the clearing.

Alex had been right. Above the distant booming of thunder, just audible, was a faint staccato crackle. Gunfire, surely. To his side, all but invisible in the dank shadows, Don Hammond nodded in agreement, showed two fingers – two clicks ahead – and pointed up the trail. *Yes*, thought Alex with fierce joy. *Yes! This is what I joined the Regiment for. This is what I'll do for as long as they'll let me.*

He grinned at the wiry sergeant and glanced round at the four other members of Zulu Three Six patrol as they melted into the dank foliage. Immediately behind him was a sharp-faced trooper named Ricky Sutton, the patrol signaller. At twenty-three, Sutton was the youngest and least experienced member of the team. Covering Sutton's back as he worked was Stan Clayton, a long-serving and famously mouthy cockney corporal, and on the other side of the clearing, shadowy in the dimness, crouched Lance Wilford and Jimmy 'Dog' Kenilworth, a corporal and a lance-corporal respectively. Like Alex, they were dressed in sodden jungle kit and webbing, and carrying M16 203 rifles and a sheathed *parang*. Beneath the frayed rims of their bush-hats their faces were blackened with cam-stick. All had compasses attached to their wrists and rifles.

13

At Don Hammond's sign, the patrol members quietly lowered their heavy Bergan rucksacks and began to cache them. Mosquitoes whined around them, settling greedily on their hands and faces. A couple of the men had leeches visible at their necks and wrists, and Alex guessed that they all had at least half a dozen sucking away beneath their wet shirts and combat trousers.

Crouching in the dank foliage, Hammond unfurled the aerial of the sat-com radio, and reported the patrol's position and the direction of the small-arms fire to the SAS base in Freetown. When Hammond had completed the report Alex resumed the lead scout position. Signing for the rest of the patrol to follow, he set off towards the distant gunfire.

This was it, he thought – *this had to be it* – and breathed a silent prayer of thanks to the gods of war. He was thirty-five years old and a commissioned officer, and both facts militated against him. SAS officers, or 'Ruperts' as they were known, were usually directed into planning roles, while the 'chopping' was done by the troopers and NCOs. As a Rupert, Alex was lucky to be here at all. Somehow, against all the odds, it seemed that he had been granted one last adventure.

Zulu Three Six patrol was searching for a missing ITN news crew.

The journalists – reporter Sally Roberts, cameraman Ben Mills and sound recordist Gary Burge – had been missing for more than thirty-six hours now. They had last been seen in the town of Masiaka, thirty-five miles inland from the capital, Freetown. Masiaka was a strategically important staging post, and its mildewed and flyblown bungalows had been much fought over in the dirty war between the Sierra Leone army and the Revolutionary United Front. At present it was in the hands of pro-government forces and so considered more or less safe for Western media teams.

According to the Agence France Presse people who'd been showing them around, Sally Roberts and her team had arrived in Masiaka intending to interview members of a notoriously volatile pro-government militia known as the West Side Boys. The ITN team had hoped to find the militia's commanders at the mildewed and bullet-pocked bungalow that served as their HQ, but on arriving there had discovered that the occupants had decamped eastwards in pursuit of an RUF raiding party.

Undeterred, and against the advice of the other Western press agencies, the ITN team had decided to follow the West Side Boys into the RUF-held badlands and at dawn the next day had set off on the Kissuna Road in a hired car. No one in Masiaka knew what had happened to Roberts, Mills and Burge after that. No one had seen them and no one had heard from them, despite the fact that all three were carrying sat-phones.

From evidence later provided by militia members it seemed that the West Side Boys had followed the raiding party far into RUF territory and that a vicious but inconclusive firefight had taken place near Kissuna, after which the militia had withdrawn back towards Masiaka. During the battle, as usual, most of the combatants had been blind drunk; the RUF on palm wine, the West Side Boys on the plastic bags of raw gin that they habitually carried. A dozen or so fighters, several of them children, had been killed on both sides.

When the ITN team neither returned that night, nor contacted anyone in Masiaka, people began to wonder. At noon the following day, fearing the worst, a BBC news crew filmed an interview with a West Side Boys militia leader called 'Colonel Self-Loading'. Within two hours of the interview, and following a swift triangular exchange of secure calls between Freetown, Whitehall and Hereford, an unedited video copy of the film was running at SAS HQ, Freetown. The HQ was a former security complex on the edge of Lungi airport – a scruffily anonymous cluster of tents, low Nissen-style huts and radio masts. Watching the video clip were Major David Ross, OC of the forty-strong detachment from 'D' Squadron, and Captain Alex Temple of the Regiment's Revolutionary Warfare Wing.

The twenty-minute clip made for grim viewing. Colonel Self-Loading's eyes were red with fatigue, ganja and trail dust but he was certain of his facts: no Western correspondent had spoken to any member of the West Side Boys since their departure from Masiaka two days earlier. And certainly no Western woman.

If the team had been anywhere near the Kissuna battle zone, the colonel told the BBC interviewer, then they had probably been lifted by the RUF. Even now, he said, the woman was probably being asked if she wanted 'long sleeves' or 'short sleeves' – amputation above or below the elbow. Hacking off arms was the RUF's calling-card. Recently, they had extended the practice to genitals. Once mutilated, victims were made to sit in bowls of caustic soda.

'And maybe they eat them, you know.' The young colonel shrugged, reaching under his Tupac Shakur T-shirt to scratch his belly. 'Food is short.'

Colonel Self-Loading was in a position to know about the RUF's dietary habits. A year earlier the West Side Boys had sided with the rebels, sweeping down to occupy Freetown on a manic tide of blood and slaughter, and to the thumping beat of the RUF anthem 'No Living Thing'. The conversion of the West Side Boys to the government's way of seeing things – a conversion which was rewarded by British mercenaries with a thirty-five-ton sanctions-busting consignment of Bulgarian weaponry – was comparatively recent. If Colonel Self-Loading said that the RUF ate human flesh, then they did.

'You see, this is a bad war,' he declared to the camera with all the authority of his nineteen years. 'A very bad war.'

Excusing himself, he explained to the interviewer that he was off to find a 'popsicle' – an iced lolly made of neat gin – and a woman.

'Doesn't look good,' said Alex levelly, when the footage came to a close.

'Nor it does,' said David Ross. 'And I've got a feeling it might be coming our way.'

Alex nodded. 'I'll put my lads on standby.'

'Do that,' agreed Ross.

The Revolutionary Warfare Wing, from which Alex's

16

twelve-strong team had been drawn, is the most secretive element of the SAS and the unit's existence has never been officially admitted. Its purpose is the execution of officially deniable tasks and contracts, including the covert training of overseas 'friendlies'. These last have included the Mujahedin of Afghanistan and the Cambodian Khmer Rouge.

On this occasion, rather less controversially, Alex Temple's team were in Freetown as part of a training package for the Sierra Leone army. They found it uninspiring work and between exercises were glad to return to the temporary base they shared with the forty men of 'D' Squadron.

At twenty minutes after 5 p.m. Alex was summoned to the OC's hut for the second time that afternoon. In a few succinct sentences David Ross put him in the picture concerning the kidnap of the ITN team. The squadron would be mounting a search operation that night, Ross informed Alex, and the RWW team would remain on standby at the base to help with the planning of a rescue.

Alex heard Ross out and proposed an alternative plan. The RWW team would mount the search, he suggested, while 'D' Squadron would stand by to effect the rescue.

Ross politely but firmly turned Alex's plan down. The RWW team were separate from his command, their presence in Sierra Leone was being paid for by that country's government and there would be an awkward convergence of responsibilities.

Alex countered that for the purposes of the operation he would be happy to place himself and his men under the direct command of Ross. If he led the search team 'D' Squadron could be kept intact for the rescue. 'If we find them,' he pleaded with the OC, 'it'll be a "D" Squadron success. If we don't, it'll be an RWW fuck-up.' What Alex didn't need to add was that he had several years' more experience than Ross and was undoubtedly the best man to lead the search.

Ross considered Alex's suggestion. The two men liked and respected each other, and the lean-faced ex–Signals officer was aware that this would probably be Alex's last chance of leading his men into hostile territory. In the end, he gave Alex the nod. Intelligence reports from RUF informers suggested that the hostages had been taken to one of two possible camps. Alex was to divide his men into two six-man patrols and prepare for insertion under cover of darkness.

As he listened to the briefing an hour later and pored over the map table with his men, Alex felt the first fluttering crawl of anticipation. This, he knew from experience, would build to the taut excitement which always preceded action. When the time came, the excitement would give way to an icy, analytical calm. Then, for better or worse, he would do his job.

And on this one, he reckoned, it might well be for worse. Looking at the aerial reconnaissance photographs – at the drab, swampy vastness of the jungle, the tiny gnat-bite settlements and the sullen clay-coloured waterways – it seemed almost unimaginable that they would locate the ITN team. How the hell could they find three people in all of that? And even if one of the patrols did locate the journalists, would they still be alive? Would there be time to scope the place out, accurately assess the enemy's strength and firepower, insert a rescue team and lift the hostages from under the noses of the notably well-armed RUF?

'We have to think positive, gentlemen,' said Ross briskly, as if reading his thoughts. 'The intelligence people have established a link with RUF commanders in the interior. We're assured that if they want to negotiate, the infrastructure exists. Having said that, of course, we can't count on any such thing. We've got to find the hostages and prepare a hard extraction.' He swept his hand over the maps. 'Now, it looks like a huge search area, but the probability is that if our hostages are still in one piece they're being held at one of a pair of jungle camps in the Kissuna sector. These are located as follows' – he overlaid the assembly of aerial photographs with a clear sheet marked up in chinagraph pencil – 'and I've coded them Arsenal and Chelsea. Both, as you can see, are on the Rokel river, and neither is more than ten clicks from our LZ here on the ridge line, which we will call Millwall.'

18

Carefully, Alex scanned the aerial photgraphs. The camps were just about visible if you knew exactly what you were looking for. They were surrounded by a hell of a lot of jungle, though.

'Search teams will be dropped off at Millwall at 2330 hours tonight,' Ross continued. 'By the time they reach their recce points, judging by past experience, the bulk of the RUF soldiery will be off their heads on dope and palm wine, and security around the camps will be piss-poor. We could approach earlier but the risk of the patrols being discovered would be much greater, with concomitant increase of risk to the hostages.' He steepled his fingers and regarded them levelly. 'As it is you're going to have to go bloody carefully, and remember that just because these buggers are part-time cannibals who like dressing up in weird costumes and chopping toddlers' arms off with machetes, it doesn't mean they aren't at home with sophisticated weaponry. They've got RPGs and all sorts in those camps, thanks to their income from those bloody diamond mines they control, and I don't – repeat *don't* – want to lose any men. You will not, under any circumstances, risk a contact, is that understood?'

Everyone nodded. Alex glanced at the other patrol members. He was the only officer.

'From Millwall,' Ross continued, 'patrols will tab in to their respective targets. Whether or not there's any sign of any hostages, we're going to need full reports concerning numbers, weaponry, fields of fire, disposition of buildings and all the rest of it, OK? By 0230 hours tomorrow, if we haven't located the TV people, I want both patrols back at Millwall for evacuation by Puma. If we have found them I want both patrols to converge on the camp in question and remain eyes-on. Alex, you and one other will then tab back to Millwall and be choppered back to Freetown to brief the Squadron. Any questions so far?'

Along with the others, Alex shook his head.

'The timing of the assault will depend on the intelligence you get back to us and the outcome of any negotiations that take place,' Ross continued. 'It's still perfectly possible that the

RUF can be persuaded to return the hostages – Roberts and Co. are an international press team, after all, and the RUF aren't completely indifferent to world opinion.'

Oh no? thought Alex, who had seen the school-age amputees on the streets of Freetown and Masiaka. *You could have fuckin' fooled me.*

'Assuming the negotiations fail, the "D" Squadron assault team will go in between twenty-four hours and a week from tonight. Again, any questions?'

And again there were none.

At 11 p.m., the two RWW search patrols boarded a Puma. Showing no lights, fitted with low-noise rotor blades and flown by a pilot in night-vision goggles, the helicopter slipped silently inland, overflew Masiaka and swung eastwards into RUF territory. At 1130, precisely on schedule, the twelve soldiers de-bussed, crouching in the rotor wash as the Puma lifted away from the ridge line and turned back towards Freetown.

Thirty minutes after caching the Bergans the patrol halted for a scheduled comms burst from base. As Ricky Sutton looped a plastic-coated aerial wire over a tree branch, a damp, over-bearing heat pressed around them. The sporadic bursts of rifle fire were clearly audible now and over the smell of decom-posing vegetation the air carried a faint drift of woodsmoke.

Were the ITN team being held at the camp ahead of them? As always in the presence of danger, Alex felt tautly, intensely alive.

Checking his watch, he joined Don Hammond and Ricky Sutton who were huddled over the 319 patrol radio, waiting for the burst to decrypt. In silence, the three men stared at the miniature green-lit VDU screen.

Black letters leapt into view. Ricky Sutton wiped away the rain.

'HOSTAGES TO BE EXECUTED 14th 1200. INFORM WHEN LOCATED. SEARCH PATROLS TO SUPPORT D SQN ASSAULT AT 1ST LIGHT. ROSS'

'Fuck me!' breathed Alex, his heart pounding. 'The

fourteenth is today. First light's in about four hours. And we haven't even found them yet.'

He'd wanted an adventure.

He'd got one.

TWO

Assault at first light.

That turned everything – *everything* – on its head. The RUF must have issued some impossible ultimatum – the freeing of all prisoners taken by the Sierra Leone army, for example.

The patrol had moved through the remaining jungle as fast as humanly possible. They were very close to the camp now and Alex recognised the random discharges as being those of British-issued SLRs. The sound was a good sign. Unless the RUF were fighting among themselves it meant that they were in party mood, emptying their 7.62 rounds into the river and the surrounding jungle out of a kind of stoned machismo. And perhaps, Alex thought, in anticipation of the killing of the news crew at midday.

'Left a bit,' murmured Don Hammond behind him.

Alex raised a hand in thanks. As lead scout, he was the only member of the team not responsible for navigation – all his concentration went into watching and listening: for the unexplained movement, the shadow that wasn't a shadow, the tiny suck of a boot in clay, the oily straining of a cocking lever.

Listening was becoming harder. In addition to the rifle fire, there was the faint thump and whisper of music. Straining his ears, Alex recognised one of Sierra Leone's big summer tunes – a favourite of the RUF, the SLA and the militias alike – called 'Titti Shaggah'.

Had they posted sentries, he wondered, stilling the five men behind him with a hand gesture. For two minutes the patrol crouched unmoving in the animal track, but there was no sound that shouldn't have been there. They moved on and the ridge line began its gradual descent towards the Rokel river. Step by silent step, Alex negotiated the gradient. The rain was still holding off, but splashing rivulets streaked the treacherous clay incline. They were five hundred yards away from the camp now and through the dense foliage below them Alex could see the yellowish flickering of electric lights. Surely, he thought, they must at least have some bloke on stag.

They had and Alex almost missed him. All he saw, in fact, was the tiny swing of a cigarette coal at the side of the track twenty yards ahead. Stilling the patrol again and deliberately steadying his breathing as the adrenalin flooded his system, Alex moved silently down the skiddy clay, feeling with his feet for the rocks and tree roots that would noiselessly support his weight. *One squelch*, he thought – *one snapped branch or kicked stone – and we're buggered*.

Ten yards now and he could see in the moonlight that the sentry was leaning against the other side of a tree trunk. A tree trunk whose thickness was approximately that of a man's chest. Once again, the arm swung sideways. The hand held a ganja spliff, not a cigarette.

Quietly, Alex drew a short Mauser stabbing knife from his belt webbing. It took him three agonised heart-thudding minutes to cover the last sodden yards of the descent and then finally he was behind the trunk, his nose and eyes full of drifting ganja smoke but his feet secure on the slippery twisting tree roots. Like a striking snake, as his right hand reached across with the knife, Alex's left hand clapped across the sentry's mouth. At the last moment, though, with a desperate outrush of breath, the SAS officer checked his blade. The face beneath his hands was smooth, the neck slender, the struggling body pitifully small. The sentry was a kid – might even have been a girl – couldn't have been more than ten, and almost immediately went limp with terror in his arms. The spliff fell to the ground and went out with a tiny hiss.

Keeping a hand firmly across his captive's mouth, Alex gestured to Don Hammond to join him. The sergeant quickly gagged the child with a sweat rag, tied the slender wrists and ankles with a length of para cord from his belt kit, and concealed the immobilised figure beneath a dense bush in the darkness to one side of the track.

The patrol proceeded warily with the descent. They encountered no more sentries and, as they neared the lights and the music, the ground began to level out until they found themselves close to the edge of the tree line. In front of them a parapet of knotted roots supported a thick tangle of rotting vegetation, beneath which was a drop of about six feet. Beneath this, either drunk or stoned but unquestionably asleep, lay two RUF soldiers. One was wearing a white nylon wedding dress, the other threadbare tracksuit trousers and a combat smock hung with plastic dolls' heads.

Ricky Sutton, keen as ever, drew his commando knife. 'Shall I do 'em?' he mouthed, but Alex shook his head. If the bodies were found the whole camp would go to a state of alert, jeopardising any potential rescue mission. As Ricky sheathed his blade, Alex scanned the area with his binoculars.

Below them, contained within the dark curving sweep of the Rokel river, lay the camp. Roughly oval-shaped, it occupied an area slightly greater than a football pitch. At the nearer, lower end was a large bonfire on to which, at intervals, silhouetted figures heaped wet branches and tree roots, encouraging a thick column of grey-brown smoke. On the higher ground to the east, lit by strings of low-wattage bulbs, two windowless cinder-block huts stood at right angles to the river. Beyond them was a cluster of mud-walled outhouses. On the far side of the river the jungle rose steeply for a hundred metres or so to the ridge line.

Of the hundred and fifty-odd figures visible in the camp, perhaps a score were dancing and drinking around the bonfire, while at least twice that number were milling around the far end, near the huts. The remainder staggered about, singly and in large drunken groups, at the river's edge. Most carried SLR 7.62 rifles, but there were a few AK 47s and RPGs in evidence too. Several of the men appeared to be so attached to their weapons that they were dancing with them.

The sheer numbers of the RUF made any assault of less than

company strength hazardous. The cinder-block huts would provide cover for anything up to fifty soldiers each and if the hostages were in this camp they were probably situated close to or inside the huts. Bringing fire to bear on the RUF without injuring them would be difficult. The most positive factor, in Alex's view, was the topography of the camp. Surrounded as they were on three sides by the vast grey-green bulk of the river, the RUF were like rats in a bag. If all of the SAS firepower was positioned along a single front in the tree line, the bag could be drawn shut. The difficult part was going to be finding, and then extracting, the hostages.

Another plus point was that despite the recent incursion into the Kissuna area by the West Side Boys militia, no serious attempt had been made to implement any form of camp security. The noise, for a start, was considerable. The crack of random discharges tore the air, as did the answering, echoing smack as these impacted in the surrounding jungle. No wonder no one wants to go out on stag, thought Alex, with all this random shooting you'd take your bloody life in your hands. From beneath the sound system, which continued to belt out 'Titti Shaggah' and other local hits, came the steady thump of a generator.

'If I'd known it was a party,' muttered Stan Clayton, 'I'd 'ave worn my dancin' trousers!'

Alex smiled and beckoned the men around him. 'No sign of our people so far,' he whispered, 'but I want to take a closer look. Those huts up the end look promising for a start. Don, I want you to stay here with three of the guys and count heads and weapons. Stan, I want you to come with me. We're going for a swim.'

The cockney grinned, grasping the plan immediately. Quickly the two men stripped off their webbing, leaving their kit in two neat piles. Then, creeping past the unconscious RUF soldiers, they lowered themselves down the tree roots to ground level.

In front of them, bordered by the river, was the camp. To their right were the black-shadowed margins of the jungle.

25

Ahead of them, and falling away behind them into the jungle, was a rough, mud-churned road. Swiftly the two men turned right, paced off twenty yards into the swampy foliage, turned through ninety degrees, took bearings from their wrist compasses and set off through the darkness on a fast-paced eastbound course parallel to the road. Ten minutes later they exited the jungle. The dark sweep of the river was now at their feet and they were well upstream of the camp.

'We'll 'ave to tuck in tight,' murmured Clayton thoughtfully.

Alex nodded. Close up, the Rokel was a vast and terrifying force of nature. The flash floods that accompanied the early days of the rainy season had torn its winter banks away and the normally placid river was now an angry torrent hundreds of yards wide. If Alex and Stan strayed out of the side eddies they could be hurtled miles downstream or drowned outright. Hard in to the bank, however, the risk of detection was much greater. The whole undertaking was very much more dangerous than it had first appeared, but it represented the SAS team's only chance of locating the hostages.

'Let's find ourselves a raft,' whispered Alex.

Soundlessly, they waded into the warm, soupy water, where a regular procession of tree limbs, bushes and other vegetation uprooted by the floods was washing past them in the current. Within a couple of minutes they had secured the perfect vehicle – a twenty-foot branch hung with decomposing foliage.

'Ready?' asked Alex.

'Sure.' Clayton nodded. 'I can always use a few dozen more leeches round my bollocks!'

Carefully they steered the branch a short distance away from the bank and began the smooth, inexorable drift towards the camp. Only their heads showed above water and behind the festoon of rotting weeds they were effectively invisible to the guards on the riverside. Slowly they rounded the bend past the camp's first outposts. It was shallower here and Alex could feel his feet dragging on the river's muddy bed.

Close up, the scene was very much more threatening than at a distance. On the bank, less than ten yards away, a crowd of drunken soldiery staggered around, clutching rifles, machetes and beakers of palm wine. Even over the muddy tang of the river the SAS men could smell the cloying reek of the home-made spirit. From the speakers the RUF anthem 'No Living Thing' punched out, bouncing from the cliffs opposite with a thudding reverberation. Along the shore the glazed-eyed soldiers screamed the choruses.

His face inches from the corporal's, Alex was conscious of Stan Clayton's attempts to still his breathing, to remain absolutely motionless behind the branch. *If they see us*, thought Alex — *if the branch catches on something and swings around — we're dead. They'll hack us to pieces in seconds. Stan's wife will be a widow, his son will be without a dad and it will all be my fault. My fault for turning an important search mission into a juvenile, hairy-arsed, straight-to-video personal fucking adventure.*

The random shooting continued. One man, standing on the bank no more than eight feet from them, casually loosed off a couple of rounds from his SLR as he urinated into the river, and the SAS men flickered an expressionless glance at each other as the 7.62 rounds passed inches over their heads and tore into the far bank. A few yards further on a woman with her dress pulled up over her back crouched listlessly in the mud as a bearded soldier drove into her from behind. Around her, a surly and impatient knot of men watched and waited, and masturbated to make themselves hard for when their own turns came.

This hellish scene was repeated at intervals along the bank and more than once Alex caught himself — or so it seemed — staring mesmerised into the eyes of an RUF warrior. His heart appeared to be beating hard enough to disturb the greasy surface of the water. It seemed impossible that he had not been seen.

But the soldiers, it turned out, were less interested in driftwood than in the slopping palm wine buckets from which, at intervals, they refilled their half-gourds and plastic beakers. Those and the half-dozen wretchedly prostrate women on the shore — refugees, Alex guessed, displaced by the fighting.

The current, perceptibly faster now, swept them past the outhouses. The first, Alex guessed from the rhythmic chugging

27

sound, housed the generator. In a second, from which the buckets were being carried, he supposed that they had some kind of distillery. The third, a mud-walled dwelling whose palm-frond roof had collapsed inwards, was anyone's guess, but as they drifted past it the palm wine stink was joined by that of shit.

And then, for no more than five seconds, Alex saw them: three pale-skinned figures, their heads bowed, their hands tied behind them, kneeling in the narrow passage between the two cinder-block huts. They were being guarded by a single uniformed soldier carrying an SLR, smoking a joint and wearing a pink bubble-cut wig.

Alex's eyes widened and he turned to Stan Clayton, saw that the other man had clocked the guard and the captives too. Then they were passing the speakers, and taking the full thumping force and screaming distortion of 'No Living Thing'.

'I think I prefer the Martine McCutcheon version,' murmured Clayton thoughtfully, as an RUF man heaved a wet tree root on to the bonfire and a shower of bright-orange sparks whirled skywards. They were only eight or nine yards from the nearest whooping, rifle-waving soldiers now, but the amplification from the sound system was such that the corporal could probably have yelled at the top of his voice without being heard.

And then, as the firelight dimmed and a column of dense brown smoke replaced the flames, Alex felt the current take sudden hold, swinging the branch and themselves into deeper water. The two men silently struggled to remain concealed and to keep the branch parallel to the shore. They were clearing the camp fast now – the bonfire was already well behind them – but they were moving inexorably towards the Rokel's racing central channel.

'We're going to have to let go,' gasped Alex and heard Clayton's grunt of agreement beside him.

'On three, underwater and kick for the side. One, two . . .'

Alex released the branch, dived, and felt himself lifted by the current and swung with doll-like helplessness through the dark, churning water. There was a roar at his ears, a sense of vast and

28

indifferent force, then a rock or a boot exploded in a vicious flash of light against the side of his head.

Somehow, even as he briefly lost consciousness, he managed to keep his mouth shut. Hours or maybe seconds later, desperate to breathe, he clawed his way to what he thought was the surface, struck mud and felt himself dragged downwards again by a hand at his collar. For some reason, there seemed to be air at the bottom of the river. He tried to inhale, gagged and found that a mud-tasting hand was clamped over his mouth. Water streamed from his nose. He could breathe again. He opened his eyes.

Clayton's worried grin was inches away. 'You all right, Alex?'

They were in deep, eddying water beneath the bank. The music and din of the camp were still loud, but no longer deafening. Stan Clayton had one elbow under Alex's chin, the other anchored to a solid-looking mangrove root.

'Are you OK?' The whisper more urgent now.

Alex tried to nod and then, retching, vomited foul-tasting water. There was blood in his eyes and his head hurt like hell. Somehow he found a root of his own and passed an unsteady hand over his face. 'Yeah . . . thanks, Stan. Lost it there for a moment. Thanks.'

I was seconds away from drowning there, he told himself. *Seconds away from death.*

'I think we're more or less clear of the camp,' continued Clayton. 'The other blokes can't be far, but I'm a bit worried about them fuckers we 'ad to duck round on our way here. Bride of Frankenstein an' his mate.'

'Let me have a look,' said Alex and with Clayton's help hauled himself up so that his eyes were level with the bank. They were less than twenty yards from where they had descended the tree roots, but of the sleeping RUF soldiers there was no sign. Instead, Don Hammond was leopard-crawling towards him through the shadows, grabbing him under the arms, dragging him by sheer brute force up the slick clay face of the bank.

'I reckoned it was either you guys or a hippo wallowing

around out there,' said the sergeant. 'Come on, Stan, grab hold.'

When Clayton was on the bank too the three of them moved back from the river and into cover, and Alex swiftly brought the sergeant up to date concerning the ITN team.

'How did they look?' asked Hammond.

'Alive,' replied Clayton tersely.

'Where are the other guys?' asked Alex.

The sergeant inclined his head towards the bush. 'Just moving the two guards that were here away from the path. We reckoned you'd be coming out about here.'

'Did you kill them?'

'Yeah, course we did.' He looked at Alex doubtfully. 'Are you OK? You look as if you've got some kind of head wound.'

'Took a whack in the river on something. Stan dragged me in by the collar.'

'Well, that'll have saved us all some paperwork. Dead officers we don't need. Are you OK to tab back to Millwall, or do you want me to go?'

'I'm fine to go, Don.'

'You sure? What's eight nines?'

Alex hesitated. The question seemed strangely unanswerable.

'And the motto of the Parachute Regiment?'

Again, Alex was silent. He'd begun his military career with the Paras but couldn't for the life of him . . .

Hammond nodded and glanced at Clayton. 'I'd say you're a bit concussed. I'll tab back to Millwall with Lance and pick up the home-bound chopper. You stay here and set up the assault.'

Alex nodded. The sergeant was right. A single navigation error between here and Millwall – more than an hour's night march through thick jungle – could cost the captives their lives.

'Put it this way, Alex.' Stan Clayton grinned. 'At least if you stay 'ere you're guaranteed to be here for the fireworks. Go back wiv a leakin' 'ead and Ross'll just send some other fucker.'

'OK, guys, OK. I hear you,' said Alex, raising his hands in mock surrender. 'Don, have you managed to draw a map of the camp?'

Hammond nodded, and pulled out a sheet of waterproof

paper marked up with outlines and co-ordinates.

'Right,' said Alex. 'The ITN people, when I saw them, were being held in the passage between these two cinder-block buildings here, which you've called Hut One and Hut Two. Was that how you saw it, Stan?'

'Yeah, it was.'

'And from what I could see they looked very tired. Their morale was poor. Each or any of them might be hurt, possibly badly. But I'd say that all three were definitely alive.'

'Guarded?'

'One guy. Pink curly wig.'

Hammond looked at Clayton, who nodded in confirmation.

'Weapons?' asked Hammond, still looking at Clayton.

'My guess would be that there are about a hundred and fifty SLRs in the camp – one for each man. I saw a few AKs and RPGs, too, and there could be anything in those huts.'

'Fields of fire?'

For five minutes Hammond submitted the two men to a detailed debrief. Evidently suspicious of the accuracy of Alex's recall, given the captain's recent knock on the head, he made a point of verifying every fact with Clayton.

With the map filled in with as much detail as Alex and Stan Clayton could provide, Don Hammond radioed Zulu Three Five patrol who were observing the Arsenal camp ten kilometres away and reported that the hostages had been located. The patrol leader, a sergeant named Andy Maddocks, replied that he was pulling out immediately and estimated that he would reach Chelsea in about ninety minutes.

Alex then set off with Zulu Three Six patrol back up the track towards the Bergan cache. En route they checked the captive child-sentry, who was frightened but otherwise unharmed. Before the fighting started, Alex decided, he would release the poor little bugger into the jungle. Would that help him, or even save his life? Quite possibly not, he admitted to himself, but he couldn't play God.

When they reached the clearing where the Bergans were cached, Don Hammond radioed in a sat-com report to David

Ross and then kept on going. It was 0145, and he and Lance Wilford had three-quarters of an hour in which to reach the Puma landing zone at Millwall. All things being equal he would be back in Freetown by 0300. The assault – the killing time – would come an hour later at first light when, with a bit of luck, the RUF forces would be sunk in drunken, exhausted sleep.

It wouldn't be a pushover, thought Alex, remembering the red-eyed fury with which the soldiers had roared out the words of 'No Living Thing'. For all their gross indiscipline – for all their raping, mutilating, torture and murder – the RUF were well-armed and they were certainly no cowards. They would fight and they would fight hard. Many of them believed themselves to be impervious to pain, and given the volume of ganja and palm wine they got through of an evening, they were probably right.

What did they intend to do to Sally Roberts and her crew if their demands were not met? Impossible to say, although given the cruelty and contempt with which the soldiers treated the African women at their disposal – gang rape being the least of it – he could hazard a guess at the female reporter's probable fate. The men would most likely be shot and dumped in the river.

But this, mused Alex, glancing at his wristwatch, was not going to happen. Instead, in just under two hours, Sally Roberts, Ben Mills and Gary Burge would be flown out of the camp code-named Chelsea in a Puma helicopter. And with any luck, they would be alive when it happened.

At the bottom of the slope, behind the tree roots, Zulu Three Six patrol sat tight. This time, as well as the sat-com and the 319 patrol radio, they'd brought their individual Motorola UHF sets with them from the Bergan cache. Precisely co-ordinated operations like this one tended to be very comms-heavy. There was a worrying amount of movement near the hostages, Alex noticed, and he found himself straining to watch as the distant figures came and went beneath the strings of yellow light bulbs.

Cool it, he told himself. *For the moment – for just a few hours more until the deadline – the RUF need the news team alive.*

At precisely 0230 Ricky Sutton set up the sat-com to receive

Ross's scheduled transmission from Freetown. The incoming message was brief and to the point: Don Hammond and Lance Wilford had been exfiltrated from Millwall and were on their way back to base. Assault time was estimated at 0400.

As the twenty-three-year-old trooper folded away the sat-com aerial, Alex divided his team in half and disposed them in the jungle line in positions commanding broad arcs of fire over the camp. He himself took the western position with Sutton; Stan Clayton and Dog Kenilworth moved to the east.

Attaching the earpieces and throat mikes of their UHF sets, the patrol worked out their individual targets. When the time came, the impression given to the RUF had to be one of devastating force – that they were under sustained attack from all sides. In truth, of course, the rebels would be heavily outgunning the SAS, but they must never be allowed to know this.

The camp's situation, Alex knew, would work against the rescue team. With the looping river at their backs the RUF had nowhere to flee to, and in the event of attack they would have no option but to face the jungle and the opposing fire team and shoot it out. Desperation would make them very dangerous, there would be a huge volume of fire directed towards the two RWW patrols and once the helicopters were on the ground it was going to be very difficult to return that fire. The hostages and the assault and rescue teams would be right in the thick of it. They'd agreed over the radio that the incoming 'D' Squadron soldiers would wear their bush-hats inside out with the orange band showing and not have any cam-cream on their faces, but it was still going to be very tricky knowing who was who – first light or no first light.

The insects were silent, now, and the temperature finally falling. Around the shallow dugout that was Alex's firing position hovered the scent of the Sierra Leone night – a pungent blend of wet clay, woodsmoke and rotting mangoes. To his left, manning the sat-com and the patrol's 319 set, lay Ricky Sutton.

Alex had agreed with Don Hammond that the patrol would try a second swim past between 2.30 and 3 a.m. to determine

33

whether the hostages had been moved inside for the night. Stan Clayton had volunteered to go again, knowing as he did where the currents were most treacherous, and at 2.45 his narrow form slipped away eastwards, upstream of the camp. As he did so, Dog Kenilworth made his shadowy way to the downstream exit point to drag him up the river's sheer clay bank.

The next fifteen minutes passed slowly for Alex. The RUF posed no great danger to Stan – they were unlikely to be awake, sober and staring into the river at this hour – but Alex had felt the massive and wilful power of the Rokel river at first hand and hoped that the outspoken cockney would play it safe. Eventually, thankfully, the two loomed out of the darkness – Stan Clayton once again dripping with river water. The news was that the ITN team were still in the same place and still tied up, but apparently asleep. As was their guard, still wearing the Barbara Windsor wig.

Ricky Sutton unfurled the sat-com's aerial and called up Freetown. The news that the hostages had not been moved would come as a relief to the 'D' Squadron team, who wouldn't have to waste time searching for them while under fire – the camp would be a hornet's nest by the time the team de-bussed from the Puma. No one had so far put it into words, but it was possible that the Regiment would take casualties. It was possible that the story would end, as so often before, at the modest graveyard of St Martin's church outside Hereford.

A few minutes before 3 a.m. Andy Maddocks called Alex on his UHF set to report that he had arrived with Zulu Three Five patrol and was in position at the bottom of the approach slope. On Alex's instructions the six newcomers worked their way into the tree line above and behind Alex's patrol, and silently took up firing positions in pairs. As soon as they were established Alex briefed them by radio as to the location of the hostages.

One hour to go. In Freetown the 'D' Squadron assault and rescue team would be boarding the Pumas, loading magazines and checking kit. There would be nerves – they would be aware that they were hitting a hot landing zone.

How would it go, Alex wondered? Was there any way he could further ensure his men's safety? Not really, he decided. The thing was risky, but it had to be done. There wasn't a man here or at the squadron base who would rather be somewhere else – somewhere where there weren't any bull-leeches, malarial mosquitoes or trigger-happy rebels. Without exception the men under his command subscribed to Don Hammond's philosophy, that life was too short to spend it buying magnolia emulsion and 'wanking over Gail Porter'.

Which was pretty much how Alex felt himself.

Would this, as he had assumed, be his last taste of active service? As an officer he was bloody lucky to be dug in here with a bandolier of grenades across his chest and ten fully loaded magazines in his pouch rather than sweating it out on others' behalf in the briefing hut.

Not that he hadn't been pleased to be sent to Sandhurst. Only two or three Regiment NCOs received a commission each year and it had been very gratifying to be singled out. In his ten previous years of SAS service he'd seen Ireland – a lot of Ireland – the Gulf, Columbia, Liberia, Bosnia (where they'd given him the Military Medal), Kosovo and now Sierra Leone. And the list was even longer if you included the deniables and the 'black bag' jobs like Somalia and Sri Lanka.

Why had he been chosen? Alex wondered. Because he'd watched his mouth over the years? Because he'd managed to survive a decade of SAS service without actually decking a superior? Something like that, probably. Whatever – it had made it worthwhile staying in the army for a full term of service. With a bit of luck he'd make major before too long. After that, if he played his cards right there was Staff College . . . But what the hell. All that lay in the future.

It had been weird, though, hanging out at Sandhurst aged thirty-four with all the teenaged officers-to-be with their sports cars and their nightclubs and their weekends in the country. There had been admin classes, report-writing classes and even an etiquette or 'knife and fork' course. Never in his life had Alex felt more like a fish out of water.

The others hadn't all been rich, but plenty of them had been, especially the ones destined for the Brigade of Guards and the other outfits where an expensive social life came with the regimental silver. Alex, whose father ran a small garage and body-repair shop in Clacton-on-Sea, and who had joined the Paras as a private to impress a girlfriend (who had immediately dumped him – thanks, Stella!) found it impossible to imagine what it must be like to have money to spend on Savile Row suits and Curzon Street restaurants and Caribbean sailing holidays at that age.

For Alex, at eighteen, it had been rockfish and chips, Kestrel lager and a brown leather jacket ('sixty-five quid mate, fully lined') from the Pakistani guy who had the stall at the Saturday market. There hadn't been any foreign holidays. 'Why pay to go to the Seychelles,' his father would ask, nodding towards Marine Parade with its icy spray and mournful winter winds, 'when the sea's right here on our bloody doorstep?'

It wasn't meanness, it was just that Ray Temple didn't hold with what he called 'all that pina colada bollocks'. What he did hold with was motor sport and lots of it. Formula One at Brands Hatch, drag races at Santa Pod, stock cars at Belle Vue, bangers at King's Lynn, night races at Snetterton – any occasion involving cigarette advertising, petrol vapour and deafening noise. The Temple family attended pretty much every event in the Castrol motor sport calendar. And went first class all the way, with enclosure tickets, steak dinners at the motel if it was an overnighter, souvenir T-shirts and the rest.

The old man had been broken-hearted when, inspired by a TV documentary series, Alex had gone for the Parachute Regiment rather than one of the mechanised units. 'Don't be a tosser, son,' Ray Temple had begged him. 'If God had meant us to walk, he wouldn't have created fuel injection.'

But Alex had been adamant and stuck to his guns throughout the tough Para-selection course known as 'P' Company. He wasn't particularly big and he certainly wasn't the archetypal tattooed, scarred-knuckled Tom, but when it came to the specialised skills of the airborne infantryman he was a natural.

He was a fast learner, excellent with weapons and always switched on in the field. His superiors marked him down as potential NCO material and posted him to his battalion's Patrol Company.

Unexpectedly, like many a town-raised soldier before him, the young paratrooper developed a passion for the wild, remote terrain in which he and his unit trained. He enjoyed downing pints and trapping WRAC girls with his Patrol Company mates, but found that after only a few days in barracks he missed the freedom and the solitude offered by the mountains and the moors. Shortly after his twenty-third birthday he was made up to lance-corporal, but by then a part of him had begun to wonder if there might be more to army life than the culture of the Aldershot brotherhood, with its relentless cycles of drinking, brawling, mooning, curry-swilling, shagging and vomiting.

On impulse, he applied for SAS selection. By then, perhaps jealous of his promotion, some of his colleagues were beginning to regard him coolly. No one made any specific accusations but the word got around that he was a bit of a loner. There was an unconfirmed rumour that he had turned down the chance to join in a game of 'freckle' – a ritual in which a fresh turd was hammered between two beer mats on a pub table and the least bespattered paratrooper got to buy the next round.

If he had failed SAS selection, Alex would have had a very hard time living it down. But he didn't fail. Along with Don Hammond, then a Royal Fusiliers corporal, and a dozen others of the forty or so who applied, he passed. Badged into the Regiment, he discovered a different sort of soldier – tough, self-sufficient young blokes like himself who knew how to have a good time but didn't need to strike macho attitudes. The best friend he'd made in the Regiment was probably Hammond. As unmarried troopers they'd shared quarters in Hereford, along with a couple of clapped-out cars and – for three ill-tempered months – a Royal Army Dental Corps nurse named 'Floss' Docherty.

When it was announced that Alex was to be commissioned, no one could have been more pleased than Don Hammond.

The two had an instinctive sympathy in the field and neither saw any reason why this should be affected by their differing ranks.

And here he was, a dozen years and a dozen dirty wars after signing up, a bloody officer! His father had laid down his plug spanner and laughed fit to piss himself when Alex had told him that he was going to Sandhurst. 'You always were a canny bugger,' he told Alex, shaking his head in disbelief, 'but this beats the bloody bank.' His mother, seeing him in his full-dress uniform for the first time alongside the public-school boys, had wept.

Well, he reflected wryly, flipping up the backsight on his M16 and taking a sip of tepid water from his canteen, he might as well enjoy it while it lasted. The system gave, but the system also took away, and took away faster than shit off a hot chrome shovel. At heart, Alex knew, he was not an Establishment man.

THREE

Shortly after 3.30 there was movement in the camp. A tall soldier carrying some kind of hooked knife was walking amongst the prostrate soldiers, stepping over outflung arms and legs. As he reached the camp perimeter he paused to kick one of the sleeping figures. It was one of the women, Alex saw through his binoculars. With infinite slowness, the woman began to get to her feet, only for the soldier to take her by the hair, wave his bill-hook, and start violently pulling her towards the jungle. Hastily, fearfully, she matched her pace to his. This looks tricky, thought Alex. This looks very tricky indeed. They're making straight for us.

'Coming our way, Alex,' murmured Ricky Sutton beside him.

'Seen,' replied Alex. For the second time that night he drew his Mauser knife. The pair were no more than fifty yards from him now. Whatever you're going to do to her, Alex pleaded silently with the soldier, do it right there. Don't come any closer.

But the man kept on coming. Whatever it was that he intended – the curved knife almost certainly had something to do with it – it was going to make a lot of noise. There were going to be screams. So he was taking the woman into the bush where her evil-spirit howling wouldn't wake the camp up.

Twenty-five yards now, and Alex could hear the woman's terrified keening and the soldier's muttering as he forced her forward. If they tried to evade, to crawl sideways out of their way, the soldier would see them. And if they stayed put . . .

When it came to the moment, instinct took over. Tripping

39

the soldier with his rifle, avoiding the scything blade as both the man and the woman fell, Alex leapt on top of him. For a critical moment the soldier must have thought that a tree root was to blame for the confusion, and that the melee consisted only of himself and the woman, for he made no noise beyond an stifled curse. And then the butt of Alex's M16 met the back of his head with bone-smashing force, and he was still.

Ricky Sutton, meanwhile, had grabbed the woman. Behind his hand she was still keening, the sound a tiny sustained ribbon of anguish. Deliberately, Sutton moved his face into a shaft of moonlight, so that she could see at a glance that despite the black cam-cream he was European, and urgently shushed her. Their eyes met – his taut and pale, hers tear-rimmed and terrified – and she nodded once. She was wearing a thin cotton dress and plastic sandals.

The soldier had to be dealt with and Alex had no choice but to do it in front of the woman. Lifting the unconscious man's head by the hair, he chopped inwards and dragged the blade of the Mauser knife hard through the front of his throat. There was a rushing wet heat from the jugular, a clicking gasp from the severed windpipe, and a brief shivering dance of the legs. Within half a minute exsanguination was complete. The sticky blackness was everywhere.

Sutton, meanwhile, gagged the shocked, unresisting woman with a sweat-rag. Wrists and ankles trussed with paracord, she lay against a shallow incline behind them. Six feet away, the corpse of her late admirer stiffened in the cooling tar of his blood. The SAS officer and the trooper settled back to wait.

At 0350, Alex noticed a tiny shift in the quality of the darkness at the head of the Rokel valley to the east. If he looked a little to one side he could make out a ridge, a tree line, where previously there had been nothing. The minutes passed, the cyclorama paled a further degree, and the misted, dew-charged vastness of the jungle began to reveal itself. There was nothing on earth, thought Alex, to beat the grandeur of the African dawn.

Not even the front at Clacton.

He raised his binoculars. There was the command-post, there were the huts, there were the embers of the bonfire. And there – everywhere – were the sleeping soldiers and their weapons.

Quickly the men re-checked the sightings on their M16 203s. As well as a conventionally calibrated rifle-sights, which they had set to two hundred yards, their weapons had sextant-sights screwed to their carrying handles.

0355, and the pilot of Hotel Alpha, the lead Puma, was now audible on the patrol's UHF sets. His voice was relaxed. 'Coming in on schedule, Zero Three Six. You should see us in three or four minutes. Over.'

'We hear you, Hotel Alpha. Ready when you are. Over.'

Raising his rifle, Alex took up aim on the door of the left-hand of the two barracks-huts. Hut One.

0358. The pilot's voice again. 'Touch-down in two minutes, Zulu Three Six. Repeat, touch-down in two minutes.'

'Everyone ready?' Alex whispered. It was unlikely that anyone had fallen asleep, but it had been known to happen.

They all heard it at the same time. At first it was just a pulse, distant and low. Could have been a heartbeat. And then, with shocking suddenness, the lead Puma was racing towards them over the grey jungle canopy.

A sentry holding a Kalashnikov was the first to stir, and Alex dropped him with a single high-velocity round to the chest.

'*Boyakasha!*' breathed Ricky Sutton to his left and opened up with a long stream of tracer at the guards around the bonfire. The other sentries ran for the cover of the huts, but met a series of lethally aimed bursts from Stan and Dog. As they fell, Alex saw Don Hammond lean coolly out of the side of the helicopter and heard the distinctive *boom boom* of the heavy 5.5″ gun. Chunks of masonry seemed to leap from the walls of Hut One and, as the RUF soldiers poured out like angry ants, Alex snapped off a fast series of shots into the doorway. The area between the huts also held armed men, but these he left alone for fear of hitting the hostages.

Fire was being returned now and with interest. Volleys of 7.62 SLR rounds were snapping through the tree line,

41

shredding the foliage around them and kicking up great gouts of earth. Unpeturbed, Stan Clayton and Dog Kenilworth kept up a lethal assault with their M16s. Behind them Andy Maddocks' patrol put down steady fire.

Lowering his rifle so that he was cradling it in his arms, Alex slipped one of the small, egg-like grenades from his bandolier into the launcher tube below the main barrel and swung the weapon towards the eastern-most point of the camp. A glance at the sextant and he fired. The grenade dropped some two hundred and fifty yards away and burst with a fierce crack amongst a group of soldiers who were attempting to bring fire to bear on the helicopter. Returning the rifle to his shoulder, Alex stilled the survivors with a series of single shots.

Working the slide to discharge the used shell-case, he loaded a second grenade into the tube, and aimed it in the direction of the generator-hut. Another miniature schrapnel storm, sending several men running from cover into the open, where Ricky Sutton's unhurried shooting dropped them in fast succession. The camp was in chaos now. The Puma had landed, its rotors still turning, and the 12-man SAS team was pouring out of it, diving for cover and snapping aimed bursts at the RUF rebels who surrounded them.

In response several of the rebels dropped their SLRs and ran. A handful threw themselves on the uncertain mercy of the river. Most, however, making up in aggression and outrage what they lacked in preparedness and training, determined to make a fight of it and attempted to fall back on the cover of the two cinder-block barracks huts. Lacking any coherent command-and-control system, however, they found themselves retreating into their own side's defensive arcs of fire. Several of them only managed to make it into cover because their colleagues' long-uncleaned SLRs had jammed.

For a moment, Alex held his fire. As he watched, the incoming SAS team split up. Half raced for the hostages, disappearing behind the huts, half assaulted Hut One. The whoomf of a grenade, a long burst of fire, a staccato flurry of single shots and the building was theirs. A moment later the rescue team reappeared at the sprint, ducking through the rebel fire towards the helicopter. Three of them had limp, half-dressed figures slung over their shoulders. 'Go!' prayed Alex. 'Get them on the chopper and out of here. *Go!*'

The Puma, as if alive to the urgency of the situation, seemed to dance with impatience on her struts as enemy rounds snapped about her. At the controls, Alex could see the helmeted pilot, motionless – a brave man, he thought – and the silhouetted figure of Don Hammond poised at the open door, waiting to haul up the hostages.

The RPG must have been fired somewhere behind the generator. It whooshed a couple of feet over the heads of the rescue team, impacted against the Puma's slanting plexiglas windshield and vapourised the cockpit and the pilot in an orange-white bloom of flame. The blast threw the oncoming rescue team and the hostages to the ground and, as they lay there, the SAS men instinctively covering the journalists with their bodies, a second missile struck the rear of the Puma's cargo compartment. The buckled and burning remains of the heli-copter canted sideways and Don Hammond pitched face forwards from the doorway – his clothes, his head and his remaining arm aflame.

Powerless to help from two hundred yards distance, his mind a stunned blank, Alex watched as Hammond tried unsuccess-fully to get to his feet. The two members of the rescue team who had not been carrying hostages rose from the ground, raced forward and between them attempted to stifle the flames on the burning sergeant and drag him into cover.

But the RUF were beginning to rally. And while the hostages and the rescuers were covered from fire by the bulk of Hut One, Hammond and the men who had run out to help him were far enough forward to be exposed. Shots snapped around them and Alex heard a lethal-sounding double smack. One of the SAS men staggered and fell. Somehow, supporting his wounded mate with one arm and half-dragging the sergeant's blackened remains with the other, the third man made it to the cover of Hut One, where the hostages were being scrambled through the doorway over the sprawled corpses of dead RUF soldiers.

The SAS team had barely vanished inside the hut when the Puma's fuel tanks went up in a third roaring explosion, and oily black smoke began to twist into the grey dawn sky.

'Zulu Three Six, this is Hotel Bravo, what is the situation?'

It was the pilot of the support Puma.

'Hotel Alpha is down, Hotel Bravo. Repeat, Hotel Alpha is down. Stay back until my signal.'

'Will do, Zulu Three Six.' The pilot's voice was expressionless.

There was a brief hiatus and, forcing himself to postpone all thoughts concerning Don Hammond, Alex undertook a swift assessment.

At least twenty rebels lay out in the open, dead, while a dozen more twitched and gaped and bled amongst them. A further dozen RUF casualties were almost certainly concealed amongst the outbuildings to the east of the camp. Even allowing for a few runners and swimmers that still left a hundred-odd rebels in good combat order.

'Dog,' Alex murmured into his UHF mouthpiece. 'I want you and Stan to cut through the jungle to the point where we got into the river and work your way back towards the camp from the east. We've got to take out that grenade-launcher before the support helicopter arrives.'

'Heard.'

'On our way.'

Still on his UHF set, Alex then called up the assault and rescue team, requested the sergeant in charge and explained that he had sent in two men from the eastern end of the camp to try and force the RUF soldiers to keep their heads down.

'Understood,' came the reply. 'I'll put another four in from this end. If you keep laying down fire from the bush we should be able to keep 'em busy enough to get the chopper in and out.'

A moment later, however, a long volley of 7.62 SLR and Kalashnikov rounds smacked into Alex's position. Heady with the destruction of Puma Alpha, the defending RUF troops had decided to take the battle back to their tormentors in the jungle.

As the firestorm swept their position, spattering himself and Sutton with bark and falling leaf fragments, Alex pressed his face and body into the damp coffee-ground soil. Beside him he heard the unmistakeable whipcrack of physical impact and a shocked gasp.

'Ricky?' he said, fearing the worst.

'I'm hit,' muttered Sutton through clenched teeth, 'in the fuckin' arse.'

Alex's heart sank. How many bloody more, he thought. If I run into Sally Roberts, the bitch'll wish she'd never been born.

Another volley raked the tree line. Somewhere behind him, the bound woman keened with fear. Reaching for the shell-dressing pack in Sutton's smock pocket and the clasp-knife in his own, Alex cut through the young signaller's blood-sodden DPM trousers, slapped on the dressing, and ordered him to sit tight. To his right Stan and Dog returned fire, pouring a steady stream of armour-piercing rounds on to the RUF positions around Hut Two.

A moment later Alex saw four SAS men slip out of the door of Hut One and disappear around the far side. From the generator area he heard the crack of 203 grenades launched by Dog and Stan and a moment later the familiar stutter of M16s on rapid fire as the assaulters completed the movement. The RUF were now under sustained assault from three directions, trapped in a lethal cage of noise and shrapnel. No RUF man was going to risk standing up for long enough to aim and correctly discharge an RPG in all of that, Alex reckoned. Quickly, he called in the reserve Puma.

The pilot acknowledged the signal and sixty seconds later the big snout-nosed chopper swung in fast and steep, dropping down next to the twisted and still burning wreck of the first. It had hardly touched the ground when the rescue team sprinted out of the barracks-block with the ITN crew over their shoulders. Hurling the journalists through the open doorway like so many sacks of coal and dragging themselves in afterwards, they were away within seconds, dipping and swaying across the grey-green jungle canopy to safety.

On the sat-com, Alex called up Ross. 'Hostages airborne,' he told the CO, 'but we've taken casualties.' Quickly, he brought him up to speed with events.

'Keep me posted,' said Ross tersely, and broke the connection.

Silence now from the RUF – all of their remaining strength pinned down in and around Hut Two. Above them, the sky seemed to be darkening again. Stalemate.

Alex slotted a fresh 30-round magazine into the belly of his weapon. Does the fight have to be to the death, he wondered. The fierce anticipation of the night before was entirely spent. The camp was a butcher's shop now and one or two of the RUF corpses looked horrifyingly young. All that he felt now was revulsion – a desperate longing for the whole thing to be over.

And then Dog Kenilworth's Brummie tones were in his earpiece. 'They're jacking it in. Slinging their rifles out.'

Alex exhaled, permitted himself a moment of relief.

'Any men followed the rifles?'

'No, not so far . . . Yeah, hang on, one's just shouting to Stan now.'

'What's he saying?'

'Dunno. Something meaning "No shooting!", I'd guess. He's coming out.'

'Watch yourselves, OK?'

'Don't worry, Alex.'

One by one the RUF soldiers processed out of Hut Two and the other outbuildings at the eastern end of the camp. From the tree line Alex saw the line of disarmed men, hands raised, shuffling towards the smoking wreck of the first Puma. There, under the watchful eye and trained M16s of the assault team, they waited in disconsolate ranks.

'Andy,' Alex ordered, 'cut across and join Stan and Dog. When it looks as if all the prisoners are under guard, I want the three of you to do a quick house-to-house, check for stay-behinds.'

'Understood,' said Maddocks.

Alex turned back to Ricky Sutton. The trooper was pale and

clearly in shock, but managed a wry grin. An SLR round had torn a furrow over the hamstring muscle at the back of his thigh, and despite the two shell-dressings blood was still welling hotly through the gauze.

'Right,' murmured Alex briskly. 'Who had the patrol med-pack?'

'I'm . . . lying on it.'

Carefully, Alex eased the pack from beneath the trooper's chest, found a morphine stick, and angled it into Sutton's thigh. Within seconds, the taut, fearful strain in the young trooper's eyes was replaced with a dreamy vagueness.

Reaching for his UHF set, Alex pressed the transmit button. 'How's it going, lads?' he asked.

'Fine,' came Andy Maddocks' voice. 'No stay-behinds, all badboys disarmed. What shall we do with the weapons? We've got a hundred-odd SLRs, few AKs, RPGs, odds and sods.'

Alex removed a saline drip assembly from the med-pack.

'All weapons, ammo, and comms kit goes into the river.' He thought of the women and children who, raped, traumatised and with one or both arms hacked off by men such as these, were still arriving daily in Freetown. 'And that includes all pangas, machetes, billhooks, whatever. Anything with a blade.'

'Understood.'

Turning to the bound woman, whom he now saw was probably no more than 16 or 17, he fingered the gag from her mouth and tied it round Sutton's thigh to reinforce the shell-dressing. Then finding a vein at the trooper's wrist, he worked in the IV needle. Beside him, crooning distractedly to herself as if to comfort a child, the girl sat blank-eyed.

Within minutes the secured camp had taken on an ordered and familiar aspect, with sentries posted, SAS casualties stretchered and ammunition checks underway. The mood was sombre – even the irrepressible Ricky Sutton lay in morphined silence on his stretcher. Where the bonfire had raged the night before, the captured RUF soldiers sat in subdued lines with their hands plasticuffed behind their backs. Others, moving with dream-like slowness, stacked the bodies of their dead comrades.

Beyond them the rain hissed and steamed as it met the smoking shell of the Puma.

On the sat-com, Alex arranged the details of the return to base with David Ross. It would probably be a question of two Chinooks, they decided – one for the SAS team, one to deliver the RUF dead to the government forces HQ. A few yards away, Stan Clayton and Dog Kenilworth manoeuvred Don Hammond into a black body-bag.

FOUR

At breakfast the mood was sombre.

They'd de-bussed at SAS HQ shortly after 6 a.m. and, calling for hot coffee in his hut, Ross had debriefed Alex immediately. Alex's account had been detailed but unemotional and Ross had heard him out in near silence, only occasionally interjecting a brief question. When they were done, an hour or so later, Ross had nodded, his lean features expressionless, and sat for a moment in silence. Alex knew he had liked Don Hammond as much as any of them.

'You did well, Alex. Bloody well. All of you. Another few hours and we would have had three dead UK nationals on our hands, not to mention egg all over our faces. Bearing in mind that we were hitting a hot DZ, it was always going to be a very high-risk operation.'

Alex nodded. At times like these, as both men knew, there was not a great deal to be said. Violent death was the everyday currency of their profession and there was no sense pretending otherwise.

'Just remind me of the daughter's name, Alex.'

'Cathy. I think she was seven last birthday.'

Ross looked tiredly down at his notes. 'Right. Thank you.'

Would I like that job? Alex wondered. *Would I enjoy sitting up and watching the clock as my men risked their lives? Would I be able to write the letters of condolence that David Ross always made a point of writing?*

The phone at the OC's right hand buzzed. He listened for a moment, then covered the mouthpiece and turned to Alex. 'It's Hugh Gudgeon at Para HQ. The TV people are all in one piece, apparently. They want to thank the leader of the rescue team personally.'

'I haven't got much to say to them, David, to be honest.'

Ross nodded and looked away. 'I'm afraid that won't be possible, Hugh, nor do I want any mention made of the Regiment in connection with this business. Would your chaps very much mind taking the credit? No? Excellent. All right, then. 'Bye.'

Alex had left the CO's hut to shower, shave and clear himself of leeches. This was a rather simpler process than that shown in films like *Bridge Over the River Kwai*. One touch of army-issue insect repellent and the fat, purple-black bloodsuckers fell off. The repellent was useless for anything else – it positively attracted mosquitoes – but it did have this one killer application. Stripping to the skin in the makeshift outside shower area, Alex managed to rid himself of twelve bull-leeches – a personal best.

In the mess tent he joined the rest of the patrol, who had got a head start on the NAAFI baked beans, pale-yolked local eggs and monkey-bananas. And beer, of course. It may only have been seven in the morning, but after a mission it was understood that you popped a few cans.

Alex helped himself to a plate of beans, one of the doughy, locally baked bread rolls and a can of Carling. The food looked none too appetising in the tent's greenish light, but at that moment Alex could have eaten practically anything. 'Cheers, lads,' he said, thumbing back the tab. 'Here's to a daring rescue!'

'Who was responsible for that, then?' asked Lance Wilford.

'The Paras,' said Alex.

'Ah.' Dog Kenilworth smiled. 'Fine body of men.'

There was silence for a moment.

'Any news on Ricky Sutton?' asked one of the troopers from Zulu Three One patrol, who had been tasked to recce the Arsenal camp.

'Should be OK, is my guess, barring a very sore arse,' said Alex.

'And Steve Dowson?' Dowson was the 'D' Squadron corporal who had been hit while attempting to rescue Hammond.

'Shoulder's a mess but he'll live.'

There were relieved nods, followed by another protracted silence, then Stan Clayton raised a fridge-frosted beer can. 'To Don Hammond,' he said loudly. 'Bloody good soldier, bloody good mate.'

The others raised their own drinks and then everyone started talking at once and the mood lifted. There was no shortage of good Don Hammond stories and it had been one hell of a successful mission.

As Alex drank and listened in silence, the elation of the successful mission faded, to be replaced by the sombre reality of his friend's death. After the third can his mood had not improved and, unwilling to spoil the others' celebrations, he slipped from the mess tent, collaring a bottle of rum as he went.

In his own tent he raised the mosquito net overhanging his camp bed, sat down and took a deep hit of rum straight from the bottle. He would say goodbye to Don alone and in his own way.

He was about to neck a second swallow when a trooper ducked through the tent flap. 'Sorry, but the Boss wants you.'

Again? thought Alex, pulling himself unsteadily to his feet. *Bollocks.* Glancing regretfully at the rum bottle, he followed the trooper from the tent.

In the hour since their last conversation, David Ross had clearly suffered a change of mood. Irritation now etched the spare features. 'You're going home,' he told Alex abruptly. 'Don't ask me why because I don't know. All I've been told is that you're wanted in London as soon as you can get there.'

Alex stared at him, mystified. What the fuck was going down? Whatever, he'd had enough of this sweaty shithole. 'Can I take a couple of the lads back with me? We can jump a Hercules.'

'No on both counts,' said Ross testily. 'They want you quicker than that. You're being choppered to Banjul and

51

boarded on to a BA civilian flight to Heathrow. For that reason you're taking civilian clothes and cabin luggage only.'

'I didn't bring any . . .' Alex began.

'One of the liaison blokes is picking some stuff up now. Should be back any minute.'

'Is this to do with last night's operation?' Alex ventured.

'Not unless there's some element to the whole thing that I haven't been told about.'

That such a possibility even existed, Alex saw, clearly rankled bitterly with the CO. 'I'll get packing,' he said.

Ross nodded.

Fifteen minutes later, dressed in a flowered bush shirt, over-tight slacks and plastic sandals from Freetown market – all that the liaison guy had been able to rustle up at ten minutes' notice – Alex was watching from the passenger seat of a Lynx helicopter as Kroo Bay and the curving northern sweep of Freetown fell away beneath him. The rain of the early morning had given way to sunshine and now the whole country seemed to be steaming in the heat. Beside him, the khaki T-shirt of the special forces pilot was dark with sweat beneath the arms and where it was in contact with the plastic seat cover.

'Another hot one,' said the pilot laconically over the intercom.

'Looks like it,' Alex replied, settling himself back into his seat. They had the best part of two hours' flying time ahead of them. In twenty minutes they would be in Guinea airspace and in half an hour would be overflying the capital, Conakry. Thereafter they would follow the coastline northwards through Guinea-Bissau and touch down at Banjul at 9.30.

He determined to enjoy the view.

At Banjul he was the last one on to the British Airways flight.

'You must be important,' said the stewardess who met him at the door of the 777. 'They've held this plane for fifteen minutes!' She looked down at his plastic sandals with a lemon-sucking smile. 'Ready to walk the gauntlet?'

His appearance prompted a slow handclap. Around him, the sea of faces was hostile. They had been waiting for him, one angry woman informed him, for over twenty-five minutes. Perhaps next time he travelled he might bring an alarm clock with him?

His seat, needless to say, was right at the back of the aircraft. Toilet class. He was shown there by the lemon-sucking stewardess, and had to endure the eye-rolling and barely disguised impatience of an almost entirely female complement of economy-class passengers.

The stewardess directed him to a seat next to an amply proportioned woman, some fifty years old, who smelt strongly of coconut tanning oil.

She looked him up and down. 'Well,' she murmured purposefully, noting the uncomfortable tightness of his trousers. 'Aren't I the lucky one!'

Alex's spirits sank. How long was this fucking flight? Eight hours? 'Are you all . . . together?' he asked, indicating the other passengers.

'Well, it'd probably be true to say that we're all here for much the same reason,' the woman said with a small smile.

'Which is?'

'To meet Gambian boys, of course. Bit of the old Shirley Valentine.'

'Ah,' said Alex. 'Right.'

'Africans are properly appreciative of the fuller figure, you see. And they know how to woo a girl without ever mentioning DIY or football.'

'Or their jobs?' ventured Alex.

'Or their jobs,' she agreed. 'Quite right. I'm Maureen, by the way.'

'Alex.'

'So what brings you to the Gambia, Alex?'

'Oh, I never talk about my job. Too boring.'

'You came here for . . . *work*?'

Mistake. Serves me right for being a smartarse, he thought. 'I'm in, er, travel,' he explained.

'So you . . . get around a bit?'

'Here and there.' He shrugged.

She nodded. Taxi-ing into the oncoming breeze, the big 777 started its long race to take-off.

'And do you like big girls, Alex?'

Blimey, he thought. Talk about cutting to the chase. 'Did you have a good holiday, Maureen?' he asked her, with what he hoped was professional-sounding interest.

In answer she fished a polaroid photograph from her purse. It showed a young Gambian man, nude except for a pair of sunglasses. He was about seventeen, slender and leaning backwards to counterbalance his evident enthusiasm. The plane hurtled into the air, pressing them back into their seats. 'There's my answer, Alex. Now can I please have yours? Do you like big girls?'

He turned to her, took in the painfully sunburnt flesh, the hennaed hair, the small hopeful eyes. 'Maureen,' he said. 'I do like them. But I've got one waiting for me at home.'

'Hm,' she said, unconvinced.

An hour or so after take-off, breakfast was served. Uncertain of what was waiting for him at Heathrow, Alex ate the lot. With a bit of luck there'd be some lunch, too. Trouble, as every soldier knew, was best faced on a full stomach. And with a well-rested mind. The adrenalin rush that accompanied violent action was invariably followed by exhaustion and Alex slipped gratefully into sleep. One of the few advantages of his present situation – perhaps the only advantage – was that he would be able to see Sophie again and he didn't want to appear completely knackered when he did.

For a long while, scenes from the previous night replayed themselves before his eyes. The smell of rotting mangoes and the river, the clicking of that severed windpipe, tracer scorching across the clearing, the screams of the maimed RUF men, the stillness of the Puma pilot as his aircraft danced beneath him, the Puma enfolded in flame against the sodden grey of the jungle, Don Hammond pitching forward, the smack of SLR rounds impacting into Steve Dowson's shoulder and Ricky Sutton's thigh . . .

The images faded. They were not ready to join the longer-established nightmares in the vault of Alex's memory – it would be weeks and perhaps months before that happened – but they had been faced. He had always tried to make horror his friend.

It showed, Sophie told him, on his face.

FIVE

Sophie Wells was the sister of Jamie Wells, who had been an officer cadet at Sandhurst with Alex and was now a Coldstream Guards lieutenant.

Jamie and Alex had met towards the end of the course. It had been a Friday night and with his ten-year-old Karman-Ghia out of commission, Alex had been looking for a lift into London, where he had arranged to meet a mate for a few beers.

Jamie had not only been driving to London but to Chelsea, which suited Alex perfectly. Dave Constantine, the colleague in question, had recently been posted as Permanent Staff Instructor to 21 SAS and Alex had arranged to meet him at the bar in the territorial battalion's King's Road HQ. Jamie, meanwhile, was going to a party in Cadogan Mansions, behind Sloane Square.

On their arrival in London Alex stood Jamie a drink at the bar at the Duke of York's HQ, where Alex was handed a note. Dave Constantine, he discovered, had been called away at the last moment to replace one of the other PSIs on an escape and evasion exercise on the Brecon Beacons.

Jamie had suggested that the SAS man come with him to the party, which was being given by his sister. Alex hadn't been keen; to spend the evening with a hundred braying Sloanes was very low on his wish-list. 'What does your sister do?' he asked doubtfully.

'You'll have to ask her.' Jamie grinned.

'Right.' Alex smiled grimly. 'I get it. It's a survival exercise. You've had to survive the beatings and the bollockings, so now I've got to survive the Taras and Tamaras.'

Jamie returned his gaze. 'Think of it that way if you like,' he said equably. 'But you might also enjoy yourself.'

'Yeah, right.'

'What have you got to lose?'

Alex conceded defeat.

The party was on the third floor of a nineteenth-century mansion block, and seemed to be taking place on the stairs and in the lift as well. Alex had expected an uncomfortable roomful of red-faced young men in corduroys and tractor-tyre shoes; what he actually encountered was the best part of an acre of dizzyingly beautiful women.

He had also expected to look out of place; in fact, although some of the handful of men present were expensively dressed, most looked as if they had bought their gear off an Isle of Dogs market trader. The look was as fake as their cockney accents and movie-gangster rhyming slang, but Alex reckoned that his cropped military haircut, Essex Stock Cars T-shirt and old Levis would probably pass muster among them.

Alex's first hint of Sophie Wells's existence was when a gold and turquoise whirlwind blew past him trailing scent, silk and male admirers. She came to rest briefly in front of Jamie – for just long enough, in fact, to present her brother with a kiss and an introduction to a dewy-faced teenager in a chiffon micro-skirt – 'she's the new "face" of Prada, so I want you to make absolutely sure she's in bed by 10.30!' – then was suddenly right there in front of him. 'So.' She smiled. 'It's Alex, isn't it? A friend of Jamie's from Sandhurst? How lovely of you to come!'

For a moment Alex gazed at her, taking in the short chestnut crop, the cool grey-green eyes, the Italian silks, the flimsy and very visible lingerie beneath. Where did you begin with a creature like this?

'I'm Sophie,' she continued encouragingly, swiping a couple of glasses of champagne from a passing waiter's tray and handing one to Alex. 'And these dreadful people' – she gestured vaguely around her – 'are my friends. Aren't they ghastly?'

Alex managed a smile. 'You should see mine,' he said. 'Is this party to celebrate anything?'

'My twenty-sixth birthday,' said Sophie. 'My entry into middle age.'

'You look well on it,' said Alex, wishing he could have found something cleverer to say.

'Do I? God, I don't deserve to. You look . . .' She hesitated. 'How old are you?'

'Thirty-four.'

'I was going to say that you look older than this lot' – she waved vaguely at the people around them – 'but you don't. You just look . . . different.'

She held his gaze, Alex noticed, rather than darting her eyes about the room in search of the next flirtation, the next conversational fix. So steady was her regard – so intimate, somehow – that they might have been alone together.

'Well, there probably aren't too many other soldiers here.'

She laughed. 'That's certainly true. But I've met a few soldiers in my time and they didn't have what you've got – that sort of wary look behind the eyes.' She dropped her voice to an enquiring murmur. 'How did that get there?'

Alex looked away, momentarily uncomfortable, breaking the cocoon that they had briefly spun about themselves. Sophie watched him patiently.

'Jamie wouldn't tell me what you do,' he said eventually. 'I'm supposed to ask you in person.'

She shrugged. 'Oh, I'm a fashion PR. I get column inches in the glossies for designers.'

'I bet some of those designers are grateful for a few inches,' said Alex.

'Alex!' shrieked Sophie in mock outrage. She turned to a man in a canary-yellow biker's outfit and Alex, taking his cue, drifted away. By one of the windows he saw Jamie, glass in hand, talking to the Prada girl. Alex caught his eye and winked, and Jamie flushed a slightly deeper shade of pink than usual. *These are nice enough people*, thought Alex, *but what the fuck am I doing here, precisely?*

He wandered into a large kitchen, fitted out with tiny laser-like spotlights and vast brushed-aluminium units and appliances.

The placed looked like a safe depository he'd once guarded. Opening the walk-in fridge, he found himself a cold Mexican beer. The champagne went down the sink.

At one end of the room was a large picture window, looking out over Sloane Street. For several minutes Alex stood there in unmoving silence, watching the northward crawl of red tail-lights towards Knightsbridge. At that moment, it seemed that he was disconnected from everything and everyone that he knew. His SAS career had separated him from his family, promotion had lifted him out of the orbit of his fellow NCOs, and he guessed that both age and background would set him apart from most of his brother officers. He didn't particularly regret any of this except possibly the distance that had grown between himself and his family. This was as much a matter of logistics as anything else: Hereford was a long way away from the Essex coast and London stood between them. He just didn't make it down there often enough.

Nor had he ever been married. He'd had lots of girlfriends over the years but had always held back from proposing to them. There was plenty of time for family life, he'd always reckoned, when he wasn't being yo-yoed around the world by the Regiment. Ireland had discouraged him, too. He'd seen brave soldiers fall apart when their wives and children were threatened. What would it be like, Alex wondered, planning a future with someone? And what sort of person would that someone have to be if they weren't going to end up at each other's throats?

Far below, in Sloane Street, an articulated lorry straddled the traffic where it had jackknifed while attempting to turn into a side street. Long lines of cars had built up on both sides of the road and the faint blare of their protest was audible through the heavy plate glass. Behind him Alex heard the suck of the opening fridge.

'You must be Jamie's friend. Sophie thought you'd done a runner.'

He turned to find a pretty fair-haired girl in jeans and a floaty top jacking open one of the Mexican beers.

'Still here, I'm afraid.' He extended his hand. 'I'm Alex.'

'I'm Stella.' She looked at him appraisingly and grinned. 'She'll be really glad you're still here. She was like *oh no*, he's *gone*, we've completely freaked him out. Not that I'm supposed to tell you that, of course.'

'I can keep a secret,' said Alex.

'Yeah, I'll bet you can,' said Stella, drawing alongside him. 'Interesting view down there?'

They peered down through the summer twilight.

'Fashion's not really one of my special subjects,' Alex told her.

Stella nodded. 'Unlike most *fashionista* babes, there's a lot more to Sophie than her job.'

'I'm sure,' said Alex. 'Are you a PR too?'

'Nah. Sophie does the London PR for my company. I'm a designer.'

Behind them there was a sudden overexcited hubbub. Alex glanced over his shoulder to discover a tall, anxious-looking girl chopping lines of white powder on one of the polished aluminium draining boards. A half-dozen other modelly looking boys and girls crowded impatiently round her. Bank-notes were produced and small hoovering sounds ensued. One evenly tanned young man whom Alex vaguely recognised had a violent sneezing fit into a paper kitchen towel. There was nervous laughter from the others, but by the sixth sneeze the blood spatters were clearly visible.

'You don't disapprove?' asked Stella, watching him watching them.

'Me? No.' Alex held up his beer and squinted at the label. 'Personally I'd rather go this way than that way, but . . .' He shrugged.

'Each to his own?'

Alex looked over at the powder-nosed models. 'Or her own.'

The kitchen was filling up. Stella introduced Alex to a film director named Danny Biggs, for whose latest project she was designing costumes.

'What's the picture going to be about?' Alex asked.

'Bunch of geezers turning over a bank,' said Danny.

'Working title "Hair of the Dog".'

'Why do you need a fashion designer to dress bank robbers?' Alex asked him. 'Most villains I've come across are fat, middle-aged white men in dodgy gold jewellery and knocked-off sports gear – the sort of stuff you can pick up in any high street.'

'Well, we 'ave to improve on reality,' explained Danny. 'Dress 'em in ruffled shirts an' Gucci whistles.'

At that moment Jamie appeared with the Prada girl and touched fists with Stella. 'You'd better watch out,' he told her, indicating Alex. 'This man gave us a lecture yesterday on ambushes and surprise attacks. Keep him in view at all times!'

Stella raised an eyebrow. 'I thought you were one of the . . . what do you call them, students? Cadets?'

'I am,' said Alex. 'But I came up through the ranks for ten years first, hence my advanced age. From time to time us old lags get called on to address the Ruperts – that's Jamie and his friends – and pass on a few dirty tricks.'

'Dirty tricks, eh?' mused Stella. 'Sounds interesting.'

As Jamie and the Prada girl exited with their drinks, Sophie reappeared.

Alex's heart thumped in his chest. She was beautiful, he realised, and beautiful in a much more interesting way than the models, with their stick-thin limbs and their dim, drug-dazed faces.

'Hey, girlfriend!' Stella greeted Sophie. 'Look who's still here!'

As Sophie met Alex's eye, the beginnings of a smile touched the corners of her mouth. 'Well! I thought we'd shocked you into flight.'

Alex attempted an answering smile. 'I don't scare quite as easily as you think,' he said.

At the draining board the anxious-looking model was rubbing the last of the cocaine into her gums.

Stella rolled her eyes at the girl. 'Tash, you should cool it with that stuff. I don't want you falling off the catwalk tomorrow.'

'I know, Stell. I've just been like, so busy, yeah? I got this option for the new Virginity campaign and everyone at the agency's like hey, you really gotta do this, they're like *really* big clients and I'm like *whoa*, cool it, yeah? I just want to, like, chill out, y'know?'

'I know,' said Stella gently. She turned to Sophie. 'Dad was asking how you were.'

'Tell him fine,' said Sophie.

'What does your dad do?' Alex asked Stella on impulse.

'He's a musician,' said Stella. 'He used to play bass guitar with a band in the Sixties. And he still does a bit of songwriting.'

Alex nodded. 'My dad's into cars. That's his thing.' He turned to Sophie. 'What about you? How's your old man fill his time?'

'He sells what he calls area-denial systems and the rest of the world calls landmines,' said Sophie. 'Mostly to third-world dictators. That's his thing.'

Alex nodded again. This was clearly sensitive territory. 'And is business, er, good?' he ventured.

'Booming,' said Sophie drily.

They looked at each other for a moment.

'Before you disappear,' said Stella, 'I've just had a thought. Why don't you and this nice young man come to dinner at my place tomorrow night?'

Sophie gazed into Alex's eyes. Her grey-green gaze poured over him like a wave. 'That would be lovely,' she said quietly. 'Are you free?'

'Yes,' said Alex.

'Good.' Sophie kissed him softly but firmly on the mouth. 'See you there.'

Alex watched her go. Stella watched him watch her. 'Smitten, I'd say.' She smiled. 'Definitely smitten.'

'Who?' asked Alex, smiling like an idiot.

'You tell me.' Stella bent and rummaged in her bag. 'Here, I'll give you the address for tomorrow night.' She wrote it on the back of an invitation to a film première. 'Be there,' she told him sternly. 'I'm counting on you, OK?'

'I promise,' said Alex.

Ten minutes later he was walking down Sloane Street with Jamie, who after a promising start had seen the Prada girl stolen away from him by the film director Danny Biggs.

'He told her he grew up hanging around the dog tracks and nicking cars,' protested the disconsolate Jamie. 'The truth is that he went to Eton with me and his father's the Lord-Lieutenant of Shropshire. Bastard.'

'I'm afraid all's fair in love and war, mate,' Alex told him. 'No prizes for second place.'

'I guess not,' Jamie agreed gloomily.

They walked on in silence for a few paces.

'By the way,' said Alex, a little self-consciously, 'it looks like I'm seeing your sister tomorrow night' – he checked his watch – 'I mean tonight. For, um, dinner.'

'Oh, yeah?' said Jamie, amused at Alex's embarrassment. 'Glad you came, then?'

'I guess I am.'

The next day Alex spent the afternoon at the Duke of York's Headquarters in the King's Road, test-firing revolvers with Dave Constantine. Wondering if he should dress smartly for dinner at Stella's – perhaps even buy some new clothes – he had eventually ditched the idea and stuck to his jeans and a T-shirt.

In the evening he took the tube to Notting Hill Gate and walked northwards up Ladbroke Grove. Stella's flat was on the first floor of a vast white wedding cake of a Victorian house and overlooked a private garden. From a dark staircase he walked into a huge room flooded with pale evening light. Several floor-to-ceiling windows had been opened outwards on to an ironwork balcony, in front of which Stella and a guy with dark hair and a lazy smile were sitting at a table drinking champagne.

'Alex,' said Stella. 'Hey. You made it!'

'I did,' agreed Alex.

Trying to recall the event afterwards, he discovered there were gaps in his memory. He couldn't remember what Stella's boyfriend did – it might have been something to do with the music industry, or possibly with TV, but then again it could have been advertising or PR – and he couldn't remember anything that they ate or drank or talked about at the long table

63

in front of the balcony. For Alex, this was one hell of a lot of information to forget in a short space of time but he didn't really give a damn because everything to do with Sophie – her skin, her hair, her smell, the way she moved – etched itself deeply and permanently into his consciousness.

She amazed him. There were her clothes, for a start – electric blue and, presumably, vastly expensive – which lent her the sheen of an exotic bird. And then there was her slender, delicately rounded body, and the limitless candour of her wave-green eyes. But more than her appearance there was her manner, her almost reckless confidence. Most women Alex had met up to that moment had seemed to watch themselves, to monitor their appearance and the impression that they were making minute by minute. Not Sophie. Sophie didn't seem to give a damn. There was a huge mirror on one wall of the twilit room and though she passed it a score of times Alex never saw her glance into it once. She was just there, beautiful if you chose to think so and if not, well, who cared?

Alex chose to think so. He was entranced and the thing that really got him – the thing that really ducked under his guard – was that she seemed to be as entranced as he was. She just stared at him, quite openly, fascinated.

'What's that smell?' she asked him as soon as she walked into the room. Walking over to Alex she sniffed at him. 'It's on your hands,' she stated. 'A kind of burnt . . .' She pressed his fingers to her nose and then touched her face to his hair. 'But you don't smoke, do you?' she murmured from behind his ear.

'It's gunpowder residue,' said Alex, realising what she was referring to. 'Cordite. You get it from using firearms in an enclosed space.'

'You've been killing people again,' said Stella disapprovingly. 'Honestly, you boys!'

Alex smiled. 'Just trying out some new toys on the range.'

'As one does,' said Stella's boyfriend. 'What sort?'

'Moorsyth .50 super-magnum,' said Alex.

'Ah.' The boyfriend was clearly none the wiser. 'Right.'

'Let's eat,' said Stella.

After dinner they split up. Spooning the sugar crystals from the bottom of her coffee cup, Sophie announced her desire that Alex take her for a walk. It was a warm evening, the streets, the cafés and the pavements were crowded, and it seemed the most natural thing in the world that she should take his arm so as to avoid their becoming separated. At one moment, outside a noisy Portobello Road pub, she stopped in her tracks and turned to face him, placing her hands on his shoulders. When he met her gaze, however, she smiled enigmatically and moved on.

Ten minutes later she suddenly dived into a bar. It was tiny, the walls were yellowed with cigarette smoke and hung with ancient photographs of boxers and footballers. 'Quick!' she told the barman. 'We need some malt whisky. Hurry, it's an emergency.'

'Do you always get what you want?' asked Alex as the waiter placed two tumblers of Laphroaig in front of them.

She frowned. The whisky made its smoky way down their throats. 'I think . . . pretty much always,' she admitted. 'What about you?'

'It's a long time since I've wanted anything as badly as . . .'

She reached for his thigh under the table. 'Do you want me . . . badly?'

'Yes,' said Alex.

Her eyes shone and she compressed her lips with pleasure.

They had finished their drinks and crossed Notting Hill Gate into Kensington Church Street. There, as if at a prearranged signal, both had raised their arms to the same cruising taxi.

In the back, ignoring the seat belts, he put his arm round her shoulders and she kissed his neck before moulding herself warmly against him. Taking his other hand, she placed it on her breast and he felt the nipple harden beneath his probing fingers.

'Mmm!' she murmured.

Laughing, but their movements urgent now, they ran up the stairs to her flat. They had kissed as soon as the door had closed behind them – a long kiss, but one which swiftly proved to be less than either of them wanted or needed.

She led him inside, somehow managing to unbelt him and to remove her blue silk top as she went. An antique velvet-covered sofa offered itself, and by then she was unzipping and stepping out of her skirt. His hand moved to the damp triangle between her legs, hers to the zip of his trousers. He sat back and she lowered herself gratefully on to him, gasping as she felt him thrust hard inside her. Her back arched and her hair fell away from the pale oval of her face. 'I can still smell the gunpowder,' she gasped and drove herself against him, hot and wet, clenching and releasing, rising and falling.

SIX

Sleepily, Alex reached for her. Eyes closed, he allowed his fingers a lazy exploration of her body, felt the desire stir inside him once more.

But Sophie seemed to have changed. Her breasts, for a start, were very much larger and heavier than he remembered, and were now suspended in a loose nylon bra and resting against several warm rolls of flesh. The smell in his nostrils was not that of Guerlain perfume and expensive hairdressing but of sweat, airline cooking and recycled air.

Cautiously he opened an eye. The face that lay inches from his and the breast that he was fondling belonged to his fellow passenger from Banjul, Maureen. And it was Maureen's hand which was firmly cupping his crotch.

'You certainly do like big girls, don't you,' she whispered hungrily. Her fingers tightened round him. 'In fact you're quite a big boy yourself!'

Alex stared at her. The whites of her eyes had a yellowish cast to them, as did her teeth. A centimetre of grey showed at the roots of her hennaed hair. In the opposite aisle, one of the few other male passengers on the flight caught his eye and gave him a leery wink.

'A little bird tells me that you and I are about to join the mile-high club,' she whispered.

Alex struggled upright. 'That little bird is wrong,' he said, searching his memory for the woman's name. 'I'm sorry, I've . . . I've been asleep.'

She looked at him quizzically. 'You seemed so . . .'

'I was dreaming,' he said firmly. 'Of my girlfriend.'

'Ah,' she said, drawing herself upright and pulling an in-flight magazine from the back of the seat in front. 'I see.'

Every detail of her deportment spelt hurt and disappointment – emotions to which Alex guessed she was no stranger. He glanced at his watch: 2.45 p.m. London time. Three bloody hours to go. He felt stale and overtired. Whatever was waiting for him at the other end had to be an improvement on this.

Three men were waiting for him.

They were standing with one of the Customs officers at the EU citizens' immigration desk. One, in a shiny blazer and slacks, looked like a run-to-seed bodybuilder. Salaried muscle, thought Alex. Ex-squaddie, 18K and a clothing allowance. The second, a florid-faced figure in a Barbour coat, had the tired, tolerant gaze of the time-serving civil servant. The third, a younger and more military-looking figure in a Brigade of Guards tie and a velvet-collared coat, Alex vaguely recognised. Box, he thought. MI5.

'Captain Temple,' asked the younger man. 'Could you step this way, sir?'

They hurried him into the Customs offices, down a flight of stone stairs and out into a car park where they convened round a nearly new Ford Mondeo.

'Alex, isn't it?' said the man in the velvet-collared coat. 'Gerald Farmilow. We met at Thames House. I'm Five's liaison officer with the Regiment.'

It came back to him now. He'd been introduced to a bunch of Security Services suits when he'd first taken over the RWW team. This Farmilow character had been one of them.

'I remember, Gerald,' he said. 'I'm sorry – it's been a bit of a long night.'

'Congratulations, by the way,' said Farmilow. 'An excellent result.'

Alex nodded. He felt dry-throated and in need of a shower. And some halfway sensible clothes.

Farmilow glanced at his watch, a wafer-thin sliver of gold and enamel, and nodded towards the red-faced man in the Barbour.

'Alex, George will tell you what this is all about.' He held out his hand. 'I've got to push off back to Millbank.'

A brief handshake and he was gone. Identification effected. Mission completed.

'I'm George Widdowes,' said the man in the Barbour, opening one of the Mondeo's rear doors, 'and this is Tom Ritchie.'

The driver mutely raised his hand.

'I'd also like to add my congratulations to Gerald's,' Widdowes continued. 'I understand you had a major success last night.'

Alex looked at him non-committally and climbed into the car. He wasn't about to discuss Regiment business with these people.

Widdowes nodded approvingly. 'Lips sealed. Quite right. Look, Captain Temple, we've got a good hour's drive ahead of us – we're going out to Goring, in Berkshire – so I'll put you in the picture as we go. Do you smoke?'

Alex shook his head.

The younger man drove, Widdowes sat in the back with Alex. Alex's overnight bag joined a laptop computer that was lying on the front seat. No one spoke until they were crawling along the exit road towards the M4 with the rest of the evening rush-hour traffic, but finally Widdowes half turned in his seat. 'I'm sure I don't need to say this, but it's essential that you don't repeat a word of what I'm about to tell you to anyone. Colleagues, senior officers, other security services people . . .'

Alex didn't bother to reply. Leaning against the back seat of the Mondeo with his eyes half closed, he felt a little of the tension leaving his shoulders.

'Good. Right, then. Had to say that. You know how it is.'

Alex nodded.

'Right . . . Well, here goes. A fortnight ago there was a murder committed in Chertsey, just inside the M25 in Surrey. Know it?'

'Isn't there an MOD arms sales place there?'

'That's right. Which is why the victim – one of our fairly

69

senior people, a man named Barry Fenn – happened to be staying in the area.'

Alex nodded. He was suddenly and acutely aware of his appearance – in his flowered shirt and flip-flops he looked and felt ridiculous. Typical of Box to get you at a disadvantage. 'Go on,' he said levelly.

'You weren't here, obviously, but even if you had been you wouldn't have heard or seen anything about it. We found him, we cleaned him up, we disappeared the body. Officially Barry Fenn died of heart failure in an ambulance en route to St Peter's Hospital, Chertsey. In fact, he was killed in the early hours of the morning in a third-floor bedroom at the White Rose Lodge by a person or persons unknown. The killer – I'm assuming it's one person – disabled the exterior floodlight warning system, scaled the back of the building, climbed in through a window, eliminated our man, returned the way he came and vanished.'

'How did he kill him?' asked Alex.

'Horribly,' said Widdowes, closing his eyes. 'Barry Fenn was a good friend of mine. Had been for twenty years odd.'

Alex waited. Widdowes steepled his fingers again.

'The killer tied his wrists and drove a six-inch nail through the side of his head. When he'd done that he cut his tongue out.'

Alex said nothing. Widdowes' words had fired off a number of warning flares in his mind, but he showed no outward sign of this. The SAS were deeply wary of the other security services, whose human resource management they considered fatally flawed. David Shayler had gone a long way towards making monkeys of Five by publicising their involvement in the Muammar Gaddafi assassination plot and Richard Tomlinson had performed much the same service for Six when he outlined plans to whack Slobodan Milosevic with the help of the RWW. In general it was not a good time to be sharing a sleeping bag with Military Intelligence.

'I'm sorry,' Alex said neutrally. 'I'm sure he was a good man.'

'He was,' said Widdowes.

Alex glanced at his plastic flip-flops and sunburnt toes, and thought of Africa and Don Hammond and the screams of the wounded RUF men. Although the leech marks were still fresh on his arms and legs and groin, the bloody events of the night before already seemed a world away. 'Let's cut to the chase, Widdowes,' he said. 'What do you want from me?'

The MI5 man turned to him. 'We're going to the site of a second murder. Another of our desk officers, a man named Craig Gidley. Exactly the same modus operandi, except that this time the killer gouged his eyes out.'

A moment's silence.

'Go on?' said Alex.

'And we've got reason to think the killer's one of our guys. Or to be precise, one of your guys. An SAS-trained undercover agent.'

Alex stared out of the window. They passed a flooded gravel pit, a coppice, fields.

'We need this man found, Captain Temple, and soon.'

The dead man's house stood a short distance outside the Thames-side town of Goring. A high flint wall surrounded the property; inside, a converted Georgian farmhouse was fronted by a neat lawn, yews and a lime tree. On the gravelled drive in front of the main entrance several cars were drawn up.

Ritchie found a space for the Mondeo, opened Widdowes' door for him and returned to the driver's seat, patting his pockets for cigarettes. Widdowes led Alex round to the back of the house, where two men and two women were sitting at an ironwork garden table. They looked as if they had been there for some time.

Widdowes led Alex round the table, first to the older and obviously senior of the two women, whom he introduced as 'our deputy director', then to the two men, who were respectively a service pathologist and a forensics officer. The final introduction was to an anonymous-looking younger woman whose name was Dawn Harding.

With these formalities complete the pathologist and the forensics man excused themselves and returned to the house. In

71

response to a gesture by the deputy director, Alex and Widdowes took their vacated chairs.

'Thank you for coming at such short notice, Captain Temple,' said the deputy director. She was an austerely handsome woman in her fifties, grey-haired.

Alex nodded cautiously.

'I believe George has brought you up to date with events?'

'In general terms, yes.'

'And with what we want you to do.'

'He's given me a fair idea.'

'And?'

'And my answer to him was the same as my answer is to you: that I'm a soldier, not a policeman. I can track a man through the jungle or over mountains, but not through criminal record databases and security services computer files. You've brought in the wrong person.'

The deputy director looked at her two colleagues and back at Alex. 'You won't need files or records,' she said quietly. 'We know who murdered Fenn and Gidley.'

Alex stared. 'You know who . . .'

'Yes. At least we've got a pretty good idea. And finding him is something we've got well in hand ourselves. What we need from you is more in the nature of disposal. Before we go into that, though, I'd like you to look at the body and see what it suggests to you. George?'

Widdowes stood and led Alex into the house through the back door. Inside, a flag-stoned corridor gave on to an oak-floored front hall, and the hall on to a small, book-lined study. To Alex, as he flip-flopped through, the set-up looked like an expensive one. The furniture was old and dark, and the gilt-framed portraits which hung on the walls looked like originals.

Disposal. Typical Box bullshit. They meant execution.

The owner of the house was lying face down on the study carpet. Although not tall he was a bulky man, and his dinner jacket and trousers looked a size too tight. His hands, blackened and swollen, had been tied behind his back with yellowish cord and it was clear from the severely chafed wrists that he had struggled violently against his bonds. Beneath his face a congealed pool of blood had blackened the worn Persian rug. The coppery smell of the blood hung in the air.

From the doorway Widdowes signalled for Alex to approach the body.

'We've taken the photos and run all the technical stuff. You can move him around if you want.'

There was nothing that Alex wanted to do less, but he put his hands to the body and pushed, and the corpse rolled heavily over on to its back. In this position the full horror of the assault was revealed. The face was an unrecognisable mask of caked blood. Where the eyes had been were now clotted black holes. At the victim's right temple the head of a six-inch flat-head nail showed a couple of millimetres proud of the skin surface. On close inspection the nail head proved to be flecked with rust. For the best part of a minute Alex stared at the body. It seemed to be expected of him.

'OK?' asked Widdowes.

Alex shrugged. 'Just fill me in again on what happened. The Gidleys were having a party, yeah?'

'A dinner party,' said Widdowes. 'A dinner party for four Service colleagues and their partners. They would have arrived at about the same time that you left Freetown to keep your appointment with the RUF.'

'And you weren't there?' asked Alex.

'No,' said Widdowes, a small note of annoyance creeping into his voice. 'I wasn't, as it happens.'

'And the deputy director?'

'The DD was there, yes. In all – including Craig and Letitia Gidley – ten people sat down to eat. By half past midnight the guests had all left, and Craig Gidley locked the front gate and let the dogs out.'

'They were Dobermanns, right? Attack dogs?'

'That's right. They'd been shut up in their kennels while the guests were around. Normally they had the run of the grounds – a couple of acres in all. Better than any alarm, as you can imagine.'

'Not on this occasion,' said Alex soberly.

'Well, no, as it happened. Not on this occasion.' Widdowes rubbed his eyes. It occurred to Alex that the MI5 man had probably had as shitty a day as he had.

'Shortly afterwards Letitia Gidley saw her husband lock the front door. She went up to bed – they had separate bedrooms – and he went into the study announcing that he was going to have a finger of Scotch and spend half an hour on the computer. That was the last time she saw him alive. She found him here at 9.30 this morning and called the DD.'

'Where's – what's her name – Letitia Gidley now?'

'At a colleague's in London. In a fairly bad way, as you can imagine. Let's go outside.'

Gratefully, Alex followed him into the hall and thence to the porch. The front door was of heavy steel-backed oak. 'This how he got access?' asked Alex.

'Yes. Picked the lock. Very expertly. Come through.'

Widdowes led him the fifty yards or so past the parked cars to the front gate, where he pointed to a telegraph pole.

'See that little box on the line running to the house?'

Alex recognised it at a glance. 'It's a sonic deactivator. Sends a false "secure" signal to the alarm monitoring station.'

'That's right. Have you ever used one?'

Alex chose to ignore the question. 'And it was just the house that was alarmed?'

Widdowes looked at him thoughtfully for a moment before nodding. 'Just the house. These two little charmers kept an eye on the garden.'

He led Alex along the lawn. In the herbaceous border, doubled up among the lupins and delphinia, were the stiffened bodies of two Dobermann pinschers.

Alex whistled appreciatively. 'He's good, this guy. And the wife heard nothing?'

'Nothing.'

Alex nodded. At the front door the two men he had met earlier were loading a body bag into the boot of one of the cars. Ritchie, cigarette in mouth, was giving them a hand.

'How would you have taken out Gidley?' asked Widdowes.

'I'd have done pretty much as this guy did,' Alex answered. 'Wait until everyone's inside and the party's under way, then climb the telegraph pole and disable the alarm. He wouldn't have gone inside the grounds at that stage because of the dogs.'

'How would he have known about the dogs?' asked Widdowes.

'He would have seen them,' said Alex. 'He'd have had this place under surveillance for days, maybe even weeks. He'd have known the dogs' names, when they were fed, everything.'

'So then?'

'Then he would have pulled back from the target and positioned himself somewhere he could count the cars out at the end of the evening. Field, maybe, or a tree. He probably had binoculars. Soon as he was sure the Gidleys were alone, he'd have returned and gone over the wall.'

'What about the dogs?'

'See the way they're lying?' asked Alex, pointing to the twisted bodies. 'I'd put money on his having used poison, meat laced with strychnine. You whistle the dogs over, throw down the meat and then assume a submissive posture face down on the ground. Instead of going straight for your throat the dogs just piss on you. Once they've symbolically dominated you, you see, you're no longer a threat and they can get on with the meat.'

'Big mistake,' murmured Widdowes drily.

'Very big,' agreed Alex. 'They're dead in seconds. Then our man takes a quick trot to the front door, boosts the lock and . . .' He shrugged. 'That's the how of it, anyway. As regards the why, you tell me.'

'Let's go back to the DD,' said Widdowes.

They returned to the back of the house, where the deputy director was making notes in a small ring-binder. The two men sat down. It was several seconds before she looked up. 'So, Captain Temple, give us your assessment of the perpetrator of this murder.'

Alex hesitated. 'Why me?' he asked her. 'Why pull me out of the Sierra Leone jungle when you could have had Hereford chopper a bloke down this morning? Why waste the best part of a day?'

The deputy director gave the faintest of smiles. 'Because I wanted *you*, Captain Temple, not just some "bloke". I've been led to understand that you're the best.'

Alex looked away. 'Who told you that?' he asked sardonically.

'Commissioned from the ranks at thirty-four after a decade's exemplary service. RWW team leader while still a captain . . . The facts speak for themselves.'

Alex shrugged. He guessed that, one way or another, he'd managed to keep his nose clean over the years. And managed it without brown-nosing the brass, which he privately considered to be his real achievement. 'Let me get this right,' he said. 'You're in the process of trying to locate the man who murdered Fenn and Gidley. Assuming that you do locate him, you want me to move in and eliminate him.'

'That's about the shape and size of it.'

Alex nodded. 'If I'm going to do that, I'm going to need to know everything you've got on him.'

'That's not a problem.'

'And I'm going to need to ask you some pretty sensitive questions.'

'And I'll do my best to answer them, Captain Temple. There'll be no secrets between us. We want this man taken off the streets, and fast. For reasons I'm sure I don't have to go into, I want the whole thing tied up before the police get wind of it. Or, God help us, the press. That means days, Captain Temple. Not weeks. All of this is *urgent*.'

Nodding his assent, Alex looked out across the evening stillness of the garden. Midges whirled in the scented air. Was it his imagination or had she emphasised the word 'captain', as if to suggest that promotion would accompany success. Or that demotion would follow refusal, perhaps . . . Not that he had a hope in hell of getting out of this.

'OK.' He nodded.

The deputy director swept her papers together. 'Good,' she

said briskly. 'I'll see you in my office at 9 p.m. tomorrow. By then we'll have photographs and the bulk of the forensic information, and I can give you some of the background to all of this. Meanwhile you'll be liaising with Dawn, who'll take you back to London. Anything you need, just ask her.' With that she got up, briefly extended her hand to Alex – he pressed it, perhaps more gingerly than was strictly polite – and swept into the house.

'I'll wrap up here, Dawn,' said George Widdowes. 'Why don't you and the captain make a move? Unless of course' – he turned to Alex – 'there's anything else you need to see?'

'I don't think so,' said Alex and turned his attention for the first time to the woman who had been sitting in silence at the far end of the table.

SEVEN

Alex's first impression was of toughness: tough grey eyes, tough posture and tough attitude. She had nondescript blonde hair, hadn't bothered with make-up and was wearing a black short-sleeved sweater, black trousers and flat-heeled elastic-sided boots.

The impression didn't last. The clothes, if plain, were clearly expensive and accentuated rather than concealed the smooth curves beneath. If she was wearing no make-up it was because she knew she looked fine without it. And she certainly wasn't tough in the way that the 14th Int women he'd known in Belfast had been tough. Women like Carol Denny or Denise Foley who would match the Regiment guys drink for drink after a good terrorist kill and would have been perfectly happy lying up in a freezing hide with a Heckler and Koch snipers' rifle and doing the job themselves. Denise, he remembered, used to bake a cross-shaped cake every time the Det or the Regiment took a player out.

Nor was Dawn Harding much like the Box girls he'd met over the water. For the most part they had been bright, ordinary-looking types, much more desk-bound and secretarial than their Det colleagues. Most of them, according to Don Hammond – who'd always had a bit of a way with words – were 'gagging for a bit of Regimental pipe'.

But not this one. This one was decidedly unimpressed and it wasn't just because he happened to be dressed like a West African pimp. It was because she wanted to impress on him from the start that there was a distinct difference in status between some johnny-come-lately ex-squaddie and a fast-track MI5 desk officer to be. When she turned to him it was with the polite but very slightly patronising look that all executive-stream Box personnel seemed to acquire sooner or later. 'So,' she said. 'Back to London. Have you got anywhere to stay?'

It was a good question. Since clearing Customs at Heathrow, Alex had not had a moment to himself and he certainly wasn't about to ring Sophie with all these wanky spooks hanging around. He didn't even want to call her from his mobile until he was well clear of them – mobile phones were a pushover in surveillance terms and although it was unlikely that a scanner was being operated from the cars at the front of the house, he didn't want to take the chance.

There was one call he could and would make, though. Tersely excusing himself and deliberately marching a good twenty yards away from Harding, he put a call through to Lieutenant-Colonel Bill Leonard, the CO of 22 SAS. This, Alex knew, was in direct contravention of Widdowes' request, but bollocks to that.

Howard was still at his desk at the Regimental base at Credenhill, near Hereford. 'Well done last night,' he said quietly. 'Overall, a bloody good show. You're in Berkshire I gather, with friends.'

On insecure lines the Regiment used the minimum of military jargon. There would be no 'sirs' or 'bosses' or departments named.

'That's right. They have some . . . cleaning they want me to do.'

There was a brief silence. Finally Howard spoke. 'I want you to lend them a hand on this one, Alex. Accepting an upgrade like you did last year means eating a shit sandwich from time to time and this is one of those times.'

'Yeah, but . . .'

'No buts, Alex. This problem of theirs has got to be dealt with and I can't think of a better man than you to do it. I'm sorry, Alex, but that's a must. What I can promise is choice of posting when you're done. You've got my word on that.'

Alex said nothing. By the time he was done, he reflected – if he was ever done – things would have changed. The 'choice' would dissolve, as it always did.

'How's Karen?' he asked. Karen was Don Hammond's widow.

'Bearing up, as is Sue. They've both got people round with them. I'll have someone call you about the funerals.'

Sue, Alex guessed, must have been the wife of the dead Special Forces pilot.

'Help our friends out, Alex. There's no room for manoeuvre on this one.'

The phone went dead.

Dawn Harding drove a two-year-old Honda Accord and drove it with an almost aggressive respect for the speed limit. When she was cut up at traffic lights outside Reading she merely slowed to let the other driver get away, while on the M4, where the prevailing speed was around 80, she seemed happy to roll along in the high 60s.

'Saving the engine?' Alex ventured at one point.

'No. Hanging on to a clean licence,' answered Dawn. She gestured towards the traffic pouring past them. 'And I've nothing to prove to a bunch of stressed-out commuters. Where is it you want to go exactly?'

Alex had tried Sophie earlier but got her voice-mail. He got it again now. For a reason that he couldn't quite put his finger on – something to do with wanting to hear her reaction to the news of his return – he didn't want to leave a message. 'Sloane Square,' he answered. 'Anywhere around there.'

'Late-night shopping in the King's Road?' Dawn archly flicked a glance at his shirt.

'No, I've got some friends at the barracks,' said Alex. *And sod you too*, he thought.

'OK. Sloane Square it is. And I'd be grateful if you didn't go chatting to all your Territorial Army mates about this after-noon's events, if that's all right with you.'

He stared at her. 'It's not my habit to "go chatting", as you put it, to my mates or to anyone else. I was a badged SAS soldier before you . . .' He faltered to silence. How old was she? Twenty-five? Twenty-six? '. . . Before you sat your GCSEs,' he finished weakly.

She smiled. 'So, have you ever killed anyone, Captain?'

'I've hurt a few people's feelings!'

Dawn nodded sagely. 'And are you very conscious of your age? Is that a problem for you? After all, most captains must be ten years younger than you. My sort of age, in fact.'

'Listen,' said Alex, 'if you think your superiors' – he stressed the word – 'have got the wrong man for the job, I'd be very happy to step down. Just stop the car and I'll fuck off.'

'You'll . . . *fuck off*?'

Alex reached over to the back seat for his bag.

'Yes,' he said. 'I'll fuck off.' He looked at her meaningfully. 'There is no aspect of this project that I'm looking forward to, none whatsoever. I've had dealings with Thames House before and regretted it every time. For my money you jokers can dig yourselves out of your own shit.'

'I see. Well, that's certainly telling it like it is. Did it ever occur to you, Captain Temple, that we might all actually be on the same side? Pursuing the same objectives?'

Alex said nothing. At that moment he was at least as angry with himself as he was with her. She'd wound him up and he'd gone off like a fucking clockwork mouse. *You're a dickhead, Temple*, he told himself. *Get a grip.*

She slowed to negotiate the lights at Barons Court. As she pulled on the handbrake, Alex watched the muscles in her forearm tauten. She had long fingers and short, square-cut nails.

'You're saying,' she went on, 'that it's really of no concern to you that some . . . some maniac is torturing and murdering our people?'

'I was only wondering why you couldn't deal with the whole thing in-house.'

'The decision has been made to do otherwise,' said Dawn curtly.

Which pretty much brought the argument to a close. She gave him her mobile and office numbers, and asked him to ring

81

her as soon as he knew where he was staying. Mentally Alex determined not to do this.

'Do you know your way to Thames House?' she asked.

'Millbank, last time I visited.'

'Tomorrow at 9 a.m., then. I'll meet you at the front desk.'

'It's a date.'

Unsurprisingly, she didn't smile. A few minutes later, as she brought the Honda to a halt outside the Duke of York's Headquarters in the King's Road, he nodded his thanks and grabbed his bag.

'Tomorrow,' she repeated, flipping a long brown envelope on to the passenger seat.

Alex hesitated before reaching for it.

'Expenses,' she said. 'According to our records, you don't have a London address. And unless you've left some clothes at Miss Wells's – and my guess is that you're not really the type for that cosy domestic scene – I'd say that you're going to need to add to your wardrobe some time between now and tomorrow. Keep it simple, would be my advice, and dress your age. Harrods is still open for a couple of hours. See you.' She didn't even leave at speed, just drew gently away from the kerb.

He watched after her for a moment, shaking his head with intense dislike. The reference to Sophie had had its intended effect: to let him know that Dawn Harding and her organisation could jerk his chain any bloody time they felt like it. 'Not if I see you first,' he murmured, but knew that his words had no meaning. He and Dawn Harding were locked together for the duration, like it or loathe it. He punched the recall button on his Nokia.

Five minutes later a silver Audi TT convertible pulled to a swerving halt at the kerb. 'Hey, sexy! Looking for business?'

For the first time that day Alex smiled. Sophie was wearing a screamingly loud Italian print shirt and, despite the lateness of the day, sunglasses. The sight of her made his heart dance. 'Jump in,' she ordered.

From that moment, things picked up. Alex explained his

clothing predicament, Sophie made a rapid series of phone calls and five minutes later a willowy young man in leather trousers was unlocking a warehouse in Chelsea Harbour. Lights flickered on to reveal at least a dozen rails of men's clothes and several shoulder-high pyramids of shoeboxes. 'Help yourself to anything you want,' the young man told Sophie and Alex. 'I'll find you some bags.'

'What is all this stuff?' Alex asked.

'Mostly bits and pieces from shows and magazine fashion shoots,' Sophie replied. 'A lot of it hasn't even been worn.'

They eventually settled on a selection of items that Alex thought slightly over-fashionable and Sophie disappointedly described as 'somewhere between dreary and invisible'.

'In my world,' Alex explained, 'the grey man is king. How much do we owe this guy?'

'Oh, give him a couple of hundred.'

'Are you sure?'

'Don't worry. It'll get written off as damaged.'

'You lot are worse than army quartermasters.'

Sophie swung the keys of the Audi from a slender forefinger. 'My place?'

In the flat overlooking Sloane Street they heated up a Sainsbury's Prawn Vindaloo, drank Kronenbourg beer from bottles and watched *Goodness Gracious Me*. For Alex, after weeks of rations consumed in exclusively male company, the evening was heaven.

When she saw that he had unwound a few notches, Sophie settled herself against him on the sofa. 'Is it good news that you're back?' she asked him tentatively. 'Does it mean that you've got some time off?'

'Yes and no,' he said. 'I'm here to . . . chase something up.'

'Anything you can tell me about?'

He shook his head. 'I'm sorry.'

'Dangerous?'

He shrugged. 'Doubt it. I've got to find someone, that's all. Brain work, not bullets. So I'm going to be around, yeah, but I'm also going to be coming and going.'

83

She nodded. 'Is it always going to be like this?' she asked. 'Me asking, you not telling?'

'For as long as I'm in, yes,' he said. 'You mustn't take it personally.'

'I don't take it personally,' she said, with a flash of irritation, quickly suppressed. 'It's just that we've been together for a year now, on and off, and I'd like to feel that I had some . . . access to your life.'

'You have full access to my life,' he told her gently. 'It's just my work that's off limits. And I promise you, you're not missing anything there.'

'But your life *is* your work,' she protested. 'I can see that in your face. All those missions in Northern Ireland and Bosnia, all those dead men . . . I can see them there behind your eyes.'

He shrugged. It was not something he'd ever talked about in much detail. The demons, it was generally accepted, came with the job.

'I want all of you, Alex. Not just the burnt-out remains.'

He frowned at his Kronenbourg bottle. At the edge of his vision an RUF soldier crouched in blood-sodden shock, his lower jaw shot away. Behind him staggered the blackened figure of Don Hammond. There was a full company of such men quartered in Alex's head now.

Blinking them away, locking on to Sophie's grey-green eyes, he smiled. 'I'm all here. And I'm all yours.'

EIGHT

Alex presented himself at the front desk of Thames House at a couple of minutes to nine. Dawn Harding was waiting for him there, briefcase in hand, and signed him in. 'We're wearing Italian today, are we?' she said, noting his Gucci loafers and running an appraising glance up and down his grey Cerrutti suit. 'I thought you Hereford boys were more comfortable in Mr Byrite.'

'I know the importance you civil service types attach to appearances,' Alex said equably, fixing his visitor's badge to his lapel. 'You wouldn't want me to let the side down, now would you?'

He followed her into the lift, where she pressed the button for the fourth floor. 'And you found somewhere to stay all right?'

'I managed to get my head down.'

'I'm sure you did.' She stared without expression at the brushed-aluminium wall of the lift. As previously, she was dressed entirely in black and wearing no make-up, perfume or jewellery. Her only accessories were the briefcase – large, black and plain – and a military issue pilot's chronograph watch. This spareness did not, however, disguise her femininity. In some curious way, Alex mused, allowing his gaze to linger around the nape of her neck, it highlighted it. Or at least it made you wonder.

The lift shuddered to a halt. 'A word of advice,' she said flatly, checking her watch as she marched out into a grey-carpeted corridor flanked by offices. 'The correct form of address for the deputy director is ma'am.'

Alex smiled. 'So who are you, then? Matron?'

85

She gave him a withering glance. 'Dawn will be just fine.'

The deputy director's office was at the far end of the corridor. Dawn left Alex in an ante-room containing a leather-covered sofa and a portrait of Feliks Dzerzhinsky, founder of the KGB, and disappeared through an unmarked door.

She reappeared five minutes later. Alex was still standing – the leather sofa was so slippery he could hardly sit on it – and she led him into an office which would have been sunlit had not the blinds been partially lowered. This, Alex guessed, was to prevent glare rendering the computer monitors illegible. There were three of these on a broad, purpose-built desk, along with a telefax console and a tray piled high with what looked like newspaper cuttings. Maps, books and a large flat-screen monitor covered most of the walls, but a painted portrait of Florence Nightingale and a signed photograph of Peter Mandelson romping with a dog went some way towards softening the room's essentially utilitarian lines. At the near end half a dozen leather-and-steel chairs surrounded a low table bearing a tray with a steaming cafetière and four civil service-issue cups and saucers.

Behind the desk, silhouetted against the half-closed blinds, sat the deputy director and once again Alex was struck by her handsome, clear-cut features and elegant appearance. Today she was wearing a charcoal suit, which perfectly complemented her shrewd blue eyes and the expensively coiffed gunmetal of her hair.

To one side of her, both hands thrust deep into the pockets of a suit which had probably once fitted him better, stood George Widdowes. To Alex, the studied informality of the posture looked like an attempt to play down his subordinate status.

The deputy director rounded the desk and held out her hand. 'Since we're to be working together, Captain Temple,' she told him with a practised smile, 'I think we should at least know each other's real names. I'm Angela Fenwick, and my full title is Deputy Director of Operations. Dawn Harding and George Widdowes you know. Welcome to Thames House.'

86

As they arranged themselves in chairs around the table, Angela Fenwick leant forward and pressed down the plunger of the cafetiere.

'Boom!' whispered George Widdowes. No one smiled.

Angela Fenwick turned to Alex. 'I'd like you to know that nothing that is said in this office is recorded, unless you ask for it to be, and nothing you say here is in any way on the record. Basically, you can express yourself freely and I hope you will. The corollary is that you are not to make any mention of what I am about to tell you to anyone, in or outside this agency – and that includes your Regimental colleagues, past and present – without my express say-so. Do you have any problem with that?'

'No, I don't think so.'

'Good. Coffee, everybody? George, will you be mother?'

When Widdowes was done, Angela Fenwick leant back in her chair, cup in hand, and turned to Alex. 'Craig Gidley's murder,' she said. 'Did that remind you of anything?'

Alex glanced at the others. They were looking at him expectantly.

'You can speak openly in front of George and Dawn.'

Alex nodded. 'PIRA,' he said. 'Belfast Brigade took out those two FRU guys by hammering nails into their heads. Early 1996, it must have been, just after the Canary Wharf bomb. Left the bodies at a road junction outside Dungannon.'

'That's right,' Fenwick agreed. 'Can you remember where you were at the time?'

Alex considered. 'In February 1996 I was in Bosnia,' he said. 'I was part of the snatch team that grabbed Maksim Zukic and two of his colonels for the War Crimes Tribunal at The Hague. But we heard about the Canary Wharf bomb pretty much as it happened, and later about the FRU guys too.'

'Ray Bledsoe,' added Widdowes. 'And Connor Wheen.'

'Yeah, that's it. Bledsoe and Wheen. We didn't see that much of the FRU when we were on tours in the province, but I probably met both of them at various times.'

Angela Fenwick frowned. 'Am I right in thinking that you

were number two on the sniper team when Neil Slater shot the Delaney boy at Forkhill?'

'Yes, that was a year later.'

'The information about the weapons cache at the Delaney farm came from a tout originally cultivated by Ray Bledsoe.'

'Is that so?' said Alex. 'We tend not be told stuff like that.'

'Why didn't you tell me last night that you thought there was a PIRA connection to the murders?' asked Dawn Harding accusingly.

'You didn't ask me,' Alex answered mildly. 'But I was pretty certain of it as soon as Mr Widdowes here mentioned six-inch nails.'

Angela Fenwick nodded. 'I just wanted to establish that you knew about the Bledsoe and Wheen incident. And you're right, the roots of this thing do indeed lie in Northern Ireland. But they go back a little further than 1996. Back to Remembrance Day in 1987, in fact.'

'Enniskillen,' said Alex grimly.

'Precisely. Enniskillen. On the eighth of November in 1987 a bomb was detonated near the war memorial in that town, killing eleven people and injuring sixty-three. A truly horrendous day's work by the volunteers.'

Alex nodded. Widdowes and Dawn, sidelined, were staring patiently into space.

'The day after the explosion there was a crisis meeting attended by six people. Two of those – the former director and deputy director of this service – are now retired. Of the remainder one was myself, one was George, and the others were Craig Gidley and Barry Fenn. I was thirty-nine, a little younger than the others, and I had just been put in charge of the Northern Ireland desk.

'The purpose of the meeting was to discuss something that we were acutely aware of already: our desperate need to place a British agent inside the IRA executive. As you'll probably be aware, we had a pretty extensive intelligence programme running in the province at the time. We had informers, we had 14th Intelligence Company people, and we had touts. What we didn't have, however, was anyone close to the decision-making process. We didn't have anyone sufficiently senior to tip us off if another Enniskillen was in the wind and there couldn't be – there absolutely couldn't be – another Enniskillen.

'So basically we had two choices. To turn a senior player or to insert our own sleeper and wait for him to work his way up. The former was obviously the preferable choice in terms of time but in the long run it would have been much less reliable, as we could never be sure that we weren't being fed disinformation. We tried it, nevertheless. Got some of the FRU people to approach individual players that 14th Int had targeted and make substantial cash offers for basically harmless information. The hope was that we could hook them through sheer greed and then squeeze them once they were incriminated. Standard entrapment routine.

'But as we half expected, none of them went for it. Even if they had any ideological doubts – and in the wake of the slaughter at Enniskillen one or two of the players certainly did have ideological doubts – they knew only too well what happened to touts. Apart from anything else, they knew they'd never be able to spend any money we gave them. So they told our people where to get off and in a couple of cases published their descriptions in the Republican newspaper *An Phoblacht*. Which, as you can imagine, made us look pretty damn stupid.

'So the decision was made to put in a sleeper. Not someone who, if he was lucky, might be allowed to hang around the fringes of the organisation and report back snippets of bar talk. Not a glorified tout, in other words, but a long-term mole who would rise through the ranks. Someone who had the credentials to rise to the top of this highly sophisticated terrorist organisation, but also the courage, the commitment and the sheer mental strength to remain our man throughout. We would need someone exceptional, and identifying him would be a major project in itself.

'Operation Watchword, classified top secret, was planned and run by the four of us – myself, George, Gidley and Fenn. It had

89

a dedicated budget and a dedicated office, and no one else in the Service was given access of any kind. It was to be divided into three stages: selection, insertion and activation. Our man, once we found him, would be known as Watchman.

'Selection began in October 1987. The first thing we did was to make a computer search through MOD records. We were looking for unmarried Northern Irish-born Catholics aged twenty-eight or less and ideally those who had been the single children of parents who were now both dead. We looked at all the armed services. From the list that we got, including those with living parents and siblings, we eliminated all the officers, all those above the rank of corporal or its equivalent and all those with poor service records – for drinking, fighting, indiscipline and so on.

'We were left with a list of about twenty men, spread across the various services, and at that point we borrowed a warrant officer named Denzil Connolly from the RWW.'

Alex nodded. He had never met Connolly but knew of him by reputation. A right hard bastard by all accounts.

'Connolly dropped in on the various commanding officers and adjutants. He didn't enquire directly about the individuals we were interested in, merely asked if he could make a brief presentation and put up a notice calling for volunteers for Special Duties, which pretty much everyone knew meant intelligence work in Northern Ireland. Afterwards, over a cup of tea or a beer, he'd ask the adjutant if there was anyone he thought might be suitable. Self-sufficiency, technical ability and a cool methodical temperament were what was needed. If the target name failed to crop up he'd bring out a list that included the man in question. He had been given a dozen possibles, he'd say. Could the CO grade them from A to D in terms of the qualities he'd mentioned?

'By Christmas we had the numbers down to ten, all of whom answered the selection criteria and had either been directly recommended or assessed as As or Bs. The ten were then sent to Tregaron to join the current selection cadre for 14th Intelligence, bumping the course numbers for the year up to about seventy. You probably know more about the 14th Int course than I do, Captain Temple, but I believe it's fairly demanding.'

'It's a tough course,' said Alex. 'I think it prepares people pretty well for what they're going to encounter as undercover operators.'

Angela Fenwick nodded. 'Well, of the ten we sent on the course, four were among those returned to their units as unsuitable by the staff instructors at the end of the first fortnight. The other six were pulled out of Tregaron by us at the same time, although they assumed that what followed was part of the normal selection course. They were housed in separate locations in the area where our Service's psychiatric people interviewed them over several days to assess their suitability.'

'Why not let them just go through the normal 14th Int selection course?' asked Alex.

'Because there was a big difference in what we wanted out of them. Working undercover is lonely and solitary work but ultimately you're still part of a team. You're still a soldier on a tour of duty, and there are plenty of times in an undercover soldier's life when he can let his guard down, put aside his cover, socialise with his colleagues and be himself. The man we were looking for, on the other hand, would have no such opportunity. Once inserted he would probably never speak to another soldier again. He'd be giving up everything and everyone he'd ever known. We needed to know that he was capable of that.'

'And there were other factors,' added George Widdowes. 'We didn't want our man known as one of those who successfully completed the course. As part of his cover story he needed to have failed. And to have failed early enough for it to be believable that he couldn't remember much about the other sixty-odd blokes on the course. We didn't want our operation to compromise the security of the ones who passed.'

Alex nodded. 'Yes, I see what you mean.'

'The other thing at that stage was that we had to separate our six men from each other in case they figured out what they had in common and put two and two together. It wasn't a huge risk, but even at that stage we had to be one hundred per cent security conscious.'

'Right.'

'We interviewed the six,' continued Angela Fenwick, 'and, as George explained, they assumed the process was part of the normal 14th Int selection. Four of them we were happy with, the other two we sent back to Tregaron. The four we liked the look of were bussed one at a time to different points in an MOD training area in the North-West Highlands near Cape Wrath, given rudimentary survival and communications kit, and ordered to dig in. It was January by then and conditions were atrocious, with blizzards and deep snow.

'Over the next three weeks, although they were never more than a few kilometres from each other, none of the four men saw each other or another human being. They were given their instructions by radio or through message drops and ordered to carry out an endless series of near impossible tasks – marching all night to food drops where there turned out not to be any food, processing unmanageable amounts of data, repairing unmend-able equipment, that sort of thing – and made to do it all on next to no sleep and in the worst possible physical conditions. The idea, obviously, was to test their mental endurance, and although the four never saw them they were in fact being monitored throughout by a three-man team from the SAS training wing at Hereford.

'At the end of the three weeks they were each put through an escape and evasion exercise. This culminated in their being captured, given a beating and driven to a camp near Altnaharra where they were subjected to forty-eight hours of hard tactical questioning by a team from the Joint Services Interrogation Wing.

'After this the four were assessed by the instructors. One was in a very bad way by then and clearly unsuitable – I think he ended up having a nervous breakdown and leaving the army. Two were reckoned to be tough enough but essentially more suited to teamwork than a solo placement and were taken back to Tregaron to continue the 14th Intelligence course. The fourth one – the one they recommended – was a Royal Engineers corporal named Joseph Meehan.

'We had been hoping that Meehan would be the one they went for. He was young, only twenty-three at the time of the Watchman selection programme, and very much a loner. So much so, in fact, that his CO had been worried about his long-term suitability for regimental life. At the same time he was highly intelligent, highly motivated, and had an exceptional talent for electronics and demolitions. As it happened, he was also on the waiting list for SAS selection.

'For our purposes he seemed to be perfect. We needed someone young – it was going to take years rather than months to get him to a position of authority within the IRA. And of course we needed a loner. As far as we were concerned he had everything.

'Anyway, Meehan it was. From Altnaharra he was heli-coptered down to London and installed in one of our safe houses in Stockwell. At the point at which George and I first met him, in February 1988, he still thought he was on the 14th Int course. He thought everyone did a month's solitary in Scotland. Even said he'd enjoyed it.

'We told him the truth. Explained exactly what we wanted of him. Said that if he took the job his soldiering days were effectively over. That he'd never be able to see his army mates again. He told us what he'd told the psych team a month earlier, that he hated the IRA with every bone in his body and would do or say whatever was necessary to destroy them.

'Knowing Joe Meehan's life story as we did, we were inclined to believe him. He was the only son of a Londonderry electrician who, when the boy was twelve, attracted the atten-tion of the local IRA for accepting a contract to rewire a local army barracks. Meehan senior was kneecapped, his business was burnt out and he was chased from the province, eventually resettling in Dorset. Joseph went with him, left school at sixteen, and apprenticed himself to his father, but by then the old man was in a pretty bad way. He was crippled, drinking heavily and going downhill fast. He died two years later.'

'Was there a mother?' Alex asked.

'The mother stayed behind in Londonderry,' said Widdowes. 'Disassociated herself from the father completely after the kneecapping. Asked Joseph to stay behind when the father left and when he wouldn't she shrugged and walked away. Ended up remarrying a PIRA enforcer who ran a Bogside poolhall.'

'Nice,' said Alex.

'Very nice,' agreed Widdowes. 'And that was the point when Joseph joined the British army. One way or another he was determined to avenge his father's treatment. His hatred of the IRA was absolutely pathological – he described them to our people as vermin who should be eliminated without a moment's thought.' Widdowes blinked and rubbed his eyes. 'And from our point of view this was good. Hatred is one of the great sustaining forces and Meehan's hatred, we hoped, would keep him going through the years ahead. When we told him the nitty-gritty of what we wanted, he didn't hesitate. Yes, he said. He'd do it. We had our Watchman.'

NINE

'Training Joseph Meehan took six months,' said Angela Fenwick, staring out over the grey-brown expanse of the Thames. 'We would have liked to have given him more time, but we didn't have more time, so we packed everything into those six months. He lived in a series of safe houses, always alone, and the instructors came to him. Without exception these were the top people in their respective fields and permanently attached to Special Forces or Military Intelligence institutions on the mainland. For obvious security reasons no serving personnel were let anywhere near him. To start with we put him in one of the accommodation bunkers at Tregaron. Isolation conditions, of course, and we bugged the room and tapped the phone.'

Alex knew Tregaron well. Two hundred acres of windswept Welsh valley, rusted gun emplacements and dilapidated bunkers, all of it behind razor wire. He'd blown up a few old cars there as part of his demolitions training. Bloody miserable place to stay on your own, especially in winter. 'Who did you put in charge of him?' asked Alex.

'An RWW warrant officer, who provided us with progress reports and so on. We started off by getting a couple of the Hereford Training Wing NCOs to put him through their unarmed combat course, and sharpen up his advanced weapons and driving skills. Apparently he managed to bring the unarmed combat instructor to his knees by the end of the third session.'

'Impressive,' confirmed Alex. 'I wouldn't fancy trying to deck one of those guys.'

Fenwick nodded. 'At the same time we had an instructor

from Tregaron taking him through his surveillance and anti-surveillance drills, and generally familiarising him with intelligence procedures – drop-offs, dead-letter boxes and so on. After this we brought in a rapid succession of people to teach him individual skills like covert photography, lock-picking, bugging and counter-bugging, demolition and so forth. You probably know most of the specialists in question?'

'Stew for locks?' asked Alex. 'Bob the Bomber for dems?'

'Well, it's not exactly how they were introduced to me,' said Angela Fenwick with a smile. 'But I think we're probably talking about the same people. We had a couple of our own Service people bring him up to speed on computers, too. The technology was obviously less advanced than it is now but it was clear even then that the intelligence war was going to be fought every bit as keenly in cyberspace as on the ground.

'Meehan learnt very fast indeed, especially the technical stuff. According to his service record he'd always been a natural with electronics and the SAS demolitions people described him as the best pupil they'd ever had. The usual routine was that he'd do the physical stuff in the mornings and the classroom stuff in the afternoon. The Tregaron people updated him on the geography of the province and told him the locations of all the drinking houses, social clubs, players' homes, safe houses et cetera, to the point where he could almost have got work as a minicab driver, and at least once a day they ran him through different aspects of his cover story. Like all the best cover stories, this had the advantage of being ninety-five per cent true. Only nine months of it would have to be fictionalised. Nine months and a lifetime's beliefs.'

Alex was impressed by Fenwick's grasp of the salient details of the operation. She certainly seemed more on top of things than most of the MI5 agents he'd met in the field. He was also beginning to feel the beginnings of sympathy for Meehan. *If the ex-Royal Engineer was twenty-three in 1987*, thought Alex, *he's just a year older than me. We were probably learning much the same things at much the same time. The difference being that I was learning them in company with a bunch of mates and going out on the town on Friday nights and he was stuck in an isolated bunker in Tregaron with a tapped phone. Poor bastard.*

'Anyway,' continued Fenwick, 'the instructors hammered away at him pretty much full-time, seven days a week. We had a couple of the JSIW people come down and take him through his story until he was practically reciting it in his sleep. And, of course, we played the usual mind games, getting him to memorise complex documents, waking him up in the middle of the night to check minute aspects of his cover, that sort of thing. Every room in the house was plastered with pictures of IRA players, so even in his time off he was taking in information.'

She paused. To either side of her George Widdowes and Dawn Harding sat in trance-like silence.

'After three months we moved him down to Stockwell for a couple of days so that the Watchman team could spend some time with him and from there it was on to Croydon for a couple of months of advanced fieldcraft training with our service instructors. By that stage we were very much concentrating on demilitarising him, on knocking the professional soldier out of him. For that reason his time at Croydon was deliberately made as unstructured as possible. We fed him junk food, beer and roll-ups, slowed his metabolism down, sent him on the sort of exercise that involves spending the day in a pub. There's a test we set field agents that involves selecting a total stranger in a public place – pub, launderette, that sort of place – and seeing what information you can extract. There was a checklist we had – name, address, phone number, car registration number, job description, place of birth, spouse's maiden name, credit card number . . . It's not an easy skill but Meehan got to be very good at it indeed – and he always made the other people think that they were the ones doing the questioning. All in all, he was a natural. A fantastic find.' She coughed and patted her throat. 'Sorry, as you can see I'm not used to doing so much talking.'

Standing, she walked to a small table beside her desk and

poured herself a glass of Evian water. George Widdowes half rose, as if about to pat her on the back, but caught Dawn Harding's eye and sat down again. The room, Alex noticed, was becoming uncomfortably stuffy.

'After Croydon,' Widdowes said, 'we put our man through his first real test. We sent him back to the Royal Engineers two weeks before the 14th Int selection course was completed – the course, that is, that we'd pulled him out of several months earlier – and told him to get himself kicked out of the regiment. Left it up to him how he managed it.

'What he did was to go around telling everyone he'd been kicked off the 14th Int course because he was Catholic and Irish-born. He made it look as if this had really dented him – he started drinking a lot, picking fights, getting his name on charge sheets and so on. He'd already visibly put on weight and was a long way from being the lean, mean fighting machine the Engineers had originally sent up to Tregaron. There was an insubordination charge, a complaint of insulting behaviour by one of the civilian catering staff and some incident with a pub bouncer in Chatham – all slippery-slope stuff. The end came when one of the warrant officers discovered some detonator cord in his locker in the course of a room search. He claimed that it was a mistake, that he'd signed it out for instruction purposes and forgotten to sign it back in again, but the CO wasn't having it and Meehan was out on his arse.'

Alex whistled quietly and Widdowes shrugged. 'It was the only way. The whole thing had to be believable – we couldn't risk asking the CO to fake up a dishonourable discharge. Enough people were in the know already.

'Immediately after his discharge Meehan moved back to London and got a bed in a working men's hostel in Kilburn. Within a couple of weeks he'd picked up work with an emergency plumbing and electrical repair outfit run by a local tough called Tony Riordan. He stuck with Riordan long enough to figure out all the scams and fiddles, and generally acclimatise himself in the role of jobbing electrician, and in the evenings, like any other twenty-three-year-old, he'd hit the bars. As we hoped would happen before too long in that area, he ran into a few exiles from Belfast and Derry, and picked their brains about job prospects over there. Wasn't a political guy, he said, just had family over there and wanted a change.

'He ended up being given a few names. Nobody who'd seen the quality of his work thought twice about recommending him. And finally, over the water he went.

'The first thing he did over there was to visit his relatives. There was his mother, of course, still living over the pool hall in Bogside, and there were the usual uncles and aunts and cousins scattered around the place. He looked them all up, said his hellos, paid his respects. He didn't advertise the fact that he'd been in the army, but he didn't try to hide it either. Just told anyone who asked that he'd got fed up and left.

'He saw his mother for the first time in more than ten years, but made no secret of how he felt about her walking out on the family. The boyfriend, by now a pissed old fart approaching sixty – bit like me – tried on a bit of Republican stuff, told him there were people he should meet and so on, but Meehan wasn't buying. Didn't want to know, he said. Wasn't interested.

'By the autumn he was living in Belfast. A cousin who was a chartered surveyor – highly respectable guy, married, kids, house in Dunmurry – offered to take Meehan in until he'd found his feet. Meehan stayed there for eight weeks or so, sorted himself out a job with the service department of a store in the city centre, a sort of Tandy-type place called Ed's Electronics, and moved into a rented place a few streets away from his cousin. He also started seeing a girl, a hairdresser called Tina Milazzo. She was a careful choice – Catholic, clearly, but not part of any obvious player set-up. Her family were immigrants and her parents ran a café in the Andersonstown Road. The Milazzo family were known to us because of Tina's brother Vince, who fancied himself as a hot-shot driver and all-round dangerous dude, and liked to hang out where the players hung out. He would never have been allowed within a mile of any real action because he was a loudmouth, but he was tolerated.

'After that, it was basically a question of waiting. We sent Barry Fenn out as his agent handler and Barry used that waiting period to run through the various communications procedures – something we always try to do if we can, because it reassures the agent in the field that the systems work. So we were pretty well informed about the assimilation process.'

'Did Fenn handle anyone else?' Alex asked.

'No. He was Meehan's dedicated handler. We didn't tell Meehan that, though.'

'Why not?'

'Well, I suppose because we didn't want to worry him by suggesting that PIRA might have sussed out the others. They hadn't, of course, but we didn't want him concerning himself for one moment with those kinds of issues. Anyway, once Meehan was in place we told him that henceforth the drops and meets would be initiated by him rather than by us, and that we'd be pulling Barry back – or 'Geoff' as Meehan knew him – until he reported that a definite approach had been made. We knew this was likely to be months rather than weeks, because we'd agreed from the start that Meehan would adopt a strictly "not-interested" posture vis-à-vis any Republican stuff.'

'Wasn't there a danger that PIRA would take him at his word and leave him alone?'

'I think we pretty much made him irresistible. As well as working at the shop he let it be known that outside work hours he was happy to do repairs at home. Transmitter-receivers and computers that no one else could fix, that sort of thing. The more complex the problem, the better he liked it. It was only going to be a matter of time before the word got around that one of the guys at Ed's was a circuitry wizard and a few quiet checks started to be made. And of course we also had Vince Milazzo shooting his mouth off about his sister's new bloke who'd been in the army but had got pissed off and walked out.'

'And they bit?'

'Eventually they bit. To our relief, as you can imagine. It had been more than eighteen months since Enniskillen by then, and in that eighteen months we'd had eight soldiers killed in Ballygawley, six at Lisburn and two in the Buncrana Road. More than thirty-five men had been seriously injured and that's just the army statistics. I can't honestly remember how many civilians and UDR members had been murdered in the period, but the pressure on this Service to get a man in place was unbelievable.

'The way it happened was that one evening in June 1989 a couple of fellows were waiting for Meehan when he finished work. Suggested he came for a quiet drink and drove him to MacNamara's, which is very much a volunteer hang-out. Asked him if he took on private work. He said he did, but nothing political, which they seemed to accept. One of them then took him out to the car park and showed him an army Clansman radio. Asked if he could fix it.

'Well, obviously he could have fixed it in his sleep, but he refused, said he wasn't touching it. When they asked him why, he told them that he recognised the radio as army issue and wanted no involvement with that sort of business. Then he thanked them politely for the drink and walked off. They didn't try to stop him.

'But of course they were back a few days later, and this time it was six of them and they didn't take him to a bar, but to the first floor of a house in the Ballymurphy area. They'd done some checking, they told him, and they had some questions that needed answering. They were still polite, but it was clear that if the answers weren't good enough he was in serious trouble.

'It was the moment he'd rehearsed a thousand times. Sure, he'd been in the British army, he told them, and he'd never tried to hide the fact. His family knew it, his girlfriend knew it and his employer knew it. He also told them what had happened to his father and how he had been chased from the country a decade earlier. With his father dead, he explained, he no longer had any family on the mainland, so he'd come home.

101

All he wanted now, to be honest, was to carry on with the work he was doing, bank a decent salary and be left alone to get on with his life.

'They heard him out. As a Royal Engineer, they said, he must have been involved in demolitions.

'Sure, he told them, and for the first time allowed a note of bitterness to creep in. He'd been a qualified demolitions instructor and at one time had considered a career in the quarrying industry after leaving the army. With his dishonourable discharge, however, all that had gone up in smoke.

'Tell us about the discharge, they said, so he did. He'd been stitched up, he explained, and all for a couple of lengths of det cord. All the instructors kept bits and pieces in their lockers – signing the stuff in and out every day took bloody hours. It wasn't as if it had been drugs or live ammunition, they'd just had it in for him for being a Mick. But then that was the Brit Establishment for you – heads they win, tails you lose. But what the fuck, he still had the skills. No one could take the skills away.

'They listened and then drove him back to his flat. Nothing much was said, but this time when they handed him the Clansman he took it. They gave him a number to ring when it was ready.

'After this encounter, which he described to Barry in detail from a public phone near his home, the communications from Meehan via Barry Fenn almost dried up. It became clear to him that he was being watched almost full-time. He was certainly being tested; a few days after mending and returning the Clansman a woman called round at his flat at seven in the morning with an Amstrad computer in a plastic bag. It had crashed, she told him, and she needed a data-recovery expert.

'He unpicked the mess, downloaded the data and discovered that it contained details of the security system of one of the city-centre banks. It was obviously a set-up: if the security was beefed up in any way they'd know he was a player for the other side. So we did nothing about it at all – didn't even bother to tell the bank. And of course there was no raid.

'A couple of weeks later the first two men turned up at his flat on a Saturday morning. As far as we can work out he was taken on some kind of tour of the city. Various introductions were made and the day ended at a drinking club.

'Over the next few months a gradual process of indoctrination took place. The people that he met were low-level players for the most part, and I guess they flattered Meehan and showed him a pretty good time. A charm offensive, if you can imagine that. Our instructions to him, relayed via Barry, were to allow himself to be drawn out. We wanted him to give the impression of "coming to life", both socially and politically.

'Tina Milazzo certainly helped with this. Sources on the ground told us that she gave the impression of enjoying the nightlife and the conspiratorial atmosphere, and the company of the other girlfriends. She probably sensed that the other men were respectful of Joe, that they had plans for him and that this reflected well on her. Whatever, she fitted in. She helped the thing along.

'Over the months that followed we heard almost nothing from Meehan. We wanted him to dig in, to live and breathe Republicanism, and we told him that he should only contact Barry if he had anything really vital to report.

'Nothing vital came up. The killings of soldiers and others continued, but we considered it highly unlikely that Meehan was anywhere near the inner circles where such things were discussed and planned. It would be years, probably, before that would be the case. But he was on his way. Shortly before Christmas 1989 a seventeen-year-old named Derek Maughan was picked up by a team of volunteers after stealing a car and joyriding around the outskirts of the city. It was not the first time this had happened, it was decided to make an example of him, and he was driven out to waste ground and a nine-mil round was put through his kneecap. From the front, as he was just a lad, rather than from the back. Now as it happened, one of the volunteers on the snatch team was touting for the FRU and within a couple of days of the shooting we had the names of all those involved.

'The driver was one Joe Meehan. That year this agency was able to give the Cabinet Office a very special Christmas present. The assurance that a sleeper was in place in the Belfast Brigade. That, finally, MI5 had a man in the IRA.'

TEN

There was a lengthy pause. Dawn Harding, as if to make a tacit point about self-control, sat motionless and without expression. George Widdowes stretched in his chair and recrossed his legs. Rising and marching briskly to her desk, Angela Fenwick lifted the telephone and ordered sandwiches for four. From a desk drawer she took a clear plastic folder. Inside was a sheaf of photographs, which she handed to Alex.

He examined them one by one. There was an early Meehan family shot taken in a kitchen: the father standing in his shirtsleeves, the blowsy bottle-blonde mother smoking by the stove and the pinched, worried-looking boy – even then the image of his dad – crouched over his homework. In the school photo, scrubbed and hairbrushed, young Joseph didn't look much happier, but he appeared to have cheered up a bit for the holiday snap in which, aged about eleven, he and his mother were sitting at a folding table by a river with a caravan in the background. Another shot, possibly taken on the same holiday, showed the boy triumphantly holding up a small trout. Almost a smile on his face.

And then there was Meehan aged about fifteen taking part in a cross-country race. The seriousness and the pinched look were back by then, and had been joined by something else – a tenaciousness, a hard intentness of purpose. The same expression was waiting behind the level gaze as the sixteen-year-old apprentice stood with his visibly frail father in front of their van ('Lawrence Meehan, Electrical and General Repairs').

And finally as a squaddie. A formal sit-down shot of the battalion in shirtsleeve order. Meehan in civvies posing with two fellow privates in front of an armoured personnel carrier. Meehan in issue overalls doing something complicated at a workbench with a soldering iron. Meehan and a couple of mates brewing up on exercise beneath a rockface.

And that was it. A life in ten photographs. Not conventionally handsome, but intelligent-looking. Not naturally one of the lads, but the sort you could rely on to stand his round. Not a natural tough guy, perhaps, but a fast learner. And without question a bad enemy. A real implacability behind the pale, narrow features and the rain-grey eyes.

'So this is him,' said Alex eventually and, catching Dawn Harding's scornful expression, immediately regretted the statement's pointlessness.

'This is him,' said Angela Fenwick. 'The Watchman. Our PIRA mole.'

'I'm assuming the story you're telling me has an unhappy ending,' said Alex.

'I want you to know everything,' said Fenwick. 'I want you to know exactly what sort of man we're dealing with. I want you to know everything we know.'

Alex nodded. He was busting for a piss. He said so and Dawn Harding stood up. En route, she officiously hurried him past several open office doors. *For fuck's sake*, he thought.

'Aren't you coming in?' he asked her when they reached a sign marked Male Staff WC. 'Just in case I catch sight of something I shouldn't.'

'There won't be much to catch sight of,' she said.

When they got back to the deputy director's office the sandwiches had arrived. In Alex's place two files had been placed on top of the Meehan photographs. They contained ten-by-eight-inch colour photographs taken at the scenes of the murders of Barry Fenn and Craig Gidley, and the respective pathologists' reports.

'None of these to leave the building, please,' said Fenwick. 'Dawn will show you a room where you can go through them when we've finished.'

Opposite Alex, Widdowes was galloping through his

106

sandwiches as if fearful that they were going to be taken away from him.

Alex picked up one of his own, and was about to bite into it when a thought struck him. He froze and Dawn Harding raised an eyebrow. 'I've just realised something,' he said. 'Yesterday morning I left an RUF sentry who can't have been more than eleven tied to a tree. I meant to let him go when we pulled out.'

'Sounds to me he's pretty lucky to be alive at all,' said Angela Fenwick.

'I doubt he *is* still alive,' said Alex. 'The survivors of the raid will be looking for scapegoats.'

'Can't make an omelette without breaking eggs,' said Widdowes through a yellow-toothed mouthful of bacon, lettuce and tomato. 'Africa's a bloody basket case, anyway. It's not what the rest of the world does to them, it's what they do to themselves. God, the stories you hear.'

'Sally Roberts is apparently telling anyone who'll listen that she was carried to safety in the strong arms of the SAS,' said Fenwick.

'We told her we were Paras,' said Alex. 'Where did she get the SAS stuff from?'

'She told the *Telegraph*'s stringer that none of the men who rescued her had shaved or washed for several days and that they wouldn't talk to her in the helicopter. The Paras always chatted her up.'

The ghost of a smile touched Alex's face but he said nothing.

'Right,' said Widdowes, placing his sandwich plate on the carpet and wiping his mouth with a spotted handkerchief. 'Shall I take over?'

Fenwick nodded and glanced quickly at Dawn. Alex sensed a current of empathy between the two women from which George Widdowes was excluded.

To begin with, Widdowes explained, things had looked good. From Meehan's occasional brief reports to Barry, and from information provided by touts and informers, it was clear that he was serving out some kind of initiation period. He was regularly called out for driving jobs, moving other volunteers from area to area, and transporting punishment squads and their victims to locations where beatings and kneecappings were administered. The IRA liked its volunteers to have a clear understanding that severe penalties were handed out to those who disobeyed them.

Meehan was also used as a 'dicker', standing on street corners looking out for manifestations of security forces personnel. Only the more experienced dickers, Alex knew, were used for 'live' operations. If a hit was planned on a border post a series of walk-pasts would be organised in the course of which the dickers would look out for any of the tell-tale signs – additional sentries, increased patrols and defences – that the operation was known about. A tout might have talked, anything might have happened, but the net result of a security lapse would invariably be the same: an SAS killing team waiting in ambush and a series of funerals attended by Gerry Adams and Martin McGuinness. The job of the dickers was a vital one to the PIRA and many operations were cancelled or postponed because of a dicker's instinct, honed to a sensitive edge on a thousand street corners, that 'something wasn't quite right'.

The first indication that Joe Meehan was moving up the terrorist ladder came in August 1990 when he reported to his handler that he'd been asked to act as a dicker on a bank robbery in the Cliftonville Road. The Northern Ireland desk made no move to inform the local security forces and the robbery went ahead. A female teller suffered a badly broken nose when she was punched in the face after attempting to press a panic button and a little over £8500 in cash was taken.

After the bank job, things went very quiet. In a twenty-second call on a public phone the following morning Meehan informed Barry that he was now being watched round the clock, although he had given his fellow volunteers no sign that he was aware of this. As far as the serious players were concerned, he said, he was still very much on probation. A lot of the volunteers couldn't quite get their heads round the idea of trusting an ex-soldier.

Somebody must have trusted him, however, for he finally got

his turn. A three-man team was assembled to recover a weapon from a cache in a churchyard near Castleblayney and Meehan was one of them. Again, he was able to inform Barry of the upcoming operation and again MI5 allowed it to take place unhindered. In the normal course of events the weapon would have been dug up by an SAS team, bugged for tracing purposes and rendered harmless – 'jarked' in special forces parlance, then reburied and left for recovery by the IRA.

On this occasion, however, it was decided that the risk that PIRA might discover the jarking and suspect a security leak was too great. No suspicion, however slight, must taint the Watchman. Whatever the cost, the weapon had to remain intact.

And the cost was very nearly fatal. Within two days a Royal Welch Fusiliers patrol had come under fire in Andersonstown and their lieutenant had had the stock of his SA 80 rifle shattered by a high-velocity round. The patrol returned fire but the trigger man escaped across the rooftops. The weapon, later identified from the spent rounds as a US Army-issue M16, was never found. MI5's silence ensured that no watch was placed on the cache for the weapon's return.

'We were playing a very dangerous game,' Widdowes admitted. 'But if the slightest suspicion had attached to Watchman, even long after the event, then we would have lost him. That M16 was our entry ticket, if you like. It's probably still out there somewhere.'

From his knowledgeable tone Alex surmised that Widdowes had spent some time on the ground in the province. 'What would you have said if that lieutenant had been killed?' Alex asked.

'I would have said the same thing that I said about the piccaninny in Sierra Leone two minutes ago: that you can't make an omelette without breaking eggs. We had to get a man into PIRA. He had to be above suspicion. At some stage we were probably going to have to weather a loss.' Widdowes delivered himself of an uneasy smile. 'I can see that you disapprove, Captain Temple.'

'No,' said Alex. 'It's just the way you put it.'

'We're in the same business, Captain Temple, and fighting the same enemy by all means at our disposal. The language is neither here nor there.'

Alex nodded. He thought of Sierra Leone, of a Puma helicopter swinging low over the jungle canopy beneath a bruise-dark sky. How would Don Hammond's relatives be weathering their loss, he wondered.

'Moving on,' said Widdowes firmly. 'The recovery of the M16 marked the end of Meehan's probationary status. He was in. One of the boys. And slowly, surely, the intelligence followed, increasing in quality as he rose through the ranks. For a couple of years between 1993 and 1995 we had really useful stuff coming in. A little of it we were able to act on; most of it we weren't — not without compromising him — but it was all grade A information.'

'The Cabinet Office was happy?' asked Alex drily.

'The Cabinet Office was very happy,' said Widdowes. 'And so were we. He gave us the location of a training camp in County Clare in the Republic, for example, and we were able to establish a covert OP in order to identify everyone who came and went. He gave us details of a PIRA safe house in Kentish Town in London, and we successfully installed a watcher team next door to monitor all arrivals and communications. Both of those represented major intelligence breakthroughs. And he gave us other things: names, vehicle registration numbers, surveillance targets, touts who had been set up to disinform FRU agents . . . It was a rich seam and while it lasted we mined it.'

'While it lasted?' asked Alex.

'Sadly, yes. For about two years Watchman gave us 24-carat weapons grade intelligence. And then, over the months that followed we began to notice a decline. At first it was barely noticeable. The information kept coming in — initially via Barry and later via a secure e-mail line to this office — and it all continued to look good. Names, possible assassination targets, projected dates for mainland campaigns — it was all there. But it had become subtly generalised. There was a lot of stuff about "policy". It had stopped being the sort of information it was possible to act on.

'Eventually there came a point where Angela, Craig Gidley and myself sat down and went through the message files, did some hard talking and came to the regretful conclusion that, for want of a better expression, we were having our pissers pulled. The general consensus at first was that Meehan had lost his nerve. On the rare occasions where he provided raw intelligence it came in too late for us to do anything about it. For example, there was an RUC officer who died because we only heard about the plan to murder him forty minutes before it took place. We put an emergency call out to his CO but the guy was in his car, driving home, and one of Billy McMahon's boys shot him outside an off-licence. You probably remember the incident.'

Alex nodded. The RUC man had been named Storey and it had been his habit of stopping off for a packet of Benson and Hedges every evening that had sealed his fate.

'The intelligence was either too late or it was second-source,' continued Widdowes, 'by which I mean that it was information that we were going to get from someone else anyway – touts or whoever. It looked OK on paper, but on the ground it was never quite good enough and we were forced to admit that we'd probably lost him. He'd gone native, lost his bottle – whatever.'

'Couldn't you pull him out?' asked Alex.

'We tried to but he went silent on us. Wouldn't respond to any request for contact. In late 1995, when it became clear that he'd moved out of his flat, sold his car and gone to ground, we started to close things down. We pulled Barry Fenn out for a start, in case he was compromised, and didn't replace him.'

'You turned Meehan loose, effectively?'

'We left the e-mail link open. He could have contacted us any time. But he didn't. By mid-1996 we were sure that he had turned – that he was now one hundred per cent PIRA's man. There were two bombs, one in a Loyalist pub in the Shankill

111

Road, one in a supermarket in Ballysillan, and the word coming in from the FRU's touts was that they'd been set by Joe Meehan. A total of seven dead. Lives might or might not have been saved in the Watchman's early days but now they were most definitely being lost. And the joke of it in the bars in Ballymurphy and on the Falls Road – the real hilarious fall-down-laughing joke of it – was that we'd trained him. That the PIRA's top electronics and explosives man was British army-trained.' He shook his head. 'What happened in February 1996 to the FRU people, Bledsoe and Wheen, you know. They were killed on the orders of Padraig Byrne – that was pretty much common knowledge. What you won't have heard is that the man who actually whacked those nails through their heads was – to our certain knowledge – Joseph Meehan.'

Alex winced. 'You had proof of that?'

'Everyone knew. Apparently there were at least a dozen people there when it happened. Word is they were blooding all the young guys.'

'And Meehan was completely beyond your reach by this time?'

'Yes, completely beyond our reach. There was only one thing we could do and we did it. We fed him into the jaws of PIRA's paranoia. We sent a story to the *Sunday Times* purporting to have been written by a former undercover soldier from 14th Intelligence's Belfast Detachment. In the article, among a lot of other stuff, the supposed soldier mentioned that for several years MI5 had been running a senior IRA mole and went on to describe three or four intelligence breakthroughs that the mole had made possible. The stories were true and in each case the information in question was known to Meehan.

'We then immediately went through the motions of attempting to place an injunction on the *Sunday Times*, but at the same time made sure that the attempt wasn't successful. A few days later we dropped the word in the Falls that Joe Meehan was playing both sides and one of his mainland bank statements arrived at the Sinn Fein office. We pay our people pretty decently and the best part of three and a half K was going into his account every month.

'After that we never heard another word – either from him or about him. He just vanished. We had a tout chat to Tina Milazzo but she hadn't seen him for months. Not since he "got weird", as she put it. Our assumption until a couple of weeks ago was that he'd been executed some time in the spring of 1996. Interrogated, probably, and then shot.'

'Until Barry Fenn's murder,' said Alex quietly.

'Exactly. At which point we realised that he was alive.'

'You were – are – certain that it's Meehan, then?'

'It has to be him,' said Widdowes. 'He knew Fenn and Gidley, he used a hammer and nail, he used entry and exit methods that only a man with highly specialised training would use.'

'So what exactly do you want me to do?' asked Alex, although he was already certain of the answer.

Widdowes looked at Angela Fenwick and after a brief pause it was Fenwick who spoke. 'There were four of us on the Watchman team,' she said tautly. 'And Fenn and Gidley are already dead.'

Alex nodded. Despite her professional control he could hear the fear in her voice.

'Basically,' she said, 'we need you to kill Joseph Meehan before he kills us.'

ELEVEN

'So give me one good reason why you can't take the whole thing to the police, let them catch the guy and have him stand trial for murder,' said Alex.

He and Dawn were sitting in the cafeteria at Thames House. Beyond the armour-plated ground-floor window, the river moved brownly and sluggishly seawards. At the end of the counter steam rose from the electric urns as the staff prepared for the four o'clock tea rush. Like everywhere else in the building, the room was stiflingly overheated.

'Too many people would be compromised,' answered Dawn, in the tones of one dealing with a child. 'Surely you can see that?'

'I can see that your Service would come out of the whole thing looking bad, yes. The press would crucify them.'

'And your Service too,' said Dawn patiently. 'We made the Watchman a spy, but your lot made him a killer and it's the killer we're after now. We're in this together, like it or not. If my people go down, your people go down too.'

'It'll come out sooner or later. These things always do.'

'Not necessarily. No one's seen or heard of this man Meehan for years. We find him, you chop him – finito, end of story. He's certainly not going to be missed.'

'You think you'll find him?' asked Alex quietly.

The grey eyes hardened a fraction. 'Don't you think we will?'

'If he doesn't want you to find him, he'll go to ground somewhere.'

She raised an ironic eyebrow. 'Somewhere that only you Special Forces boys can follow, right?'

Alex shrugged. 'I might be able to help you with the way that he thinks. Give you an idea of the sort of place he'd look for.'

She sighed. 'Look, we have the Service's best psych team dealing with the way that this man thinks and our best investigators looking for him. Any suggestions would, I'm sure, be very helpful, but we do, in fact, have the matter well in hand. What we'd really like you to do is wait and, when the moment comes, move in and eliminate him.'

'Is that really all you think we're good for?'

'On this occasion, I'm afraid that it's all we need you to do.'

They sat in uncomfortable silence. Outside on the river, a succession of interlinked barges moved upstream against the current. She had no real idea, thought Alex, what she was asking him to do. What it was like to look another human being in the eye and then kill him. How, in those moments, a few seconds could stretch into infinity.

It's all we need you to do.

A belated flicker of concern crossed her face. She frowned. She seemed to be aware of the direction his thoughts were taking. 'It's not up to me,' she said. 'I'm just here as a go-between.'

He nodded. It was as close to an apology as he was ever likely to get. 'So when did you join the Service?' he asked.

'Six years ago.' She forced a smile. 'I answered the same advert as David Shayler, as it happens.'

'What did it say? "Spies wanted"?'

'It said: "Godot Isn't Coming".'

'Who the hell's Godot?'

'A character in a Samuel Beckett play called *Waiting for Godot*. The other characters wait for him.'

'And he doesn't come?'

'No.'

'Sounds unmissable. So you knew this was an MI5 advert?'

'No. But I knew it had been placed by an organisation with a bit of . . . sophistication to it.'

'Right,' said Alex. 'Because of this Godot stuff.'

'Exactly.'

'We watch a fair amount of Samuel Beckett's stuff up in Hereford. Are you glad you answered that advert?'

'Yes.'

'And are you free this afternoon?'

She looked at him suspiciously. 'No. Why?'

'When I've looked through the photographs and the pathology reports, I'd like to go back to Gidley's place. There are a couple of things I need to check.'

'I thought we'd established that you were leaving that side of things to us.'

'Dawn, I need to see what Meehan's exact movements were the night before last. If I'm going up against him, I have to know how he operates.'

'I very much doubt there'll be anything to see.'

'That depends on what you're looking for. Trust me, I'm not going to be wasting your time.'

She regarded him expressionlessly for a moment and nodded. 'OK, then, but like I said, I'm tied up this afternoon. It'll have to be tomorrow morning.'

'I guess that'll have to do. Tell me something off the top of your head.'

'What?'

'Why is Joseph Meehan murdering the MI5 officers who ran him?'

'I heard you ask Angela Fenwick the same question. She said she didn't know.'

'I heard her say it. But what do you think?'

'I think he went native, like George said.' She shrugged. 'Why do any terrorists do what they do? It's an armed struggle. We're the enemy.'

'But why choose such an extreme method of killing people? And why take out Fenn and Gidley who, let's face it, were pretty much at the fag-end of their careers?'

'He killed the people he knew. To Meehan, Fenn and Gidley represented the heart of the British Establishment. As do George Widdowes and Angela Fenwick, presumably.'

Alex shook his head. 'I don't think he killed them for

116

symbolic reasons. As Brit oppressors or whatever. I think he killed them for a specific reason.'

She narrowed her eyes. 'What makes you think that you can see inside this man's head?'

Alex shrugged. 'We're both soldiers. Soldiers are methodical. They believe in cause and effect. What's the point of carrying out an elaborate, ritualistic murder that no one will ever know about? That you know will be immediately covered up?'

'Perhaps he's mad.'

'Do you know something?' said Alex. 'For a moment there we were almost having a conversation.'

Dawn held his gaze for a moment, then reached to the floor for her briefcase. When she straightened she was her usual brisk, businesslike self. 'As well as the photographs and reports on Fenn and Gidley I've got some keys for you. They're for a top-floor flat in St George's Square in Pimlico. You can stay there if you need to or' – she hesitated for a fraction of a second – 'you can make your own arrangements.'

'Thank you,' said Alex neutrally.

Barry Fenn, he saw, had been a weaselly, narrow-shouldered man. From the photographs, in which he was wearing blood-stained pyjamas and was sprawled half in and half out of bed, it was clear that he had been woken from sleep. According to the pathologist's report he had struggled briefly and ineffectually before being struck on the back of the head with some sort of cosh. The six-inch nail had been hammered into his temple while he was semi-conscious and his tongue, it appeared, had been hacked out as some sort of afterthought. Livid and hideous, it had been placed in the unused glass ashtray beside the bed alongside a book of matches. There was less blood than there might have been.

Looking at the photographs, Alex realised that his earlier identification with Meehan had been dangerous and stupid. Beyond their training and a similarity in age, he had nothing whatever in common with this maniac. Dawn was right: the man was a psychopathic murderer and had to be stopped.

The pathologist's report on Craig Gidley indicated that, like Barry Fenn's tongue, the victim's eyes had been cut out after the fatal hammerblow had driven the nail through his temple. To Alex this confirmed that the mutilations were there for a purpose other than to cause suffering. As a message, perhaps?

But a message for whom? For MI5 as a whole? For George Widdowes or Angela Fenwick in particular? Whatever the message, it was clear that either Widdowes or Fenwick was next on the Watchman's list.

Would he get them? Alex wondered dispassionately. Would he catch them and kill them? Forewarned and with all the protective resources of MI5 at their disposal, they would be much harder targets than Fenn and Gidley had been.

But then the Watchman was clever. He had been taught by the best – in many cases the same people who had taught Alex – and he had clearly forgotten none of it. The combination of professionalism, sadism and sheer insanity he embodied was terrifying.

What did he want? What was the man trying to achieve?

Alex stared at the photographs of Meehan as if his gaze could somehow penetrate their surface and unlock the man portrayed in them. But the more he shuffled them around, the less they seemed to reveal. Just those pale, skinned-whippet features and that watchful, guarded gaze.

He looked tough. Not in the sense of being intimidating, but in the sense of being a hard man to break. He'd duck and he'd dive but one way and another he'd keep on going. There were a thousand looking like him on the streets of Belfast – dingy, forgettable figures hunched into donkey jackets. Alex could see why he'd been such a perfect undercover man.

Would MI5 find him? Meehan would have to make a serious mistake first and there was nothing to indicate that that was going to happen. Mad he might be, but careless he clearly wasn't.

Alex turned to the large map of Britain on the wall. Where would Meehan be hiding out? No, turn the question round. Where would he – Alex – be hiding out if he were Meehan? In

118

a city, among the crowds? No, he'd be in danger if he revisited his old London stamping grounds. He couldn't risk going anywhere there was an Irish community. The arm of the IRA, like its memory, was long.

Meehan would know that MI5 would leave no stone unturned in their search and that unless he had built up a completely watertight new identity they would find him. He'd have to have a new passport, driving licence, social security number – everything. Just checking in and out of bed-and-breakfast houses was not going to be enough. He'd have a base somewhere. Somewhere he could hide.

Somewhere he could plan the next killing.

Alex arrived back at Sophie's flat shortly before seven, having arranged to meet Dawn Harding at nine the next morning. She'd pick him up, she told him, where she had dropped him off the night before – outside the Duke of York's Headquarters in the King's Road.

He found Sophie changing. 'We're going out,' she told him, swinging round so that he could zip up the fastening of her cocktail dress. 'One of my clients – Corday – is launching a new fragrance range and I've helped organise a little party for them. The perfume's called "Guillotine" and all the women have to wear a red velvet ribbon round their necks as if they've been beheaded.'

'Do you mind if I give it a miss?' Alex asked wearily, loosening his tie. 'I'm not really in the mood.'

'Oh, don't be boring, darling! I'm sure you've had a horrible day doing whatever secret things you've been doing but so have I. It's been impossibly grim at the PR coalface. Come and drink some champagne at Corday's expense, and then . . .'

'And then?'

'And then you can take charge of the evening. How's that?'

Alex agreed. If Five were going to leave him twiddling his thumbs while they pursued their investigation, then he might as well enjoy himself. And he wanted to please Sophie who, after all, was putting him up. He didn't even have to drive the next

119

morning – Dawn would be doing that, presumably at her usual infuriating crawl. So he might as well chill out. 'So where are we going?'

She raised her chin to tie her red velvet ribbon. 'Hoxton Square.'

'Where's that?'

'Alex, sweetie, which planet have you been living on for the last few years? Hoxton is only the most desirable *quartier* in London. You can barely throw a stone without braining some famous artist, model or designer. It's celebrity city!'

'Right, well, just introduce me as a friend of your brother's. Say I work in security or something.'

She frowned and pouted into the mirror, checking her make-up. 'Security's a bit dingy-sounding, darling. Can we manage something a bit more upscale? Something dot.com, perhaps?'

'OK. I'll have a think.' He rubbed his eyes. Various sub-conscious worries were still nagging at him. 'I realised something dreadful today, that I'd left a rebel sentry – a boy, can't have been much more than ten – tied to a tree in the middle of the Sierra Leone jungle a couple of days ago.'

Sophie wriggled her toes experimentally in her raw-silk shoes. 'I know. It's awful how forgetful one gets. Do you want to ring someone about it?'

Alex stared at her disbelievingly. 'He's probably dead by now, or at the very least missing an arm.'

'Shall we go?'

As they swerved through the traffic in the silver Audi TT, with Sophie impatiently cutting up every vehicle that had the temerity to draw alongside her, Alex tried to improve his mood. Things could be worse, he told himself. He was being paid to waste time in London – an opportunity that most soldiers would give their eye-teeth for – and he was sleeping with a rich, beautiful and highly sexed girl who gave every sign of thinking he was the cat's pyjamas. He was on his way to a party to drink champagne with said highly sexed girl, and in two or three hours they would tumble into bed and tear each other to pieces.

So what was pissing him off, exactly? Was it that he seemed to be spending his life being shuffled about by women? Alex had nothing against working with women but right now his life seemed to be run by them. In the past whenever girlfriends had started making noises about permanence and commitment, Alex had started making noises about the incompatibility of soldiering and married life. And he had meant it. He had seen his colleagues go down like ninepins, their tiny independence skewered by the demands of ratty, frustrated wives. The wives hadn't started ratty and frustrated, but they soon got that way when they discovered that the system could only accommodate them and the kids as sideline players. As Stan Clayton had once explained to him: getting the trouble-and-strife up the duff before an overseas posting was like spitting in your beer before you went for a piss!

Seeing the results – vengeful, careworn wives, fragged-out blokes worrying about money and their families' security from dawn till dusk – Alex had sworn to have nothing to do with any of it. As far as he was concerned the deal was that you promised nothing that you weren't prepared to give, had a good time for as long as it lasted and got out before things turned nasty. He had a sort of honour system, which went something along the lines that if a woman made it plain from the start that she wanted marriage and kids then you didn't waste her time. Otherwise, you went for it.

Something told him, though, that with Sophie it was going to be different. For a start he was not in control of things. He didn't automatically call the shots, as he'd always done before. She moved easily and fluently through a world in which, if he was honest, he felt insecure. And while she respected his skills and knew that there was another, darker world in which he moved with ease and fluency, she never allowed herself to be overimpressed by him.

Ultimately, he wasn't sure of her. This made things exciting, but it also made things . . . difficult.

As they swerved round a traffic island in the TT, tyres screaming, Alex told himself that he ought to take a train up to

Hereford and pick up his car. Behind the wheel of the Karman-Ghia he could at least pretend that he was in control of his life. For the time being, though . . .

What the hell?

TWELVE

When they reached Hoxton Square Sophie ignored the double yellow lines and parked right outside the venue. This was a former electricity showroom turned gallery, and paparazzi were already drawn up at either side of the entrance. As Alex and Sophie hurried in there was a brief burst of flash – presumably in case they were celebrities whom no one yet recognised.

The party was on the first floor and the place was already crowded. On the far side of the room Alex caught sight of Stella laughing with a group of models. The sound system was playing Juliette Greco, two women in tricolore hats were spraying perfume at anyone not fast enough to get out of their way, and the sharp smell of 'Guillotine' cut the air.

'Come and meet Charlotte,' said Sophie, taking Alex's hand and sidling purposefully towards a slight, dark-haired woman who seemed to be dressed in 1970s wallpaper. 'She's the oldest of the Corday sisters. You've heard of the Corday fashion house, haven't you?'

'Why don't I go and find us a drink?' Alex suggested, disengaging his hand.

Within moments he had been swallowed up by the crowd. Around him brief snatches of conversation and shrieks of laughter rose like waves above the music and were inaudible again. A gravel-voiced broadcaster whom he vaguely recognised but had never met threw her arms round his neck, kissed him on the mouth and asked how the new restaurant was going. He told her that it was still serving human flesh and moved on, leaving her open-mouthed.

People pushed past, flickered a glance at him in passing to

establish for certain that he was not someone that they needed to know and vanished. Alex wanted to speak to none of them – he simply couldn't summon up the interest. Over the months that he'd been seeing Sophie he'd attended quite a few of these occasions and he'd come to the conclusion that London society was peopled almost entirely by fuckwits. From the outside it looked glamorous, all late-night restaurants and beautiful girls and champagne, but in truth, he had discovered, it was very, very dull. For every genuine achiever there were a hundred style journalists, fashion parasites and cokehead aristocrats desperately jockeying for recognition. None of them seemed to have any awareness of a world beyond their own tiny circuit, and listening to the endless loop tape of their conversation about clothes, accessories, drugs and parties bored him out of his mind.

There were exceptions. He liked Stella and of course he liked Sophie – more than liked her, in fact.

But why was it, he wondered, that the whole scene that she was involved with made him feel so dead inside? And – equally importantly – why was it that situations involving real death made him feel so acutely alive? How was he supposed to square those facts with the idea of – one day, at least – settling down?

'Bloody Mary?'

Alex looked down to see a tiny, large-busted girl in a tricolore cap, holding a tray. She giggled. 'Or Bloody Marie-Antoinette, I suppose I should say.'

Alex took one of the glasses and drank. It was almost fifty per cent pure vodka and fiery with tabasco. 'Bloody strong, whichever.'

She laughed. 'I know. I thought I'd loosen this lot up a bit. Come the revolution, they'll all be for the chop.'

'They certainly need culling,' said Alex morosely, taking a deep hit of his drink. It occurred to him a few seconds later that he was feeling rather over-sorry for himself. These people weren't so bad. He threw back the remains of the drink, helped himself to another and took a deep swig. He began to feel very much more cheerful. Get a life, Temple, he told himself. Have some fun for a change!

'Shall I just stay here?' she asked. 'Let you help yourself?'

He smiled. Small girl plus big tits equals hard-on. 'You could do worse,' he said. 'Are you one of the caterers?'

'Sort of. Part-time. I'm actually trying to get into the fashion business.'

'You should speak to Sophie Wells. She's over by the entrance, or was when I last saw her.'

'She's a right snotty cunt,' said the girl, as Alex took a third glass. 'D'you know her?'

'Mm. A bit.'

'Which bit?'

'Go on.' He smiled. 'Piss off before we're all in trouble!'

'Hey, Alex from Clacton!'

'Stella! How's it going?'

She gave him an uneven grin. 'All right, apart from the smell of this perfume. It's like fish guts at low tide.'

'I guess the original guillotine wasn't too fresh,' said Alex.

'What have you been up to?' she asked. 'I haven't seen you for a bit.'

'I've been in Africa,' said Alex.

'Yeah? How was that?'

He shrugged. 'Tell me something, Stella.'

'OK.'

'If you wanted to hide – if you absolutely had to hide, life or death – where would you go?'

'I'd go where I always go,' she said, as if the question were the most normal one in the world. 'The past.'

He stared at her. Heard someone calling her name.

She smiled and the crowd drew her away. 'Believe me,' she said, fluttering her fingers. 'There's nowhere like it.'

He found Sophie again and was just about to hand her her drink when something irregular registered at the edge of his vision.

At the entrance, by the glass doors, two tall heavy-set figures were forcing their way past the security guards. The guards were doing their best, but they were no match for the red-faced, guffawing newcomers. One of them, a beef-fed, tiny-eyed giant

125

of at least six foot two inches in height, was wearing a rugby shirt while the other, city-suited, was only a shade shorter. The crowd backed away from them uneasily.

'Shit!' said Sophie quietly at Alex's side. 'Gatecrashers.'

She stepped with confidence into the path of the two men. 'Look, guys . . .' she began. 'This is a private . . .'

'Charlie,' roared the taller man, throwing a massive arm round Sophie's shoulders. 'Take a look at what I've . . .'

But the other was forcibly slapping a passing guest on the back. '*You, sir*!' he brayed. 'Are you – by any chance – an *arse-bandido*?'

Both gatecrashers had public-school accents, Alex noted. Everything about them spelt money and arrogance. Well, they were about to get what was coming to them.

'So, my darlin'.' The bigger of the two reached drunkenly for Sophie. 'You were saying . . .'

A split second before his hand reached Sophie's chest, a fist crunched into his nose. The blow carried with it every ounce of resentment that Alex had ever felt towards the privileged classes.

'*Alex*!' he heard Sophie scream. '*No!*'

The man turned to Alex, amazed. Blood poured from his flattened nose as if from a tap and streamed down the front of his rugby shirt. The other man stood there, swaying. There was a moment of absolute silence, then the bleeding man drew back a fist the size of a bowling ball.

Alex swerved, felt the wind of the blow pass his cheek and, half turning, seized the oncoming arm by the wrist. Forcing his shoulder into his attacker's armpit, and using the Hooray's own weight and momentum, he threw him hard on to his back. The giant frame seemed to pinwheel in the air for a moment and then crashed down over a crate of champagne bottles.

'*Alex*!' screamed Sophie again.

He sensed rather than saw the second man's rush. Grabbing a Bollinger bottle by the neck he turned and swung it with all his strength. The bottle smashed against the man's skull with a crunching, gassy sigh and in a white explosion of foam. With spectacular effect his head turned blood-red, his eyes rolled upwards and he crashed to the floor. Screams joined the spatter of broken glass and the groans of the first attacker who was writhing beneath one of the caterers' trestle tables.

The pushing started, then, and the panic. A drinks table went over, then another, and within seconds the floor was covered in spilled champagne, canapes and broken glass. Someone activated the fire alarm. Hanging over everything was the acrid stench of 'Guillotine'.

'*Alex!*' Sophie screamed for a third time, waving her fists at him. 'What do you think you're doing?' Around them, people were jostling for the exit.

'What do you mean?' asked Alex, dropping the smashed bottleneck. 'Did you really want those pissed-up yobs grabbing at you?'

'They were two boys who'd had too much to drink, that's all. It's *you* who's ruined the party!' She stared despairingly at the departing guests and then down at the fallen men. 'Could someone please ring an ambulance?' she pleaded.

'*Boys?*' asked Alex, amazed. 'Look at the fucking size of them. I can't believe you're siding with them.' He turned to her thoughtfully and smiled. 'But then I suppose they're your type, aren't they?'

'Don't be so *stupid*. You *totally* overreacted and you know it. You could have . . .' She shook her head, incoherent with anger. Beside her, one of the caterers was dialling 999.

'Killed them?' Alex regarded the fallen and bloodied figures dispassionately. The first man, still groaning, appeared to have badly injured his back and the second was unmoving and bleeding copiously from the head. 'No such luck, I'm afraid. I'd say your perfume got its publicity, though.' He sniffed the air. 'Stella was right, it is a bit fishy.'

She rounded on him, eyes blazing. 'And what the hell would you know, you . . . you *psychopathic hooligan*?'

Alex began to laugh. He couldn't help himself. 'I'm sorry!' he managed eventually. 'Really, Sophie, I'm sorry.'

Drawing back her hand she slapped him as hard as she could across the face and marched furiously off.

Alex caught up with her. 'Please,' he said. 'I'm sorry, Sophie. Really I am. I wasn't laughing at you. It's just the whole thing.'

She shrugged him off. Her voice was shaking with anger. 'The *whole thing*, as you call it, has turned to shit. I open up my life to you, introduce you to my friends, and you just . . . just crap all over them. You can make your own fucking way home and you needn't bother to call me again. Find someone else's life to smash up.'

At this moment, as they stood there facing each other, speechless, the little waitress with the big bust appeared at the foot of the stairs. 'So, is this a good moment to talk about work?' she asked Sophie brightly.

Sophie glanced at her uncomprehendingly. 'No,' she said quietly. 'It isn't.'

The waitress shrugged. 'Told you she was a cunt!'

Alex watched Sophie slam the door of the silver Audi. When the snarl of her exhaust had died away he reached into his suit pocket. The safe-house key was still there.

THIRTEEN

The first hour of the drive up to Goring in Dawn Harding's Honda was conducted in near silence. Alex had a mild hangover and was feeling a bit guilty about the way the previous evening had turned out. He shouldn't have laughed, he told himself.

The trouble was, the row had exposed all the differences that existed between them. He couldn't be bothered with most of her friends, when all was said and done, and he couldn't be bothered to obey the rules that people obeyed in her world. She considered him an unreconstructed macho dinosaur, and in return he found her spoilt, shallow and overprivileged. They brought out the worst in each other.

And yet they wanted each other. Often.

The night in the Pimlico flat had been a cheerless one. A 1970s Bulgarian defector might have felt at home in the place, with its stained orange carpet and fusty, boarding-house smell, but Alex could have done with something a little less Cold War.

He should get some flowers, he told himself, present himself at Sophie's front door that evening with an apologetic face and a big bunch of roses. Would roses do the trick? They were supposed to, but then in Sophie's picky and obsessive circle roses might be considered naff.

'Do you like roses?' he asked Dawn.

She looked at him suspiciously. 'Why?'

'If someone gave you roses, what would you think?'

'A man, you mean?' she asked.

'For the sake of argument, yes.'

'I'd think either he was trying to get something from me, or he was apologising.'

'Right.'

'If they were really special, though . . . I mean if they weren't just those boring, limp, half-frozen things you buy at the tube station in a twist of cellophane but properly scented old English roses grown in a garden, well, I might at least listen to what he had to say.' She glanced at him shrewdly from the driving seat. 'In trouble, are we?'

'No. Just wondering.'

'Ah. Wondering. Well, my experience is that most girls do, in fact, quite like to be given roses.' She narrowed her eyes at the road ahead. 'Even the posh ones like your Sophie.'

He nodded. He guessed he was going to have to say goodbye to any kind of private life for as long as he was working with Box.

'Can I ask what you're actually doing to locate this Watchman character?' he asked.

Her expression remained unaltered but her eyes froze over. 'Put it this way,' she said. 'We've got pictures, we've got DNA, we've got dabs, we've got handwriting, and we've got vocal and facial recognition systems in place. I think you can say that we're adequately covered.'

'And Widdowes? What are you doing to protect him?'

'George Widdowes is an experienced intelligence officer.'

'So were Fenn and Gidley. Didn't help them much when laughing boy showed up, though, did it?'

'Forewarned is forearmed.'

Alex shook his head despairingly and rubbed his eyes. 'You don't get it, do you?' he said quietly. 'Meehan will kill him. He's programmed to do it and he will do it.'

She was silent for a minute or two.

'OK,' she said. 'I'll tell you. We're setting up a lookalike at his house. A Special Branch guy. We've got the place ringed with police marksmen. George himself has been pulled out of circulation.'

'You think that'll work?'

'Look, I admit we were a little bit slow off the blocks with Gidley, but we're very much on-message now.'

'On-message,' said Alex. 'Right.'

'This Watchman,' Dawn went on patiently. 'He's one man, he's on his own, he's got no support system to speak of. It's not constructive to be too afraid of him.'

'He's a murderer,' said Alex. 'He's Regiment-trained. And he's spent several years in the field with the most sophisticated terror organisation in the world.'

'You sound as if you admire them.'

'Professionally speaking I do admire them. If I'd been born a working-class Catholic over the water I'd probably be a volunteer myself and most Regiment blokes will tell you the same thing. It doesn't mean you aren't prepared to do your job and waste as many of the fuckers as you can, but ultimately when you put a bullet through one of those boys and you look into his dying eyes you can see yourself as you might have been, and that's the truth.'

From the long habit of counter-surveillance, Alex glanced up at the rear-view mirror. The small movement and the dizzying motion of the reflected cars reminded him how much vodka was still in his bloodstream and he pressed the button to lower the passenger window. Fresh air rushed in. The sun had not yet burnt off the dew in the fields. 'The PIRA are good,' he continued, 'and the thing they're better than anyone else at is security. They won't hesitate to cancel a hundred-man operation if one dicker's instinct tells him or her there's something not quite right – that one too many cars has passed or that a man's coat's hanging wrong or there are no birds in a hedge where there should be birds. Our man Meehan will have absorbed all that. He'll wait as long as it takes. That's why I respect him. And that's why you people should respect him too.'

'Respect him, yes,' Dawn agreed, her eyes fixed on the road ahead. 'Fear him, no.'

'Given a choice between fear and arrogance,' said Alex mildly, 'I'll take fear every time. Nothing gets you killed faster than arrogance.'

'We'll see, shall we?'

'I'm afraid we will, yes.'

They settled into a sour, antagonistic silence.

When they got to Goring, Alex asked Dawn to park several hundred yards from the house. 'I want to approach the place as the Watchman would have done,' he explained. 'See it as he would have seen it the first time he came down here.'

'No one noticed any strangers in the village,' said Dawn. 'We've asked a few questions about that.'

'He wouldn't have been noticeable,' Alex told her. 'My guess is that he would have come on foot first time round, probably in hiking gear and on a wet Saturday. Or by bicycle, perhaps. Anorak hoods, clear glasses, cycle helmets – they're all good disguises. Those just-passing-through, rambler-type people are invisible in a semi-touristy place like this. You see them at the side of the road eating a sandwich and swigging a soft drink, but you don't really see them. You couldn't describe them two minutes later.'

She nodded. They continued in silence along the roadside.

Dawn frowned. 'But what would he . . .'

'Shush a minute,' said Alex, cutting her off. The Gidleys' house was just coming into view and he wanted to see it – had to see it – through the Watchman's eyes. At his side, as he marshalled all his senses and instincts to this end, he was vaguely aware of Dawn bristling with irritation.

Women, he thought.

Meehan would want an OP – a place he could observe from without being seen. Somewhere away from the road and out of range of the dogs, but close enough to check out the arrangements. He'd have planned for at least a week's surveillance. He wouldn't have compromised with just a day or two. He would have gone up with food and water and a bag to crap into, and noted everything. Where would he have watched from? A building? Were there any other buildings in sight? No. No farm sheds, garages, outhouses, nothing. Their absence would have been one of the factors that attracted Gidley to the house in the first place. So was there anywhere at ground level he could lie up? Didn't look like it, because wherever he lay the wall surrounding the property would block his vision. He wouldn't be able to get enough height on the place. The contours were against him.

Man-made OPs? There were telegraph poles running along the road and connecting to the property, and it was theoretically possible that he'd nicked a BT van and overalls to fit the deactivator. But he wouldn't have been able to stay up there for long enough to establish anything worthwhile – within moments of his appearing the Box security people would have been on to BT to check him out.

Trees, then. Alex had reckoned from the start that Meehan had gone for a tree, but he'd wanted formally to eliminate all other possibilities. There were a horse chestnut and a sycamore overhanging the road on either side of the Gidleys' perimeter wall, but he dismissed these. Tempting, but just too close to the house and the orbit of the dogs. Besides, in consideration of the security hazard they posed, all the trees near the property wall had had their lower limbs sawed off. Climbing them would have necessitated scaling equipment and any climber would have had to take the risk of being seen either from the house or the road.

On the opposite side of the road was a field of young corn bisected by a public footpath. Mature trees stood at the side of this path at irregular intervals. Alex scanned them from the road. The ideal observation point was a large beech, from whose boughs a clear hundred-and-fifty-yard sight line on the house and grounds was available. Without a word, with Dawn sighing behind, he marched down the road, swung his leg over the stile into the field and moved at pace towards the tree. His head was clear now, his brain singing with the pleasure of the pursuit. 'I'll have you, you bastard!' he murmured to himself. 'I'll fucking have you!'

They arrived at the foot of the beech and Alex climbed expectantly over the elephantine grey roots. Meehan, he was sure, would have climbed the trunk on the far side from the road, using ropes and scaling equipment. Carefully, he examined the trunk. Nothing. No sign, no scar. *Shit*! It *had* to be this tree. But the trunk showed no sign at all, not a single scratch, scar or abrasion that might have been made in the last month. After searching the fine-grained silvery surface for more than twenty minutes he was forced to concede that if Meehan had used this tree he had not climbed it by the trunk. Nor were there any branches hanging anywhere near the ground.

Dawn remained expressionless, but Alex could tell that his frustration gave her quiet satisfaction. Finally, and meaningfully, she glanced at her watch.

'Come on,' he said, marching her further up the path.

The next tree that might have afforded a view over Gidley's property was a horse chestnut. Its large leaves and candle-like white blooms made it a lot harder to see out of but at the same time, Alex noted, a lot harder to see into.

Maybe, he thought. Maybe. Warily, he circled the trunk. Like the beech, it was fine-skinned and any scratch would have shown. But once again, there was nothing.

'Is it possible,' asked Dawn demurely, 'that you might just be barking up the wrong . . .'

'No!' he snapped. 'It bloody isn't. He was here somewhere.'

'You're sure?'

'I'm sure. Now please . . .' Desperately, he scanned the tree's spreading skirts and his eyes narrowed. There was one place, just one, about ten feet from the ground. 'Come with me,' he ordered her. 'Step where I step.'

Followed by Dawn, he moved into the shadowed, dew-sodden grass. When he was below the lowest point of the bough he motioned her to be still and crouched down. Half closing his eyes, he felt carefully around the wet ground as if he were blind. It took five minutes, but eventually he found what he was looking for: a plug of pressed soil the size and shape of a cigarette packet. 'Got you,' he breathed.

'What is it?' asked Dawn.

In answer he felt quickly around and eased another plug from the ground a foot away. 'He had a ladder,' said Alex. 'He didn't want to go up the trunk using a scaling kit and leave marks, so he used a ladder and a rope and went up here. Then afterwards' – Alex held up the soil – 'he filled in the places where the feet of the ladder went. It hasn't rained since then, so . . .'

'Why go to that trouble?' asked Dawn. 'Since we know it's him and he knows that we know.'

'He's a perfectionist,' said Alex. 'It's about doing it right, whatever the circumstances. About leaving no trace.'

'A sort of Samurai code?' mused Dawn.

'That sort of thing,' Alex agreed. 'What I think he did here was to get a decorator's ladder – one of those aluminium self-supporting jobs – tie one end of the rope to it, throw the other over the branch, pull the branch down and tie off the rope. Then he grabbed the branch and up he went.'

'Dragging the ladder up behind him on the rope. Neat. Too bad we haven't got a rope or a ladder.'

'We've got me,' said Alex. 'And we've got you.'

'Oh, no!' said Dawn firmly. 'No *fucking* way!'

'Way, baby!' said Alex with a grim smile. 'Shoes off.'

'Tree-climbing's not part of my job, *baby*!'

'And saving your colleagues' life? Is that part of your job? Personally I couldn't give a monkey's, but . . .'

'Why can't you go up alone?'

'I could, but it would mean my standing on your shoulders and I'm not sure you could manage that.'

'Try me.'

'I'd love to.'

'You know what I mean.'

They tried it. She genuflected; he took her hands and stepped on to her shoulders with his bare feet.

'Do you have any idea how much I paid for this sweater?' she breathed, trembling with strain.

'Take it off,' said Alex cheerfully. 'I won't be shocked.'

'Fuck you!'

She couldn't straighten up. She tried – gave it her best shot – but in the end she simply couldn't.

'Why don't we try it the other way round?' he suggested reasonably.

'Why don't we just get a ladder from the house?'

'If this doesn't work we will, OK?'

Sullenly she took off her shoes, placed them together on the wet grass as if on a wardrobe shelf, took his hands, stepped on to his shoulders.

'And . . . up.' He straightened. 'Take your hands away from mine when you're ready. Grab the branch. Good, now pull yourself up. Try and get your leg over.'

'I thought that was your speciality,' she gasped. Then she looked down at him nervously. 'What now?'

'Move as close to the end of the branch as possible, so that it's weighed down.'

She did so. He took off his shirt and threw it up to her, ordered her to tie it round the branch, which she did. 'And now these. Tie the legs together so that they make another link of the chain.' He threw her his trousers. She tied them to the shirt. He was now naked except for his boxer shorts. 'How silly do I look?' he asked.

'From up here? Very.'

'You sure the knots are sound?'

'I've done some sailing. Trust me, they're sound.'

He hauled himself up as if using a rope ladder, unknotted his shirt and trousers – part of the haul he had bought with Sophie – and quickly re-dressed. 'OK, do you want to stay here? Or climb with me.'

She hesitated. He could see a small muscle working in her jaw. 'I'll come up,' she said eventually.

'Right. You know what we're looking for. Anything, basically.'

'You really think we're going to learn anything?'

'I think we have to look.'

They climbed for ten minutes, the ground fell slowly away beneath them and the dark-green leaves enveloped them. As they moved upwards they found tiny but unmistakable signs that someone else had recently done the same thing and by dint of hard searching were able to follow a trail of lichen blurs, pressure marks and trodden fungi.

'Look up,' said Alex at intervals, which Dawn correctly interpreted as 'Don't look down'.

Finally, breathless, she turned to him. 'I can't get up there.' 'There' was the broad junction of several branches with the trunk some thirty feet from the ground.

'He managed it,' said Alex.

'Well, I can't,' she breathed. 'It's just too long a reach.'

'I'll get you up there,' Alex said.

'Must you?'

'Yeah. I'm pretty sure that's where he watched from. I'm going to lift you and sit you there, OK?'

'OK,' she said uncertainly.

He braced himself opposite her, placed his hands on her waist and looked into a pair of grey eyes from which she was struggling to keep all signs of fear. Beneath his grip, however, he could feel a faint involuntary trembling. When he lifted her she almost made it – she was absurdly light, somehow, for someone so bad-tempered – but the fine black wool of her sweater gave a poor grip and she slipped down again between his hands. The sweater, meanwhile, slipped up.

'I'm sorry,' he said sincerely, staring at the neatly voluptuous contours of her scarlet satin bra. 'I didn't mean that to happen.'

She wrenched down her sweater. *Blimey*, he told himself. *Who'd have thought that beneath that stroppy exterior . . .* 'Try again?' he suggested.

Now sheer anger got her up there. Once settled, she stared out over the fields.

He clambered up behind her and saw what she saw. The trunk and the adjoining branches formed a solid enclosure within which, without too much discomfort, it would have been possible to remain for hours. Before them the alignment of the heavy, densely leaved chestnut branches afforded a perfect long-distance view of the Gidleys' property. Only the area directly behind the house was invisible.

'He was here,' said Alex. 'He was here for days. Look, you can see the worn place in this fork where he wedged his foot.

137

And here, this shined place where he sat. This was where he planned Gidley's murder.'

'If I weren't so utterly terrified of heights,' said Dawn quietly, looking around her, 'I'd say it was rather beautiful up here.'

Alex stared at her. 'You're really afraid of heights? Phobic?'

She returned his stare openly and frankly. 'Like I said, terrified. This is the highest I've ever been off the ground outside a house. Skyscrapers make me feel faint. I couldn't even go up the Eiffel Tower.'

'So why didn't you tell me?'

She looked him in the eye. 'You didn't exactly make it very easy, did you?'

He was silent for a moment. 'I guess not. I'm sorry. You're a trooper, Dawn Harding, and I'm a bastard.'

She nodded thoughtfully. 'Yes, I'd pretty much go along with that. I might add the words "patronising" and "sexist" while I was about it.'

'Fair enough.'

'And request that if we're going to continue working together you don't take out your frustrations on me every time you get an order you don't like, or your Sloaney girlfriend gives you a hard time, or you don't get laid, or whatever.'

'OK.'

'And most importantly that you get me to the ground in one piece.'

'I promise.'

Together, as best they could, they searched the branches around them for anything that Meehan might have left. In the end it was Dawn who found it: an inch-long stub of pencil slipped into a knot hole near their feet. Working it out with his pocket knife, Alex managed to slip the pencil into his shirt pocket without directly touching it.

'Forensics'll be interested to see that,' said Dawn. 'Do you think there's anything else?'

They searched every inch, but found nothing else. Ten minutes later they were back on the first branch, ten feet above the ground.

'Ever done a parachute course?' Alex asked her.

She shook her head.

'OK, I'll jump and then catch you.'

He hit the ground, rolled and stood himself up. Soon, she was hanging from the branch with her bare feet on his shoulders. One after the other, he took her hands. She wobbled.

'OK,' he said. 'Now put my hands under your arms.'

'No funny business?'

'As if!'

Gently, he lowered her down the front of his body. When their faces were level and her mouth inches from his, he stopped. He looked into her eyes. Was there the ghost of a smile there?

They had lunch in a nearby pub. Ploughman's lunches, with in his case a beer and in hers mineral water. A sharp morning had turned into a warm day and they sat outside at a bench.

'You did something today you wouldn't have thought yourself capable of,' Alex began.

'Oh, spare us the squaddie pep talk, please. I went up that tree this morning because . . .'

'Because the thought of being bested by a yob of a soldier was something you couldn't face. Worse even than your fear of heights, right?'

She shrugged and smiled. 'Perhaps. I never said you were a yob, though.'

'No?'

'No. Though you certainly are one. And proud of it – after all, it's a solid-gold chick puller, isn't it, being in the Regiment?'

'Didn't you get laid last night either?'

'As a matter of fact I did,' said Dawn mildly.

There was a heartbeat's silence.

'So, who's the lucky guy?' Alex asked, rather more sharply than he intended.

In answer Dawn just laughed and shook her head. 'That pencil was a good find,' she said, cutting a pickled onion in half. 'Forensics can get stuck in. There should be dabs.'

'There won't be,' said Alex. 'He meant us to find it. It's a message.'

'How d'you know that? How d'you know he didn't make a mistake? Just leave it there?'

'He wouldn't do that. He doesn't make mistakes.'

'That's just your ego talking. You're Regiment-trained, he's Regiment-trained. In your mind you can't make a mistake, therefore he can't make a mistake.'

'All that I'm saying is that trained guys like him don't make mistakes concerning operational procedure. You arrive at an OP with a pencil, you leave with a pencil, end of story.'

'OK. So what, in your opinion, is the message?'

'I think it's part and parcel with the nails. Some kind of reference to the undercover days. That knot hole was rather like a dead-letter drop, didn't you think? Perhaps returning the pencil is his way of saying that things have gone beyond words. That the only possible medium of communication left is murder.'

She stared at him.

'My guess is that he's way ahead of us,' said Alex. 'My guess is that he knew you'd bring in someone like me and so he put that pencil where only someone like me would find it.'

'I found it,' said Dawn.

'You know what I mean. It's a message for me. As if to say hello, brother. I was wondering when you'd be along.'

'You think he wants to be caught?' asked Dawn.

'I don't know about that – but I know he means to do a fair bit more killing first.'

Dawn frowned. 'I'm not supposed to tell you this, but there's something that probably wasn't in those reports you were given. They analysed the nails that were used to kill Fenn and Gidley, and found something very strange indeed.'

Alex looked at her.

'They were well over fifty years old. Nails haven't been made by that process or of that particular alloy since before the Second World War.'

'The pencil,' said Alex. Using a paper napkin he removed it

140

from his shirt pocket. It was of dull, plain wood, and bore no marking of any kind.

They peered at it. 'I'll bet you anything you like it turns out to be the same age,' said Dawn.

'Any idea what that's all about?'

'Search me.' Dawn half smiled. 'Except that you've already done that once today, haven't you?'

'Not as thoroughly as I'd have liked,' said Alex. 'I'm sure there are a few more surprises in store.'

'More than you'll ever know,' said Dawn.

FOURTEEN

That afternoon Alex took a train to Hereford, picked up his car from the garage where it had been repaired, collected some clothes from his flat and drove out to the SAS base at Credenhill. There he went straight to see Lieutenant-Colonel Bill Leonard, the CO. Howard was expecting him, and the Adjutant showed Alex straight through to the spare, utilitarian office with the steel furniture and the black-and-white photos on the wall.

'So how's it going with the Box investigation?' asked Howard, pushing away the laptop computer at which he had been tentatively poking. The CO was a short, broad-shouldered Yorkshireman with untidy brown hair, an enquiring blue gaze and fists the size of frozen chickens. A few years back he had played rugby for the army and many of his former opponents still bore the scars to remember him by. Bill Leonard was a far cry, Alex had always considered, from the public-schooled Ruperts who had preceded him. This was one of the reasons why Alex had decided to approach him and to disregard the order from Angela Fenwick not to discuss the Watchman case with his SAS colleagues.

'They're not letting me anywhere near it,' said Alex. 'My job is basically to wait on the sidelines until they find the guy, and then go in and waste him.'

'Are they going to find him?'

'Doubt it. He may be nuts but he's still a lot faster on his feet than they are. They've set up some lookalike in the home of the guy they suspect is next in line, but he'll suss it a mile off.'

Howard nodded. 'I've seen his file. He looks pretty switched on. Or he certainly was then. You think he'll whack this next bloke?'

'I reckon I can probably cut down the odds of that happening if they'll let me. But you know what they're like.'

'I know exactly what they're like. What *are* you doing?'

'Well, I'm doing what I'm told, which basically means fuck all. The trouble is, I suspect this guy's expecting someone like me to come after him.'

'He'd be a fool if he didn't expect that,' said Howard, studying his massive fingers. 'You think he'll have a go at you?'

'If I get in his way, yes.'

'You want to draw a Sig or something from the armoury?'

'It might be sensible. What I'd really like to do is speak to anyone who trained him. Are any of those blokes still contactable?'

Howard frowned. 'It was a fair old time ago, but you could give Frank Wisbeach a ring. His name's in the file as one of the Watchman instructors.'

'Do you know where I could find him?'

'He was driving a minicab in town the last I heard of him, poor old sod. Clarion cabs, I think they're called.'

'It might help to have a word,' said Alex. 'Anything that gives me an angle on Meehan and on the way his mind might be working.'

'If you do get an inside track, there could be a lot we can learn. About agent stress, breaking points and so on. We need a lot more information on that sort of thing.'

'Well, if I find myself face to face to him, I'll ask him what exactly turned him into a serial killer,' said Alex.

'How many people do you have to take out before they classify you as a serial killer?' Howard wondered aloud.

Alex shrugged. 'Four, I read. Up to that point you're just a killer. After four you're serial.'

Howard smiled wolfishly. 'Like us, you mean?'

It was an hour before Frank Wisbeach returned Alex's call and when he did he was apologetic, explaining that he had been on

143

an airport job. He was free that evening after 7.30, he told Alex, and they arranged to meet for a drink at a small pub on the outskirts of the city.

Driving back into town, Alex wondered what he should do about Sophie. For starters give her a call, he thought, and dialled her home number on his mobile. It rang unchecked; she hadn't put the answering machine on. He tried her mobile number but got the message service.

He didn't want to leave a message, he wanted to speak to her directly. Something about the morning's encounter with Dawn Harding had made him want very much to sort things out with her.

Later, he told himself. Later.

The Black Dog was not a pub that many Regiment members went to and this was why Alex had chosen it. It was a dim, dingy sort of place with an over-loud jukebox and the sour smell of spilt lager and cheese-and-onion crisps. Frank Wisbeach arrived shortly before eight and Alex was a little shocked by the sight of the gaunt figure in the cheap windcheater who had been his first Close Quarter Battle instructor.

'How are you, son?' asked Wisbeach, transferring a crumpled inch of roll-up to his left hand for the duration of their handshake. 'I heard they made you an officer.'

'They did,' said Alex. 'I'll be shuffling paper for the next few years.'

'Don't knock it, son – think of the pension. You're knackered before your time in this game. If it's not your knees it's your back. All those bloody Bergan runs.'

Wisbeach certainly looked knackered, Alex reflected as he bought the first round. It was the old story – that of the regimental hard-man who couldn't quite hack it without the army's visible and invisible support systems. Frank Wisbeach had left the SAS at the end of the 1980s after a distinguished career as an NCO which had taken in Oman, the Falklands War and several tours of Northern Ireland, and signed up with a private security company with training contracts in the Middle East. Alex was uncertain of the details, but the word was that a big client had then defaulted on months of back pay and expenses, bankrupting the company and several of its employees.

A series of bodyguarding jobs followed, but by then Wisbeach had been too old a dog to learn the ways of spoilt pop stars and bored Arab wives. A short fuse, an unwillingness to suffer fools gladly and a taste for the drink had ensured a swift professional decline, and by the mid-1990s he was living in a caravan and manning the doors in a provincial nightclub.

'So what brought you back to Hereford?' Alex asked, placing the other man's pint of bitter in front of him. 'I heard you were down in Luton.'

'Marriage, mate. Marriage brought me back. I came up for a reunion with a few of the lads from the Regimental Association and somewhere along the line – I can't quite remember the details but a pub lock-in was certainly involved – I found myself proposing to Della. Arse on her like a four-tonner but a nice smile and a half-share in a hairdressing business on Fortescue Road. Frank, my lad, I thought, it's time you settled down. Ever drink so much you pissed yourself?'

'No, I don't think so.'

'I was doing that most nights. And shitting myself too at weekends. There comes a point you review your options.'

Alex nodded sympathetically.

'So I married Della – fuck knows what she sees in me, but there you go – and picked up a bit of cabbing to help with the bills. Best thing I ever did. You ever been married?'

Alex shook his head.

'Take my advice, son, save it. Let the army look after you for as long as it wants to and then find a woman with a comfy pair of tits on her and a bit of money of her own, and hang your fucking boots up.'

'Sounds good,' said Alex.

'It is good, mate,' said Wisbeach, one-handedly rolling himself another cigarette. 'It is good.'

The deftness of the gesture reminded Alex of the skilful combat instructor that the older man had once been. 'You taught me a lot, Frank.'

145

Wisbeach shrugged and put a match to his roll-up. 'You were a good soldier, son. Saw that straight away.'

'That's not what you said at the time!'

'Well, you've got to dish out the old bollocks, haven't you. That's what you're there for on Training Wing.'

Alex smiled. 'I guess. Do you remember a guy called Joe Meehan?'

Sparks of wariness appeared in the other man's eyes. He seemed to sink into his cigarette smoke. 'It's a long time since I heard that name mentioned. A very long time.'

'You trained him, didn't you?'

'Who wants to know?'

'Bill Leonard suggested I speak to you.'

Wisbeach nodded slowly. 'Did he indeed. What's the whisper on the lad you mentioned, then?'

Alex wondered how much to confide. Sober, Wisbeach retained the Special Forces' soldier's habit of discretion. He hadn't even admitted to knowing Meehan. But pissed-up . . . 'The whisper is that he went over the water and they turned him.'

Wisbeach looked Alex in the eye and Alex saw from the slow freeze of his expression that the former NCO had guessed what he had been ordered to do. Knew that he was looking for Meehan in order to kill him.

For several moments neither man spoke. Above their heads, a pseudo-Victorian fan paddled stale cigarette smoke around the ceiling. On the jukebox, All Saints sang in mournful harmony.

'I'm sorry for the both of you,' Wisbeach said eventually, regarding his nicotined fingers with a kind of depthless exhaustion. 'There's no fucking end to it all, is there?'

'No,' Alex agreed. 'There isn't.'

'How will you . . .'

'I don't know,' Alex said. 'I just have to locate him.'

Wisbeach seemed to come to a decision. 'Joe Meehan was very good,' he said briskly. 'Technically you couldn't touch him. He was one of those people weapons always worked for. I was the same, so I knew it when I saw it. Mentally, too, he was very tough. Not in a laugh-it-off sort of way like most Regiment blokes – more like one of those Palestinian or Tamil Tiger suicide bombers. He was a true believer, if you know what I mean.'

'Was that a strength or a weakness?'

'Well, you wouldn't have wanted to go out on the piss with him, put it like that. He was a total loner and dead serious all the time. But then we weren't training stand-up comedians, we were training secret agents and assassins. In fact, I felt sorry for the poor bastard.'

'Why?'

'Because guys like that always destroy themselves in the end. They just bash on and on, never giving up, until there's nothing left of them.' He stared at the huddle of customers near the window and took a deep swallow of his beer. 'I'm told they're burying young Hammond in the morning.'

'That's right,' Alex confirmed.

Wisbeach shook his head. 'Africa, eh. What a fucking dump of a place to cop it. Get you another?'

'Yeah. Same again please.'

Wisbeach made his way to the bar. As he returned with the two full glasses three teenagers wearing earrings and flashy sports gear pushed roughly past him, spilling both drinks. None bothered to look round or to apologise.

'Excuse me, lads,' said Wisbeach mildly, turning to them. 'Bit of an accident. Do you mind filling up these glasses?'

The three looked round, incredulous and sniggering. 'Fuck off, Grandpa,' said the heaviest, whose doughy features were topped by a greasy centre parting.

Bloody hell, thought Alex. Here we go. 'Forget it, Frank,' he called out across the room.

But the ex-NCO was not of a mind to forget it, and placed the spilt drinks carefully on the bar. 'Come on, lads,' he said, the ghost of a smile touching his features. 'Don't let's spoil the evening with bad manners.'

At waist level, where the barman couldn't have seen it even if he'd been looking, there was the flash of a blade.

'You heard me,' said greasy-head. 'Now *fuck off!*'

Wisbeach frowned, as if disappointed. Then a heavy-knuckled hand shot out, grabbed the knife-wielder's neck and squeezed hard. There was a moment's absolute stillness. The Baha Boys boomed on the jukebox.

Wisbeach's knuckles tightened. The knife dropped to the floor and its owner's mouth snapped convulsively open, issuing a spray of half-chewed potato crisps and phlegm on to Wisbeach's sleeve.

The ex-NCO grinned. 'Good here, isn't it?' he said to the other two louts. His tone was conversational. For the first time that evening, thought Alex, the old bugger looked genuinely cheerful.

As anoxia kicked in, greasy-head's eyes crossed, the shiny nylon of his Adidas track pants darkened with urine and he sank half-conscious to his knees. When Wisbeach finally released him he lay retching and sobbing on the floor beneath the bar. If the barman had noticed anything, he showed no sign of having done so.

'Two pints please, lads,' Wisbeach said quietly, addressing the two survivors of the incident. 'You can bring them over to our table.'

Stunned by the sight of their leader's humiliation, they nodded their agreement.

'Better?' Alex smiled when they had taken delivery of their drinks.

'Much,' said Wisbeach. He leaned forward. 'Listen, son, don't go around saying you got this from me, but if you really want to know about Joe Meehan, the person to talk to is Denzil Connolly. Denzil was on one of those Khmer Rouge RWW training packages with me – a really shit-hot instructor – and he was in charge of Meehan at Tregaron before they dropped him over the water or whatever the hell they did with the poor sod. The two of them spent two or three months living in each others' pockets. So if anyone knew him . . .'

'Any idea where I'll find Connolly?'

'Sorry, mate. Not a clue.'

Alex nodded and the two men drank their beers in silence.

'Want another?' asked Alex eventually.

'I won't, thanks,' Wisbeach replied. 'I've got a couple more hours' driving.' He stood up, gaunt and tall, and extended a hand to Alex. 'Fuck of a business, son.'

'Yours or mine?'

The ex-NCO smiled. 'Watch yourself, OK?'

FIFTEEN

Five minutes later Alex was walking towards Hereford city centre. The encounter had depressed him, Don Hammond's funeral was tomorrow and he felt like cheering himself up.

As he left the outskirts of the city the streets got busier. There was a slight drizzle but this hadn't deterred the good-time crowd and noisy groups were swinging from bar to bar along the shining pavements, anxious to pour their salaries down their throats as rapidly and with as much shouting and laughter as possible. As the noise and the Friday night smell of beer and cheap perfume swallowed him up, Alex felt his spirits lift. A fat blonde girl winked at him and her friends giggled and screeched – he recognised them as part of the troopy-groupie crowd that often hung out at The Inkerman in the hope of being 'trapped' by young SAS troopers.

'Yo, Alex!' It was Andy Maddocks from 'D' Squadron and Lance Wilford of the RWW, dressed to kill in their civvy going-out clothes.

'Hey!' said Alex, moving out of the way of the lurching crowd on the pavement. 'What are you flash buggers doing back here?'

'Big turnaround after the hostage-rescue,' said Andy Maddocks. 'They're sending another squadron out next week.'

'And the RWW team?'

Lance Wilford shrugged. 'You disappeared, Don's dead, Ricky Sutton's having his arse mended in hospital . . . I guess they felt they ought to send in a new lot. Give the SL government their money's worth.'

Alex nodded. 'They pulled me out for a liaison job,' he told the other two men in answer to their unspoken question. 'I'm up here for Don's funeral tomorrow.'

The others nodded soberly and then, brightening, Maddocks turned to Alex. 'Why not join us for a few bevvies? And possibly a chat about the weather with a trio of nymphomaniac nurses, preferably still in their uniforms?'

'And suspender-belts,' added Lance wistfully.

'Sounds good to me,' said Alex.

A few minutes later they were crammed into a smoky corner table with pints in front of them. Andy, unwilling to waste time, was craning his head from side to side, looking for spare women.

'I thought you were married, Andy,' murmured Alex.

'Separated. Wendy binned me when the squadron got back from Kosovo.'

'Any particular reason?'

'Mental cruelty's what she told the lawyer. Which I suppose is as good a way as any of saying that she was shagging a footballer.'

'A footballer? You're kidding?'

'No, she and some friend of hers who goes out with one of the reserves took to going to all the United home games. With predictable fucking consequences.'

'Manchester United?' asked Lance.

'No, you womble, Hereford United.'

Lance reflected. 'I was going to say, if it'd been a Man U player it'd almost've been worth it. I'd let Ryan Giggs shag my wife.'

'You haven't got a wife. Giggsy wouldn't want to shag any woman that'd marry you. What'd he want to bother with some slag from . . .'

'Are you calling my future wife a slag?'

'Well, she is, isn't she? Be honest.'

They all laughed, Lance loudest of all.

This is good, thought Alex. This is real.

'So, do you reckon you'll be getting any Hereford United tickets?' Lance asked, after a short drinking break.

He ducked just in time to avoid Andy's fist.

151

'Where did the mental cruelty come in?' asked Alex.

'Told Wendy I didn't want kids,' said Andy. 'Couldn't bear the thought of having a son or a daughter who lost its dad. It's one thing being killed, it's another lying there knowing you're going to break your child's heart.'

'So why d'you marry her in the first place?'

'Price she put on her virtue. No white dress, no snakey-snakey.'

Alex nodded. 'Where did you go on your honeymoon?'

'Belfast,' said Andy. 'With the rest of the squadron . . . Lance, mate, I think we're in business. Go and ask those three to come over. Her in the blue top and the two with her.'

'Why me? You go!'

'You're a fucking corporal, now get your arse over there.'

Alex would have said it was impossible to get anyone else round the table but somehow the three managed to jam themselves in. One of them, a cheerful, round-faced girl with what Frank Wisbeach would without question have called 'comfy tits', was practically sitting on his knee.

'Whassat?' she asked, squirming uncomfortably.

'My mobile,' said Alex apologetically. 'What's your name?'

'Gail,' said the girl, snapping her lighter beneath a king-size Pall Mall. She smelt of make-up and Pernod and synthetic perfume and her hair – inches from his face – was a curtain of wheatish blonde, as flat as if it had been ironed. Next to him, Andy Maddocks was very seriously informing the girl in the blue top that the three of them were gay.

'Bollocks!' said the girl in the blue top. 'We know what you are. We sussed you ten minutes ago from the tans.'

'And the muscles,' said Gail, reaching across the table to tweak Lance's tattooed bicep.

'And the crap haircuts,' volunteered the third girl to shrieks from the other two. 'We're not fucking stupid.'

'It was worth a try,' said Andy. 'I was going to suggest you try and convert us to heterosexuality.'

'And just how would we do that?' asked the girl in the blue top.

'Well . . .' began Andy.

For an hour the six of them sat, drank and laughed. Alex could feel himself getting drunker and drunker but the fact didn't worry him in the least. He had never been a regular pub-goer but right now he was having the best time that he could remember. This was the reality, this smoky bar corner and the press of the crowd and the laughter of his mates and the weight of Gail's thigh against his and the tableful of empty glasses. If he was going to take his officer status seriously, he supposed glumly, he was going to have to wind this sort of activity down.

So how should he play it? Up or out? Stay with the army in the knowledge that the best was behind him or bale out and take his chances in civvy street? The latter sounded more tempting but what would his life actually consist of, given that soldiering was the only trade he knew? Babysitting overpaid celebrities who – at best – would treat him as a paid accessory? Waiting in the rain outside the fashionable restaurants where Sophie and her friends went? He couldn't see himself taking that route. He didn't want to end up like Frank Wisbeach, taking his frustrations out on delinquent teenagers.

Contract soldiering, perhaps. Working for the highest bidder. Fucking up the lives of third-world citizens on behalf of multinationals like Shell or Monsanto?

All in all, he thought, he'd rather go back to Clacton and take the garage off his dad's hands. But then he couldn't quite see Sophie hunched up against the sea wind eating haddock and chips from the bag, or chucking a rubber bone for the dog, or watching *EastEnders*.

Sophie. He should give her a bell.

'You're a quiet one, aren't you,' said Gail. 'You haven't said a word in ten minutes.'

'Sorry,' he said. 'I was thinking.'

'What about?'

'The future, I suppose.'

'Well, we could start off with another drink.' She glanced at her two friends, who were subtly but definitely paired off with Andy and Lance.

'Same again?' he asked her. 'Pernod and black?'

'Yeah. I'll come with you.'

On their unsteady way to the bar, he found his arm encircling her waist and her body moving into alignment with his. He felt her hip-joint articulating beneath his hand, the soft weight of her breast against his side.

'You're an officer, your mate said.'

'Er, yeah.'

'You don't sound like an officer.'

He grinned. 'What do I sound like?'

She frowned and pouted up her lips. 'Oh . . . I don't know. Like the others, I s'pose.'

'Well, that's what I am like.'

'You're not, though. They're, like, dead laddish and up for a laugh, and you're not like that at all. You just pretend to be.' She narrowed her eyes, leant against him and lowered her voice. 'I bet you're a right hard bastard. Have you got a girlfriend? Don't answer that – of course you have. Just don't tell me about her.'

'As long as you don't tell me about your boyfriend.'

'I haven't got a boyfriend.' The crowd propelled them forward against the bar. 'I've got a bloody husband, worse luck.'

Alex turned to stare at her but at that moment the barman materialised in front of them, eyebrow raised. Alex ordered himself a sixth pint and a Jameson's whiskey chaser, and Gail her fifth Pernod and blackcurrant. 'Married?' he asked flatly.

'He's away. With someone else.' She glanced up at him. 'Don't ask, just be nice to me.'

She was pretty, he thought. Pretty eyes. And a mouth and body to chase the ghosts away. He slipped his hand under the bottom of her sweater, felt the taut waistband of her jeans and the warm flesh above.

The drinks arrived and they backed away from the bar.

'Where d'you live?' he asked her.

'I don't want to go there,' she said. She touched his cheek with the back of her fingers. 'What about you?'

'Walking distance.'

In the flat he bolted the door and closed the curtains as she walked slowly around, touching things.

'There's dust everywhere.' She smiled.

'I've been away. Coffee? And I've got some Bushmills somewhere?'

'Sounds good.'

In the kitchen area the strip light was on the flicker. Alex was kissing her against the wall and she was running her hands up his back when the kettle boiled.

In the bedroom there was a jumble of mostly green kit against the wall – waterproofs, thermals, medical packs, a water purifier, sleeping bags and stuff sacks – into which, earlier that day, Alex had tossed the shoulder-holstered Glock pistol and accessories he'd signed out of the armoury at Credenhill.

If Gail noticed this, she made no comment, just lowered her drink and kicked off her shoes. 'Music?'

In answer Alex directed her to the miniature sound system and pile of CDs that sat, as dusty as everything else, on a shelf.

'This is the strangest collection I've ever seen,' she said wonderingly. 'Miles Davis, Britney Spears, Johann Sebastian Bach, the Teletubbies, *Bridget Jones's Diary* . . .'

'It belonged to a guy who got killed last year,' said Alex. 'I think there were some Christmas presents for his family among it.'

She shook her head. 'The lives you people lead.' She switched the system on and selected the Britney Spears CD.

On the bed, or rather on the double mattress that served Alex as a bed, they undressed each other. She was wearing a tight lilac sweater which she pulled away from her face as he took it off so as not to smear her make-up. Beneath it, she amply filled a black lace bra. Smiling, she allowed him to search behind her back for a moment before pointing to the rosebud clasp at the front. He undid it and lowered his head. Her fingers knotted in his hair.

Finally they were both naked. She was pale-skinned and soft as ice cream, and there was a dreamy-eyed passivity about her which he found a vast relief after Sophie. She was his – all of her, unconditionally and for as long as he wanted.

Breathing in her muskily synthetic aura – part pub, part Boots perfume counter – he ran his hands over the impossible softness of her breasts. When he reached the inside of her thighs she gasped and drew her knees apart.

She tasted, in some curious way, of Alex's memories of his childhood, of sweat and closeness and sea spray, of the time before he had killed anyone. She moved like the sea too – slowly and from somewhere deep within herself. After a time he moved back up her body, manoeuvred himself inside her and forgot about Sophie altogether.

SIXTEEN

She left early, while he pretended to be asleep. He woke for a second time to find a note on the pillow and a daytime telephone number – a work number, he guessed.

Why had she left? Not wanting to spoil things with the awkwardness of a morning after? He smiled – in many ways theirs had been the perfect relationship.

He shook his head and immediately wished he hadn't. It felt as if there was a cannon ball rolling around in it. The inside of his mouth was parched and sour, his stomach felt uneasy and he had a morbid thirst. Not for the first time he reflected that it wasn't the drinks that made you pissed that fucked you up, it was the completely unnecessary ones that you drank when you were already pissed. It was those Scotches that you ended up with just because it felt right, somehow, to wind the evening up with a glass of spirits in your hand.

The thought of whisky made his gorge rise, and he staggered to the bathroom and the cold tap. On the way he trod heavily on his old Casio Neptune watch – it had survived worse – and arrived at the sink just in time to throw up. Don Hammond, an enthusiastic drinker who had always tried to persuade Alex to put in more pub hours, would have been proud of him.

It wasn't until he had showered and dressed that he remembered the Glock. It was still there, thank God, as were all the heavy little boxes of 9mm ammunition. What would have happened if any of it had left the flat in the pocket of a girl he'd picked up in a pub, he shuddered to think. He'd always been the first to take the piss out of those Box clowns who had their laptops nicked from their cars.

The Glock that he had chosen was the model 34. In the past he'd used the 17, the most popular 9mm Glock model. It held up to nineteen rounds, hardly ever jammed and in general was a dream to use. The 34, developed for competition use, was basically the same gun but with the accuracy advantage of another inch of barrel. It wasn't the easiest weapon to conceal, but it still weighed in at just under two pounds fully loaded and if it came to aimed shots, Alex had decided, that extra inch between the sights might just make all the difference. He had fired off a few magazines on the range and had been stunned by the weapon's performance, given that the general rule for automatics was that at a range of more than twenty yards you were lucky if you could hit anything smaller than a front door.

From the armoury he'd also drawn a silencer and a laser dot-marker sight, which he reckoned ought to cover most eventualities.

And a knife. A standard-issue Government Recon commando knife with a 6.25-inch blade. The instinct that Alex had about Meehan was that he wasn't a firearms man. Firearms were crude, noisy and remote – he would regard it a failure to have to resort to them. Meehan, Alex was sure from his modus operandi so far, was a close-up man. A blade man.

Retrieving his watch, he saw that it was almost 9.30 and rang Dawn. She was no party girl. She would be up and about.

Her mobile rang twice and then she answered it.

'Up and about, Miss Harding?' he asked her. 'Bright-eyed and bushy-tailed?'

'Is that Captain Temple?' she enquired in a brisk, businesslike way that told Alex immediately that she was not alone.

'Yes. It is. Can I talk, or are you . . .'

'No, I'm not. What do you want?'

'I just wanted to make sure you were enjoying this' – he peered through the curtains – 'rather damp morning. And not fooling around in bed. Did you tell me what his name was, by the way?'

'Look, Captain Temple, if you've got something to say . . .'

158

'I thought I'd let you know where I was. In case you were missing me.'

'In your dreams. Where are you?'

'Hereford. I'm chasing up one of our man's ex-teachers.'

'You think that'll be useful?'

'I think it's all we've got, for the moment. I'll keep you abreast.'

'You do that. Oh, and, um, the object we found. It was the age we thought it might be. And bearing the right prints. Congratulations, Captain.'

The phone went dead. Why did he have this irresistible desire to wind Dawn Harding up? Alex wondered. Because she was such a straight arrow? Such a company girl? And whom had she been sleeping with, anyway? Some keen young computer buff from Thames House, no doubt. Some pillar of the Orienteering or Mountain Biking Club. Alex could just see him, weedy and pale, leaning back against the pillows, having a moody post-shag Dunhill. Except that he wouldn't smoke. He'd probably be a vegetarian. A vegan. Drink ground-up acorns instead of coffee.

By ten, having gulped down a half-pint glass of lager from the store in the fridge (an old morning-after trick of Don Hammond's) Alex was feeling a little better. Ready, in fact, to undertake part two of the standard hangover cure – a full English fried breakfast.

More cheerful now, and gratified that the fingerprints on the pencil stub had conclusively linked Meehan with the killings, Alex made his way to a café. The downside to the discovery was his certainty that the find had been intended by Meehan. It had almost been a greeting to his pursuer.

For all his instincts concerning the Watchman, Alex mused, he really had no idea where the man might be holing up. One possibility was that he was moving around the fringes of one of the larger cities with transients and unaccountables – squatting, perhaps, or moving between cheap hostels and bed-and-breakfast houses, or hanging out with travellers. If in trouble, the rule went, seek out those who also have something to hide. The Watchman, however, also had to avoid the Irish Catholic communities among whom visiting PIRA players moved, so perhaps he was avoiding the cities.

A second possibility was that he had constructed himself a completely false identity – driving licence, bank accounts, credit cards and the rest of it – and was living in a rented flat and passing himself off as a salesman or some other itinerant professional in a small provincial town.

But something told Alex that this was not the man's style. Frank Wisbeach's words reinforced the idea of Meehan as the victim of some grandiose delusion. A man of unwavering seriousness, the old NCO had said. No detectible sense of humour. A 'true believer'. Alex had met 'true believers' before. The phrase was used to describe soldiers who believed that the purity of their calling somehow singled them out from the rest of humanity. They tended to subscribe to ideas of 'the warrior's path' and 'the mediocrity of civilian life'. 'Green-eyed boys' they'd called them in the Paras. This didn't stop them being good soldiers – quite the opposite in many cases – but it did mean that their behaviour could get a bit weird if unchecked. The Watchman's murder project definitely had the 'true believer' edge to it and it was for this reason that Alex didn't quite believe that the man was pretending to be Mister Average and driving a Ford Escort. It didn't go with the apocalyptic nature of his actions. If he saw himself as some mystical bringer of vengeance (as so many of these nutters seemed to) then he would ensure that his surroundings were appropriately Gothic and elemental. A forest, perhaps. Something like that.

Did he own a vehicle? Probably, but Alex guessed he would use it only sparingly. Vehicles showed up on CCTV, people noticed and remembered them and they were powerful transmitters of forensic evidence. Stolen cars were especially bad news if you wanted to keep your head down.

Alex addressed his breakfast – black pudding, bubble and squeak, eggs, beans, mushrooms, two fried slices and a mug of tea. The business.

He was just supposed to do the chopping, he reminded himself. Fine, except that the only time Five were likely to get anywhere near Meehan was when the former MI5 agent had finished his killing spree and was ready to give himself up. Killing Meehan at that point would be little more than a gesture.

Right now Meehan would be watching Widdowes, just as he had watched Fenn and Gidley. He'd be lying up nearby, entirely aware of the lookalike and the rest of their strategies, waiting for the moment when they stopped fully believing that the attack would come. The moment when they persuaded themselves they had won. And then, with blinding and brutal speed, he would strike.

Alex had to persuade the Box team to let him take over – or at least participate in – the guarding of George Widdowes. He'd have to get the MI5 officer back into his house so that, like a tiger to a tethered goat, Meehan would be drawn to his prey. The idea was a good one. It could work. He'd have to talk to Dawn about it. They would have yet another row. He discovered he was rather looking forward to it.

Don Hammond's funeral was the usual sombre affair. There was an obvious police presence, some blocking off the traffic, with many of the officers carrying side arms.

Less obvious was the standby squadron, who were waiting in Range Rovers at several of the surrounding crossroads, armed with MP5 Heckler and Koch sub-machine guns.

Alex arrived in the dark Principles suit that he used for Regimental funerals and metropolitan area surveillance, and was nodded through by the adjutant, also suited. In the church there were somewhere between a hundred and fifty and two hundred people. There were several rows of soldiers from the Credenhill base, all looking uncharacteristically smart in their Number Two uniforms, and in front of them a tight group of friends, relations and other uniformed soldiers surrounded Karen Hammond, Don's widow, and Cathy, his daughter.

Moving hesitantly forward, Alex met Karen's eye. She smiled and beckoned him, and a place was made for him in the row behind her. Silently she reached out her hand and equally silently Alex took it. She's as brave as Don was, he thought, turning to the coffin which stood, flag-draped, in the aisle. On it lay his friend's medals, his blue stable belt and his sand-coloured SAS beret.

Who dares wins.

Not every time, thought Alex, catching sight of eight-year-old Cathy Hammond's grief-whitened face. Not every time.

In the churchyard Alex allowed his attention to wander as the chaplain spoke the now familiar words of the funeral service. His eyes travelled over the bare heads and the bemedalled uniforms, and the relatives' dark coats and suits. Karen and Cathy were both weeping now, and Karen's family pressed protectively around them. The eyes of the other soldiers, for the most part, were downturned. Alex himself felt empty. Tears were not what he owed Don Hammond.

And then, as the three shots were fired over the open grave, Alex's wandering gaze met a pair of eyes that were not downturned – that were levelled with deathly directness at his own. The man, who was wearing a nondescript suit and tie, and had a curiously ageless appearence, was standing on the other side of the grave behind Karen's family, and Alex realised with stunned disbelief that he knew this narrow face and pale unblinking stare, that he had seen photographs of this man in Thames House, that he was standing just three yards away from Joseph Meehan, the Watchman.

As their eyes locked, Alex felt his scalp crawl and his heart slam in his chest. *No, it was impossible.*

Impossible but true. It was Meehan and he had come to scope out his pursuer. In the icy flame of his regard was a challenge, a statement of ruthlessness and contempt. I can come and go as I please, it said – even here, even now, in the secret heart of your world – and there is nothing that you can do to prevent me.

And Meehan was right. At that moment there was nothing in the world that Alex could do. Sympathy for Karen Hammond and the dignity of the occasion paralysed him. He couldn't speak, let alone jump over the open grave and grab the man by the throat.

There was a loud clatter overhead as three Chinook helicopters flew past in formation. Alex held Meehan's pale gaze, but the ranks of mourners shifted as they looked upwards, and when they re-formed, moments later, the cold-eyed face had vanished.

Alex peered desperately over the open grave as the churning helicopter blades faded away, but the fly-past had marked the end of the service. As the Hammond family and their friends moved away from the graveside, the regimental personnel held back, Alex among them. Short of elbowing his way through the uniformed men he was trapped.

Finally, the crowd began to disperse. Moving as fast and as forcefully as he was able, given the circumstances, Alex made his way to the churchyard exit. There was no sign of anyone resembling Meehan either inside or outside. Running to the head of the road he challenged the two uniformed troopers on duty there. Had a man in his mid-thirties just passed them – fair-skinned, dark-haired, five ten, grey suit . . . tough-looking . . .

The words spilt out but the troopers shook their heads. No one like that. No one on his own.

Ignoring the curious stares of the exiting mourners, Alex ran on ahead of the roadblock to the nearest Range Rover and repeated the questions.

Same answer. No one answering that description.

Shit. *Shit.* Had he imagined seeing Meehan? Had the image of the man been preying on his mind to the point where he was beginning to hallucinate? Was Meehan now stalking *him*?

Tucking himself into the roadside, Alex called Dawn on his mobile and – in guarded terms, given that he was using an open line – reported the incident.

'How sure are you that it was him?' Dawn asked.

'Not a hundred per cent. And if it was he could be anywhere by now.'

163

'Why would he want to show himself like that?'

'Check me out, perhaps. Let me know he can come and go as he pleases.'

Dawn was silent. Alex could tell that she was unconvinced that the man had been Meehan.

'Look,' he went on, 'I've got a possible regimental lead. It's not much but it's a possibility. Someone who knew our man. Someone he might have talked to.'

'Do you need my people's help?'

'No. Leave it to me.'

'OK, then. Keep me informed.'

She broke the connection and Alex looked around. Several people were staring at him and he self-consciously brushed down his suit. He had meant what he said to Dawn. Meehan could be anywhere by now. There was no chance of catching him without involving the entire Hereford and Worcester police forces and probably not even then. And, if he was honest with himself, he *hadn't* been a hundred per cent sure it was Meehan.

Much more constructive to work out where his base was. There had to be some secret location he returned to between the killings. An inner-city flat? A hostel or bed and breakfast? A caravan park? The only person who might possibly have a clue as to the whereabouts of that location – and it was still a hell of a long shot – was Denzil Connolly. Of those who trained Meehan, according to Frank Wisbeach, Connolly was the only man who really got to know him. If he could find Connolly, Alex reflected, he was in with a chance of finding Meehan. He might, at the very least, learn something about the man he was pursuing.

'Looking for a lift back to camp?'

It was the driver of one of the Range Rovers and Alex accepted gratefully. At the Credenhill base he made his way to the sergeants mess, where he was formally invited in – as an officer, he no longer had the automatic right of entry.

After an SAS funeral there was always a big piss-up. Alex had been to more of these than he cared to remember and if there

164

were ever times that the Regiment genuinely resembled the family it claimed itself to be these were they.

The mess was a large room dominated by a bar and furnished with oxblood Chesterfield furniture. The floor was carpeted in regimental blue and the walls were hung with paintings of former SAS soldiers, captured flags and weapons, and the plaques of foreign units. An impressive collection of silverware was also on display.

Men poured in in groups, animated now and relieved that the austerity and the tears of the funeral were behind them. A sheepishly grinning Ricky Sutton arrived on crutches, newly released from hospital, and was greeted with a ragged cheer. Most of the men headed straight for the bar, and by the time the Hammond contingent and the other wives and relatives were ushered in there were the makings of a fine party.

Alex, still shaken by the incident at the funeral, did not immediately move to join his friends. Seeing Bill Leonard, he cornered him and asked him if he had any idea of Denzil Connolly's whereabouts.

The burly lieutenant-colonel did not look best pleased to be questioned on this subject. Curtly he assured Alex that the Regiment had no contact information of any kind on Denzil Connolly. Then, excusing himself, he moved away.

The Hammond family came in, and Alex was among the group who moved to greet them.

'Don really loved looking for trouble with you fellers,' said Karen, teary-eyed and shaky but somehow still smiling. 'I'd never have tried to take him away from all that.'

'He was the best,' said Alex gently. 'Best soldier. Best mate.'

She wept against his shoulder for a few moments, then wiped her eyes and put on a brave grin. 'Where's that posh girl of yours, then? Don told me she was a smasher!'

'She couldn't come,' said Alex. 'She got stuck in London. Work.'

Karen smiled. 'Well, don't leave it too long. You'll need a nice smart wife when they make you a general.'

'Yeah, well, it hasn't quite got to that yet.'

'Don't leave it too long, Alex. Promise me.'

He smiled. 'I won't, Karen. I promise.'

For now, though, there was something he had to follow up and he made his way to a knot of old lags who were clustering around the RSM at the bar.

'Afternoon, Alex, you warry old bugger. I mean sir,' said the RSM, addressing his beer glass. 'Word is you enjoyed yourself last night!'

The others smirked.

'I may have taken a drink,' admitted Alex. 'Or two.'

'In mixed company?'

'That's not impossible either.'

The RSM nodded. 'Well, you look like shite today. Serves you right. Poor old Don, eh.'

'Poor old Don,' Alex echoed. 'He had a very bad last minute and I hope Karen never hears the details of that. But you should have seen him hanging out of that chopper with the SLR and Kalashnikov rounds screaming around him, blazing away with the old five point five. Talk about Death from Above.'

The RSM nodded approvingly. 'I hear you didn't do so badly yourself?'

Alex shrugged. 'We were lucky. We could easily have lost a lot more guys. Next time they should just let the hostages get eaten or chopped to pieces or whatever.'

'You said it,' said the RSM, wordlessly handing his glass back for refilling. He glanced at Alex's suit. 'Heard you'd been pulled out of Freetown ahead of time. Spooky business, I heard.'

'That sort of thing. I'm trying to get hold of someone you may be in touch with. Denzil Connolly.'

The NCOs looked at each other.

'Long time since I heard that name,' said a sniper team leader named Stevo. His tone was careful.

Alex said nothing. There was no communications web more intricate, secretive and subtle than that which existed between British army sergeants. He had been part of it once, but it was closed to him now. He could only file his request and wait.

'There was some strange stuff with Den Connolly,' said the

166

RSM, glancing at Alex. 'And that looks like an empty glass in your hand. I thought you officers were supposed to set an example.'

For the time being, Alex knew, that was as far as things would go. An overfull pint glass was handed splashily over. Someone spoke through a microphone over the laughter and hubbub. There was going to be an auction of Don Hammond's kit, with the proceeds going to Karen and Cathy.

Two hours later Alex's head was singing with Stella Artois and the shock of seeing Meehan at the funeral had receded. Stepping out into the sudden silence of the evening drizzle, he made his way across the tarmac to the guardhouse. After the original Sterling Lines barracks in Hereford, the Credenhill camp seemed a vast high-tech sprawl – more like a software park or an airport than anything else. Sticking his head into the guardhouse, he asked if someone could ring for a minicab to take him back into Hereford. As it turned out, one of the duty policemen was going that way and offered him a ride.

Denzil Connolly. The name bounced back and forth in Alex's mind. In case anyone just happened to remember anything, he'd left his mobile number with Stevo and the RSM.

There were two ways to catch a predator like Meehan. One was to peg out a bait and lure him into the open, the other was to find his lair and stake it out.

If necessary, Alex intended to try both.

Back at the flat, he rang Sophie. Her home number was engaged, her mobile switched off. Depressed by the afternoon's events, fuzzy-headed with alcohol, he considered giving Gail a ring. For a long and tempting moment he felt her body against him, soft and unresisting.

At the last minute he decided otherwise. Changing into a sweat top and shorts, he made his way outside to the pavement and began jogging towards the outskirts of the city. It was raining harder now, the light was beginning to go and most of the shops were closed. The pavements were all but deserted, but once again Alex was visited by the unpleasant suspicion that he was being watched.

Get a grip, he told himself. *Paranoia isn't going to help.*

Soon he was on an empty road leading southwards. The rain, cold and clean, lashed his face and hands, his breathing steadied and found its rhythm, and his mind began to clear. He had to watch his step, he told himself, or at least be a bit more discreet. Last night he would probably get away with on the grounds that his best friend had just been killed and everyone was entitled to go crazy from time to time, but if he made a habit of it people were going to start thinking he was losing his grip. And when that occurred, well, you only had to look at Frank Wisbeach to see what happened when a good soldier started to unravel.

Fired with a new resolve, he pushed himself hard on the five miles or so back to Hereford. The rain continued, it was lancing down now as the light faded, and he could feel the beginnings of a new blister on one heel.

Back in the flat he showered and tried Sophie again. Same result: home engaged, mobile switched off. Quickly he dressed, packed a suitcase, locked up the flat and climbed into the pearl-white Karman-Ghia. Pointing the bonnet towards the Ledbury Road, he set out for London. He was glad to have the car back and to feel the cheerful growl of the 1835cc engine as the rain lashed the windscreen in front of him. Ray Temple had accepted the thirty-year-old shell in lieu of a debt two years earlier and rebuilt the car from the wheels up, selling it to his son for the altogether bargain price of £5000.

The car could really move, but on this occasion Alex made sure to keep well within the speed limit. Whatever the alcohol limit was these days, he was uneasily certain that he was in excess of it. He'd only had a couple of pints at the funeral – well, perhaps it had been three – but there had probably been a fair bit left over from the night before. Having said that, he'd run the best part of ten miles before starting to drive, which would have burnt off a few units, surely?

Best to take no chances, to take a leaf out of the Dawn Harding school of motoring. While waiting at traffic lights

168

outside Cirencester he dialled her number. 'So what are you up to?' he asked her.

'What business is that of yours?'

'What's his name, Harding?'

'Grow up, Temple.'

'Can we make a date for tomorrow morning?'

'Any particular reason?'

'Nothing I can talk about on an open line. How about breakfast?'

'OK. Eight o'clock outside my office building.'

The phone went dead.

In Western Avenue, as he entered London, he spotted a rose seller standing in a lay-by. He was unlikely to find any florists open, Alex thought, so he bought twelve quid's worth – the rest of the man's stock. Mindful of Dawn's words, he took off the cellophane wrappers and bunched the blooms all together. The roses were pretty knackered-looking and certainly had no scent to speak of – they still looked as if they'd been bought in a lay-by, in other words – but they were better than nothing.

Half an hour later he was parking the Karman-Ghia in Pavilion Road, off Sloane Street. The rain had stopped and the pavements and the roads shone silver beneath the street lights. Tucking the roses under one arm and tidying his hair with the fingers of the other hand, he made his way towards the building containing Sophie's flat.

Glancing up at her window he saw her, wearing the white towelling bathrobe that she'd stolen from the Crillon Hotel in Paris. She was in her bedroom, staring out eastwards over the city. And then a second dressing-gowned figure appeared beside her, placed an arm round her shoulder.

Who the fuck was that, Alex asked himself, his heart plummeting. Stella, perhaps? But he already knew it wasn't Stella. Running back to the car he rummaged inside his travel bag, pulled out a pair of image-stabilised Zeiss binoculars and focused on the two figures.

It was a bloke. Some fashionably stubbled fucker. And very much at home, thank you very much, with his arm round

169

Sophie, who looked like the cat who'd had the cream. Well, she certainly hadn't wasted any bloody time, had she?

Stupid bastard, he thought, hurling the roses up the middle of Pavilion Road.

Stupid bastard!

SEVENTEEN

'So,' said Dawn, stirring the cup of brick-red tea that the café owner had just placed in front of her. 'Is this going to be a long argument or a short one?'

'I've paid for a long one,' said Alex.

She regarded him bleakly. His call to her after the funeral, Alex realised, had counted as a mark against him. She thought that he was getting flaky, that he had started seeing things.

'Look, I've got a hell of a lot to get on with. What is it you want?'

'I want to talk to you about George Widdowes. I don't think your lookalike idea is going to work. I think the only way we're going to stop Meehan is by setting a trap. By putting the real man back into the house as bait.'

'No way. We're on top of the Widdowes business. The man we've got looks very like George indeed. He's wearing George's clothes, driving George's car into London every day . . .'

'Meehan will have guessed that you'd try that,' said Alex impatiently. 'He'll have checked him out.'

'Only from a distance, going by our find at the Gidleys'. That tree must have been a hundred and fifty yards from the house. He'll never know the difference from that sort of range.'

'The tree was a general OP for watching security procedures and checking out the dogs. He'll have had a closer look than that at Craig Gidley before killing him, believe me. Probably set himself up at the side of the road earlier in the day and checked him in through the gates. He knew Gidley, just like he knows Widdowes. A glance would have been enough. And a glance has probably been enough to tell him that you're using a lookalike right now. That's why nothing's happened. That and the fact that the area is almost certainly swarming with Box employees with sniper's rifles. You have to remember that our man's served in Belfast and South Armagh. He's got a nose for that sort of thing.'

Her silence told him that he was right about the concealed marksmen.

She placed her teaspoon carefully in her saucer and frowned. 'Look, at least as things stand we're keeping George Widdowes alive.'

'Sooner or later Meehan's going to discover where you're keeping him,' said Alex. 'He'll follow him back from work. There are only so many exits from Thames House and yes, I know about the underground car parks and the tunnel and the rest of it and so, sooner or later, will he. Meehan will stake them all out, one by one. It may take a month, it may take him a year, but sooner or later he'll do it. He'll catch Widdowes leaving the building and follow him back to wherever it is you've put him. Where is it that Widdowes lives, officially?'

'Hampshire,' said Dawn.

'All these guys tied up in Hampshire while Widdowes goes off his head in some crummy safe house in Docklands or Alperton or Gants Hill, waiting for a bullet between the eyes? At the moment Meehan's calling all the shots – we've got to stop retreating and take control of this thing.'

Dawn pursed her lips thoughtfully.

'At least put the idea to Fenwick,' Alex continued. 'And if she agrees in principle, then let's go down to Widdowes' place and check out the possibility of setting up an ambush.'

'I can't promise anything,' she said eventually. 'But tell me what you want to do and I'll put it to the deputy director.'

'Can you please slow down,' said Dawn, 'we're not going for the land speed world record.'

They were heading up the M3 to Hampshire, this time in the Karman-Ghia. Alex had told her that he didn't think he could take another journey with her at the wheel and she had retorted that she was perfectly happy to be driven – it would make a change, in fact.

To Alex's surprise – and to Dawn's irritation, he suspected – Angela Fenwick had agreed to his request to recce Widdowes' house with a view to returning the agent there and luring Meehan into a trap.

George Widdowes lived a short distance outside the village of Bishopstoke in the Itchen valley. Longwater Lodge, where he lived alone, had once been attached to the much larger Longwater House, now a management college. Surrounded by trees and shrubberies, and set back some fifty metres from the road, the lodge was bordered at its far end by a carrier stream of the River Itchen, which flowed through the grounds of the main house.

Alex and Dawn had parked a quarter of a mile away outside the Pied Bull pub in the village's main street and had ambled out towards Longwater Lodge as if they were a young couple who, on impulse perhaps, had taken the day off. After the rain of the previous day the fields had a summery freshness and the steady hum of bees rose above the grumble of the distant main road.

The Lodge looked empty. The curtains were drawn, no cars stood outside it and a brand-new For Sale sign stood at its gate. The sign had been Dawn's idea and she had somehow ensured that it was up within the hour. Any enquiries to the London estate agent whose name it bore would have been met by the explanation that while the owner of the property wished to announce his intention to sell in the near future, the agency had not yet received full instructions.

Alex had been surprised by the speed with which the idea had been implemented and that Winchester estate agents were quite so receptive to sweet-talk from the security services. 'Oh, we've got friends everywhere,' Dawn had glibly informed him. 'We're quite big players in the property market.'

The purpose of the sign had been to enable her and Alex to reconnoitre the property. If we want to have a good look, she had told him, then we might as well do it the easy way and walk straight up the drive. Anybody watching will simply assume that we're a couple who are interested in buying.

Turning his back on Longwater Lodge, Alex scanned the surrounding countryside. Still green cornfields bordered by hedgerows and oak trees on the higher ground; water-meadows in the valley, with willows and poplars shading the river. Hundreds of acres visible and a thousand places where an experienced man might be lying up. The Watchman was out there somewhere, keeping the house under observation, but you could send in a battalion of paratroopers with dogs and helicopters and still not find him. With the first indications of a search he would simply fade away.

Alex stared over the road into the sunlit green valley. He knew he would never be offered an obvious give-away like the flash of a binocular lens, but for an optimistic moment or two he stared anyway.

From the humpback bridge crossing the river, the two of them examined the Lodge and its surroundings. The property comprised about an acre and a half in total. The road on which they stood swept right-handed round the front of the garden, and was separated from it by a wall of about five feet in height and a neatly clipped yew hedge.

'That's where our people go in at night,' Dawn told him. 'They climb over the wall once it's dark and keep the place under surveillance through night-vision goggles.'

'How do they get here?'

'By Land Rover. Park up a hundred yards away round the corner.'

'He'll have sussed them out on night one,' said Alex. 'You can count on that.'

Dawn shrugged. 'You may be right.'

'I am right,' said Alex. 'He's almost certainly watching us right now. Give us a kiss!'

'In your dreams.'

'I mean it. That's what normal couples do when they're looking at houses. They hold hands. They kiss each other. It means they . . .'

'I know perfectly well what it means.' Turning, she kissed him glancingly on the left cheek.

He frowned. 'Oh, come on, Bunnykins, you can do better than that. Think how happy we could be here. Think of little Bethany and Jordan and Kylie running into the house with bunches of flowers and bouncing on our bed on Saturday mornings. Think of the songs you'll sing as you bake the bread and scrub the floor. Think of the jam you'll make.'

'You're sick, Temple.'

'I'm not sick, Bunnykins, I just want a proper kiss. I'm not necessarily talking tongues at this stage, but I do think it should be convincing.'

'Don't be disgusting. And stop calling me Bunnykins.'

'I will if you kiss me right now, mouth to mouth, for a minimum of five seconds. If not, I'm afraid you go on being Bunnykins.'

With a long-suffering sigh she turned to him and placed her arms round his neck. Her mouth was very soft. She even closed her eyes.

'There,' he said finally. 'That wasn't so bad, was it?'

She was silent for a moment. 'I've had worse,' she said.

He placed his arm round her waist, sensed her body stiffen, then felt an answering arm creep unwillingly round his waist.

'How many marksmen?' he asked.

'Most nights two, I think. One somewhere in the front here, one round the back of the house. I doubt anyone could get past them to the house without being seen.'

'I'm not so sure,' said Alex. 'Let's walk around the garden. Lots of pointing to the ground, please. Lots of saying that's where we'll have the sweet peas and let's put some crocus bulbs in here and oh dear, we'll never get camellias to grow in this chalky soil.'

'You're really determined to make me look and feel absolutely as stupid as possible, aren't you,' she murmured.

'No, I'm not. I'm just trying to stop you looking like an MI5 desk officer – someone Meehan would suss at a glance. Like I said, he's probably watching us right now. If I were him, I'd be. Let's look round the back.'

'What are you hoping to find, exactly?'

'He'll have scouted the place, looking for a way in at night. Somewhere he can get into the property without being bumped by the security people. I'm searching for that way in.'

'Do you know how you'd do it?'

'I'm pretty sure I do but I'd just like to walk around for a bit. What about you? How would you get in?'

'Shoot the guards, perhaps? Silenced rifle with night sights?'

'That'd certainly do it,' said Alex, pointing at the house as if discussing a loft conversion, 'but he hasn't killed anyone except his targets so far.'

'He killed Gidley's dogs.'

'Dogs are just security products. Everyone kills dogs. But my take on Meehan is that he doesn't want to leave a trail of supplementary human corpses. Pride in his work would prevent that.'

'Is this you identifying with him again? Is this the way you see killing? As work to take a pride in?'

He laughed. 'You're the one who's hiring the hit man. You tell me. And follow this path round, please. I want to have a quick look at the river bank.'

'You think he'll come by river?'

'That's the way I'd do it. Quick cuddle here, I think, under the weeping willow.'

'Must we?'

'I'm afraid so. It's just too romantic a spot to miss.'

'Oh, yeah? And just what constitutes a romantic spot, in your view?'

'I think anywhere can be, if you're with someone you really, really . . .'

She folded her arms. 'Go on.'

'Kiss me, Harding!'

Her eyes were as flat as a snake's. Slowly, she placed her arms round his neck and her lips against his. Through his shirt and hers he felt the small pressure of her breasts. Then she stepped back.

'That didn't register very high on the Richter scale,' he protested.

'We're supposed to be married,' she said, turning to look at the house. 'Not in love.'

They continued along the bank. The river was slow and deep, its shining surface almost viscous-looking in the sunlight, the bank-side foliage perfectly reflected. Six feet below, emerald weeds wavered and trailed over polished gravel and chalk.

He's watching us, thought Alex with absolute certainty. And he's saying to himself: are these two the nice young couple that they seem to be, or have they come to hunt me down and kill me? 'Here,' he said. 'This is where he'll come. Don't stop. Keep walking. He'll approach silently from a couple of hundred yards upstream – no one will see him in a black wetsuit once the light's gone – and he'll climb out between these two banks of bullrushes.'

'Are you sure of that?'

'I'm positive. It's exactly where I'd do it. You're covered by the bushes on the bank and the rushes in the water, you're the minimum distance from the house – you definitely don't want to have acres of lawn to cross – plus there's a sort of underwater chalk bar like a step you can use to climb out. He's already tried it. When we walk back past you'll see a boot scrape in the algae on the chalk bar and a couple of reed clumps that look as if they've been twisted by someone pulling himself out. He's rehearsed it.'

Dawn crouched to examine a clump of yellow flag iris. 'How do you know it was him?'

'Well, who else is going to have been climbing in and out of the river in George Widdowes' garden? He'd probably have been wearing a weight belt to counteract the buoyancy effect of the wetsuit and keep himself low in the water on his approach. There was a snapped root where he might've tried hanging the belt in the dark. He wouldn't want to leave the water wearing it.'

'You spotted all that in the time it took us to walk past that bit of bank?'

'I knew what I was looking for. What I expected to see.' He thought of Sierra Leone and the frothing brown torrent of the Rokel. 'I've made the odd river approach myself. Bit rougher than this, but the principle's the same.'

'So what are you suggesting? That we have one of the marksmen up a tree, waiting for Meehan to climb out. Sort of a hippo shoot?'

'While your shooters are here he won't come,' said Alex. 'It's as simple as that. Plus he already knows about the lookalike. Probably knows his name, address and home phone number by now.'

'So what are you saying?'

'Get rid of the shooters, the lookalike, everything. Pull them all out and move George Widdowes back in. I'll move back in too, along with a back-up guy, and we'll set up an ambush of our own – a proper killing team. Sooner or later Meehan will have to come and then we'll waste the bastard.'

'What back-up guy?'

Alex's immediate thought was of Stan Clayton. 'Someone from Hereford. One of my people.'

'There's no question of any other non-Five people being involved, I'm afraid. This is a top-secret operation, not a get-together of your barrack-mates.'

'Listen,' he said quietly. 'They aren't just my barrack mates, they're the people with the best training and experience of this kind of close-up surveillance in the world. Guys who've spent days at a time lying up in the undergrowth next to IRA arms caches, or waiting for Bosnian war criminals. With all due respect to your guys, I've seen them in action and they stick out like the bollocks on a dog. One other guy from my RWW team, that's all I'm asking.'

'I can pass on the request, but I can tell you right now what the answer's going to be.'

Alex shook his head. 'You still don't get it, do you?'

'I get it only too well. You want to turn this into a Regiment operation. Well, I'm afraid it's all a damn sight too sensitive for that.'

'What you mean is that you don't trust anyone else to keep his mouth shut about what is basically one of the most disastrous fuck-ups in your service's history. You're afraid that if word gets out that one of your agents not only turned into one of PIRA's top nutting boys but crowned his brilliant career by torturing and killing a choice selection of your desk officers, that people just might start asking questions about your service's competence to handle intelligence affairs in the province. They might decide the Treasury got better value for its money from some other agency. The Firm, for example.'

At the mention of MI6, Thames House's hated rival, Dawn Harding all but bared her teeth. 'You are out of your depth by some distance, Captain Temple. You have been placed under the authority of my service and you will kindly respect that authority.'

'Even when its orders are illegal?'

Dawn's expression tightened. 'Let's behave like grown-ups, shall we? We both know what has to be done, we both know why. Like I said, I will pass on your request but I can tell you now what the response will be: if you need back-up, MI5 will provide it. Assuming, that is, that they go along with your plan at all.'

Alex nodded expressionlessly. 'Let's go and check out the house.'

She nodded and followed him towards the Lodge.

'After all,' he added drily, 'we have to make sure there's going to be room for the children's play area.'

Half an hour later the two prospective buyers of Longwater Lodge were sitting in a quiet corner of the Pied Bull. On the walls framed photographs of local cricket teams were displayed, along with horse brasses, winnowing fans, malt shovels, scythe handles and other redundant rural artefacts. A truce had been agreed between them.

'It strikes me,' said Alex, when their sandwiches and drinks had been served to them, 'that your deputy director is probably in the clear. That there's a good chance she's not one the Watchman's targets.'

Dawn narrowed her eyes. 'What makes you say that?'

'Fenn had his tongue cut out, OK?'

'OK.'

'And Gidley had his eyes cut out?'

'Yup.'

'Widdowes, if he gets him, will have his ears cut off.'

'What makes you say that?'

'Well, I figured it might be that three wise monkeys thing. See no evil, speak no evil, hear no evil.'

She nodded. 'I thought of that as soon as I saw what he'd done to Craig Gidley. The suggestion being that when they were alive they saw, spoke and heard evil, and only now that they're dead . . .'

Alex nodded. He had thought it was a pretty brilliant deduction on his part and was rather disappointed that she had reached the same conclusion, and reached it first.

'The thing I was going to say,' he pressed on, 'is that there are only three wise monkeys. So assuming your man Widdowes is supposed to be the third, that puts Fenwick in the clear.'

'Two points,' she said. 'One, we're dealing with a psychopathic murderer here. Assigning logic or structure to his actions and assuming that he will abide by this logic and structure is asking for trouble. He will do what he will do, period. Two, look at this. I did an Internet search for the expression "wise monkeys".'

From her jacket pocket she took a folded piece of paper. It was a printout, Alex saw, a printout of a London auction house web page.

Lot 42 – 'Four Wise Monkeys'. Netsuke, Thirteenth Century
    This is a highly rare and important piece, in that it shows four wise monkeys, rather than the more coventional three. The monkeys were introduced into Japan from China in the eighth century AD by a Buddhist monk of the Tendai sect,

and are believed to have been associated with the blue-faced god Vajra. Originally there were four monkeys, namely Mizaru (see no evil), Mazaru (speak no evil), Mikazaru (hear no evil) and Iwazaru (know no evil). As in this piece, Iwazaru was always represented with his hands placed over his heart. By the fourteenth century, however, the fourth monkey was absent from most representations, as he is from the best-known example, the seventeenth-century carving over the doorway of the Sacred Stable in Nikko, Japan. The presence in this early piece of the fourth monkey emphasises the essentially ambiguous nature of the traditional instruction. For while at one level the refusal to see, hear and speak evil will afford spiritual protection, at another level it lays the postulant open to charges of moral disengagement – of a closing of the heart.

Alex read the sheet and handed it back to Dawn. 'Four monkeys, then,' he muttered. 'Do we reckon that our Watchman knows about the fourth?'

'It took me less than a minute to find this on the web.'

'I guess you're right,' said Alex.

'And there's another thing,' Dawn went on. 'Do you remember the pictures of Meehan you saw in Thames House?'

Alex nodded.

'Do you remember the one in the kitchen of their house in Derry? The one with both his parents in it? Well, if you enlarge it you can see that there are some brass ornaments on the shelf. There's a bell shaped like a Dutch girl, and a miniature camel, and a little square thing that I'd bet a month's salary is a statuette of the wise monkeys.'

Alex nodded. 'Well, that does seem to wrap it up,' he said. 'And to put your Miss Fenwick squarely in the frame as the fourth monkey.'

'That's rather what we feared.'

'You might have mentioned it,' said Alex. 'Like I said before, anything that helps me to know him better will help me to deal with him.'

181

'We were rather hoping you might deal with him before the projected number of his victims became . . . an issue.'

That evening he was changing into a tracksuit in the Pimlico safe house, preparing to go for a run, when his mobile rang. It was Dawn, although she didn't announce her name. 'You've got what you wanted,' she said peremptorily. 'Our friend returns to his house in Hampshire the day after tomorrow.'

'Do I get any of my people?' asked Alex.

'No. You either use ours or you go without.'

'Understood.' He frowned. 'Look, you don't fancy a drink or something, do you?'

'Didn't the roses work, then? I forgot to ask.' Her tone was amused.

He paused. Took a deep breath. 'Do you fancy a drink or not?'

But the phone had already gone dead.

EIGHTEEN

'So,' said George Widdowes. 'You're really sure about this? You're sure that you'll be able to tackle Meehan when he comes?'

'Yes,' said Alex. 'I am. So far he's had everything his own way. He's been able to pick the time and the place. Now we're going to force his hand.'

The MI5 desk officer and the SAS captain were sitting in the ante-room to Angela Fenwick's office in Thames House.

'Tell me,' said Widdowes.

'Basically,' explained Alex, 'we bait a trap. As you know, there's a For Sale sign outside your house. What's going to happen is that you're going to move back there for a few days and in three days' time you're going to supervise the loading of all your stuff into a removals van. Is the place very full?'

Widdowes shook his head tiredly. 'Not very. This is strictly necessary, is it, all this house-moving routine?'

'We've got to do it properly. And it'll make sense to Meehan. You're afraid and you feel isolated out there by yourself, so you're moving back to London. Maybe you've even been ordered to move back to London. Whichever, you're going to miss the place and, given that there are a couple of armed policemen patrolling the property, you decide it'll be safe to stay there for the last few nights.'

'You reckon that'll bounce him into having a go?'

Alex nodded. 'I reckon it will. And if he doesn't come in the next forty-eight hours he certainly will after he sees the furniture van being filled. He'll know that this is his last chance – that if he doesn't take you now all his surveillance has gone to waste and he'll have to start from scratch again.'

'You think we can set the whole thing up without spooking him?'

'Well, that's the question. Anything smells funny and he won't come – he's PIRA-trained, after all. If you just moved back into the place without any security, for example, he'd be very suspicious indeed and let the whole thing go. My guess, though, is that when he sees those armed cops he'll think that you reckon you're safe.'

'The armed police won't put him off?'

Alex smiled and shook his head.

'So why won't he just wait until that evening and follow the furniture van? Follow it to my supposed new house or flat?'

'Because it won't be going anywhere. The loading'll finish about six, and then the van will be driven a couple of hundred yards down the road and parked up in a lay-by to wait for the next morning. Local removal firms often do that so that they don't have to pay their crews overtime.'

'Why not wait until the next day and then follow the van?'

'Because it might go anywhere – a storage facility, for example – and then he'll have to start searching for your new place from scratch. Besides, he'll know that wherever you go will be ultra secure in comparison with your present place. He'll know that the Hampshire house offers by far the best chance he's likely to get.'

'And you'll be waiting for him?' said Widdowes doubtfully.

'Basically, yes. I'll hide up by the river and when he comes I'll shoot him at short range with a silenced weapon.'

'How will you make sure he doesn't know you're there waiting for him?'

'He won't know,' said Alex quietly. 'Count on that. I've set up ambushes before.'

In the car park beneath Thames House, a little over twenty-four hours later, Alex squeezed into the boot of the car that was to masquerade as Widdowes'. The BMW saloon had been customised with a boot-fitted surveillance lens and bullet-proof windows.

'Are you going to be all right in there?' Widdowes asked.

'Yeah, I'll be OK. Hand us in my kit, could you, and put your own stuff on the back seat.'

The drive took an hour and a half in total and by the end of it Alex was feeling light-headed and nauseated from the exhaust fumes. When Widdowes finally sprang the boot open, it was in the near darkness of the garage at Longwater Lodge. Illuminating his watch, Alex saw that it was a few minutes before 5 p.m. 'Right,' he said, when he had stretched his legs for a moment or two. 'This door leads directly into the house?'

'Yes.'

'And is there a room without any windows?'

'There's a cellar, yes.'

'Perfect. I'll set up my stuff down there. Can you get me there without leading me past too many windows?'

Widdowes nodded and opened the door to the house. Alex, feeling slightly ridiculous, followed the tall Barbour-coated figure on his hands and knees. They reached a door, which Widdowes opened. Alex swung himself on to a descending staircase and took his bag from the older man, who then flicked a light switch and followed him down into the cellar.

It was a decent-sized place, and not too damp. In front of him was a large Potterton boiler, switched off. Against the other walls stood a wine-rack, a carpentry workbench, several bundles of magazines bound with baler twine, a case of Eley shotgun cartridges and a battered travelling trunk.

'I've got a camp bed,' said Widdowes. 'I'll bring it down for you.'

While he was upstairs, Alex unpacked his case. He left the clothes inside, and arranged the weaponry and kit on the carpentry workbench. There was the Glock 34, its silencer, the laser dot-marker sight on its factory-fitted slide, a spare lithium battery for the laser sight, two boxes of twenty-five hollow-point 9mm rounds and the Recon knife. There were also a sleeping bag and a tin of black waterproof cam-cream from a survival shop in Euston, a pair of fisherman's felt-soled boots from Farlow's of Pall Mall, and an all-black Rip Curl wetsuit, weight belt and jet fins from a diving equipment store in Fulham. For Alex, not usually an enthusiastic shopper, the knowledge that he'd been spending MI5's money had made for a pleasant morning.

When he reappeared with the camp bed Widdowes appeared disconcerted by this array. In fact, he looked badly scared. His features were flushed and his eyes flickered uneasily about him. Hardly surprising, thought Alex. It couldn't be anything but terrifying to know that you were next on the list of a proven psycho like Meehan.

'Are you OK?' Alex asked.

Widdowes nodded. 'Yes, I'm OK.' He laughed nervously. 'You've certainly brought the full armoury with you.'

'I'm not taking any chances with this bastard,' said Alex. 'He's going straight in the fucking ground. Have you got your own weapon?'

Widdowes reached inside his jacket, withdrew a Colt .38 revolver, spun the chamber and returned it to the shoulder holster.

Alex nodded. Privately he thought that if it ever came to a one-on-one between Widdowes and Meehan the MI5 man was as good as dead, but he guessed that the heft and weight of the Colt were a good confidence booster. He turned to Widdowes. 'Look, I know you're an experienced field agent and I don't want to get your back up, but a handful of rules for the duration, yeah?'

Widdowes nodded.

'Avoid windows. I doubt he'd try and shoot you but better to be safe than sorry, so if you must go past a window keep moving. Whether inside or outside the house, don't ever present a static target and don't whatever you do speak or shout out to me – don't worry about warnings, if he comes anywhere near here I'll see him before you do. I'll have him covered. Behave at all times as if you were alone in the house. Have you met up with the two police guys?'

'Yes. They're MI5 people, in fact, in police uniforms.'

'That's fine. Basically what we need them to do is mooch

around the front of the house. Just wander about between there and the road, and stick their necks into the back garden every so often. They should stay together most of the time, smoke the odd fag, that sort of thing. They've got to look like lazy and incompetent jobsworths: out to grass and no threat to anyone. Can you make sure they understand that?'

Widdowes nodded again.

'Otherwise, just observe your usual routine. It might help if you put an empty bottle or two out each night – give the impression you're hitting the old vino. That'll encourage him to think . . .'

'Yeah, I know what you're saying. Nerves shot, soft target . . .'

Alex looked at Widdowes. His darting glances, uneven colour and paper-dry lips confirmed that he was very frightened indeed. He put a hand on the older man's shoulder. 'George, mate, we're in this together and I'm fully aware that your part is the harder one. Honestly. If you can think of a better way of nailing this fucker I'm on for it, believe me.'

Widdowes pursed his lips and nodded.

'I'm also sorry to put you through a non-existent house move, but again . . .'

'That's OK,' said Widdowes, forcing an unconvincing smile. 'I've been meaning to sort through all this junk. Get my life into some sort of order. What do you want to do about eating?'

'Well, it gets dark at about eight o'clock and I want to get into position about then. So if we have a feed at seven-ish?'

'I'll knock something up. You're going to wait for him in the river, aren't you?'

'That's the idea.'

'Have you considered how you're going to get into position without him seeing you? I mean, we have to assume he's watching the area around the house. Quite possibly from close up.'

'You're going to have to drive me downstream to somewhere I can get into the river and work my way back here. Somewhere he won't see me get out of the car.'

'That's no problem. I can take you up to the next road bridge

187

and you can get back through the grounds of Longwater House. There's no one there at the moment, the place is closed up.' Widdowes frowned. 'But how do you know Meehan won't be down there? How do you know you won't run into him?'

'Because he won't want to go in blind. He'll come from the direction he can watch the house and the guards from, which is upstream. You can't see anything at all from where I'm going, except trees.'

Widdowes slowly nodded. 'Right. Got you.'

'Is there a pub in the downstream direction? Some reason you might be going that way?'

'There's an off-licence in Martyr Worthy. If I come back ten minutes later with a Thresher's bag . . .'

'Good enough. Now I'd suggest you get upstairs. Maybe take a cup of tea to the two cops – give you an excuse to brief them about looking useless.'

'What will you do?'

'I'll be OK, don't worry. See you at seven.'

Widdowes nodded and smiled wryly. 'I'll tell you one thing,' he said. 'If this guy Meehan succeeds in taking me out there are going to be some long faces at Thames House.'

Alex looked at him.

'Angela Fenwick, for a start,' continued Widdowes. 'She's in line for the directorship, that's why the deaths of Fenn and Gidley have pissed her off so royally. If she loses any more of her desk officers it's going to start looking very much like carelessness. Her star and that of her familiar could well start to decline.'

'Her familiar?' asked Alex, surprised by the bitterness and vehemence of his tone.

'Dawn Bloody Harding. Zulu Dawn. Dawn of the Living Dead. From the moment she joined the service she hitched her wagon to Angela's – that's why her progress has been so meteoric. For as long as Angela's riding high, Dawn's up there with her. But if Angela falls, then Dawn goes down too. Don't overlook the political side of all this, chum. You've been brought in to safeguard the upward mobility of a political cabal.'

188

'I'm here to safeguard you, George. The rest doesn't interest me.'

Widdowes nodded philosophically and shrugged. 'I'm sorry. You're right – it's not your worry. Getting cynical in my old age, that's all.'

When he had gone Alex unrolled his sleeping bag on the camp bed, lay down and stared at the cellar's plasterboard ceiling. Eventually he closed his eyes. It was going to be a long night and he would do well to get some rest. In his pocket, his mobile throbbed.

'Yeah?'

'It's Dawn Harding.'

'Zulu Dawn!'

There was a silence. 'Where did you get that name?' she asked accusingly. 'Have you been . . .'

'It's one of my favourite films,' said Alex breezily. 'How are you?'

'Fine,' she said curtly. 'Is everything OK down there?'

'So far, yes.'

'How's George holding up?'

'He's under a bit of stress but he's keeping it all together.'

'You think Meehan will come tonight?'

'Might. Bird in the hand and so on.'

There was a pause.

'Are you . . . OK?' she enquired.

'Do I detect a note of concern?' asked Alex, unable to keep the smile from his voice.

'No, you don't!' she snapped. 'I simply need to know you're in good shape. I don't want any more corpses on the pathologist's slab.'

'Don't worry,' said Alex, the vision of Dawn suspended high above the ground in her scarlet underwear flashing past his eyes. 'I'll keep myself in good shape for you.'

She disconnected. Alex returned his gaze to the ceiling and his smile faded. He had ninety minutes in which to rest up. He closed his eyes.

Shortly after seven Widdowes woke him. The MI5 officer

was carrying a plateful of cheese and ham sandwiches, a Granny Smith apple, a Mars bar and a two-litre bottle of still mineral water. 'Sorry,' he said. 'It's not quite up to Gordon Ramsay standard. I assumed you'd want mustard on the ham?'

'Yeah. Great.'

'I meant to ask. What do you want to do about washing?'

'I don't,' said Alex. 'You can smell toothpaste and soap on the air. I won't be using either until Meehan's dead. And hopefully I won't be needing a crap till then, either. As far as pissing's concerned, well, from time to time you'll find this Evian bottle on the stairs.'

'Got you,' said Widdowes without enthusiasm.

Alex ate and drank for five minutes in silence, then loaded the Glock's magazine with nineteen rounds and slapped it into the butt. Pointing the handgun at the wall, he pressed the button activating the laser sight. A small red dot appeared on the wall, scribbling fine lines of light as Alex moved the weapon. Satisfied, he thumbed the system off again. Then he stripped, pulled on the wetsuit and buckled the sheathed Recon knife round his calf. The Glock went into a plastic thigh holster on a lanyard. Blackening his face and hands with the cam-cream, he pulled up the neoprene hood of the wetsuit. The clothes that he had just been wearing went into the waterproof stuff sack that had previously held the wetsuit. The boots and fins went into a carrier bag. 'OK,' said Alex. 'Let's do it. What's the light like outside?'

'Going fast,' said Widdowes.

They made their way back to the garage, Alex climbed into the boot and Widdowes drove off, stopping briefly to converse with the uniformed men at the gate. The ensuing drive took no more than three minutes, but took them well out of the sight of anyone who had been observing the house. Quickly, watching out for other cars, Widdowes let Alex out of the boot, handed him the stuff sack and drove on. The whole operation had taken no more than ten seconds.

Crouching in the cow-parsley on the river bank, Alex peered around him in the fading evening light. Above him was the road, which was narrow and unlikely to see too much traffic between now and tomorrow morning. To his left was the road bridge. He could just make out a narrow walkway beneath this, but access to it was largely obscured by nettles, elder and other roadside vegetation. Sliding down the bank, Alex pushed through undergrowth into the darkness beneath the bridge and cached the stuff sack of clothing there. Attaching the weight belt round his waist, he undid the Farlow's boots and tied them to the belt by the laces, then pulled on the jet fins and lowered himself into the water.

The carrier stream was about six feet deep at the edge and deeper, he guessed, in the middle. Despite its smooth surface, the current was considerable. Cautiously, he began to move forward. The boots at his waist dragged a little, but this was more than compensated for by the powerful jet fins, just as the buoyancy of the wetsuit was compensated for by the weight belt. With it he was able to move silently with only his head above the surface, without it he would have been wallowing about on the surface, leaving a wake like a speedboat.

Tucking in to the side of the river, trailing his arms at his side, he concentrated on moving with absolute silence and the minimum of water disturbance. After fifty yards he passed a high fence, which he guessed was the boundary of the Longwater estate. A few hundred yards, Widdowes had said. He swam silently on. At one point the river shallowed, running over a broken bottom no more than a couple of feet deep and Alex was forced to leopard-crawl six inches at a time against the weight of the tumbling water. With relief, however, he soon felt the river bed falling away beneath him.

After a hundred yards, he grabbed on to an overhanging root, swung himself into the bank and took stock. Soon he would be coming into the area that he had to assume was under night sight surveillance. Meehan might be several hundred yards away, scoping out the property from a concealed hide, or he might be much closer. He could be lying up in the river as little as fifty yards upstream. From now on Alex would have to move with extreme caution.

A couple of yards ahead there was a faint splash. A small sound, but enough to set Alex's heart racing. Something had been thrown or dropped into the water. Was Meehan waiting on the bank above him? Had he seen him? Shrinking into the knotted roots beneath the river's mud and chalk banks, Alex froze, his heart pounding. Slowly, an inch at a time, he reached for the knife, withdrew the razor-sharp blade from the scabbard, held it inches beneath the surface. And then, against a faint patch of light, he saw the questing head of the otter, cutting an arrowhead wake through the water. Going hunting, he guessed with dizzying relief.

When he had caught his breath he moved on, keeping hard in to the bank, driving against the current with the fins. Through the trees to his left he could see the vast dim bulk of Longwater House, now, and ahead of him the lights of the Lodge. What was Widdowes up to? he wondered. In the short time they had spent together he had developed a sympathy for the man. Not much in Widdowes' manner suggested it now, but he'd probably been a competent enough operative in his time. Box's Belfast agent handlers were not fools, for the most part (although one or two of them were and Michael Bettany had been a traitor too, jailed for spying for the Soviets), nor were they cowards. No one who had seen what had happened to Fenn and Gidley, though, would be anything but afraid.

Alex was suddenly filled with a loathing of Meehan. They all moved in a dirty world, that much was accepted, but to do what he had done, well, that was something else. Chopping bits of people's faces off, hammering nails into them . . . What the last hours of those two poor bastards from the FRU must have been like was beyond imagining.

Alex moved silently upriver in the deep black shadows beneath the bank. He was invisible now, a creature of the night. He came to a halt beneath the slender curving trunk of a willow, a place he had noted when he visited the house with Dawn. Above him was the yellowish haze of the lights from the Lodge, five to six yards ahead of him was the silhouette of the reed-bed and the bushes through which he had calculated that Meehan would make his exit.

Feeling beneath the water, Alex found a sturdy root and, quickly exchanging his fins for the Farlow's boots, attached the fins to the root by their straps so that they hung in the current a foot beneath the surface. Could he find them again? Yes, they were just below this willow root. Should he take the weight belt off? He tried it, felt himself rising in the water and hastily reattached it. Where to go? Inching forward, his feet found a shelf that would take his weight. Gratefully he sensed the thick felt soles of the fishing boots grip the slippery chalk. If he'd settled for commando-soled boots, as he'd originally considered, he would have had a hard night ahead of him. His right arm found a corresponding elbow of willow root to hook through. He was now facing the current and the direction that Meehan would come. Between him and Meehan's projected exit point was a clump of sedge and the outer skirt of the willow's foliage. As long as he kept still, he would be invisible, even if Meehan was using night sights.

For his part, Alex had decided against night sights. Partly because of their unwieldiness in the water, partly because the intensified green images would compromise his night vision. He knew what he was looking for and he knew where to look. Even when the lights went off in the house there would be a close to full moon. And it would be when the lights went off that Meehan would come.

For an hour Alex remained there, unmoving, his eyes scanning the river ahead of him. In low light conditions, he knew, you saw better with your peripheral than your direct vision. Very slowly, a limb at a time, he kept himself moving underwater, gently contracting and relaxing his muscles. Partly to stave off cold and avoid cramping, which despite the wetsuit was a very real threat, and partly in order to remain alert.

Of all the ambushes that Alex had ever set up, this was by far the least satisfactory, in that he was operating alone and without back-up. He would go for a heart shot as Meehan pulled himself out of the water, he decided, when both his hands were occupied. The silenced double tap would punch the life out of the former agent before his brain had had a chance to take in what was happening. He'd be dead before his knees bent and the Watchman's rule of terror would be over.

The first man Alex had killed had been during the Gulf War in 1991.

He had been part of a four-man Sabre team tasked to knock out a Scud missile dump at al-Anbar, west of Baghdad. Under the command of an NCO named Neil Slater they'd been choppered in by night and left to forage for cover. The cold had been extreme – they'd been sent in wearing little more than lightweight 'chocolate chip' battledress and shirts – and there had been no cover of any kind. Within the hour they were frozen to the bone. The four of them – Alex, Neil Slater, Don Hammond and Andreas van Rijn – had made a quick recce and Slater had made the decision to lie up for the rest of the night in a disused berm a couple of hundred yards from the dump. None of them had slept; instead they had huddled together against the cold and the wind-borne snow that whipped mercilessly about them.

The next morning, half-frozen, they had seen a convoy of Iraqi T-55 tanks rumbling towards them – the most terrifying sight Alex or indeed any of them had ever witnessed. Desperate, they had buried themselves in the detritus at the bottom of the berm – Iraqi ration tins, ammunition boxes, rubble, old tyres, discarded cam-netting and the decaying corpse of a goat – and prayed. The Iraqi tank crews, anxious to relieve themselves after several hours in their T-55s, had surrounded the berm. The Sabre team were pissed on, they were shat on and Alex's thigh was agonisingly burnt by a discarded cigarette end, but they were not discovered. And eventually, after four ghastly hours, the tanks had rumbled away into the desert.

As soon as the SAS team had judged it safe to move Slater had radioed in the tanks' position and direction of travel, and called in the air strike on al-Anbar. Its purpose was twofold: to destroy the missiles grouped there for transportation to mobile missile launchers and to kill a man known as Marwan.

'Marwan', to the Allied intelligence forces based in Saudi Arabia, had for several weeks been little more than an occasionally occurring code name in the welter of enemy radio traffic. It was thought from the contexts in which he was mentioned that he might be a senior technician of some sort. Then an intercepted transmission between the al-Anbar base and Baghdad command had suggested that 'Marwan' might be a man known to the Allies as 'Guppy' – an Iranian scientist who had changed sides during the Iran-Iraq war and now ran the missile research plant at Sa'd 16, in north Iraq. It was the Sa'd 16 team who had developed the al-Husayn – the long-range version of the Russian Scud that could be fitted with chemical and biological warheads. According to the transmission, 'Marwan' was due at the al-Anbar base that evening, suggesting that the missiles might be about to be checked over and dispersed.

If 'Marwan' was indeed 'Guppy', then it was essential that he be killed, just as it was essential that the missiles should be destroyed while they were all in one place. Neil Slater's instructions were to call in the air strike, assess the subsequent damage and ensure that there were no Iraqi survivors.

The air strike was at the same time the most dramatic and the most appalling event Alex had ever witnessed. The Tornados had screamed in, their missiles drawing a deceptively faint diagonal trail, and the Scud jet-propellant had gone up in an eyeball-searing roar of light and heat, hurling vehicles, machinery, weapons and human body parts in all directions. The explosions had been followed by a terrible screaming and by the sight of disjointed figures writhing on the charred ground. And by the smell, the meaty stench of burning human flesh.

'Go!' Neil Slater had screamed. 'Go, go, go!'

And they had gone. Above them the sky was black with smoke, as if a solar eclipse were taking place. Initially Alex had thought that they would encounter little or no resistance, that the entire Iraqi strength had been killed or maimed in the air strike. But this was not the case, as rapidly became clear. As the team advanced, moving in skirmish order across the twilit noon landscape, they came under sustained fire from a slit trench. A group of Iraqis must have been lying up in a bunker and escaped the firestorm unleashed by the Tornados.

The four SAS men hurled themselves into cover behind a Panhard Landcruiser which had been blown on to its side by the blast. From directly in front of them the Iraqi fire team immediately brought a withering hail of 7.62 rounds to bear on the vehicle from their Kalashnikovs. Between the two sides lay the charred, twisted and smoking bodies of the missile support crew, the lingering screams of those who had not yet died cutting through the stinking air. Thirty yards in front of them was an anti-aircraft gun emplacement, surrounded by the bodies of the men who had manned it. To twenty-six-year-old Corporal Alex Temple, who had never been on a full-scale battlefield before, it was a scene straight from hell.

'What range do you reckon?' Neil Slater asked him calmly, as Kalashnikov rounds screamed and ricocheted against the Landcruiser's blackened and twisted flank.

'I'd say fifty metres,' said Alex, struggling to keep his voice steady.

Slater nodded and removed a grenade from his bandolier. The grenade's gold top told Alex that it was the high-explosive type, rather than anti-personnel or white phosphorus.

From the other side of the Landcruiser came the whoomfing crack of a Russian grenade. Hand-thrown, guessed Alex, but not quite far enough.

Calmly Slater checked the sextant sight on his weapon's carrying handle and slid the HE grenade into the 203 launcher tube beneath the barrel of his M16. 'Fifty metres it is,' he said. 'Cover please, lads. Time for a delivery of Gold Top.'

'Pasteurise the fuckers,' whispered Andreas van Rijn, Slater's second-in-command.

As the three of them poured aimed shots from their M16s at the Iraqi position, Slater leaned coolly from cover, glanced down once at the sextant sight and fired.

The egg-shaped grenade hit the ground a few feet beyond the

trench, bounced once and exploded noisily but harmlessly on the desert floor, shredding a thorn bush.

Quickly, Slater reloaded. This time the grenade fell short, but close enough to blow a half-hundredweight of sand and scrub into the trench.

The fire from the Iraqi trench intensified, and it was at that moment that the SAS team guessed they were facing elite troops and 'Marwan' was in the enemy trench. This was the only possible explanation for the Iraqi team's failure to surrender, given that they faced almost certain obliteration: they had been ordered to defend the missile scientist with their lives.

A second Russian pineapple grenade bumped laboriously towards the Landcruiser, exploding deafeningly up against it. A spatter of Kalashnikov fire followed.

'Our turn, I think,' said Slater grimly, shaking his head against the blast. This time the gold-top 203 grenade fell straight into the enemy trench and Alex watched as a shattered assault rifle flew into the air alongside the severed arm that, until a moment earlier, had held it.

'Full fat!' murmured Andreas van Rijn appreciatively. 'Full fucking fat!'

The firing did not cease. At least three Iraqi soldiers were still capable of manning a weapon and were bravely continuing to do so, forcing the SAS team to remain flattened behind the wrecked vehicle. At intervals Alex and the others were able to squeeze off a few rounds, but not to great effect. In small-arms terms it was a stalemate. But the SAS had their 203 grenade launchers.

Inexorably Slater reloaded. He had the range now, and dropped a fourth HE grenade into the Iraqi trench. This time the explosion was followed by silence and then a low groaning sound.

With his hand, Slater ordered absolute stillness. The SAS team froze. Nothing, just that long-drawn-out groaning. All of them were uncomfortably aware that sooner or later more Iraqi troops would converge on the place. Probably sooner. The destruction of al-Anbar would certainly not have passed unnoticed.

Quickly, Alex switched magazines and as he did so his eye caught a blurred movement behind the anti-aircraft emplacement to their left. A fraction of a second later a tall khaki figure was sprinting towards the Landcruiser, holding a Kalashnikov and – Alex noted in something like slow motion – a pale-green Russian cylinder grenade.

From a kneeling position Alex pulled the heavy M16 203 to his shoulder. The moment seemed to go on and on. He saw the courage and the blazing intention in the Iraqi's eyes, heard his sawing breath and the desperate driving of his feet, dropped his foresight to the oncoming man's chest, saw his upper body half turn to accommodate the grenade throw – only twenty-five yards to go now – aimed, smoothly exhaled and punched six high-velocity 5.56mm rounds through his sternum.

For a moment, as a little over a pound of bone, muscle and lung tissue leapt from the Iraqi soldier's back, his eyes met Alex's. There was surprise there and perhaps a measure of disappointment, but not much more.

Is that all, Alex asked himself wonderingly? Is that all it is to kill a man?

The volley pitched the Iraqi backwards on to his own grenade, from which he had withdrawn the pin before starting his run. Untypically of the item in question and of exported Russian grenades in general, it worked perfectly, shredding the soldier's heart through his ribs after a delay of exactly four seconds.

A frisson passed through Alex as he clenched and unclenched his toes in the Farlow's boots. He had been in the river outside Widdowes' house for nearly three hours now, his dark-accustomed eyes endlessly quartering and scanning the space ahead of him, his senses pricked for any noise or smell that was in any way foreign to the place. He was cold, but not critically so – a layer of body-temperature water lay between his skin and the wetsuit's neoprene lining. The stiller he kept, in fact, the warmer he was.

The MI5 men had played their parts perfectly, pacing loudly

198

around the grounds with cigarettes and torches, announcing their flat-footed presence to any who might be observing. You certainly wouldn't need night sights to know that the Thompson Twins were in town.

But of the Watchman there had been no sign. A heron, broad-winged and graceful, had lowered itself from the sky a little after nine o'clock and taken up residence among the reeds close to where Alex expected the Watchman to exit the river. The perfect early warning system, thought Alex. Not even Joseph Meehan could shimmy past a heron without disturbing it.

He'd felt nothing at the Iraqi's death. And nothing afterwards, when they'd killed all of those still alive. In most cases the double taps that they had delivered had represented a merciful release from the terrible burns caused by the Tornado's incendiary missiles and the exploding Scud propellant.

They'd found a man who might or might not have been 'Marwan' in the trench, dead from shrapnel wounds to the head and blast injuries. He'd been unarmed and wearing khaki overalls of a different design from the others. In his pockets they had found a Tandy calculator, an ID card and a wallet containing pictures of his family. All these, along with a half-melted Toshiba laptop computer found near the anti-aircraft emplacement, had been bagged and returned to base. The operation had been judged a one hundred per cent success.

Alex had felt nothing and thought he'd got away unscathed.

NINETEEN

The Watchman did not come and with first light Alex swam silently downstream to the bridge, exited the water and re-dressed himself in the clothes that he had left hidden there. The cold of the river and the length and intensity of his eight-hour vigil had left him desperately tired, and for a long time he could not stop himself shaking. He couldn't even bring himself to think about further nights spent the same way.

In truth, it had always been unlikely that the Watchman would come on the first night of Widdowes' return. He would want to watch and wait, to weigh up the chances of the whole thing being a set-up. In Meehan's position Alex wouldn't have come on that first night.

But now, hopefully, Meehan would have had a chance to see that the arrangement was exactly what it seemed to be: a nervous public servant guarded by a pair of competent if rather dilatory policemen. Widdowes was getting the sort of protection that an important criminal witness might get, or the senior officer of a regiment that had served in Northern Ireland.

Alex sat beneath the bridge for a further couple of hours. Slowly the darkness became wet grey dawn, and at 6 a.m. he heard a car come to a halt above him and a voice quietly call his name. Hurrying out with his kit, he dived into the boot of the customised BMW and lay there while Widdowes went through the motions of going for an early-morning drive.

Back in the garage the MI5 man looked at him with concern. 'You look completely knackered,' he said. 'Are you OK?'

'I'll live,' replied Alex. 'How are you?'

'I did what you said: cooked myself supper, watched *Newsnight*, and hit the sack. Even managed to sleep.' Widdowes hesitated. 'I'm grateful for this, Alex,' he said quietly. 'Man to man and forgetting all the inter-service bullshit, I'm really grateful. You're putting yourself on the line and that means a lot. Is there anything I can do in return?'

'Yes,' said Alex wearily. 'Stay alive. And sort us out some breakfast.'

'Any preferences?'

'Everything,' said Alex. 'The full bollocks.'

'My pleasure. Would you like a bath?'

'When Meehan's dead,' said Alex.

Widdowes nodded. From the drive came the sound of a car on gravel and voices. The MI5 'policemen' were handing over to a new pair.

In the cellar, meeting his exhaustion head-on, Alex pushed himself through a hard exercise routine followed by a series of stretches. The wetsuit, the boots and the rest of the kit were laid out to dry – a pointless exercise, really, but one which imposed a level of formality and routine on the situation.

When the breakfast came, preceded by the smell of fresh coffee, Alex ate fast and in silence.

'You're sure you want to stay here while I go to work?' Widdowes asked eventually.

'He won't try to kill you in the car,' said Alex with certainty. 'And I doubt he'll even bother to follow you. He knows where you're going, he'll know from the cops on the gate that you're coming back here. Just keep the windows up, the door locked and head straight for Thames House. You'll be fine – the guy has to sleep some time.'

Widdowes nodded. 'I'd better make a move. Sure you'll be OK?'

'I'll be fine.'

The two men shook hands and Widdowes departed. Placing the Glock 34 on the ground beside the camp bed, Alex climbed into his sleeping bag, closed his eyes and slept.

★

For the next two nights the Watchman did not come. Each evening Alex lowered himself into the river by the bridge, swam upstream and began his long vigil. He went to exactly the same position each time, hooked his arm round the underwater root, lodged his feet on the chalk shelf and waited.

Time passed with unreal slowness. As his eyes searched the gloom ahead for any sign of movement, his mind seemed to separate itself from his body, to undertake journeys of its own. Sometimes it seemed as if he were not in the river at all, but flying, or sleeping, or driving. He was visited by the familiar ranks of ghosts – the Iraqis with their charred faces and smoking chest cavities, the bullet-shattered IRA volunteers, the blood-slicked Colombians and RUF men, the frost-stiffened Serbs. All of them milled about him in an ever-changing tableau, gravely displaying their wounds, endlessly reprising the instant of their deaths. To kill a man, Alex had long understood, was to fix a moment in time, to have that moment with you for ever.

And now, with considerable formality, he was planning another death. A death that, in his mind's eye, he had seen many times. The Watchman, carried downstream by the current, would surface in the moonlit water three or four metres away and begin his silent ascent of the bank. With his right hand Alex would thumb on the infra-red sight, move the red dot to the centre of his target's chest, fire and keep firing. The coughs of the silenced Glock would be all but inaudible. The body would fall back into the water, swing towards him on the warm stream. That was how it would be.

But the Watchman didn't come. Alex waited, primed to kill, but the river remained just a river, a place of gnats and weed and flag iris. And with each grey morning he doubted his sanity more, wondered whether despite all his experience he had miscalculated. Would the BMW come and collect him once more? Or had his instincts finally deceived him? Was Widdowes even now lying mutilated and dead on the floor of Longwater Lodge?

Each morning, however, the car did come and the routine

was the same. Breakfast, coffee and then sleep. A heatwave struck, and the windowless cellar became stifling and airless during the hours of daylight.

Daylight that Alex never saw. He woke each afternoon at around three, exercised, cleaned the Glock and prepared himself – all without leaving the cellar. Dawn Harding usually rang at about five thirty, shortly after she had seen Widdowes leave Thames House. Their conversations were brief – beyond discussing the ups and downs of Widdowes' state of mind there was little to say.

When Widdowes returned he would cook supper for the pair of them, take Alex's food down to the cellar as if the SAS officer were a medieval prisoner and then – at Alex's insistence – eat his own in front of the TV upstairs, as he had always done.

On the fourth day the furniture van arrived and the loading-up began. Alex managed to sleep through most of the bumping and swearing that was taking place on the floors above, but was still awake by 2 p.m.

Tonight, he thought, squinting through the 5.32-inch barrel of the Glock at the smooth curl of its rifling. Tonight the bastard has to come.

And if he doesn't?

If he doesn't then I bow out. Apologise. Kiss Dawn's stillettos. Submit to whatever grim routine she and her department choose to inflict on me.

It was a full moon that night as Alex waited for his prey and the sky was cloudless. Even after midnight a little of the heat of the day seemed to hang about the river and above Alex's head a cloud of insects danced on the warm air. In front of his hooded, blackened and immobile face water-boatmen made tiny dashes over the surface film.

The lights had been switched off in the house for more than two hours when he saw the faintest of dark shapes drifting downstream towards him. It was about thirty yards away and a foot or two out from the bank. An otter? he wondered. No, too large and immobile. Too dead. A log, then? Maybe. Or maybe just a large clump of weed. River keepers had been cutting the weed on the fisheries upstream and great rafts of it had been drifting downstream earlier that night.

But weed was usually lower in the water than this. Quickly, Alex scanned the area to either side of it, allowing his peripheral vision to play on the shape. Nearer now, he saw that it was a large branch, splayed and leaved. But a branch which was holding hard to the bank and moving steadily towards him.

Behind his cage of roots and reeds, Alex narrowed his eyes. Was the branch going to barrel into him? Why was there a branch in the river at all in the middle of this breezeless night? Adrenalin began to trickle into his system. He pressed the Farlow's boots hard into the chalk and stealthily withdrew his arm from the grip of the underwater root. His hand held the Glock now and the safety catch was depressed for action.

Opposite the reeds, several yards upstream, the branch seemed to catch and halt. Alex's heart slammed against his ribs and his left hand joined his right on the butt of the Glock. Inch by inch he raised the weapon.

Nothing.

No movement of any kind.

Certainly no sign of anything human making for the bank.

Perhaps the branch was just a branch. Perhaps it had just happened to snag itself at the exact spot that he had been watching. Perhaps . . .

Alex blinked. Before his dark-accustomed eyes the moonlit ripples jazzed and swung.

And then – with blinding, heart-stopping force – a shining black figure exploded out of the water just inches from Alex's face. Its teeth were bared in subhuman fury, a blade was whistling downwards in its fist.

Instinct wrenched Alex from the knife's path, but a moment later a rock-like fist slammed into the side of his jaw, white light burst before his eyes and he tasted blood. Alex went down, dropping the Glock, but somehow managed to draw the commando knife from its sheath on his calf. Twisting as his attacker's blade sliced through the water, desperate to regain the initiative, he hurled himself straight at the other man's throat.

The other's reaction was identical: defence by attack. The two met in a ferocious dogfight of stabbing and flailing limbs and Alex felt an icy sharpness rip down his thigh. He was losing this fight, a part of him realised dispassionately, and it was a novel experience. His opponent was at least his equal in speed, determination and sheer savagery.

If not his superior. Alex struggled to get his knife arm out of the water and into his opponent's face but the other seized his wrist and forced it down with vicious and almost inhuman strength. A knife flash in the moonlight, a desperate swerve and the neoprene hood was flapping loose at the side of Alex's head and his cheek was hot with blood. The two men's legs locked taut – stalemate – and then in the moment before they bore each other underwater Alex drew back his head and slammed it into his opponent's nose, felt the smashing crunch of breaking bone.

Desperately swinging at the broken nose with the heel of his free hand, Alex attempted to drive the shattered bone chips backwards into his opponent's brain, but managed only a glancing blow. For a fraction of a second the eyes of the two men met and they were each other's mirror image: hooded, bloodied and snarling like wolves.

Underwater now, throwing his whole weight into the attempt, Alex wrenched desperately at his own knife arm, but the other's grip on his wrist was as inexorable as a steel vice. Baring his teeth, Alex bit into the fist that enclosed him until he felt his teeth meet through the gristle, but still the grip did not weaken. Instead, the blade flashed past his face again and although he wrenched his head away he felt the icy burn of its passage through his cheek. He should shout for the MI5 men, he realised numbly, but then there was a second explosion of light as his opponent's knife hilt hammered into the base of his skull, his face was forced underwater and there was no longer any breath to shout with.

Soon his lungs were screaming and his legs flailing beneath him, kicking at the Glock as it swung on its lanyard. He grabbed for the other's knife hand, couldn't reach it, punched at where he thought the smashed nose ought to be and clawed blindly for the eyes. But the grip on his head was as immovable as that on his knife arm, he'd had no chance to grab any air and finally his mouth gagged open to admit a choking inrush of water. Anoxia came fast and he felt his hands sleepily release their grip on the commando knife.

And then, in some dim, drowning corner of his consciousness, Alex sensed that he was being dragged upwards. Retching, he vomited up the best part of a litre of river water and as he struggled for air he was aware of a hooded face poised above him.

'So,' said the face quietly. 'You're the one.' There was a hint of a Belfast accent.

Alex said nothing. His chest was agony and points of light danced in front of his eyes 'Do it,' he rasped contemptuously. 'Kill me and be on your way.'

'I'll not kill you,' the Watchman murmured, reversing his knife in his hand. 'That'd be too much like killing myself.'

The Watchman's arm became a blur, a third blinding whipcrack of pain bloomed behind Alex's eyes and this time he lost consciousness altogether.

TWENTY

Dawn Harding arrived at 5 a.m. with a Service doctor and the same forensic pathology team that had attended to the body of Craig Gidley. Above him, Alex heard them take the stairs up to George Widdowes' bedroom at a run, heard the abrupt halt of their footsteps as they discovered the horrendous carnage there.

Alex himself was lying naked on the camp bed wrapped in a single blood-sodden sheet. The MI5 security duo who had found him unconscious on the bank had removed his wetsuit and dressed his wounds as best they could from their first-aid kits, but in the end he'd told them to leave it for the doctor. His left cheek had a deep transverse gash along the line of the bone and his right ear had been almost cut in half – two hours after the event blood was still welling down both sides of his face. With the left arm he'd been exceptionally lucky – the cut was deep but the knife had missed the subcutaneous muscles and his hand function seemed unimpaired. The wound to the left thigh was over a foot long and had bled copiously but again no important muscle function seemed impaired. Alex guessed that the tough double-layer neoprene of the wetsuit had gone a long way towards preventing more serious damage.

He supposed that he ought to be a bit more worried about his skull. He'd always been a thick-headed bugger – his dad and several of his instructors had told him that – but he had received two very violent blows indeed and the pain when he tried to move his head was excruciating: of a different order even from his gashed face.

But the pain at the back of his head shrank into insignificance when he considered the scale of his failure to protect the life of

George Widdowes, who now lay upstairs in a three-foot-diameter pool of clotting blood with a gag in his mouth, a six-inch nail through his right temple and his severed ears on his pillow.

As soon as he could move Alex had insisted that the security men help him up there and the huge blood loss had told him immediately that Meehan had cut Widdowes' ears off before ending his victim's life with the hammer and the six-inch nail.

What can those last moments have been like? Alex wondered speechlessly. What had been the order of the fear that Widdowes had felt when faced with Meehan and his knife? And the pain as the ears were sawn through? What had that been like, coupled with the knowledge of the obscene killing that was to follow?

Impossible to imagine. And whatever the nature of these experiences, it had been he – Alex Temple – who had gifted them to George Widdowes.

Arrogance had overruled caution. He had placed himself in the front line without back-up and by doing so put another man's life at risk. In part, he realised with appalling clarity, his actions had been driven by sheer competitiveness, by the simple urge to prove Dawn and her organisation wrong.

He had dared and George Widdowes had lost.

His failure, personal and professional, was absolute.

He had never felt such despondency. Never felt such icily unquenchable rage.

Dawn made her way downstairs with the doctor, a T-shirted man in his forties with a faint South African accent whom she introduced as Max. Both looked stunned by the slaughter upstairs.

Without hesitation the doctor stripped the sheet from Alex and scanned his body.

Dawn glanced down at his bloodied nakedness and then turned to the wall. '*Shit*!' she murmured. 'What a *fucking* mess. I see he almost took your ear off too?'

'Didn't mean to,' said Alex blankly. 'Just slashed at me, going

208

for my eyes. I asked your colleagues to stick the bulldog clip on to hold the whole thing together.'

'Probably saved the ear,' said Max. 'I assume this was all done with a knife?'

'Yeah. Commando type.'

'Had any tetanus shots recently?'

'Three months ago.'

'AIDS test?'

Alex closed his eyes. 'He was trying to kill me, not fuck me.'

'Get one done. Any other injuries?'

'Couple of good bashes to the base of the skull. Probably with the steel hilt of the knife.'

Max felt gingerly beneath Alex's head. 'Does that hurt?'

'Doesn't feel great.'

'Could be fractured. I'll book you an X-ray. Meanwhile, I'd better get you stitched up. You'll probably find that it hurts less and the time goes quicker if you talk.'

Alex raised an eyebrow at Dawn.

Max caught the look. 'Yeah, you can talk in front of me. I've certified three murdered desk officers as having died of natural causes in the last month, I think I'm suitably compromised.'

Dawn took a deep breath and, as Max selected a suturing needle from a case, moved back a pace or two. 'What happened?' she asked, looking coldly down at Alex.

'He got the jump on me. Basically, I was wrong to have continued with the set-up here after you refused me a back-up man.'

Dawn caught Max's eye and with a flick of her head indicated that he wait upstairs. Pulling his needle through, the doctor left it hanging.

'So George Widdowes' death was my fault, was it?' Dawn demanded as soon the door had closed above them.

'No,' replied Alex levelly, 'it was my fault. It was an error of judgement on my part. I'm not ducking responsibility for that.'

'So you had a Glock and he wasn't carrying a firearm of any kind?' asked Dawn.

'That's correct,' Alex confirmed. 'Or if he was carrying a

firearm he dropped it pretty early on in the game. So we both pulled knives.'

'Go on,' said Dawn.

'I broke his nose, bit his left knuckle pretty deeply and stabbed him a couple of times in the upper body. It obviously wasn't enough to put him down or stop him doing what he wanted to do, but I hurt him, I think. He won't be feeling good right now, and his face and hand will be visibly damaged.'

'How long did this fight go on for?'

'Oh, three or four minutes probably.'

'And how would you rate him, professionally speaking?' she asked.

Alex shrugged and immediately wished that he hadn't. 'Better than me, obviously,' he answered wretchedly. 'It was weird, though. He was totally aggressive, but . . .'

'But?'

'But when the point came he chose not to kill me.'

'Why, do you think?'

'Well, he said something just before he hit me on the head and knocked me out. Something along the lines of . . . oh, killing me would be like killing himself or something. Some psycho bullshit.'

'You saw him clearly?'

'No. For a start he was covered with black cam-cream, for seconds he was wearing a wetsuit with a hood.'

Dawn remained expressionless. 'Can you remember anything at all about him?'

Alex looked away. Once again, he saw the icily staring figure at Don Hammond's funeral. Had he simply constructed that image in his mind from the MI5 photographs?

'He's about my size and build. And right-handed. And he hasn't got a beard or moustache. That's all I'm certain of.'

'That doesn't exactly narrow it down a great deal.'

'I know,' said Alex. 'And I'm sorry. I'm sorry about the whole thing.'

Dawn looked at him, shook her head and punched out a number on her mobile. At the pick-up she relayed Alex's description and the nature of the Watchman's injuries. Afterwards she walked round the cellar, examined the gashed wetsuit and the small pile of Alex's belongings.

'We've got people covering the ground for a ten-mile radius,' she told him. 'Helicopters, tracker dogs, everything. Country-wide the police'll be looking for a man in his mid-thirties, around five foot eleven and strongly built, with a broken nose and injured hand. We've put it around that he's a paranoid schizophrenic, armed, who's escaped from the high-security wing of Garton Hill. Do not approach, et cetera.'

Alex was silent. There was nothing useful left to say.

Five minutes later Max whip-finished the sutures on his cheek. 'Right,' he said. 'Let's get on with that ear. Tell them upstairs I'll be at least another forty minutes.' He turned back to Alex with a rueful smile. 'Think sweet thoughts, my friend. This is going to hurt.'

That afternoon Alex was driven in a private ambulance to the Fairlie Clinic in Upper Norwood, London. In theory this facility is available to the paying public; in practice it is reserved for the use of the security services. Several supergrasses, Alex had heard, had received reconstructive facial surgery behind its unremarkable doors.

There, he was walked to a windowless private room and his clothes were placed in a locker. A male nurse brought him a cup of tea, a painkilling dose of Volterol and Coproxamol, and the use of a radio tuned to Classic FM. The rest of the day passed slowly.

Shortly before midnight Alex awoke to hear his mobile phone juddering in his locker. It was still switched to vibrate, he realised. He was lying in total darkness against cotton pillows, the painkillers had worn off and his stitches were burning.

'Alex,' came the voice, quiet but insistent. 'It's Stevo, man.'

'Stevo?' he asked blankly, then remembered talking to the sniper team leader at Don Hammond's post-funeral piss-up. 'Stevo, yeah, tell me! How are you?'

211

'Fine, man — listen, I don't know what you want Den Connolly for but I can tell you we've had all manner of lairy buggers asking after him recently.'

Box people, thought Alex. Might have guessed it.

'Basically the lads have kept schtumm,' Stevo continued. 'But I'll tell you what I know.'

'Go on.'

'He left after the Gulf and hooked up with some outfit doing marine security in the Mediterranean. Don't know the details, but apparently he started hitting the Scotch or the job went arse-up or whatever and the next thing anyone heard was he was into armed robbery.'

'Yeah?'

'Word is, he was the trigger man on that job off the North Circular.'

'Park Royal?' murmured Alex. 'A security van? Something to do with cashpoints?'

'Yeah. Basically three of them did the Bank of Scotland for a million and a half. Not a massive take, but good enough for Den and he fucked off to Spain.'

'D'you know where?'

'A village outside Marbella called El Angel. One of the lads went down there last summer. Apparently Den got some Spanish front guy to buy a bar for him and hangs out there.'

'What's the bar called?'

'Pablito's. Nice little place, apparently. Den's in a bit of a downward spiral, though.'

'And officially no one knows about this place?'

'Bill Leonard certainly doesn't, because he called us in a week ago and asked if anyone had any ideas where to find him. Then there were a couple of obvious Boxheads in Saxty's asking after him. We all assumed it was something to do with the Park Royal job.'

'How do you know it isn't?'

'I don't know. I reckon you'd tell us the form if it was anything like that.'

'I promise you, I'm not going to grass him up.'

There was a brief silence. 'The RSM was wondering: is it anything to do with a certain former student?'

Alex smiled and, as so often before, marvelled at the subtlety and accuracy of the Regiment's NCO grapevine. 'Speak no evil, hear no evil, see no evil,' he said eventually.

'Like that, is it? Wise monkeys?'

'Something like that. Thanks, Stevo.'

TWENTY-ONE

He offered Dawn his resignation the next day.

'You can't just . . . *walk out!*' she protested. 'You're the only one to have seen Meehan face to face.'

'He's the one who's seen me, not the other way round, and I don't look exactly anonymous with these stitches all over me. I won't be able to get within miles of him.'

'And Angela Fenwick? What's going to happen when he comes after her?'

'Your people are going to have to stop him,' said Alex. 'It's as simple as that.'

She stared at him. 'Alex.' She hesitated over the use of his name. 'Please. Don't make me beg you to finish the job.'

'It's more likely to be Meehan who's finishing the job,' said Alex wryly, touching his bandaged face.

'Alex.' she lowered her voice. 'You can catch him and you can kill him. You're the best. That's why we came to you.'

He glanced over at her. Today she was dressed completely in steely grey – the grey of her eyes. 'What would it take,' she murmured, 'to keep you on the case? In charge of the case, calling the shots?'

Would you credit it, he thought. *She's actually schmoozing me.* He closed his eyes. He'd never yet walked away from a challenge.

'You could have whatever . . .'

'Spain,' he interrupted her flatly.

She stared at him.

'We have to fly to Spain. There's someone we need to see.'

He gave her a censored version of the facts. She listened in silence.

214

'I don't see why you can't simply tell me who this man is, so that I can send someone over to talk to him.'

'He won't talk to you or to anyone you send,' said Alex firmly. 'It's got to be me. Once I've talked to this guy I'll hand the information over to you and you can do what you want with it. You brought me in for my specialised knowledge – you might as well get your money's worth.'

She looked at him uncertainly and he shrugged. If he could help MI5 nail Meehan it might make up in some small way for his negligence towards George Widdowes. It was all that he had left to offer.

'If anyone knew Meehan,' Alex continued, 'it was this guy. Day after day, week after week, down at that bunker in Tregaron . . . You get to know someone pretty damn well under those circumstances. You talk to each other because there's nothing else to do. Blokes I've trained – I know things about them their wives certainly don't.'

She nodded, took her mobile from her bag and left the room. By the time she returned he had finished the coffee. Her eyes travelled over the ugly, black-scabbed stitches that cut across his face.

'Angela's flying to Washington this morning for two days and I think we can assume she'll be safe from Meehan during that time. But it means we have to get to Spain pretty much immediately and be back within forty-eight hours. Do you think you can travel in that state?'

They went first-class that afternoon. At the Fairlie Clinic they knew all about short recovery times, and the male nurse who had attended Alex the day before gave Dawn a swift tutorial on the care of knife wounds and packed a kit containing all the bandages, dressings and painkillers that she would need.

At Heathrow, at Alex's insistence, they had bought a beach bag and swimming kit. In Alex's case this had meant a pair of blue shorts, in Dawn's a red bikini that Alex had exchanged for the severe one-piece she herself had chosen.

'We've got to fit in,' he told her as the plane circled Malaga

215

airport. 'The more official we look the less he'll tell us. If we look like a couple of civil servants on expenses I can guarantee that he won't even speak to us. And we both know you look good in red!'

She'd ignored the last comment and reluctantly agreed, as she had agreed that no official mention would be made of their contact's name or location, and that whatever she learnt from the visit no criminal prosecution would be set in motion.

'The other thing you have to remember,' Alex had told her, 'is that the world our man occupies is not run by *Guardian* readers but by hard-core criminals. The deal with girlfriends is that they wear a lot of lipstick, they're treated like princesses and when it's time to talk business they make themselves scarce. So when I feel that point's coming I'll expect you to do just that, OK?'

'I don't know why you need me along at all,' she complained.

'To make the whole thing kosher. Our guy's sure to have some sort of woman in tow and a single male visitor unbalances the household. He constitutes a threat, a sexual challenge, a physical invasion – all sorts of negative things. A man with a girl-friend, however, is quite another matter. You and his *chica* can push off and talk about blonde highlights or vibrators or what-ever and leave the men to put the world to rights over a bottle of ten-year-old malt.'

'I can't wait.'

'Look, we want a result, we've got to press the right buttons.'

She narrowed her eyes. 'And all that male-heroic, bimbo-girlie stuff is a million miles from your own enlightened, neo-feminist views, right?'

'Absolutely,' said Alex. 'I'm the original new man, me.'

The seat belt sign came on and a broad swathe of brilliant Mediterranean blue appeared beneath them. It was 4.15 local time.

The drive from Malaga airport took the best part of forty minutes in their hired Mercedes. It was a beautifully clear day, the air was warm and the pace of the traffic on the coast highway leisurely. From Malaga to Marbella seemed to be one long strip of holiday, golfing and marina developments. Some of these were completed, some were still at the bricks–and–mortar stage and all offered extravagantly generous terms to potential buyers.

'We should put a deposit down on a condo.' Alex yawned contentedly as they bypassed Marbella. 'We can retire here and play golf when we finally hang up our shoulder holsters.'

'Endless boozing with retired villains,' said Dawn acidly. 'I think not.'

'Oh, get a life, girl! The sun's shining. We're on the Costa del Sol. Let's at least try to enjoy ourselves.'

'There's something very creepy about this place. Where are all the young people, for a start?'

'Having sexy siestas would be my guess. That or lying on the beach.'

'Hm. Planning the next Brinks-Mat robbery more likely.'

'Look,' said Alex, 'there's the sign for El Angel.'

They drove past the turning and on to Puerto Banus, where they had booked accommodation for two nights. The Hotel del Puerto, they discovered, was a class act. A fountain surrounded by dwarf palms played in the reception area and their luxurious balconied room overlooked the port.

The room was a double. Alex had no reason to suspect that Connolly would check their accommodation, but he knew two singles would definitely spook him in the unlikely event that he did bother. Dawn had not been enthusiastic about a shared bed and Alex had drily promised to sleep on the floor.

And here they were. Beneath them sparkling white yachts rocked gently at anchor, and on the quayside expensively dressed holidaymakers sauntered past the bars and shops. Even Dawn brightened at the prospect before them and when Alex suggested they went down for a snack she readily agreed.

He unzipped his bag on the double bed, stripped uncom-fortably to his boxer shorts – the wound in his thigh was particularly painful after the journey – and replaced his jeans and T-shirt with lightweight chinos and a Hawaiian shirt printed with dragons. The stitches he covered up with Elastoplast. 'How do I look?' he asked Dawn.

217

'Like a beaten-up pimp,' said Dawn. 'If you'll excuse me, I'll change in the bathroom.'

She re-entered in a short cocktail frock in her signature dove-grey and the faintest suggestion of scent. Her hair and her eyes shone. Alex stared at her.

'You look . . .'

'Yes, Captain Temple?'

'. . . as if you're on holiday.'

'Good,' she said. 'Let's go.'

They chose a bar more or less at random. It was a little past five in the evening, and the glare had lifted from the sea and the gin palaces in front of them. The tables near them held middle-aged men in yachting gear and much younger women with implausibly huge breasts.

Their food arrived, plus a couple of Cokes. Alex had warned Dawn that some fairly serious drinking lay ahead. From his pocket he took a small plastic container holding a dozen ephedrine tablets. These, drawn from the Fairlie Clinic, had the dual effect of sharpening the senses and keeping drunkenness at bay. 'Bottoms up!' He grinned, downing two of them and handing the container to Dawn.

'Cheers!' rejoined Dawn rather more soberly. She took two and placed the container in her bag for safe keeping.

'Glad to see you're taking deodorant,' observed Alex, peering down into the bag. 'Things could get a bit sweaty.'

'Funny guy,' said Dawn. 'It's actually a can of Mace. Anyone tries any monkey business – including you – they go down.'

'Riot girl, huh?'

'You bet.'

The drive took fifteen minutes.

El Angel was a very different proposition from Puerto Banus. Not so much a village as an arbitrary strip of land between the highway and the sea, it comprised a clutch of new and not-so-new hacienda-style developments. The largest of these – a bowling and fast-food centre – was windowless and uncompleted, and from the weathered appearance of its plasterwork had clearly been so for some time. A large painted sign showed the development as its architects had envisaged it – bustling, youthful and cosmopolitan – but in truth it looked merely forlorn.

Parking the Mercedes on the highway, Alex and Dawn followed the track towards the sea. This passed through low scrub and between areas which had clearly once been intended to be gardens. Now, however, they only contained builders' rubble, rusting angle iron and other construction detritus. The evening breeze carried a strong smell of dogshit.

Dawn winced as thistles tore at her ankles. 'Perhaps I'm not so ideally dressed after all,' she remarked, glancing down at her strappy sandals.

'You look fine,' said Alex.

The path led on to a custom-built road flanked by white-rendered houses. Some of these were occupied and had cars on their drives and defiant little gardens of bougainvillea and hibiscus in front of them, but most stood empty.

Alex was struck by the desolation of the place. These deserted villas were, in a very real sense, the end of the road. You would come here and slowly forget everything.

Dawn must have been feeling the same, because to his amazement she slipped her arm through his. 'In every dream home a heartache,' she murmured.

'Yeah. I'm beginning to feel seriously in need of a drink.'

'This bar *is* actually on the sea, is it?'

'That was the impression I got,' said Alex. 'Shall we ring one of these bells and ask?'

They looked at each other, laughed nervously, then Dawn strode over to the nearest house. The sign read 'Tangmere'.

The door was opened by an elderly man in a cravat and an RAF blazer. A vague housecoated figure, presumably his wife, peered nervously behind him.

'We're looking for Pablito's,' began Alex, shielding his stitched-up ear with his hand.

'Over the road, face the sea, track at eleven o'clock between Sea Pines and Casa Linda. ETA three minutes. Calling on young Denzil?'

'Yes.'

'First-rate chap. Darkish horse, of course, but then that's the rule rather than the exception out here. Tempt you inside for a minute or two? Raise a lotion to the setting sun?'

'Perhaps some other time,' said Alex guiltily, seeing the poorly concealed desperation in the other man's eyes.

'Very good. Dunbar's the name. Usually here.'

Alex and Dawn set off down the track and saw the bar almost immediately. It was a blockhouse of a place, finished in a rough brownish render which matched the stony seashore. A neon design, not yet illuminated, showed palm trees and a sunset. Around the building stood half a dozen wooden benches and plastic-topped tables. A rusting motorcycle leaned tipsily against one wall.

'I am *definitely* overdressed,' said Dawn, picking her way awkwardly over the shingle.

'Whereas my pimp's outfit is spot on.' Alex grinned.

As they approached Pablito's they saw that they had taken a very indirect back route and that, in fact, a narrow road led straight to the front entrance. The swing doors in front of the building were half open. Inside, the place looked more spacious than its exterior suggested. A bar ran the length of one wall and on one of its stools a fat, heavily tanned man in a sarong, perhaps forty-five, was watching football on a wall-mounted television. Behind the bar a twenty-something woman with bleached blonde hair polished lager glasses. A cigarette smoked in an ashtray at her elbow.

As Dawn and Alex peered over the swing doors, the woman assumed a practised smile. 'Come on in, loves. We're still in injury time, as you can see, but make yourselves at home. What can I do you for?'

Alex turned to Dawn. From the corner of his eye he could see the blonde woman staring at the dressings on his face. 'What's it going to be, pet?'

Dawn smiled sweetly at him. 'Ooh, I think a Bacardi Breezer might just get me going!'

'One BB coming up. And for you, my love?'

'Pint would be nice.'

The man on the stool scratched his stomach and looked up. 'Tell you, that Patrick Viera's a bloody liability. Someone's going to put his lights out one of these days. Staying locally, are you?'

'Puerto Banus,' said Alex.

'Very nice. Come over on the 1615?'

Alex nodded, helped Dawn on to a bar stool and with due consideration for his lacerated thigh, sat down himself.

'Exploring the area, then?'

The features were puffy with alcohol, but the eyes were shrewd. And beneath the gross brick-red body, Alex saw, were the remains of a disciplined physique. On the broad forearms were the marks of tattooes removed by laser.

'We wanted to get away from things for a few days.' Alex winked at Dawn and allowed his hand to stray to the dressing on his cheek. 'And as you can see, I've had a bit of a bang-up in the motor. We reckoned we were due some quality time.'

'Well, you've come to the right place for that.' The fat man's eyes flickered over the knife wounds. 'What game you in, then?'

'Den, love, leave the poor man alone,' said the woman, clattering over to the optics in her high-heeled mules. 'He hasn't set foot in here more'n two minutes and already you're . . .'

'No, it's OK,' said Alex. 'I'm a physical training instructor. And Dawn, well, Dawn's one of my best customers, aren't you, pet.'

She giggled. 'I hope so.'

This was the explanation that they had agreed on. If pressed, the suggestion was to be that Dawn was married to someone else.

The fat man nodded and returned to the football, shaking his head at intervals to mark his disapproval of Arsenal's failure to wrest control of the game from Sturm Graz. As the final whistle blew he swung round on his bar stool and extended a large hand to Alex. 'I'm Den. Big Den, Dirty Den, Fat Bastard, whatever.' He moved behind the bar and slapped the woman's

221

tight, white-denimed rump. 'And this is Marie. Pull us a bevvy, love.'

'Leave off! And for Gawd's sakes put on a bleedin' shirt.' The woman reached for a lager glass and winked at Dawn. 'He wouldn't stand for it if I went about with my chest hanging out – I don't see why I should when he does!'

'When you've got a body like mine,' said Den, 'you should share it with the world.'

He emptied a half-glass of Special Brew in a single swallow, slapped his vast belly, reached for his cigarettes and leant confidentially towards Dawn. 'You know, I'm known locally as something of a fitness guru,' he murmured.

Dawn giggled again. 'Well, I approve of your gym,' she said, looking around her at the football pennants and the signed *EastEnders* posters.

Other customers began to arrive. Alex and Dawn nursed their drinks at the bar and listened to the amiable banter around them. Everyone else, it was clear, was a regular. Equally clear was that this unremarkable beach bar was a meeting place for expatriate criminal aristocracy. For the most part they were expensively if a little garishly dressed. The women looked a lot more like Marie than Dawn, favouring bleached-blonde feather cuts and uncompromising displays of orange cleavage. The men went for Ross Kemp buzzcuts, pastel leisurewear and extensive facial scarring.

Den acted as host, drinking steadily and determinedly himself and ensuring that others' glasses were full. To Alex there seemed to be no clear line between paid-for and complimentary drinks. No money was demanded of him and he assumed that he and Dawn were running up a tab.

At nine o'clock on the dot the Dunbars appeared, nodded courteously to Dawn and Alex, shook hands all round, drank a whisky and soda and a gin and tonic respectively, and left.

'The old boy flew Spitfires over the Western Desert,' Den told Alex afterwards. 'Ten confirmed kills. Now he's living on twenty-five quid a week. I let him run up a tab and then cancel it when Remembrance Sunday comes round. Least I can do.'

Alex nodded.

'I get him talking sometimes,' Den continued, lighting a cigarette. 'Dogfight techniques. Aerial combat. And I tell you, get him on to all that stuff and you see the old hunter-killer light come back into those eyes. Know what I mean?'

Alex nodded again. He could feel the ephedrine now, racing through his system. Beside him Den ashed his cigarette and took a deep draught of Special Brew. The big man was sweating. Behind them the wives shrieked, Dawn among them.

Alex excused himself. He needed a piss.

Edging through the crowd he made his way outside into the neon twilight and peered around. By the palm trees would do. Behind him he heard feet crunching on the shingle – some other bloke on the same errand, he guessed.

Then something determined in the tread – some grim regularity – told him that it wasn't. As he half turned, glimpsing a heavy-set silhouette topped with the shine of a shaven head, a massive forearm locked chokingly round his throat.

'Forget the fitness bollocks, chum, who the fuck are you and what the fuck do you want?'

The voice was low – almost a whisper. Alex struggled desperately to break free and lashed back with heels and elbows. The blows landed on flesh and bone but without result. The arm at Alex's throat was as solid as teak and tightening. Pinpoints of light appeared before his eyes and there was a rushing at his ears. His attacker clearly didn't expect an immediate answer.

It was probably the ephedrine that gave Alex the extra couple of seconds of consciousness in which his scrabbling fingers found the other man's crotch. Grabbing a sweaty handful of trouser, he clamped his left fist tight over the other man's scrotum and squeezed with all the force he could muster.

A high-pitched gasp of pain sounded in his ear and the arm at his throat loosened a fraction. Enough for Alex to whirl around, still clutching and twisting the other man's groin in his left hand, and hammer two rock-hard punches into his lower ribs with his right.

Evading a furious, windmilling series of counter-punches Alex staggered back, gagging for breath. He could see the man clearly now, a muscle-bound enforcer with a spider's-web tattoo inked across his thick neck. Alex had vaguely registered him in the bar earlier. The tattoos were certainly prison work.

His face distorted with pain, the gorilla advanced on Alex, who backed away fast. This wasn't about interrogation any more, it was about revenge. At that moment a slender figure rose from the shadows beside the entrance and a jet of spray cut the air.

The enforcer roared with the unaccustomed shock, pain and anger. His hands clamped themselves to his eyes, and Alex took advantage of the moment to kick him as hard as he could in the balls. With an agonised sigh, the man crumpled to the shingle.

'Can't leave you alone for a moment, can I,' said Dawn, stepping into the light from the neon sign and returning the Mace to her bag with a self-satisfied smile.

'I guess not,' said Alex, his heart pounding with adrenalin. He looked down at the groaning figure at his feet. 'Did you follow me out?'

'Put it like this – I thought all that traditional East End hospitality was a bit too good to last.'

'Well . . . Thank you!'

'What the bloody 'ell's goin' on 'ere, then?'

Framed in the bar's entrance was Connolly, drink in one hand, cigarette in the other. From the surprised look on his face the scenario was not at all the one he expected. I was supposed to be the one on the ground, thought Alex. Begging for mercy and admitting to being a police officer, presumably.

Connolly's look of surprise was quickly suppressed and he gave the fallen man a brisk kick in the guts. 'Get up, yer big fuckin' nelly!'

The enforcer writhed and Connolly turned concernedly to Alex. 'Sorry, chum, was Kev here being impertinent?'

'He asked me a question and then tried to strangle me before I had a chance to answer.'

224

Connolly shook his head, marched into the bar and returned with a jug of water, which he emptied over Kev's head. 'You just can't get decent help for love nor money these days . . .'

Slowly and unsteadily Kev dragged himself to his feet, clutching his groin. His T-shirt was sodden and a dark orange stain covered the left side of his face, where the Mace pepper spray had struck him. He managed a rueful grin, his eyes still streaming, and extended a shaky hand to Alex. 'Sorry, mate, overreacted a bit there!'

'No problem,' said Alex, amazed that the man was able to stand at all. Now that the adrenalin from the fight was ebbing away the stitches on his own face were beginning to throb.

'All friends again?' asked Connolly with a dazzling smile. 'Marvellous. Kev, take the lady inside, open a bottle of champagne — the Moët, not that dago muck — and make her comfortable. And wipe yer boat race while you're about it!'

The gorilla nodded meekly and signed that Dawn precede him through the swing doors.

'I'm sorry about that, mate,' said Connolly, turning back to Alex. 'But you'll understand I've got to keep an eye on the security side of things.'

Alex nodded.

'You're not Old Bill, I know that much. But you're something. That's no sunlamp tan on your hands and neck, any more than those are car crash injuries on your face and arm. And I didn't see the rumble just then, but . . .'

'Stevo sent me,' said Alex quietly. 'I didn't want to alarm Marie.'

Connolly emptied his glass. 'Stevo? I don't know any Stevo.'

'Jim Stephenson from "B" Squadron in Hereford. That Stevo. I'm Regiment, Den.'

'Go on.'

'I'm in "D" Squadron. Seconded to RWW, like you were.'

'So when did you join?'

For five minutes Connolly subjected him to a series of questions about Regiment personalities, extracting details that only an insider would have known. He slipped in a trick

225

question, asking if that idle short-arse Tosh McClaren was still around and Alex confirmed that yes, Tosh McClaren was still around, and he was still 6 foot 2 tall. After a time, Connolly appeared satisfied that Alex was who he said he was.

Sensing this, Alex looked him in the eye. 'Listen, Den, I'm not trouble, OK? I just want to talk.'

Connolly stared at him in silence. He looked tired, puffy-faced and a little sad. And strangely vulnerable, thought Alex, for a man who had once been known as the SAS's toughest NCO.

'You're not a talker, son, you're a shooter. It's written all over your face.'

'I'm looking for someone, Den, that's all. Help me and you can rest easy about the Park Royal job. No more cover stories, no more looking over your shoulder for the cops.'

'What the fuck's the Park Royal job?'

'Den, I'm family. Trust me.'

'Oh, yeah? So who's the girl? Well handy with the Mace, it looked like.'

'She's just a girl. Nothing to do with anything.'

Den stared at his empty glass in silence, flipped his cigarette into the gathering darkness and nodded. For a moment, behind the flushed features, Alex saw the taut wariness of the Special Forces soldier. Then the dazzling smile returned and a large hand was placed on Alex's shoulder. 'Come on, son, we're wasting good drinking time. Tonight's on the house, yeah?'

He steered Alex back inside and moments later Marie was sliding Alex a glass of champagne and a shot-glass of Irish whiskey. Someone, to applause and laughter, began to sing 'My Yiddisher Momma'.

Some time later Dawn reappeared beside him. Her cheeks were flushed and she seemed to be genuinely enjoying herself. Under the circumstances it seemed natural for Alex to slip his arm round her waist, and for her in response to incline herself against him. For a moment he felt the soft pressure of her breast against his side.

'Thank you,' he said again. 'That could have turned nasty,

one way or another. How are you getting on with the gangster wives?'

She placed her champagne thoughtfully on the bar. 'They're good fun. I like them. Any progress?'

'I've dropped a name or two. Told him who I really am. Not who you are, though. Far as he's concerned, you're just my girl.'

'Mm. Lucky me.'

'The main problem is that he thinks I'm some sort of hit man. Possibly even come over here to whack him. He's very jumpy. I think the best thing I can do is to tell him the real reason I'm here and hope that calms things down.'

'I agree. And this is looking like a rather serious conversation if I'm supposed to be some no-brain blonde bimbo.' She pouted. 'Which I clearly am!'

He ran a finger down her cheek. 'It's just that you play the part so well.'

'Now why am I suspicious of a compliment like that, I wonder?' she asked.

There was another burst of singing from the floor of the room. Someone had sat themselves at a piano and was banging out old Cockney songs.

'Are we within earshot of Bow Bells here, do you think?' mused Dawn, throwing back the remains of her drink.

'Basildon, maybe,' said Alex. 'Not that I've got any quarrel with that, as an Essex man myself.'

Den Connolly suddenly appeared beside them, sweating and massive. 'Before I'm too pissed to understand a word you're saying,' he asked Alex, 'who exactly was it you was after?'

Alex dismissed Dawn with a nod of his head and a pat on her dove-grey behind. 'Joseph Meehan. Code-named Watchman. You finished him for Box.'

Connolly nodded. 'I ain't officially here,' he said eventually, his words slurring. 'I ain't officially anywhere. But you know that.'

Alex nodded. 'I know the score from Stevo. No one hears your name. Ever. And if you can give me what I need you can rest easy about that other business.'

227

'You gimme your word on that?' Connolly glanced meaningfully down at the assembled company. 'My friends'd be very pissed off if . . . They're my family now, y'understand – forget fuckin' Hereford, RWW, all that old bollocks.'

Alex looked him in the eye. 'I give you my word.'

Connolly pursed his lips and nodded slowly and vaguely to himself. 'Tomorrow. Lunchtime. Bring your . . .' He gestured vaguely towards Dawn, who was whispering confidences to Marie. 'Meanwhiles, order anything you want. Open bar, like I said.'

They left around 2 a.m. Not because Alex thought that Connolly might relent and talk to him that night, but because he felt that he needed to prove his credentials to the ex-NCO. He had to show proper respect. Leaving early would have been regarded as very graceless. So he had stuck around, downing drink after drink, and looking suitably impressed by the tales of blags, slags, grass-ups, fit-ups, bent coppers, unnumbered shooters and all the rest of the hard-man mythology. Dawn meanwhile rested wide-eyed at his side, with her arm draped lightly round his waist. They looked, in short, like any impressionable young couple who happened to have stumbled into a bar full of criminals.

When the last goodbyes had been said and they'd finally reached the car, Dawn blinked hard several times and reached in her bag for the key.

'You OK to drive?' asked Alex blearily.

'I've actually drunk comparatively little,' said Dawn. 'I always get rum and a Coke in that situation – that way you can just keep your glass filled with Coke and no-one's the wiser.'

'Well, ephedrine or no, I'm well and truly bladdered, I'm afraid,' Alex slurred. 'But mission accomplished, sort of.'

'Get in,' said Dawn.

At the hotel they stood together for a moment in front of the open window. The port and the yachts were lit up now, and the sea was an inky black below them. A tide of drunken benevolence washed over Alex. 'You were great,' he said

228

feelingly, placing a hand on her warm shoulder. 'Especially Maceing that bonehead of Connolly's.'

She smiled and inclined her cheek to his hand. 'You've already thanked me for that. I enjoyed myself. What d'you think tomorrow holds?'

'Dunno. All that lunch invitation stuff was just to buy himself time. The more of his hospitality he can persuade us to soak up, the less bad he's going to feel about us leaving empty-handed. At the moment he accepts that I'm kosher and you're just the sweet thing I happen to be travelling with, but he's worried about who comes after me. Where it's all going to end.'

'What's he got to hide, Alex?' she asked gently.

'Enough.'

'So what promises did you make him?'

Careful, Alex told himself woozily. She doesn't know about the Park Royal job. 'Oh, I strung him along . . .'

'You think he'll talk to you tomorrow?' Dawn asked sharply. 'Because tomorrow's all we've got. In thirty hours Angela gets back from Washington and any time after that . . .'

Alex nodded. She didn't need to spell out the danger that Meehan posed. Privately, he was far from convinced that Connolly would talk to him, but he couldn't see how else the situation could have been handled. The alcohol was pounding at his temples now and the knife cuts were beginning to pulse in unison.

'Why don't I get those dressings off?' she asked him. 'Let a bit of fresh air at your poor face. Lie down on the bed?'

He could quite easily have removed the dressings himself, but lay there breathing in her jasmine scent and her smoky hair, and the faint smell of rum on her breath. She was OK, was Dawn, he decided. A bit of a bitch at times and the most irritating bloody driver he'd ever met, but what the hell? She had a tough job. He could live with her downsides.

And she really was quite seriously pretty with those cool grey eyes and that soft, secretive mouth. Without especially meaning to, and with a vague stab at discretion, he glanced down the grey linen front of her dress as she inched the dressing from his cheek.

She didn't seem to be wearing any sort of bra and he recalled with a rush of pleasure the feel of her breasts against him in the bar.

'That's not fair,' she said reproachfully.

'What's not fair?'

'Here I am, doing my big Florence Nightingale number and all you can do is stare down my front, panting like a dog. You're supposed to be an officer and a gentleman.'

'No one ever said anything about being a gentleman,' said Alex. 'And I'm not panting, I'm breathing.'

'Well, stop it. And shut your eyes, or I'll rip your ear in half again and you wouldn't like that, now would you?'

Alex smiled, and tried not to think about George Widdowes' ears lying grey and bloodstained against the pillow. The same thought evidently occurred to Dawn, for her movements abruptly hardened and became businesslike.

When she had finished she stepped out on to the balcony with her mobile phone. 'Can you give me a moment?' she asked, punching out a number. 'Personal call.'

He took himself into the bathroom. The boyfriend, he thought, and felt a sudden urge to hit Dawn's unknown lover very hard in the face. Several times, preferably.

He glanced in the mirror, at the angry black stitch-tracks across his face. *You look like shite, Temple*, he told himself. *You'd be lucky to trap some swamp donkey from Saxty's looking like that, let alone this foxy little spook. Get real.*

By the time she returned he was down to his boxer shorts and looking for the Nurofen.

'Turn round,' she said. 'Let me look at that thigh.'

Alex obeyed. Five minutes later she folded her arms. 'OK,' she began. 'This is the deal. You get the bed and the blankets from the cupboard, I get the quilt on the floor.'

'I'll go on the floor. You take the bed.'

'Normally I'd accept like a shot, but given the extent of your injuries I've decided to be generous. No arguments, Temple, OK?'

Alex inclined his head and climbed into the bed. Dawn went

into the bathroom. When she returned to the quilt on the floor she paused for a moment in front of the window, a slight and entirely feminine figure in her white T-shirt and knickers.

Alex groaned. For the first time that day he found himself in severe physical pain.

TWENTY-TWO

'You're not going to throw up again, are you?' Dawn enquired.

'I don't think so,' whispered Alex. 'But you couldn't just ask that waiter for a half of lager, could you?'

'Are you insane?'

'No, I know it sounds bad but it works. And since it seems to be impossible to get a decent fried breakfast in this hotel . . .'

'This is Spain, Alex, not the Mile End Road. Why don't you just lie back and get some sun, and stop being so scratchy?'

It was 10.30 and they were on adjoining sunloungers by the hotel pool. Dawn was wearing the red bikini they had bought at Heathrow, but not even this could raise Alex's spirits. A bad hangover had coincided with an acute bout of guilt and depression concerning George Widdowes.

The day before had been enjoyable and there had been an air of promise about things – a sense that the mistakes of the past might somehow be redeemed by a little energetic detective work. Now, everything seemed curiously pointless. If he weighed up his career and balanced the harm he had done and the deaths he'd caused against the long-term good, he was unable to state – as he'd once been able to – that on balance the good came out on top. It didn't. The bad came out on top.

Den Connolly had clearly felt that moving from unattributable operations for the RWW to boosting security vans on the North Circular Road was little more than a side shuffle. It wasn't a question of going into crime – you were already there. You had already spent so much of your career so far outside the normal boundaries of behaviour that almost anything seemed logical and reasonable.

The trouble with crime, though, was criminals. They were stupid, for the most part, and greedy. And boastful, judging by last night, and sentimental, and seriously lacking in taste. No, he decided, you'd have to put your own outfit together. A few good, reliable blokes. Apply military standards of security, planning and execution.

And then what, assuming you did the bank and made your wad?

Buy a bar and a big telly, and listen to war stories and get fat?

Dawn raised her head from the sunlounger and peered at him irritably. Her face was shining with sunscreen. 'What was it you said yesterday? Cheer up? Get a life? The sun's shining?'

Alex turned to face her and felt the day's first pale flicker of lust. The red lycra strap of the bikini top hung undone on either side of her and a single pearl of sweat lay in the small of her back. For a moment he stared at it, wondering how her skin would taste, then a waiter with a tray approached.

'*Una cerveza para el Señor, por favor,*' murmured Dawn. '*Y un naranja fresca para mi, gracias.*'

'*Si, Señora.*' The waiter nodded and disappeared.

'That sounded very fluent,' said Alex.

'Yes, I told him you needed an enema for your bad mood.'

'What I need is not to have drunk so bloody much last night.'

'I expect you've done worse in the service of your country.'

He grunted. The knife wounds were beginning to heal, and in consequence to itch like crazy. 'I forgot to ask – did you manage to rescue my weapon from the river?'

'The Glock? Yes. Plus your knife and a silenced Sig Sauer that Meehan must have been carrying. And while you were out for the count, by the way, we managed to get tissue scrapings and a couple of hairs from under your fingernails.'

'Well, I certainly held on tight. But surely you don't need any proof of who you're dealing with?'

'Every confirmation helps. But our main hope is that we might be able to learn something about his whereabouts. The Forensic Science Service can tell you a hell of a lot from a hair.'

Alex looked at her doubtfully. 'Good luck with that. The hair

233

may well turn out to be more helpful than laughing boy down the road.'

'If he's not going to tell us anything, why ask us to come back?'

'He'll probably produce something just to swing the immunity deal I promised him. The question is whether we'll be able to rely on what he produces.'

Dawn frowned at him. 'Look, about this immunity deal . . .?'

'Dawn, the chances are that if you've got nothing on him now then nothing's going to come up in the future. And you can swing it, can't you, if he leads us to the Watchman?'

'It's a hell of a big "if".'

The drinks arrived. Alex drank down his beer in three long swallows, thought it probable for several minutes that he was going to vomit, then suddenly felt better.

Dressed, they strolled through the port, where Dawn bought herself a scoop-neck top and a pair of skin-tight white jeans, and high-heeled mules. To look the part, she explained. Basic tradecraft.

Back at the hotel she changed into it all, adding a Wonderbra.

'Blimey!' said Alex, impressed. 'All you need now is a forty-a-day Rothman's habit and a boyfriend on *Crimestoppers*!'

'If we hang around at Pablito's long enough I'll probably end up with both.'

Alex raised an eyebrow. 'I thought you were already taken. Mr Lucky-boy in London.'

Dawn rolled her eyes and swung her bag over her shoulder. 'Let's go.'

Pablito's appeared deserted. The swing doors were locked, the tables untenanted and wasps swung threateningly around an overflowing litter bin.

Checking his watch, Alex knocked at the entrance.

The door was opened by Marie, who was wearing a pink velour tracksuit. 'Come in. 'Fraid Den's still sleeping it off. You look a treat, my love. Cup of Nes?'

'Lovely,' said Dawn.

When the coffee was ready they carried it upstairs. Above the bar was a small landing giving on to a bedroom and bathroom, and a sun-baked roof terrace. On a large rectangle of plastic matting at one end of this, naked but for a faded pair of Union Jack underpants, lay Denzil Connolly, snoring. An ashtray had overturned at his side and a nine-tenths-empty bottle of Bell's whisky lay just beyond the reach of his outstretched arm.

'He likes to sleep under the stars,' said Marie. 'I had to put down the matting 'cause the bottles kept smashing and then he'd roll on the pieces in the night. He's a big feller, as you can see.' She folded her arms in a long-suffering gesture. '*Den, love, we've got company.*'

The sleeping figure stirred and the eyes half opened in puffy suspicion. 'Wha' the fuck you . . .' Seeing Alex and Dawn, he closed his eyes again, groaned and writhed like a hippopotamus. 'Wha's fuckin' time?'

'Twelve. And Alex and Dawn are here.'

'Who? Oh, yeah, right. Give us a hand up.'

He struggled to his feet and Marie led him inside. There were unpleasant noises from the bathroom.

By the time they sat down to lunch on the terrace half an hour later, however, Connolly appeared fully recovered. Bullish, even, in his vast shorts and polo shirt. They ate fish and oven chips with vinegar and mushy peas cooked by Marie and drank ice-cold Spanish beer.

'You two should get a place over here,' Connolly said expansively. He winked at Dawn. 'Can you cook, love?'

'You betcha.'

'Well, then. Sorted.'

'It would be nice, wouldn't it, Alex?' said Dawn.

'I'm afraid I'm not quite in the early-retirement league,' said Alex. 'Maybe I could set up a little security outfit, though. Country clubs, golf clubs . . .'

'Protection?' asked Marie brightly.

'Well, I wouldn't put it exactly like that . . .'

The meal, and later the afternoon and early evening, wore on pleasantly enough. Alex had taken a couple more ephedrine tablets at the hotel and so was happy to maintain a steady intake of cold beer. Connolly drank Scotch from the start, occasionally topping up his drink with a splash of mineral water, and by mid-afternoon Alex estimated that the big man had sunk a good third of a bottle. This, he knew, was when you got the best of a heavy drinker: in the five- or six-hour window following recovery. The whisky seemed to have little effect on Connolly other than to cheer him up and he proved a vastly entertaining host, telling story after story about the criminal fraternity who were the bar's main – if not only – clientele. No mention was made of his own exploits, however, nor of his military past.

At four o'clock Marie drove them to San Pedro, where Connolly was a member of a country club. In practice this simply meant a change of bar and Alex tried to moderate his alcoholic intake. Dawn did her rum-and-Coke trick, always managing to have a full glass at her side, but for Alex it was harder. Connolly, he sensed, needed to know that he was in the presence of a kindred spirit. He needed company on the long alcoholic journey that would end in oblivion in the early hours of the morning. He needed to see Alex keep pace with him. This was the price for the information that he had to offer.

At six they returned to El Angel, where Maria prepared the bar for the night's trade and microwaved a frozen chicken-and-pineapple pizza to keep them all going. Despite having drunk more than two-thirds of a bottle of Scotch, Connolly appeared solid as a rock and capable of continuing for ever. Alex, by contrast and despite the ephedrine, was beginning to feel decidedly light-headed. It was a very hot day and he had downed a good dozen beers in half as many hours. Surreptitiously palming a glass and a salt cellar from one of the tables he disappeared into the Gents. There he poured a good teaspoonful of salt into the glass, added water and waited while it dissolved. Gritting his teeth, he took a hefty swig. As soon as the salt hit the back of his throat he retched convulsively, bringing up the last few drinks in a warm gush. Twice more, he forced himself to repeat the exercise. By the end of it he was white-faced and nauseated, but reckoned he had probably bought himself another couple of hours of drinking time.

Soon, the first customers started to arrive and the routine of the night began to repeat itself. Connolly appeared to be in expansive form again, greeting every new arrival with huge enthusiasm, roaring with laughter at their jokes and dispensing drinks liberally.

Alex began to despair of ever getting him alone. Had the big man, he fell to wondering, remembered a single detail of their conversation the night before? Or had he and Dawn simply been two vaguely recognised faces who, for reasons unknown, had turned up to keep him company?

The evening passed in a beery, pissed-up blur. He had drunk himself sober, Alex found, and with every minute that passed his irritation grew. He should have known better than to force through this trip on the word of a known head case like Stevo. All that he had done was compound his failure to protect Widdowes by promising information that, when push came to shove, he couldn't deliver. 'I'm not confident about all of this,' he confided to Dawn at about 11 p.m. 'Last night I was convinced he had something to tell us but now I think he's just stringing me along. That is, if he remembers what I said to him last night, which I'm seriously beginning to doubt.'

'I think you're wrong,' said Dawn. 'I think he's trying to come to a decision. I think we're in the best place we could be right now.'

Alex stared at her, amazed. Her tone was both complicit and intimate. Her usual operational scratchiness was nowhere to be found.

'Trust me, Alex,' she added, turning her back to the bar and placing a proprietorial hand on his shoulder. 'I've seen this sort of thing from informants before. It's a sort of dance they do, like cats walking round and round a place before they sit down.'

'I'm glad you think so,' said Alex, pleasantly conscious of the small pressure of her hand. 'I was going to say that I thought we'd blown several grand of your agency's budget on a wild-goose chase. That you might have some serious explaining to go through when you get back to Thames House. Swanky hotels and bikinis and all the rest of it.'

'Oh, the bikini won't be wasted,' said Dawn airily. 'But take my advice. Let Connolly come to you. He knows why you're here, all right.' She winked. 'Trust me!'

'I do trust you.'

'Well, I'm not sure if I should trust you with all these Costa Crime *femmes fatales*. I've seen a couple of real vampires eyeing you up.'

'Well, then your observational skills are better than mine, girl, because I haven't clocked them.'

She tapped the mobile phone in her jeans-jacket pocket. 'Would it surprise you that there was a call made to the hotel this morning asking to be put through first to your room and then to mine?'

'And?'

'And the caller discovered what he wanted to know, which is that we had the same room number. That I'm really your girlfriend, not some scalp hunter from Box or Special Branch.'

Alex smiled. 'Well, I'm glad we've got that straight.'

She gave him a long, cool glance. 'Will you do something for me?'

'What?' he asked, inhaling the smoky jasmine of her scent.

'If we get anything from Connolly will you go all the way for me?'

He narrowed his eyes. 'What exactly do you . . .'

She leant towards him, took his bottom lip between her teeth and bit him. Not hard, but not softly either. 'Stay on the case. You and me together. As equals. No more bullshit, no more fighting. After all,' she murmured, 'we are supposed to be sleeping together.'

He stared into her level grey eyes, dazed by her closeness.

'So, lovebirds, whassup?'

It was Connolly, swaying in front of them.

And Marie. 'Dawn, love,' she said, 'I've come to borrow you. You know the words to "Stand by Your Man", don't you? We need more chorus members.'

'Ooh, lovely,' trilled Dawn.

Connolly waited until the women had gone, then nodded towards the stairs.

On the roof terrace they drew up chairs. A bottle of Paddy's whiskey, two glasses and Connolly's cigarettes were arranged on a low table. The fat man poured the drinks. 'Joe Meehan, then,' he said, raising his glass. 'What's the story, morning glory?'

'How much do you know about what you were finishing him for?' asked Alex, sipping the whiskey, feeling the dark burn of its descent.

'Officially, nothing. Except that it was clear he was going over the water. And going in very deep, given the attention he was given. And I also knew that he was very good. Almost certainly the best man I ever trained.'

'No one told you anything?'

'No, we were left to draw our own conclusions. I'll tell you something, though. They made a big thing about the secrecy of the operation. It was an RTUable offence even to mention it.'

'Well, notes are being compared now.'

Connolly waited, his glass steady in his hand, immobile.

Alex leant forward. 'You were right about Ireland, obviously. He went in deep, joined the Provies, worked his way up.'

'Brave lad.'

'He was,' agreed Alex. 'Until the whole thing went arse-up. They turned him, Den.'

'Not possible,' said Connolly flatly. 'They never turned that lad, I'd bet the bar on it. He was the best I ever saw. The most committed. He'd never have fallen for all that tinpot Armed Struggle bollocks.'

'They turned him, Den,' Alex repeated. 'He joined Belfast Brigade's Nutting Squad. Made bombs for them. Personally tortured and murdered those FRU blokes – Bledsoe and Wheen.'

'Not possible, mate,' said Connolly again matter-of-factly, tapping the filter of a cigarette on the table and lighting it. 'I just don't believe you.'

'It's true and it's verified. The province's worst nightmare, and the Regiment and Box put him there.'

Connolly shook his head in disbelief. Closed his eyes, briefly. 'So now you're after him, yeah?'

'Look, I don't know what happened over the water, Den, but the man's certainly killing people now. Three in the last couple of months.'

'And so you've been pulled in to kill him.' Connolly took a drag of his cigarette, sipped reflectively at his whiskey and stared out over the sea.

'I need to find him. Put any spin on that you like.'

Connolly shook his head. 'You can fuckin' whistle, chum.'

'Den, mate, you've got a nice set-up here, and you've been good to me and Dawn. But do you really want to spend the rest of your life looking over your shoulder, worrying that some-one's going to grass you up? Worrying that every new customer might have an extradition order and a warrant in his pocket? Armed robbery, Den. Think about it. It pulls down a heavy score.'

From the other man's expression Alex could see that he had thought about it, often. 'Are you threatening me?'

'No. What I'm saying is that I can make that worry disappear. For ever. But I'm going to have to have something very solid to offer in return. If you've nothing to give me I'll disappear, and everything will carry on as it was before.' He emptied his glass and poured himself another. 'I'm not threatening you, Den, I'm just making you an offer. Take it or leave it.'

For several minutes they both stared out at the sea. From below them, in the bar, came the muted sound of singing and laughter.

'There was a thing Joe told me once, about his childhood,' Connolly began abruptly. 'He spent his teens, it must have been, with his dad in the West Country – Dorchester, was it, some-where like that – and every summer they'd go caravanning. Lake District, New Forest, Norfolk Broads, all over. Just the two of them. Now on one of those trips, he told me – can't remember which – his dad parked up the caravan and they set off for a hike across country.

'Usual enough story – they went a bit too far, weren't quite

240

sure of their bearings, weather turned nasty on them, so rather than footslog it back they decided to try and find a bed and breakfast. No B&B for miles, as it turned out, but what they did find was the entrance to a big old house. Deserted, with boarded-up windows and that kind of thing. The place had obviously been secured at some point, but the padlocks and the notices on the gate had been vandalised and it was pouring with rain and in they went. It was getting dark by then, and the plan was to shelter for the night and make tracks back to the caravan park in the morning.

'So anyway they got inside, found a dry corner and got their heads down. The old man's a bit worried by this point, being a law-abiding sort of bloke, but the boy's in heaven: he and his dad are having the adventure of a lifetime! Morning comes and they find that there's not just the house – there's a ruined church and a river and some falling-down cottages and a couple of shops – a whole village. All completely deserted. Obviously been locked away for years.'

'Like Imber, on Salisbury Plain? Or what's that Royal Armoured Corps place in Dorset – Tyneham?'

'Exactly. Just like that. So they have a bit of an explore. The dad's still a bit jumpy but as I say, the boy's having the time of his life. He climbs into the church through a window, jimmies a door open and finds his way down to the crypt. Now I can't remember the exact details but somewhere down there, locked away in boxes or cupboards or something, is all this antique gear.'

'Gear?'

'Covert resistance stuff. Transceivers, morse sets, one-time pads, time-pencil detonators – that sort of thing, all packed away in greaseproof paper. So he takes some bits and pieces up to his dad, who can't believe his eyes, because although the gear's all World War Two vintage it's still in mint condition.'

'A cache in case of enemy invasion,' suggested Alex.

'That's what they eventually figure. And they find other stuff, too, hidden away beneath the other houses. Electrical bits and pieces, radio components, ironmongery, what have you. A real Aladdin's cave for a young lad.'

241

'So how come no one had found this stuff before them?'

'I dunno. I'm guessing that it was because the only other people who'd been near the place for decades had been dossers and tramps. A few bikers, perhaps, and maybe the local satanist coven but . . .'

Alex nodded. 'Go on.'

'Well, the boy's all for helping himself to the gear but the old man puts his foot down. They haven't committed any offence yet, he says – it's not trespassing to walk through an open gate, after all – and he doesn't object to their having a look at all this stuff, but they're not taking it away. So they poke around, Dad explains how it all works, and then they pack it away again, reseal the boxes and off they go, make their way back to wherever they left the caravan.

'Anyway, to cut a long story short, Joe persuades the old boy to shift the caravan to a farm a couple of miles away and they go up to the old house every day – creeping around like a couple of commandos, Joe said, and having a good old sticky beak at all this secret resistance gear. Happiest time he ever knew, Joe says. Best days ever. And when it's time to go home, he tells me, he does a funny thing. He goes and buys his own padlock and chain, and locks the place up properly. Puts up all the old notices again – MOD Property, Strictly no Entrance to the Public and so on.'

'Why does he do that?'

'Not sure. My guess is that it was something to do with deep-freezing the experience. Sealing it away. And also to do with the fact that his dad could have made a lot of money out of flogging the gear without anyone being any the wiser but chose not to out of principle. There were a few of the old Mark III transceivers down there, apparently – the SOE suitcase jobs. They'd have to be worth a few grand apiece now. I suppose Joe didn't want anyone else having them away.'

'You know what I'm going to ask you next, don't you?' said Alex.

'Yeah and I'm afraid I honestly don't know the answer. I really don't. All I can remember is that the place was on the edge

242

of one of the national parks – Peak District, Snowdonia, Dartmoor . . . You must've trained people yourself – you know how you listen to what they say and you don't quite listen, and sometimes you deliberately forget.'

Alex nodded. He knew what the other man meant. Part of you kept friendship at arm's length when you were sending a man into a situation of acute danger. 'So why was he telling you all this?'

'It was a place we went in Wales – an MOD property in Eppynt Forest we were using for an escape and evasion exercise. There was a line of clapped-out cottages there and he said it reminded him of this place he'd once discovered with his dad, and told me the story.' Connolly frowned and blinked, and downed his whiskey. 'There was one other thing. The last time I saw him before the Box people came to take him away, we were up at the camp at Tregaron. We shook hands and I wished him luck, and he smiled and held up a key. At the time I had no idea what he was on about, but . . .'

'You think it was the key to that property?'

Connolly shrugged. 'Who knows?'

'And you can't think of any detail that might point to where this place was?'

'Alex, it was a dozen years ago. Anything was possible in those days and everyone you met had a weird story to tell. These things wash over you.'

'Happiest time he ever knew?' mused Alex.

'Best days ever,' confirmed Connolly and flicked his cigarette butt over the low parapet on to the beach.

'Leaving out Scotland for the moment,' said Alex, thoughtfully kicking off his deck shoes, 'you've got the Lake District, the Peak District, the Cheviots . . .'

They had been back from Pablito's for less than ten minutes. Marie had called them a taxi and they'd left the hire-car at El Angel.

'. . . the North York Moors, the Dales, Kielder . . .'

'Alex,' said Dawn quietly, turning to the open hotel window

and the twinkling lights of the port, 'could you please shut the fuck up and kiss me?'

Alex blinked. A warm tide of ephedrine-tempered alcohol raced through his bloodstream but for some imponderable reason his mind was clear. He stared at her. The Dawn Harding that stood before him now was no relation whatever of the vengeful bitch that he had been so unwillingly paired with in London. This Dawn Harding's face was flushed, her eyes were bright, her posture was challenging and expectant. A warm breeze touched her hair. With great care – this was definitely no time to fall flat on his face – he crossed the room towards her. His hands found the small of her back. Her eyes closed at his touch, her lips parted and she pressed against him, breathing hard. Wanting all of her at once – mouth, eyes, neck, breasts – he practically lifted her off her feet.

'Quick,' she murmured, her fingers in his hair. 'Get me out of these clothes.'

Alex kissed her again until she was gasping and her fingers had left his hair and were scrabbling at the buttons on his shirt.

She tore the last two, but by then he had pulled the tight white top over her head and unsnapped the fierce little Wonderbra. Her breasts were pale, their upper curves touched by a slight pinkness from the morning's sun and very faintly damp. She tasted of sweat and smoke.

Falling to his knees, he forced himself to slow down, explored her stomach with his mouth, ran the tip of his tongue down the line of tiny translucent hairs that descended towards the gilt stud of her jeans. Popping the stud, he eased down the zipper and began to pull down the jeans.

They stuck. He pulled again and she staggered, giggled drunkenly, and fell on to the bed with her legs in the air and the white Versace jeans around her knees. Taking one of the leg-ends, he tried to pull it over her feet. 'They're too bloody tight,' he breathed, swaying.

'Come on, Captain,' she said, looking up at him archly. 'If you can take down a Scud launch site behind enemy lines, surely you can manage my jeans in a hotel bedroom!'

Bracing his foot against the edge of the bed, Alex gave an extra-hard tug. They jeans came off in a rush and he fell heavily backwards on to his stitched thigh. The pain was intense and for a moment he lay there on the floor in his own half-undone trousers, swearing and laughing.

After a moment Dawn peered over the edge of the bed and saw the blood rapidly beading through the cotton. Lowering herself to Alex's side, she eased the trousers off and then hurried to the bathroom for cotton wool and surgical spirit. 'That's rather blown the romantic mood, hasn't it?' she murmured, pressing a swab to the wound. 'Still, while I'm down here I might as well have a look at the rest of the damage.'

As she poured and dabbed, Alex said nothing. The surgical spirit was cold against his skin. The sway of her small, neat breasts over his body proved a very effective anaesthetic.

He lay there as she eased off the dressings on his face and arm. He had been right in his early guess that a sensuous body lay beneath all that formal puritan grey. Her palely curvaceous form was overlaid with the faint musculature of one who exercised when there was nothing better to do with her time, but not otherwise. Her stomach was flat but soft, tapering towards the dark-blonde scribble of her pubic hair.

To tend to his arm she hunkered down over his hand. As bees to honey – as she must have known they would – his fingers moved upwards to meet her. She closed her eyes, pressed herself briefly and slickly against his palm, then continued in a businesslike way with her ministrations. 'Wait,' she told him a moment later. 'I'm concentrating.'

'So am I!'

'Let me get these bandages off – I'm not into sex with Egyptian mummies.'

To remove the dressings from his face, she sat astride him so that Alex could feel the damp heat of her crotch against his chest. But her expression was serious, and when he reached for her breasts she frowned absently and slapped his hands back down to his chest. 'I hope you don't behave like this with all those army nurses.'

245

'We don't get nurses in the SAS,' breathed Alex. 'We get some sweaty corporal called Dave or Ginge.'

'I told you to leave them alone. I'm going to have to be very rough with you if you don't.'

'I've been roughed up by experts.' Alex grinned. 'I can take it.'

A moment later she straddled him and lowered herself on to him. For a moment she was still, then he felt a series of hot, updrawing waves. Nothing mattered except the absolute intensity of the feeling that – for all their antagonism – he knew they shared at that moment. And then, with a desperate dying cry which might have come from either or both of them, it was over and Dawn gently subsided on top of him. She seemed very young – almost childlike with her scrubbed face and sleepy eyes. 'That was fun,' she murmured. 'Wasn't it?'

'It beats arguing.'

She settled herself against his shoulder. 'Please, will you be nice to me from now on?' she asked. 'I mean really, really nice?'

'I promise,' murmured Alex.

'And will you kill for me?'

He looked at her.

She wrinkled her nose at him and grinned. 'Well?' she asked. 'Will you?'

He smiled. 'OK.'

TWENTY-THREE

'OK,' said Angela Fenwick. 'The position is this . . .'

It was 10.30 a.m., and Alex and Dawn were seated with the deputy director in her office. Florence Nightingale looked benignly down from the walls; the cafetiere steamed on the table between them.

Despite her overnight flight from Washington Fenwick looked fresh, groomed and alert. Alex and Dawn, by contrast, who had taken an 8 a.m. flight from Malaga, were looking rather less impressive. Alex, in particular, had a raging thirst and a cracking headache that reminded him of its presence with every step that he took. The knife cuts, well on the mend now, were itching crazily.

Dawn, for her part, was paler and quieter than usual. They had not discussed the events of the night before – their departure from the hotel to the airport had been a hurried one – nor had her behaviour towards him changed greatly. But there had been little things. In the queue for Customs she had turned to him and pressed her face into his shoulder. In the taxi from Heathrow she had settled herself, catlike, beneath his arm. There was a complicity between them.

And for all that he was feeling lousy, the time spent with Dawn – and the few hours spent in bed with her – had reshaped things in Alex's mind. He didn't want to back out now, he wanted to go all the way, whatever the cost. He wanted to see the Watchman dead at his feet.

And it was possible – more than possible. Meehan had seemed uncatchable but he wasn't uncatchable. He was a man and men sooner or later made mistakes.

Confiding his childhood memories to Denzil Connolly had been Meehan's first mistake and sparing Alex's life had been his second.

'We got the analysis of those Meehan tissue samples back yesterday evening from the Forensic Science Service labs,' Fenwick continued. 'And they told us something rather interesting.'

She opened her briefcase and removed a paper. 'The hair that Captain Temple extracted for us has been confirmed as Meehan's against DNA samples from the other crime scenes, and it showed abnormally high medium-term traces of a substance known as perchloroethylene. Known as PCE, perchloroethylene is a solvent used in the tanning process. Due to its high toxicity – I won't bother you with the details – PCE is on the European Community's black list of chemicals whose use is strictly controlled. In this country, however – never a front-runner in environmental terms – these controls are regularly ignored by industry and run-off from tanneries into rivers is often accompanied by excess PCE levels.

'Now we've been on to the various ministries overnight, and we've talked to the National Rivers Authority and all the water companies this morning, and between them they've provided us with a list of nine tanneries from which high levels of PCE run-off have been . . .'

There was a knock at the door, and a hurried entrance by a young man holding a folded document and a book. 'Excuse me, ma'am,' he said, handing the articles to her. 'These have just been couriered over from Room 1129 at the MOD.'

'Excellent,' said the deputy director. 'Thank you.' She glanced at the document – a map, as it turned out. 'Dawn, would you be so good?'

Taking the map, Dawn rose from her seat and pinned it out on the display board opposite them. It was a map of England and Wales, flecked with larger and smaller areas of red.

'Following your call early this morning about the possibility of our man holing up at an old MOD property,' said Fenwick, 'I spoke to a couple of people in Whitehall. This map apparently shows everything, large and small, that they own. Quite a portfolio, isn't it? Billions of pounds' worth of land.'

Alex stared at the map, daunted by the sheer scale and number of the holdings. There had to be several hundred of them.

'If we could add the tanneries, please, Dawn,' said Fenwick, handing the younger woman a printed list.

Dawn stared at it, and reached for the first black mapping pin. 'Hurley, Staffordshire,' she read out. 'On the River Blithe.'

And the second: 'Mynydd, Powys, on the Afon Honddu.'

And the third: 'Beeston, Lancs on the River Douglas.'

She continued to the end of the list.

She stood back and the three of them stared at the map. The pins were spread erratically over the country, with a slight cluster detectable between Birmingham, Coventry and Northampton.

'From what the FSS people say,' Fenwick went on, glancing down at the report, 'PCEs in this sort of concentration would only to be encountered within a few miles of source. So in the case of somewhere like Hurley, for example, we don't have to follow the river system seventy miles across country to the coast. We can just draw a circle of a few miles' diameter around the plant. The FSS figure was three miles, so let's say six to be on the safe side. Any of these locations strike anyone as the sort of area you might take your son on a caravanning holiday?'

'The mid-Wales one looks good,' said Alex. 'So does the north Yorkshire and the Dartmoor. Any of those three, definitely.'

Fenwick nodded. 'Dawn, take all the data down to the computer people. We need Ordnance Survey printouts of the tannery areas, with all suitable MOD properties highlighted. It's almost certainly safe to eliminate airfields, working bases et cetera – the details of the various properties seem to be listed in this book they sent over.'

Dawn nodded briskly and gathered up the materials.

When she had gone Fenwick turned enquiringly to Alex. 'Everything healing satisfactorily? I understand you put up quite a fight in poor George's defence.'

'The Watchman did what he came to do,' said Alex shortly.

Fenwick pursed her lips and looped an errant gunmetal tress behind one ear. She was a handsome woman, Alex thought, if a bit on the cold side. Those blue eyes could freeze you to the bone in seconds. 'It doesn't take a Nobel prize winner to work out that the next in line for Mr Meehan's attentions is myself,' she said with a slight smile.

'I'm afraid it looks that way,' Alex agreed. 'What precautions are you taking?'

'As few as possible, I'm afraid. I have to continue doing my job and I have to continue to be seen to do it.'

'Have you moved house? Varied your routine at all?'

'There's no point, I'm afraid. I live as if expecting an assassin as it is and I have done ever since I inherited the Northern Ireland desk. I know you have your doubts about some of our people, Captain Temple, but I assure you the arrangements in place are good. Apart from anything else I have to receive ministers and diplomatic visitors and, well, all sorts of people. I can't just up sticks and move to some suburban safe house.'

'Bet you wish you could at times,' said Alex. The image flashed into his mind of Fenwick lying in a pool of blood with a nail through her head. She was certainly keeping up appearances, he thought. Perhaps she's worried that if she looks rattled or fails to show up for work she could lose out on the directorship.

'Perhaps I do, Captain Temple.' Fenwick folded her hands in her lap for a moment, then one of the phones on her desk started flashing, and she marched over and picked it up.

'I'll wait outside,' said Alex and left the office.

A minute later Dawn reappeared in the ante-room. In a couple of sentences Alex told her of his concerns for her boss's safety.

'She lives in a private block in a gated estate in Chelsea,' said

250

Dawn. 'It's one of the most secure addresses in London. There's CCTV everywhere, a security guard on the entrance, passes to get in and out, everything. No one – no window cleaner, no visitor, no one – gets within fifty yards of the building without security clearance. The whole place is fully modified for at-risk personnel – one-way windows, departure from an underground car park, the police a couple of minutes away in Lucan Place . . .'

'He'll be checking the place out,' said Alex. 'Probably even as we speak.'

'I know,' said Dawn. 'And that's why we're checking out anyone who goes near it and pulling in anyone who can't be personally vouched for by a resident or security staff member. Believe me, the job is being done and done properly.'

'Does she live alone?'

'Drop it, Alex, please,' Dawn said sharply. 'Our job now is to find the wasp's nest – the place he always returns to – and kill him there.'

He nodded. 'OK. Just wanted to . . .'

'I know. Let's go back in.'

For a couple of minutes Dawn's fingers raced over one of the keyboards on Angela Fenwick's desk and the large flat-screen display on the wall opposite them flickered into life.

First, an enlarged area of Ordnance Survey map came up, with the village of Hurley, Staffordshire at its centre.

'No National Park or particular tourist area nearby,' said Dawn. 'There's Blithfield Reservoir, but I don't think Meehan Senior would have driven a caravan halfway across the country to see that. Otherwise, the area on the screen is at the central point of a square formed by Stoke, Derby, Wolverhampton and Telford. Not high on the list of tourist must-sees, I'd say.' She struck the keyboard and two small areas of red appeared on the screen. 'Vis-à-vis suitably sized MOD properties in the area, we've got an RAF storage facility here near Yoxall and an old TA depot outside Colton but neither of them is less than a couple of miles from the River Blithe.' She looked up at Alex. 'I'm assuming that the conclusion we're drawing is that he is staying beside the river and using it for drinking water, rather than gathering water from the river and drinking it somewhere else.'

Alex nodded. 'He's probably got some sort of filtration system, but obviously nothing too sophisticated. Could well be using standard issue Puritabs. In the UK you tend to allow for water-borne bacteria and pesticides but not for heavy-duty chemical toxins like these PCEs or whatever they're called. And yeah, he'll definitely be holed up somewhere with its own water source rather than transporting a heavy canteen several miles across country. He'll be on the river itself – we know he likes them.'

Angela Fenwick nodded grimly. 'Next possibility?'

Another section of map flashed up.

'Mynydd, Powys. Much more deserted, obviously. Area of outstanding natural beauty and definite tourist area in the summer months. Good for fishing, too, and we know Meehan and son enjoyed that. But no MOD properties nearby. The army and marines pass through the place pretty regularly on exercise but we don't actually own anything in the catchment area at all. Not so much as a Nissen hut on the Afon Honddhu.'

'Go on,' said Angela Fenwick.

'Beeston, Lancashire, on the Douglas, halfway between Wigan and Southport. No MOD facility on or near the river. Nothing touristy about the area, particularly.'

'Go on.'

They went through all nine of them. For Alex's money there was one definite front runner – a small tanning plant on a stream named the Hamble, which ran off Black Down on the western boundary of Dartmoor. This was the one he would have chosen – this or the Mynydd one in Wales. Both were remote but served with metalled roads; both were close to popular tourist destinations; both offered vast areas of wild country in which, if need be, an experienced soldier could survive for weeks. 'It'll be one of the two, I'm sure of it,' he said.

'We've got nothing registered to the MOD on either river,' said Dawn doubtfully.

'Suppose the MOD has recently sold the property,' suggested Alex. 'For the last hour we've been looking for MOD properties and for a small village with a church, because we know that Meehan specifically mentioned the existence of a church. But if the property was classified secret, at some point, and so not marked on any map, and was recently sold . . .'

Fenwick nodded. 'Yes, that's true. There's no reason to suppose that it's marked on current maps – I can't believe the MOD bothers to inform Ordnance Survey whenever it sells and declassifies property. And of course it wouldn't be included in the MOD's current portfolio either.'

'From Meehan's story,' said Dawn, 'doesn't it sound as if this place, or at least its original purpose, has been forgotten? That nobody really knows why it was classified in the first place? It can't have been set up much later than 1940 and there's been a lot of inter-departmental paper shuffling since then.'

Fenwick reached for a phone, pressed the scramble button and dialled a number. 'Is that 1129? Jonathan? Angela Fenwick here . . . Yes, bless you for that, Jonathan. Look, I want you to do something further for me. Go back five years and check for top-security-rated but untenanted MOD properties abutting the following rivers and within five miles downstream of the following grid references. Got a pencil?' As Dawn scrolled back through the maps, Fenwick read out the tannery locations. 'And if five years doesn't throw anything up,' she continued calmly, 'then try ten and then fifteen . . . Yes, soonest, please. Ring me back the moment you find anything.'

Replacing the phone, she turned to the others. 'With a bit of luck he won't be too long,' she said. 'Shall we call up for some more coffee and some sandwiches?'

In the event, they finished the sandwiches before the call from Room 1129 came in. As she listened, Fenwick took notes. 'And that's the only one?' she concluded. 'Right. I'm grateful. Thank you.' She turned to Dawn. 'Can you get the Hamble map back up?'

Alex felt a sharp prickle of excitement.

From her chair, Fenwick aimed a red laser pointer at the screen display. 'Right,' she said. 'A recent source of per-chloroethylene pollution is this building here – a small tanning plant presently engaged in litigation with the National Rivers Authority. One and a half miles downstream of the plant is Black Down House and its outbuildings, including the shell of a church, standing on some forty acres of land. Evacuated in August 1940 by order of the War Office for reasons pertaining to national security and later classified as a secret location under the Act in relation to Operation Gladio. For the last eighteen months, following sale by auction, Black Down House and its outbuildings have been the property of Liskeard Holdings, an Exeter-based property development company. Their present condition is unknown.'

The three of them looked at each other.

'What was Operation Gladio?' asked Alex.

'An anti-communist stay-behind network set up immediately after the war by SOE and MI6, and funded by the CIA. To be activated in the event of a Soviet invasion. The idea was that agents should be put in place and materials hidden at secret locations so that any Western European country that was rolled over would be in a position to resist, communicate with the outside world et cetera.'

'And Black Down House was one of those locations?'

'So it seems,' said Fenwick.

'So all that kit Meehan found as a kid has sat there for fifty years, waiting for an invasion that never came?'

'Longer, probably. Britain established a stay-behind force as early as 1940 in case of German invasion. After the war a lot of the facilities were simply reassigned. Everything to do with Gladio and the stay-behind units has been classified top secret ever since, although bits and pieces have come out, particularly in Italy. Returning to the present day, however, it looks as if we might have found our man's base. Congratulations, captain.'

'How do you want to handle it?' asked Dawn.

'I think I should just get down there as soon as possible,' said Alex. 'Stake the place out, try and identify him, and, uh, kill him, basically.'

'Killing him would be best,' confirmed Angela Fenwick.

TWENTY-FOUR

Dawn drove. They were carrying too much unusual baggage, she insisted, for them to risk being picked up for speeding. And Alex, sooner or later, would nudge the car up to 80 or 90 mph. It was in his nature.

Alex shrugged and sat back, and with the Range Rover tucked well into the slow lane, they made their steady way westwards. Their purpose, Alex had reluctantly agreed with Angela Fenwick, was to recce the area and determine their next step. There were to be no cowboy heroics or one-man initiatives as there had been at Longwater Lodge. If further manpower was needed then MI5 would provide it. And with this Alex had had to content himself. On his right he could see Stonehenge, like an assembly of frozen NAAFI chips.

'I'm beginning to enjoy our little trips away together,' said Dawn.

Alex squeezed her thigh. 'This might not be quite the honeymoon that Spain was,' he warned her. 'Worst-case scenario we could run into a contact. Have you had any time on the range recently?'

'Just the odd twenty-five rounds at lunchtime,' she answered. 'And then mostly for fun. I did my time on a watcher team, though, and I can't imagine surveillance has changed much since then.'

'So what weapon did you draw this morning?'

'A Walther PPK. Call me old-fashioned but . . .'

Alex was surprised. The PPK was a highly serviceable weapon but famously unforgiving in the hands of a beginner. As a straight blow-back pistol it had a very stiff recoil spring and a

256

pretty snappy perceived recoil as well. 'You don't have any trouble racking the slide?' he asked her. 'Or working the double action trigger?'

'I've got nice strong fingers,' she replied, flexing them on the steering wheel. She glanced at him sideways and he smiled.

Turning, he cast an eye over the rear of the vehicle. He had tried to think of everything and if in doubt he had overspecified. There were sleeping bags, a stuff sack of spare clothing, dry boots, maps, compasses, binoculars and a jumble of other articles that a couple on a hiking holiday might carry with them. Mounted on a steel frame on the back of the Range Rover was a trail bike. It hadn't occurred to Alex to drive a motorcycle down to Dartmoor, but the moment he saw it in the MI5 vehicle pool he realised just how useful it might prove in that terrain. For that reason two sets of motocross goggles and helmets lay among the hiking gear.

There were also a handful of rather less common items: two pairs of night-vision goggles for a start, and a box each of 9mm and .38 hollow-point rounds. Had the car been stopped and searched by the police there would certainly have been a raised eyebrow or two.

'When we get there,' said Alex, 'I want you to promise to do what I say. If I say pull back to the vehicle, for example, I want you to do just that, OK? No arguments, no bullshit.'

'Fine by me. Just run through the schedule.'

'We'll do a single pass past the place, see what we can see. Then push on for a couple of miles and park up – I've chosen somewhere on the 1:15,000 map – a car park by a transport café. Then we'll cut back across country – there's a streamside path that should take us to the boundary of the estate – work our way round, and see what there is to be seen.'

'You think we'll find him?'

'Who knows what we'll find. Or how long we'll have to wait.'

'This is just a recce, right? You're cool with that?'

'Just a recce,' Alex confirmed.

'On the other hand, if you get him bang to rights . . .'

257

'You don't get men like Meehan "bang to rights",' said Alex flatly.

'Negative thought leads to negative action,' said Dawn.

'Spare me the fucking zen, Harding.' He intertwined and cracked his knuckles. The slow drip of adrenalin into his system had begun. 'Don't worry, you'll get a corpse, one way or another.'

Two and a half hours later they were driving north from Tavistock across the western plain of Dartmoor Forest. The roads were narrower now, and Dawn edged the Range Rover carefully between high banks edged with fern, hawthorn and bracken as a solitary kestrel pinwheeled above them. At intervals, as the banks fell away, a vast and baleful reach of heather revealed itself.

'Follow the sign for North Brent Tor,' said Alex, 'and then for either Chilford or Hamble.'

To their left a series of rocky outcrops stood like iron teeth against the sky. This was the Watchman's terrain, Alex was sure of it.

'We should pass Black Down House on our right any minute now,' said Alex. 'Take it as slowly as you can without looking suspicious.'

They drove for ten minutes down a side lane which was little more than a farm track. Not many people came down here, Alex reflected, noting the lane's poorly maintained surface and overgrown verges.

And there the house finally was, set well back from the road, its windows boarded and its decades-old paintwork weather-streaked and flaking. Beyond it the ground fell away sharply towards the river. There was no sign of any other buildings. Nor, apart from a temporary steel barrier which had been erected in front of the former gateway, was there any indication that the property had been developed in any way since its sale. No structural supports had been erected, and the overgrown trees and bushes surrounding the building had clearly been untouched for years. The air of neglect surrounding the place was palpable.

'Not the most inviting place in the world,' said Dawn as the property slid from view.

'I think that's rather the point,' Alex observed. 'Like the fact that you can't see much of it from the road. There's a church and several outbuildings down there somewhere, plus twenty-odd acres of woodland.'

'No vehicle anywhere near it.'

'No. Which makes me think he might not be around. After all, he'd have no particular reason to to hide it.'

'But it does beg the question as to where the hell he is,' said Dawn worriedly.

'First things first,' said Alex. 'If we're going to recce the place I'd much rather he wasn't around. As long as your boss goes straight from Thames House to the Chelsea flat she should be safe enough – assuming the security's everything you say it is.'

Five minutes later they parked the Range Rover on the cinder forecourt of the Cabin Café. For appearance's sake they went in for a cup of tea and a slice of sponge cake. There were several other people in there, the majority of them wearing brightly coloured anoraks and carrying map cases.

Alex's and Dawn's appearance, by contrast, was decidedly sombre. Alex was wearing grey wind-proof trousers and an old combat smock; Dawn had on black jeans and a lightweight forest-green jacket, and her hair was concealed beneath an army surplus jungle hat. Both were wearing nondescript hiking boots.

When they had paid, Alex and Dawn began to walk back up the road in the direction from which they had come. Both were carrying rucksacks and Alex now had a pair of high-powered binoculars round his neck. Once out of sight of the café, the pair cut left-handed into a field and descended the few hundred brambled yards to the river.

Or to the stream, for the Hamble was hardly a river. Not at this time of year, anyway. Such water as it contained tumbled quietly from pool to shallow pool, brimmed darkly for a moment and hurried on. A sheep path ran above it, disappearing at intervals but soon reprising its dry erratic track. Hanks of wool hung from a barbed-wire fence.

They slid down the nettled bank to the water and for twenty minutes Alex set a fast pace up the stream bed. The day was a warm one, despite the fact that afternoon was swiftly becoming evening, and soon they were both sweating. Alex's thigh swiftly began to throb where the stitches pulled at the wound, but he consigned the discomfort to a distant part of his mind.

They covered the ground fast. The banks of the stream were eight or nine feet high and the foliage had clearly not been cut back for years, allowing them to stay well-concealed from any watching eyes. Despite the absence of any vehicle, Alex was not convinced that the Black Down estate was unoccupied and a careful study of a large-scale map had convinced him that this was the safest approach. Meehan could not watch the entire half-mile perimeter, he could only patrol it, and Alex suspected that he slept through the day.

The estate, they soon discovered, was surrounded by a chain-link fence topped with razor wire. This was not new – long streaks of rust discoloured the galvanised metal – but at ten feet high it was still effective enough. The banks flattened at the point the stream met the perimeter, so that the lowest chain-linked strands went to within inches of the stream bed. The fence continued in both directions and there was every reason to suppose that it surrounded the estate entirely. It was clearly not proof against determined assault, but it would undoubtedly have deterred the curious over the years.

Alex and Dawn crouched in the shadows beneath the bank.

'What d'you reckon?' asked Dawn.

'I reckon I'm going to have to go in underneath it,' Alex answered.

Removing his rucksack, he took out a lightweight folding shovel and began digging in the stream. After ten hard minutes, and having hauled out several large rocks by hand, he had cleared a twelve-inch space beneath the lowest strands of the fence and the stream bed.

'OK, all clear?'

They looked around them and Alex quickly undressed. Naked, he burrowed up the stream bed and under the fence.

260

The water was surprisingly cold. When he was through Dawn wrapped his clothes in a bin liner and threw them to him over the fence. The other kit followed. 'Remind me to take those stitches out,' she hissed as Alex re-dressed.

Quickly, they ran through their contingency plans. She would wait where she was and call him on his mobile if there was anything to report, and he would attempt a search of the Black Down estate. Switching his mobile to vibrate, he melted into the woods. His progress was slow. He moved in total silence, continuously scanning the ground in front of him for trip wires and booby traps, and the landscape as a whole for any sign of surveillance.

Soon he was at the edge of the woods and from a well-concealed position among a patch of overgrown thorn bushes was able to rake the area with his binoculars. There was no sign of life and as far as he could see the area of tall grass, nettles and cow-parsley in front of him was untrodden.

Slowly, and with infinite care, he moved from the cover of the woods into the shadowed stream-bed. The water was deeper here and he was soon soaked to the waist. It wasn't the approach route he would have chosen, given a choice, but unlike the nettle-choked field, the exposed rocks would leave no trace of his passing. The day was still warm. The sugar in the tea that he had drunk had made him thirsty and with a flash of irritation Alex realised that he had not filled his canteen. Drinking the stream water, as they had discovered from the forensic samples, was probably inadvisable.

Rounding a corner he saw the church. It had a square tower and a blankly ruined look. Where there had once been windows there were now gaps around which, at some long-ago point, mortar had been roughly trowelled. At one time a road had led past the main house and down alongside the river. The church and its small graveyard lay at the end of this road, or what remained of it. Trees and bushes had forced their way through the dried-out surface and long-unchecked vegetation pressed from both sides. Beyond the church was a line of dilapidated single-storey dwellings.

Having noted the layout of the place, Alex drew himself back into invisibility beneath an overhanging alder bush. With his binoculars he used the slowly failing light to scour the area around the church and then rang Dawn. 'I'm in position,' he murmured. 'Since I've got no idea where our man sleeps or even if he's here, I'm just going to hang back and sit tight. How are you?'

'OK. Nothing to report here.'

Where would Meehan stay, Alex wondered. In the house? In the church? In the crypt, underground? Did the house have cellars? Wherever it was, it would be somewhere where he would have plenty of warning of any arrivals.

By the property's new owners, for example. Angela Fenwick had discovered that Liskeard Holdings were having trouble securing planning permission for the hotel and conference complex that they hoped to build on the site, and that was why the property remained in its ruined state. But presumably there had been a fair amount of coming and going by architects and others.

Alex reasoned that Meehan probably slept and concealed himself somewhere beneath the church. The chances were that if the house had a cellar it would be damp and uncomfortable, and subject to occasional visits – the church was much older and much more securely built. Church crypts were stone-walled. They were usually dry.

At 8 p.m. Dawn rang. 'Still waiting for Godot?' she asked.

'Yup, you?'

'The light's almost gone, as you can see. I was thinking I should get back to the Range Rover. Twitchers don't twitch in the dark.'

'OK. Be in touch.'

Two hours later his thigh was itching unbearably and his back aching from immobility. How many hours have I spent lying up like this, he wondered. A hundred? More? And how many times has the whole thing ended in failure, in merely getting up and going back to base?

He was going to have to make a decision, sooner or later,

about whether to risk taking a closer look at things. Was Meehan due back tonight? Was he already there? Was he, at this minute, watching Alex – the hunted turned hunter?

Alex shuddered, both at the thought of being scoped out by Meehan and at the memory of the former agent's terrifying strength.

No, he thought. *I'll go in now.*

Slowly he eased himself from cover and continued the silent passage upstream that he had started hours earlier. In his pocket, fully loaded, was the Glock.

Soon, the house was in view above him. The ruins of a flight of steps led down from the road fronting the house to the stream at the bottom of the slope. If he started to climb, he would greatly increase the chance of being spotted if Meehan was in residence. If he stayed where he was, however, he would never learn anything.

A step at a time, he moved up the slope. With the passage of years and neglect, the brickwork steps had cracked and he could feel their uneasy shift beneath his feet. Finally he reached the top and the front door. Was it locked? No, the lock had been kicked in and the flaking door swung open easily. Glock in one hand, Maglite torch in the other, Alex went in. He was in a front hall, a place of rotting floorboards, fallen masonry and the smell of dead animals. Fag ends and empty bottles greyed with plaster dust lay about and there was an old coat in the fireplace. Anything of any conceivable value had been stripped away – there was nothing there except walls and floor.

Taking a pair of thick socks from his rucksack, Alex pulled them over his boots. They would muffle the crunching sound of his movements and help conceal the tracks of his Danner boots on the floor. Quickly he moved from room to room on the ground floor, but found nothing. A few empty tins and a gutted mattress lay around, but there was no sign that the place had been occupied by anyone other than tramps and vagrants – and that a long time ago. There was no cellar.

Upstairs the story was the same: gutted rooms, fallen plaster-work and the darkness of the boarded-over windows. At some point a pigeon had trapped itself in there and its half-feathered skeleton lay on a bedroom mantelpiece.

Where had Meehan and his father slept that night all those years ago? Wherever it was, there was no sign that he had bothered with the place since.

Outside, it was now quite dark. Pulling on his night-vision goggles so that the scene leapt into eerie green daylight, Alex descended the slope again. At his ear was the tiny mosquito whine of the goggles' battery-powered electronics.

Carefully he made his way towards the dilapidated cottages. As with the church, a rough attempt had been made to make these safe by slapping mortar around the gaps where there had once been windows. One of them – the only one with an intact roof – seemed to have been designated a store of some kind, and its back room proved to be packed with ancient cardboard boxes containing electrical and woodworking items. Raising the goggles and flicking a pen torch beam on these, Alex identified dark-brown bakelite transformers and junction boxes, rows of dusty radio valves, plaited electrical flex, fibrous early Rawlplugs and other items whose use he could only guess at.

And nails, of course. From half-inch to six-inch. Alex pocketed a couple for the forensics team, flicked off the pen torch, lowered the goggles and went outside again.

The mobile throbbed against his thigh.

'You OK?' asked Dawn.

'Looking around,' murmured Alex. 'No sign of him yet. This is definitely the place, though – I've found a stack of those old nails. You OK?'

'Fine. Take care.'

'Sure.'

He slipped the phone back into his pocket and moved towards the pale bulk of the church. This time the door was locked. Alex considered climbing in through a window, dismissed the idea as too likely to attract attention and reached into one of the chest pockets of his smock.

It was a couple of years since he'd done the lock-picking refresher course at Tregaron and the goggles didn't help, but

Alex's movements were reasonably confident as he inserted a pick into the church door. The lock was a standard pin-tumbler type and it was no more than a few minutes before the door swung inwards.

Pocketing the pick and the torque wrench in favour of the Glock, Alex scanned the place. As in the house, anything of any value as architectural salvage had been removed and above him only a few roof beams remained. Broken tiles and mounds of pigeon shit littered the stone floor.

The door was to one side, low and arched. Again, it was locked, and this lock was no high street Yale. It took Alex almost half an hour of delicate work with the spring-steel pick to solve all the pins and bring them to the shear line, and he breathed a heartfelt sigh of relief when he felt the plug's smooth rotation beneath his torque wrench.

Beyond the door was a descending spiral staircase. The stone treads felt worn beneath Alex's soles as he crept downwards, peering before him through the goggles. There was very little ambient light for them to magnify and he seemed to be descending into a dim green haze.

The crypt appeared to be empty but for a wooden bier of the type once used in funerals. Lifting the goggles, Alex risked a quick sweep with the Maglite torch, only to have his initial observation confirmed. There was nothing else – no chests, no cupboards, no sign of habitation – merely walls and floors carved with memorial inscriptions and a cool stone emptiness. Nor were there any doors to further chambers.

Think, Alex told himself. *Go back to basics.* Meehan told Connolly that the equipment he found was in the church. The Operation Gladio hiding place had to be proof against sophisticated enemy search teams and a locked door would have constituted no protection whatever against a determined GRU or Spetznaz outfit.

Once again, he searched the place with his torch, running its beam over the walls and floors, and the inset stone tablets with their florid carvings.

He almost missed it, and he would never have found it had

he not known that it had to be there somewhere. A memorial brass inlaid into the floor in one corner of the room. Worn, as if by the passage of many feet, and inscribed 'To the memory of Samuel Calvert, born 1758, laid to rest 1825. My sword, I shall give to him that shall succeed me in my pilgrimage.'

Gladio, thought Alex. The word means a sword, doesn't it?

The brass lifted with a knife tip. Beneath, supporting it, was a heavy iron grille. And beneath the grille were steps.

TWENTY-FIVE

Alarm screamed in Alex's mind. He was getting himself deeper and deeper into a situation from which retreat was impossible.

His plan, to which Angela Fenwick had agreed, had been that he should make an initial sortie into the property to search for evidence of Meehan's presence and then pull back, so that an MI5 team could replace him. If Alex encountered Meehan while undertaking his recce, however, he was to kill him on sight. From Fenwick's point of view, Alex knew, this would be the ideal outcome. No more Watchman, no more complex and expensive deployment of Service personnel, no more threat to herself or to her ambitions.

And to be honest, thought Alex, it would suit him too. It would balance the books for George Widdowes' death. There was also the undeniable truth that a happy Angela Fenwick meant a happy Bill Leonard, and a happy Bill Leonard could mean promotion.

Plus, of course, the world would be rid of a psychopathic murderer. If Meehan were waiting in the darkness at the bottom of those steps, or if he were to return to the church right now, Alex would be trapped. Better by far to pull back, to get Fenwick to send reinforcements.

Pulling out his mobile he tried punching in Dawn's number. The sudden beep indicating that there was no signal strength made him jump and his heart race, and he realised just how on edge he was.

Meehan could come back at any moment.

Pulling the grille and the brass plate back into place from below – the gaps in the grille had deliberately been made wide

267

enough to allow this – Alex began to descend the steps. The room at the bottom, he saw with a quick, relieved sweep of the goggles, had no human occupant. It was a burial chamber and the rectangular stone slab at its centre had probably once supported a tomb.

But not now. Now the walls were piled deep and high with green-sprayed steel cases whose contents, according to the white stencilled legends on their sides, included time pencils and other varieties of detonator, delay fuses, carborundum grease, pocket incendiaries, Eureka beacons, S-Phones, Mk III Transceivers, Welrod pistols and an assortment of grenades and mines. It was a far more comprehensive list than Connolly had described, thought Alex, staring for a wondering moment at the scores of cases. Overcome by curiosity, he prised open the lid of a case marked 'Grenades – Gammon type'.

Inside, neatly packed, were a dozen bizarre-looking appliances, each consisting of a bakelite fuse housing and a cotton bag. The idea, Alex assumed, was that you filled the bag with plastic explosive – maybe chucking in a handful of nuts and bolts for good measure – and lobbed the whole thing into the middle of an enemy patrol. Very nasty indeed.

The transceivers packed into their little leather suitcases, by contrast, were objects of great fascination, with their miniaturised sockets and grilles and dials. If I get through this in one piece, thought Alex, I'm coming back for a few of these, and perhaps a couple of the Welrods too. Take them up to Sotheby's or Christie's . . .

This sub-crypt, it was clear, was where Meehan lived. At one end of the room were cardboard boxes containing new own-brand supermarket tins – soups, beans, spaghetti, peas – chocolate bars, and packet foods. A packing case held fresh oranges, potatoes and green vegetables. No onions, probably because of the strong smell they gave off while cooking. Among the food was a small plastic rubbish bag containing crushed tins, sweet papers, withered orange peel and a brown apple core. The last two looked less than forty-eight hours old.

There was also a plastic water-purification system, a tiny

MSR stove and fuel bottles, a pair of mess tins, plastic cutlery, a comprehensive medical kit – the suture-set recently used, Alex noted – and a washbag. In the corner of the room above this area a fresh-air duct led upwards into the darkness, presumably voiding behind some decorative element on the tower.

At the other end of the chamber, folded neatly on the floor, were Meehan's clothes – nondescript camping-store items for the most part, and a pair of worn cordura hiking boots. From one of these an inexpensive Suunto compass trailed a para-cord lanyard.

On the slab, weighed down at each corner, was a good-quality photocopy of an architectural blueprint. The building in question was entitled Powys Court (Block 2), Oakley Street, London SW3. A roll of similar blueprints lay to one side and a flash of the Maglite served to confirm that all related to the same building.

What was it that Dawn had said about Angela Fenwick's flat? A private block? In a gated estate? One of the most secure addresses in London?

Heart pounding, Alex scanned the place, felt through the modest pile of clothing. There was no sign of any weaponry – Meehan had it all with him. He tried thumbing Dawn's number on his mobile but couldn't get a signal.

Shit!

Racing up the steps, he hurriedly replaced the grille and the brass plate. Moments later, pulling the crypt door shut behind him, he was running from the church towards the main gate. Meehan was about to move on Angela Fenwick – he was sure of it.

He was over the gate in less than a minute and, having got well clear of the premises dialled Dawn again. This time he got a tone and she picked up immediately. 'Powys Court mean anything to you?'

'Yes, it's Angela's place. Why?'

'Meehan's got the architectural blueprint. He's probably there right now.'

'Where are you?'

269

'Couple of hundred yards beyond the entrance to the house there's a lay-by and a sign saying Chilford.'

'OK. Two minutes.'

Packing the night-vision goggles into the rucksack, he waited impatiently for the headlights of the Range Rover.

She was closer to five minutes. 'I've rung Angela,' she told him. 'Told her to get out.'

'And go where?'

'Safe house. She's agreed to stay there for the next twenty-four hours and surround the place with Special Branch people.'

'Can she get there without being followed?'

'She was on her way home from Downing Street. The driver will throw in every move in the book, make sure they're not followed.'

Alex looked dubious.

'Don't worry,' said Dawn. 'He's very good and very experienced. Ex-army, as it happens.'

'Go on.'

'She wants me up there soonest. I have to help her run things from the safe house.'

Alex nodded. 'And I'll stay down here. Sooner or later this is where he's going to come back to and when he does I'll be ready.'

'I'd have liked to stay with you.'

'I could certainly have used an extra pair of eyes and ears,' said Alex, unloading the gear from the back of the Range Rover.

'Is that all I am to you?' she asked with a half-smile. 'A handful of body parts?'

'You know what I mean.'

'Have you got everything you need?'

Alex patted his smock pockets and checked the rucksack. 'Torches, lock-picks, Glock, ammo, night sights, knife, scoff, first aid, spare clothing, waterproofs, cam-netting . . . Looks OK. To be on the safe side I might take the bike and some petrol. Don't like being without a vehicle. Oh, and some drinking water – I'm not poisoning myself with that shite from the stream.'

He opened the back doors and collected a couple of bottles of water and the helmet, goggles and ten-litre fuel can that went with the motorcycle.

'Sure you'll be OK?' Dawn asked as he lifted the bike from the transportation frame on the back of the Range Rover and rolled it towards the pile of supplies.

'Yeah. He's not getting the drop on me twice, don't worry.'

'Professional pride.' She smiled. 'Honour of the Regiment!'

'Something like that.'

She nodded. 'OK, then. Take care. And remind me about those stitches.'

'They can wait.'

She kissed him on his good cheek. 'So can I. Be careful, Captain Temple.'

'On your way, Harding,' he said, touching his hand to her hair.

He hid the bike in the woods opposite the entrance to Black Down and covered it with bracken and pine branches. The machine was an Austrian KTM 520cc EXC, and had been sprayed a matt khaki. The green plastic fuel can was full, and attachable to the rear of the seat by means of a rucksack and bungee cord. He left a helmet and pair of goggles attached to the handlebars. Then, shinning backwards and forwards over the steel barrier, he moved the rest of the kit into the grounds of Black Down House.

No cars passed. There had been traffic on the road earlier in the evening but now it seemed to have dried up. Crouching by one of the gate piers, he checked his watch. It was twenty minutes before midnight.

Quickly Alex considered his position. His target could arrive at any time, and the sooner he got himself out of sight and into position the better. But into which position – Meehan was far too security-conscious simply to climb over the barrier each time he wanted to get into the property and might approach the church from any point along the half-mile or so of boundary fence.

But whichever direction the man was coming from, Alex knew it was to the church that Meehan would go.

He settled himself to wait. He had chosen a position in daylight – in the long grass midway between the woods and the church. The Watchman would return tonight, he was sure.

This was the end game.

TWENTY-SIX

As the night progressed the temperature fell. Dampness enclosed the Black Down estate, the waning moon clouded over and shortly after midnight the first drops fell. Within the hour the grass was bowed and the stream hissing with rain.

Alex tried to ignore the increasing cold and the sodden weight of his clothing. He was lying on uneven ground behind a fallen and rotting tree with the rucksack cached at his side. His face was blackened with cam-cream, long grass surrounded him and cam-netting covered his body. Rain streamed down the grip of the Glock 34. The rain would conceal him, but it would also conceal Meehan. 'Come on, you bastard,' he murmured. 'Come on.'

He prayed that Meehan would return. Surely the man didn't have a place in London. London was a very tightly regulated city, it was next to impossible to sleep rough without some helpful cop or social worker directing you to the nearest shelter. And asking for your name. And having a bloody good look at you.

Nor would he be able to return to his Kilburn haunts. Irish London was far too dangerous a place for him to approach since MI5 had spread the word that he'd been touting for them. Every Provo sympathiser would know his face, unless he'd had it altered beyond all recognition – and that was a damn sight harder to do than was popularly supposed.

No, he'd come back down here, lie low for a bit, catch his breath. He'd been successful so far by dint of extreme caution, he wouldn't want to blow it now with only Fenwick left to kill.

And something told Alex that the tide had turned. Something about the sight of those supplies – the tinned supermarket food, that austere little pile of kit – told Alex that the Watchman was nearing the end of his watch. And when that happened he – Alex Temple – would be ready. He welcomed the hardness of the earth beneath him and the cold sting of the rain. It kept him on edge.

Shortly after 4.10 – he had just checked his watch – there was the low sound of a vehicle passing by on the road and the brief flicker of headlights. The sound was swallowed by the falling rain, the lights faded to nothingness.

Ten minutes passed. Alex hunkered down beneath the cam-netting, his body taut with anticipation, his eyes narrowed against the rain which streamed from his forehead. In front of him the foresight and backsight of the Glock were aligned on wet darkness.

'Come on,' he mouthed, adrenalin jolting through him as he thumbed down the safety catch. '*Come on.*'

Nothing.

It had just been a passing car.

The sick ebb of anticipation.

Or had it been Meehan? Had he parked up nearby and made his way back over the fence? Alex scanned the darkness in front of him through narrowed, night-accustomed eyes, methodically quartering the jigsaw of interleaving grey shapes. From the subtle difference in tones, he identified the faint outline of grasses, ground foliage and tree branches, and noted their sodden, rhythmic response to the driving rain. All was move-ment, but movement of an inanimate regularity.

And then a blur of grey within many blurs of grey, Alex's peripheral vision caught a movement that was irregular, hesitant, pulse-driven. He looked directly at it, lost it, looked away and had it again. The shape was frozen now, as if scenting the breeze.

And now moving again. Could it be a fox? A badger?

Not that shape. That animal was human.

Adrenalin kicking in.

Heart-rate increasing.

Thumb to safety catch. The Glock streaming rain. Range what? Perhaps thirty-five yards?

Come on, you bastard. Come on . . .

Thirty, perhaps, but the rain dramatically reduced visibility. *Shit!* As the foresight and backsight wavered into grey alignment so the target seemed to disappear.

Come closer.

Should he charge him. Just race over there and try and drop him as he ran?

No. His target had the advantage. Knew every inch of this . . .

The figure crouching now, half standing.

Alex hugged the sodden ground. *Come on*, he prayed. *Come this way.*

But the figure seemed to be in no hurry. Infinitely cautious, it moved against the monotone backdrop of the woods, seemed to dissolve, reappeared further away. Alex could hear movements now, footfalls through the undergrowth.

He decided to follow.

Leopard-crawling through the wet grass, he made his way slowly to the edge of the woods. The figure was standing beneath a tree now, scanning his surroundings.

Five more yards, thought Alex, and I'll be close enough for a shot. There was a broad beech trunk in front of him and Alex used its cover to stand up. In front of him the figure had moved away again.

Silently, Alex followed. They seemed to be on some sort of grass path; their progress was soundless.

Grandmother's footsteps.

He had him now. The figure – it had to be Meehan – was standing motionless against some dark evergreen bush. Three more silent paces and the kill was a certainty. Alex raised the Glock in front of him, straightening his arms, minimising the distance.

First pace. Fast. *Step it out.*

Second pace. *Keep going.*

A split second before the trip flare exploded, Alex felt the

275

wire just below his knee, ligament-taut, and then the world around him exploded into blue-white light.

Out of sheer instinct he hurled himself sideways to the ground. Blinded, and with his hard-won night vision destroyed, he could see nothing outside the area lit by the phosphorous glare. All beyond it was black.

Shit!

The flare smoking and crackling. The sound of running feet and Alex stumbling blindly after them, Glock in hand, face whipped by branches.

Meehan was making not for the church, but the house. Fifty yards behind him now, Alex tried to blink away the searing blast of light imprinted on his retinas. But it stayed there, dancing in front of his vision so that he could barely see as he ran.

He slipped in the mud, went down hard and, picking himself up, ran straight into a tree stump and fell again, setting the knife wounds screaming in protest. A hundred yards ahead of him he saw the other man race into the house. Meehan's night vision was unimpaired – he had deliberately kept his back to the trip flare.

Somehow Alex reached the front door. Behind him, in the wood, the flare was no more than a popping smoulder on its steel picket. His night vision was shot and he was following a presumably armed man into a lightless house.

Shit, just when the Maglite could have helped him, he'd left it outside in the rucksack. On the other hand the torch would betray his own position . . . Crouching motionless just inside the front door in the musty darkness, Alex listened intently.

The crunching of feet on fallen plaster, then silence except for the rain on the roof tiles. Meehan was above him.

How did the layout of the house go . . . *Think.*

Twenty stairs up, that much he remembered. The top corridor T-branching to left and right – Meehan was in the left wing, his location confirmed by a dull thump. *What did he have up there?*

Do or die, thought Alex. Let's go and see.

As silently as possible he crept up the stairs. The photo

imprint of the flare was still in front of his eyes, but the beginnings of night vision were returning to him. He could see the top of the stairs now and the corridor. To the left were three doors, one of them opened.

He had left them all closed, he remembered.

Bracing himself, readying the Glock, he burst into the room. It was empty, but the boards previously covering the window opening had been booted outwards and rain was spattering the floor. Alex raced over towards the opening, guessing that Meehan had had some sort of rope or other escape route readied there. The thump must have been Meehan hitting the roof of the porch below.

An instant before Alex reached the window, however, the floorboards collapsed beneath his feet with a desiccated sigh. There was a burst of dust and crumbling lath and plaster, and then there was no support at all and Alex felt himself pitched downwards through the choking darkness. He hit the hall floor below hard and unevenly, smashing on to one elbow and the back of his skull.

Son of a bitch – Meehan had booby-trapped the floor with rotten boards and cut out the beams. Painfully, Alex got to his feet. His parachute training had ensured that he had automatically rolled with the fall and saved himself a broken limb but he was badly shaken.

Had Meehan made a break for his vehicle, or was he waiting outside with his weapon cocked, ready to blow his pursuer away?

A distant scream of tyres on the wet road gave Alex his answer. Still dazed, he shook his head, dislodging a gritty cloud of dry plaster. Time to go, he whispered mechanically to himself. Time to go. Meehan already had a clear two minutes' start.

The rucksack. Run. Find it.

He slipped on the wet ground again, wrenching the stitches, but was beyond pain now. Safety-locking and holstering the Glock, pulling the rucksack of kit to his shoulders – both sets of actions seemed to take for ever – he forced himself in the direction of the main gate. The fall through the floor seemed to have affected his balance and he had to concentrate hard in order to place one foot in front of the other. Keep going, he repeated to himself, desperately attempting to order his thoughts. Not dead yet. Not dead till you're dead. *Keep going.*

It took him a clear minute to climb the gate and he managed to gash his thumb badly on the barbed wire while doing so. When he finally made it to the top, he sucked the blood from his shaking hand and looked blearily around him. To his left, perhaps a mile away, a tiny thread of light showed for a moment. The Watchman had gone east.

Keep going.

Even pushing the bike was difficult to begin with, but eventually he got it to the road, hauled off the night-vision goggles and pulled on the motorcycle goggles and helmet. With the aid of the pen torch – his hands were still shaking badly – he checked the tank. It was full and probably held nine or ten litres of unleaded petrol. The jerrycan in the cotton rucksack bungee-corded to the rear of the seat held approximately the same again.

The KTM had an electric start and burbled immediately into life. Cautiously, Alex let out the hydraulic clutch and moved forward. The power was there, smooth and immediate, but the knobbly motocross tyres gave him the sensation that he was riding on marbles. The seat was hard, narrow and unyielding. This was not a machine that lent itself willingly to roadriding.

Go, he ordered himself. *No lights.* The roads were empty and Meehan had to be allowed to think that he had got away. Alex had no night vision, though. He had been wearing the image-intensifying goggles for too long.

Too bad. Drive. And fast.

No lights.

At speed, it was like riding a road drill. The KTM could do 80 mph on tarmac but it wasn't what it had been designed for, and the knobbly tyres shook Alex to the bone, blurred his vision, made the teeth dance in his mouth. And with no lights . . .

Faster. Risk everything.

Rain lashed his face, the white lines on the road were barely visible and when the front wheel touched them the whole machine seemed to twitch and skate.

Accelerate into the bends. Find speed.

The main road. North to Okehampton, south to Tavistock.

Roulette: 50–50; red or black.

South. His fists tight on the domino grips, his body ice-cold in the sodden clothing, the black sutures biting into the knife-cuts.

Ignore the pain.

He saw nothing for two miles and then, far ahead of him, a tiny worm of light travelling not south, but east. If it was Meehan, he had turned off the main road at right angles. He was heading for the centre of Dartmoor and taking the narrow road at well over 70.

Shit. Bastard still had at least four miles on him. Once he made it to a road with a bit of traffic on it he'd just vanish.

Taking a deep breath, Alex swung the KTM left-handed off the road and into the wild darkness of the open moor. His only chance of staying with Meehan was to cut across country. As the crow flew Meehan was only a couple of miles away, but by road he was more than twice that.

Alex accelerated aggressively, felt the near sublime sensation as the tyres bit hard into the rough moorland. Doing the job it was designed for, the bike seemed to gather Alex up, to bind him furiously to itself. The supercross suspension had been set at a very harsh level with a minimum of compression and rebound, but Alex was soon glad of this when the front wheels hit a rock. For a moment man and machine were flying through the darkness, then the wheels came down with a testicle-crunching double smash that would have consigned a non-performance bike to the scrap heap and a less blindly determined driver to an Intensive Care ward.

But with body and brain screaming vengeance, Alex didn't give a fuck. The pain and fatigue were distant things now – all that mattered was that he dominate this leaping, howling beast of a motorcycle. He could see nothing. He was aware of a track of sorts beneath him and the glow-worm thread of the vehicle ahead and to his right, and that was all. The rest – the whipping cold, the shotgun volleys of rain and mud, the desperate grip of his hands and heels – barely registered.

In a rational state of mind he would never have been able to do it. In the event, instinct grabbed the controls from fear and good judgement. Instinct looked ahead, instinct held its line, instinct squared the front wheel into the rain-slicked rocks and hummocks, and as the four-stroke engine screamed beneath him Alex knew a crazy, weightless release. *What the fuck*, he thought. *If I smash myself to pieces, then so be it.*

Gradually, he closed the gap between them. Did the Watchman have a plan, he wondered, or was he just distancing himself from Black Down with all speed.

Almost there. Almost within safe range of him. The road across the moor was about twenty miles long, and Alex needed to be well locked on to Meehan before they encountered any more traffic. As things stood he didn't even know what sort of vehicle the other man was driving.

But he could at least see his lights now, all the time. Assuming that it was the man he was after. If it wasn't, well, that was the end of it.

Shit. Another vehicle had joined the car that he hoped was Meehan's. Swinging hard right-handed, Alex made for the road. Within the minute the front wheel of the KTM had dived into a cut and Alex found himself flying over the handlebars to land in an awkward heap in the marshy heather. He was not badly hurt, but his confidence in his bike-handling abilities took a dent. And by the time he had got himself up and righted, and restarted the KTM, neither car was in sight. More carefully now, Alex steered the bike to the road.

After the thrill of flying over moorland, it was back to the murderous vibration of the road. Speed helped a little, but only a little. Throttling back, Alex pushed the KTM up to 85 mph, and after five minutes, to his vast relief, tail-lights appeared in front of him.

The rear of the two cars was a newish red Toyota driven, as

far as Alex could see through the rainswept rear window, by a man in a hat. A Countryside Alliance sticker showed in the back window.

Swinging outside the Toyota, Alex peered through the rear window of the front car, a battered-looking dark-blue BMW. This driver seemed to be bareheaded. The car was much muddier than the Toyota.

It could be either of them. Alex stayed hard on the tail of the rear car, his eyes locked to the driver. The hat looked like a tweed one, the sort habitually worn by Inspector Frost on TV.

Both cars slowed down and Alex fell back fifty yards. They were approaching a village – a sign read Two Bridges. The Toyota driver seemed to be waving his right hand about inside the car – what the fuck was he up to?

And then something about the patterns he was inscribing suddenly made sense to Alex. *He was conducting!* He was listening to a classical music station and conducting it with his finger.

Nothing anyone had said about Meehan had suggested that he was a music fan. Nor was it credible that, at a moment potentially fraught with danger, he would be allowing his concentration to be dispersed in this way. Joseph Meehan was, as Frank Wisbeach had said, a 'true believer'. He had just survived an expert assassination attempt. Under the circumstances he was hardly going to be singing along to Classic FM.

Meehan had to be the guy in the BMW.

Alex was glad he had reached a decision because the two cars separated on the eastern side of the village. The Toyota swung right towards Ashburton, the BMW forked left to Mortenhampstead.

The first fingers of light were now visible at the horizon, and Alex braked and waited at the roadside as the BMW pulled away from the village. He had no intention of being spotted in Meehan's rear-view mirror. As long as he kept his lights off, he told himself . . .

As soon as the BMW was out of sight Alex restarted, gritting his teeth against the pulverising vibrations and dropping back the moment the red tail-lights came into view again. The

281

signpost indicated that it was ten miles to Moretonhampstead and he very much doubted that Meehan was going to turn off the main road.

More worrying was the petrol issue. Meehan, it was logical to suppose, had just returned from London when he appeared at Black Down House. He must have had some nearby place to park the car. Would he have a full tank of petrol? Was he carrying any with him?

The KTM's tank probably held about nine litres. Four-stroke engine, thirty miles to the gallon . . . say a hundred miles, max, before he needed to fill up again. If Meehan needed a refill before then, fine. Alex could ride in and shoot him with the silenced Glock at the petrol station. Ride away before anyone realised what had happened.

If Meehan didn't need petrol before Alex did, then Alex was in trouble. Meehan would simply outrun him.

He came to a decision. He would follow Meehan until his own petrol gage indicated half-full. Then he would call Dawn Harding on his mobile, give her Meehan's position and let her Service's people take over. This was their speciality, after all.

The arrangement was professionally responsible, but also gave him a reasonable chance of sorting the whole thing out himself, which he very much wanted to do. He needed closure, as – he suspected – did Meehan. Their destinies had intertwined. One of them had to kill the other.

TWENTY-SEVEN

From Moretonhampstead the dark-blue BMW took the Exeter road and then turned sharply northwards up the valley of the river Exe towards Tiverton. Hanging well back in the half-dark, Alex was still fairly certain that he had not been seen.

At Tiverton the BMW turned eastwards again. He was making for Taunton, but it seemed that caution was leading him to avoid motorways in favour of much smaller roads. From Taunton, Alex guessed, he would work his way across country to Salisbury.

At first it appeared that Alex was right. Meehan drove through Taunton and continued eastwards on minor roads for twenty-five minutes. And then, a mile or two short of the village of Castle Cary, Alex rounded a corner to see the BMW at a lay-by three hundred yards ahead of him. Meehan must be taking a piss, he thought, braking sharply.

Shit! The fact that he had stopped on seeing Meehan's car rather than driving straight past would unquestionably have set alarm bells ringing.

As nonchalantly as he could, he wrenched open the cotton bag, pulled out the jerrycan and filled the KTM's half-empty petrol tank. Then he slipped the jerrycan back in the bag, bungee-corded it to the back of the seat and stretched as if he'd only woken up ten minutes earlier. With luck, Meehan would mistake him for a local. The muddy trail bike was hardly the most likely pursuit vehicle.

A palely anonymous figure – a figure that Alex had last seen lit by a trip flare – exited the roadside hedge. Unhurriedly, Alex swung his leg over the KTM and pressed the start button, intending to pull level with the car and shoot Meehan where he stood.

When he was still forty yards away, however, he saw Meehan turn towards him, handgun at full stretch. A series of rounds whipped past Alex's head, and as he desperately braked and ducked he saw Meehan leap into his vehicle and accelerate at high speed down the road.

Pulling out the Glock, Alex fired half a dozen rounds after him, but without visible effect. Right, he thought. Gloves off. Let's cock, lock and rock.

There was no hanging back now. As Meehan took the BMW screaming through the village at close to 80 mph, Alex followed close behind. For the first time in his life he prayed for a police vehicle. A whooping siren and a set of flashing blue lights and his problems would be over.

But of course there was no police vehicle to be seen. Instead, Meehan hurled himself northwards, pulling every trick out of the evasive driving handbook that he could remember. But Alex had done the same course with the same instructors and was driving the more manoeuvrable – if also by far the more dangerous – vehicle. He quite simply locked on and stayed there, dropping back and outwards a few yards every time the road straightened in case Meehan slammed on the brakes at high speed – generally considered the most effective countermeasure against a following motorcycle.

In this fashion – Meehan racing ahead, Alex hanging grimly on to his tail – they screamed up through Radstock and Weston to the M4. Still no police and precious little traffic. It was Saturday, Alex realised belatedly. And it couldn't be more than six thirty. Seven at the latest.

At junction 18 of the M4 Meehan pulled hard over on to the motorway and joined the slow-lane traffic at 70 mph. Flattening himself to the KTM's narrow seat, eyes streaming behind his goggles, Alex followed as the BMW swung across to the fast lane: 90 mph, 95. The vibrations from the KTM's tyres were turning his muscles to Plasticene. His body ached, he had a cracking migraine and was having difficulty focusing his eyes.

Touching 100 mph now.

Just hang on. One of us, sooner or later, is going to run out of petrol.

There was nothing, now, beyond staying with Meehan. It was all he had to do. Just stay on.

The Severn Road Bridge. At breakneck speed, Meehan crashed the barrier and Alex followed. He had a momentary impression of a man in a fluorescent yellow rain jacket peering from a cabin, then the tableau was far behind them and they were swerving through the buffeting winds and rain of the westbound motorway towards Newport.

A screaming turn north next, up the Usk valley. Alex was all machine now and all pain. There was no thought beyond pursuit. At times it seemed as if he and the Watchman were one, controlled by the same hand, racing to a final rendezvous that they both craved.

Which of them would last longer? They roared through Usk, Abergavenny, Tredegar and Cefn Coed. And still the unearthly emptiness and the sense of driving the dawn before them. They were in the Black Mountain country now, among hills known by name to every SAS member, past and present. There was Cefn Crew, rearing blackly over the reservoir, there was the foreshortened bulk of Fan Fawr, there was the jagged ridge line of Craig Fan-ddu. These were the rocks that they had trained over, month after month, sweating and freezing and cursing as they dragged their aching bodies and their rock-filled Bergans over the windy granite peaks.

And then, as the dark blue BMW hurled up the thread-like Cwm Taf valley ahead of them, Alex suddenly knew where the story was going to end. For there, towering over them all, was the pitiless mother of all the Black Mountains – Pen-y-Fan. Every SAS selection cadre knew Pen-y-Fan – they were harassed up and down its grey, shale-strewn sides until they hated every unyielding inch of it. One of the final elements of selection into the Regiment was named 'the Fan Dance', as it started and finished with an ascent of the mountain.

The track briefly straightened. On the wet, potholed surface the trail-bike was coming into its own and the gap between the two vehicles was narrowing. Slamming to an angled halt, pulling out the Glock and wrenching the goggles from his eyes, Alex released a fast volley of shots at the disappearing BMW. The first few missed, ricocheting from the roadside shale, but then as Meehan threw the car into the approaching bend his rear driver's-side tyre was suddenly shredded rubber.

The BMW's overturning was both appalling and beautiful. The right-hand side of the car seemed to tuck into the shale-strewn verge for a moment and then the black guts of the machine were suddenly skywards, the roll completing itself with a shuddering crash back on to four wheels.

The vehicle came to a smoking rest beside the road, its windows glassless, then Alex saw the wiry figure of Meehan drag himself painfully out. The former agent was obviously injured, perhaps seriously, but he began climbing immediately, scrambling desperately over the rocks and fallen slates up the western face of the mountain. Slowly, warily, Alex rode the KTM towards the abandoned car. Reloading the Glock and unscrewing the silencer – silencers tended significantly to reduce muzzle velocity – he set off after the fleeing figure.

The two men climbed for several minutes, Alex remaining a steady fifty metres behind Meehan, until the vehicles were toy-like on the road below. As they climbed so the wind's roar grew, dragging at them, deafening them, and punching at their clothes. Meehan, despite his injury – he seemed to be dragging a leg – was setting a ferocious pace and Alex felt the sweat streaming down his back as he followed.

At a thousand feet a shadowy rain squall crossed the face of the mountain. Meehan turned, his face pale and contorted with pain, and sent several rounds spattering about his pursuer.

Granite chips flicked lethally about Alex's face and then a rogue shot, deflected by a rock, punched through the cordura rucksack on his back. Ricocheting from the Maglite torch, the 9mm round tore downwards and outwards through the flesh of the SAS officer's back.

Shit. *Shit!*

It felt as if someone had laid a block of ice across him. There was no pain, although he knew that the pain would come. He could feel the blood coursing down his back.

Ignore it. Eyes on the target.

Flattening himself against the rock face, Alex saw Meehan's progress was becoming erratic. He was flailing around – the shock and the injury sustained in the BMW shunt were taking their toll.

Finally, in a shower of flaky shale, he fell, rolling limply down the hillside to a grassy outcrop a little above Alex's position. His automatic – dropped – spun past Alex on to the rocks below.

Warily, Alex approached Meehan, who lay face down on the springy turf. Correct procedure would have been a double tap to the back of the skull, but he felt he owed this man more than a dog's death.

He turned the fallen man over. The thin, pale features were instantly recognisable and twisted themselves into a wry smile. Blood oozed from a cut in his head.

'Lucky shot, boyo, blowing that tyre.'

The accent took Alex straight back to Belfast. 'I've no doubt of it,' he said and quickly began to search the fallen man. There was a sheathed Mauser knife and several spare magazines, and a pocketful of loose 9mm rounds, but no other firearm.

Meehan pursed his lips. 'Did I hit you back there?'

Alex felt around his back. The hand came back bloody. 'Yeah. Another lucky shot, I'd say.'

Meehan looked away. 'So are you going to waste me or what?'

Alex didn't answer. Reaching for his mobile he dialled Dawn's number.

She answered on the first ring. 'Alex. Thank God. Where are you?'

He told her.

'And Meehan?'

Something made Alex hesitate. He looked down at Meehan. 'Dealt with.'

A faint smile touched the former agent's lips.

'Stay there,' Dawn ordered. 'Don't move. I'll pick up a flight to Brecon — be with you in an hour.'

'We're not going anywhere,' said Alex wearily, and rang off.

'So,' Meehan repeated, almost bored. 'You goin' to follow orders, soldier, and waste me?'

'You didn't waste me when you had the chance. Why?'

'Wasn't part of the plan.'

'Can we talk about that plan?'

Meehan was silent for a moment, then the corner of his mouth twitched. 'Good place for us to meet, don't you think?'

Alex smiled and nodded.

Curiosity touched the pale features. 'How did you find out about Black Down?'

'A conversation you had,' said Alex.

'Connolly?'

'Yup.'

Meehan nodded. 'I never told Den Connolly where the house was. Something stopped me, even then.'

Briefly, Alex explained how forensic analysis had discovered the solvent in his system.

'Poisoned, was I?' said Meehan thoughtfully, looking across the valley towards Fan Fawr. 'I hadn't allowed for that, I'll admit.'

'Connolly said you never turned tout.'

'Nor I did. Not ever.'

Alex stared at him. 'So what . . .'

Meehan looked wearily away. 'Just do your job, man, and give us the double tap. Get the fuck on with it.'

'I want to know.'

'Just do it.'

'None of it makes sense. Don't you at least want it to make sense?'

'You wouldn't believe me.'

'I might.'

The two men stared at each other. Around them the wind scoured the rocks and flattened the grass. The place was theirs alone.

'How much do you know?' asked Meehan eventually.

'I know about Watchman. I know what you were sent over the water to do. I know that the whole thing went bad, agents were killed, all hell broke loose.'

Meehan nodded. 'Whatever you've been told by Five, who I'm assuming you're working for right now, remember that it had a single purpose: to persuade you to kill me. Would it be fair to say that?'

'I guess so,' said Alex.

'Right. Well, remember that. And remember too that I'm a dead man. I've no need to lie.'

'I'll remember,' said Alex and moved down the slope to collect Meehan's weapon.

TWENTY-EIGHT

'The first thing you have to understand,' said Joseph Meehan, 'is just how much I've always hated the IRA. My father was a good man, religious and patriotic, and they crippled him, humiliated him and expelled him from the country he loved. Drove him to an early grave. And there have been thousands like him – innocent people whose lives have been destroyed by those maniac bastards. Whatever else I tell you I want you to remember that one fact. I hate the IRA, I always have hated them and I will take that hatred to my grave.'

He paused and the lids narrowed over the pale, fathomless eyes. 'I'm assuming that Fenwick and the rest of them told you the background stuff – the Watchman selection process and the rest of it?'

Alex nodded.

There was a curious blankness to Meehan's words. They were passionate, but delivered without expression. 'When I got over there I started off living in a flat in Dunmurry and working at Ed's – they tell you about that?'

'The electronic goods place?'

'That's right. Ed's. Ed's Electronics. And I was dating this girl called Tina. Nice girl. Grandparents came over from Italy after the war. Had a loudmouth brother called Vince who worked in a garage and fancied himself as God's gift to the Republican movement. Tried the bullshit on me a couple of times but I told him to fuck off – said I didn't want to know.

'That pissed him off, and he made sure that the local volunteers found out that I'd served with the Crown forces – thought they might give me a good kicking or something.

290

Course they did no such thing, they're not that stupid, but a couple of them started watching me and asking the odd question, and they soon found out I knew my way around an electronic circuit.'

Meehan touched his head and regarded his bloody fingertips.

'I'll spare you the details but there was the usual eyeing-up process and I started to hang out with these half-dozen fellers who thought of themselves as an ASU. They weren't, of course – they were just a bunch of saloon bar Republicans. I did a couple of under-the-counter jobs for them – radio repairs – and then a much heavier bunch showed up. Older guys. Heard I was interested in joining the movement. I'd said no such thing, but I said yeah, I was sympathetic – more sympathetic than I'd been in the past, anyway.'

'And?' asked Alex.

'And they didn't fuck around. Asked straight out if I wanted in. So I said yeah, OK.'

'Must have been satisfying after all that time.'

'Yes and no. These guys were pretty hard-core. I knew there'd be no going back.'

'So what happened next?'

'There was a whole initiation process. I was driven to a darkened room in north Belfast and interviewed by three men I never saw. What was my military history with the Crown forces, what courses had I done and where had I been posted? Was I known as a Republican sympathiser and had I ever attended a Republican march? Had I ever been arrested? Where in Belfast did I drink . . . Hours of it. And why the fuck did I want to join the IRA?

'I told them I was fed up of living as a second-class citizen simply because I was a Catholic. I told them that I'd been in the Brit army and felt the rough edge of discrimination over there. Said since my return to Belfast I'd come to feel that the IRA spoke the only language the Crown understood. Parroted all the stuff I'd learnt from the Five instructors, basically.'

'And they bought it?'

'They heard me out and it must have gone down OK,

291

because I was told that from that moment on I was to make no public or private statement of my Republican sympathies, not to associate with known Republicans, had to avoid Republican bars et cetera. I was put forward for what's called the Green Book lectures – a two-month course of indoctrination which took place every Thursday evening in a flat in Twinbrook. History of the movement, rules of engagement, counter-surveillance, anti-interrogation techniques . . .'

'The old spot on the wall trick?'

'All that bollocks, yeah. And at the end of it I was sworn in.'

'How did that feel?'

'Well, there was no going back, that was for certain sure. But I was finally earning the wages I was being paid.'

'Go on.'

'I started off as a dicker. I was told to hang on to my job so my volunteer activities were all in the evenings and at weekends. And this started to cause problems with Tina. She was a sympathiser, but not to the point where she was prepared to give her life over. She wanted to do what other girls did – go out in the evening, go round the shops on a Saturday . . . Anyway, I arranged a meet with Geoff, my agent handler – you would have known him as Barry Fenn – and he just said do whatever the fuck makes the bloody girl happy. Buy her a ring, get her up the duff, whatever. He felt it was vital for what he called "my integration into the community" that I stuck with her.

'So we got engaged, which was fine by me. And almost immediately afterwards I'm told I'm spending my two weeks' summer holiday in a training camp in County Clare in the Republic. So Tina hits the fucking roof. Me or the movement – choose. So of course I chose as I had to and she walked, and that was the end of it.'

'Was that . . . difficult?'

'I saw it as a sacrifice. A sacrifice for the greater good, which was nailing those PIRA bastards.' He paused for a moment, then the toneless voice continued: 'At that time I thought that all the evil was coming from the one direction.'

Alex watched him thoughtfully. Squaddies, by and large, did not express themselves in such abstract terms. Even the average regimental padre tended to steer clear of words like 'good' and 'evil' and 'sacrifice'. For the first time since they had found themselves face to face, Alex wondered about the other man's sanity.

'How was the camp?'

'Pretty basic. Weapons drills, surveillance, interrogation scenarios. I had to wind down my skills to volunteer level, which is a fuck's sight harder than it sounds.'

'I can imagine. Were you upset at the break-up with Tina?'

Meehan looked away. 'There was something I only found out later. She was pregnant at the time. She had the child – a boy – but never let me see him . . .'

Alex nodded, letting Meehan take his time.

'After I came back from Clare I was either working at Ed's or on call for the movement. I did a year or so's dicking and then I was seconded as a driver to one of the auxiliary cells, which is what they call their punishment squads.'

Alex grimaced. 'Shit!'

'Yeah – *shit!* – exactly. In theory we were supposed to be keeping the streets safe for Catholics to go about their business, in practice we were kneecapping teenage shoplifters. It was fucking evil – especially since I'd seen the same thing done to my dad. But that was the point. To make it as horrible as possible. To see if I had what it took. A bit of interest was being paid to me by then.'

Alex raised his eyebrows.

'A man called Byrne. Padraig Byrne. CO of Belfast Brigade at that time and later on the Army Council.'

'Ah.'

'Yeah. He'd been told I'd been a Royal Engineer and had bits and pieces sent to me for repair. Computers, mostly. There was one job where some information had to be recovered and it turned out to be details of a bank security system.'

'Fenwick told me about that.'

'Yeah, well, it wasn't too difficult to figure that one out as a

293

plant – if the security was beefed up, they'd know that I was passing the information on.'

'But you did pass it on.'

'I passed everything on. But London's policy was not to move on anything that might compromise my cover. Which at that stage I was bloody grateful for, because my impression was that the Provos still didn't a hundred per cent trust me. Especially Byrne. It was like . . . have you ever done any fishing?'

Alex shook his head.

'It was like when you've got a fat old carp nosing at your bait. He wants it, he's desperate to believe that it's safe, but his instinct tells him no. And that's how Byrne was. I could tell that he wanted to believe in me, but . . .' Meehan shrugged. 'I'd been doing a lot of driving. Scouting jobs mostly, with me in the lead car keeping an eye out for trouble and the players or weapons or whatever in a second vehicle following behind. Important, I guess, but still auxiliary stuff. I was never allowed anywhere near any operational planning.

'And then in late 1990 early 1991 things moved on. I was contacted by Padraig Byrne at Ed's and told that I was part of a weapon-recovery team. We were to dig up an Armalite from a churchyard in Castleblayney and deliver it to a stiffer back in Belfast – some ex-US marine sniper, I think it was. I reported all this to Fenn via a dead-letter drop and he told me to go ahead and not to worry, they'd jark the weapon and follow it in.

'Well, they followed it in all right, but they didn't jark it and the stiffer used it against a patrol in Andytown a couple of days later. Luckily – for all that he was supposed to be a real deadeye – he missed, but that was more to do with the patrol spotting him than there being anything wrong with the rifle. We returned it to the cache the next day, it was never jarked and as far as I know it's still in circulation . . .'

For a moment Alex saw an expression of murderous bitterness flash through Meehan's eyes, then the blankness was back.

'Whatever – I must have passed some sort of test in Byrne's eyes, because immediately afterwards I was sent to join a bomb-making cell who were working out of a basement on the

Finaghy Road. The cell had a problem. What they were trying to do was to get bombs into police or army bases, which could then be detonated remotely and the problem was that the Crown forces maintained a twenty-four-hour radio-wave shield around every vehicle, building or installation that could possibly be of interest. They needed someone to work out a signal that could penetrate the shield.

'Well, I found one. I found a frequency they hadn't thought of, and as soon as I had, and it had been tested by a feller we had working as a cleaner in one of the police stations, I passed it back to Fenn and told him to factor it into the installation defences. The next thing I knew I was being congratulated by Padraig fucking Byrne. They'd had a success down in Armagh, detonating a remote-controlled bomb inside a base there. Bessbrook. Three soldiers had been seriously injured and a cleaner – a Catholic woman, as it happened – had been killed. And serve the bitch right, according to Byrne, for taking Crown money.

'I rang Fenn that night from one of the public phones at Musgrave Park Hospital and asked him what the fuck was going down. He told me they'd had to let the bomb go by. There had been several failed detonations in the previous few months and there was suspicion at the top levels of the organisation that a British agent was defusing them. I told him it was more likely that the button men were so fucking solid they couldn't do the job properly and that was why the bombs hadn't been going off, but he just changed the subject. I was to carry on as usual. The O'Riordan woman – the cleaner – was an unavoidable loss. The soldiers would be well cared for. Finish.

'I realised that part of what Fenn said was true. There was no question mark in Byrne's mind now – I was well and truly in. That's how it seemed at the time, anyway. Looking back, I can see that I was so preoccupied with the O'Riordan woman's death that I missed the single vital fact I'd been . . .' Meehan doubled up and bared his teeth. For several long moments he was silent, neither breathing nor moving. Finally he seemed to relax and slowly straightened.

'Are you OK?' asked Alex, aware of the question's ludicrous inadequacy.

Meehan managed a smile. There was now a dark, wet stain on his shirt-front. 'Never better!' he gasped. 'Top o' the world!'

Alex waited while Meehan drew breath.

'I worked with the cell for about eighteen months. There were five of us. A QM, an intelligence officer, two general operators – one of whom was a woman – and myself. We were a bomber cell, which is why we had Bronagh with us. It was reckoned that a woman was better for planting devices in public places.'

'And all the time you were reporting to back to your London handler?'

'I was.'

'What sort of stuff?'

'Names and addresses of volunteers, registration numbers of cars, possible assassination targets, anything.'

'By dead-letter drop? By phone?'

'By e-mail mostly, from about 1991 onwards, using machines that had been brought into the shop. I'd bash away in my back room and no one took a blind bit of difference: I was just the anoraky bloke that fixed the computers. Dead-letter drops and meets are all very well, but if you're discovered you're dead. This was perfect: I'd transmit the information then delete all traces of the operation. And I was usually able to make sure that the owners of the machines I used got a cash deal, so there was no record of their having passed through the shop.'

'Sounds as if you were earning your Box salary.'

'Fucking right I was.'

'Fenwick said you lost your nerve.'

Meehan closed his eyes for a moment. The accusation didn't merit a reply.

'Our cell was involved in shooting an RUC officer at the off-licence in Stewartstown Road. I scouted in the stiffers and drove them away from the scene. London knew the hit was going to happen because I'd told them a couple of days earlier what the

296

score was – in fact, I e-mailed them a detailed warning – but the hit went ahead.'

'I heard you gave less than an hour's warning.'

'Bollocks. They had forty-eight. And an hour would have been enough anyway. No – they let it happen and that was when I understood that something strange – no, let me rephrase that, something fucking *evil* – was going down. That the reason I thought I was there – to get intelligence out to where it could save lives and do some good – wasn't the reason at all.'

'So what was the reason?'

'I'm getting there. Does the name Proinsas Deavey mean anything to you?'

'No.'

'Proinsas Deavey was a low-level volunteer who occasionally did some dicking and errand-running. A nobody, basically. I saw him about the Falls from time to time and the word was that he was involved in low-level drug-dealing. Anyway, apparently he tried flogging the stuff to the wrong people and he was picked up by the auxiliaries, who gave him a good kicking. Bad idea, because by that stage Proinsas has a habit himself. He's desperate for money. So when he gets a call from the FRU he's a pushover.'

Alex nodded.

'Now I don't know about any of this until I get a call at work from Padraig Byrne. Some time around Christmas 1995, it must have been. Padraig was what they call a Red Light by then, meaning he was known to the Crown forces as a player, so he had to keep a very low profile. I was told to go round to his place after closing time, making sure I wasn't followed.

'When I got there he told me that Proinsas had got drunk, turned himself over to one of the nutting squads and confessed he was touting for the FRU. In theory PIRA's always run an amnesty system for touts – spill your guts and you're off the hook – but in practice it's more likely to be a debriefing followed by two to the head. In this case, untypically, the nutting squad was bright enough to consult Byrne and he told them to hang on to Deavey – he'd debrief the man himself.

Which he did and then set up Proinsas to feed disinformation back to the FRU.

'Now at this stage you have to remember what's going on politically. The Crown forces don't know it yet, but the ceasefire is at an end. Southern Command's England Wing is about to detonate the Canary Wharf bomb and Padraig Byrne – a very ambitious man, remember, keen to move from the Army Council to the Executive – sees a chance for a spectacular of his own. He's going to take out a pair of FRU agents.

'He tells me this. He tells me something else. I'm a junior member of PIRA GHQ staff by then – a sort of assistant to the Quartermaster General. There's been a major technical updating and I've had to play a big part in that – training operators and so on.

'Byrne wants me to kill the FRU guys. In person, in public, in front of a big volunteer crowd. The ultimate commitment, the ultimate statement of loyalty. Do that, he says, and you're on the Army Council, guaranteed. You can forget all that paperchasing at GHQ – you'll have proved yourself heart and soul. So of course I say yes – what the fuck else can I say – and ask for details. And he fills me in. Tells me exactly what's going to happen.

'So the next day I work late at Ed's. File an encrypted report to London on a client's machine, wipe the hard disk – people are wising up to the insecurity of e-mail by then – and hope to God that the FRU people are pulled out in time. I ask to be pulled out too: the finger's going to be pointed straight at me if these guys are miraculously whipped off the streets just days before they're due to be whacked. Byrne, like I said, is a very sharp, very switched-on operator.

'The next day I got a call from the rep of a company called Intex, saying they'd ceased production of the software I'd enquired about. Intex was Five, of course, and the call meant that my message had been received and I was to sit tight.'

Alex stared at him. 'Let me get this right. Are you saying that Five knew that Ray Bledsoe and Connor Wheen were due to be picked up, tortured and murdered, *and did nothing?*'

'Yes. That's exactly what I'm saying. A bunch of us were driven down to a farmhouse on the border that the nutting squad often used for interrogations and executions – a horrible bloody place, stinking of death. The boyos, needless to say, were pissing themselves with excitement at the chance of seeing a pair of Brit agents chopped at close range. The hours passed and I tell you I have never prayed like I prayed then: that London would pull those boys out in time.

'They didn't, of course, and Bledsoe and Wheen were brought down to the border that evening. I had drawn a Browning and a couple of clips from the QM, so that I could at least make it fast, but in the event I wasn't even able to do that.'

Meehan fell silent. His eyes were as cold and blank as pack ice.

'They had a generator there and one of those heavy-duty compressed-air staple guns . . . Do you have any idea what happens when you fire one of those things into someone's eye?'

Alex opened his mouth to speak, but found that he could say nothing.

'As the eye explodes – and it goes fuckin' *everywhere* – the staple blasts its way out through the roof of the mouth. The guy's kicking, meanwhile, and pissing himself, and generally going berserk, but the thing he can't do is make any sound, because his blood and his sinuses are pouring out of his nose and mouth. The pain has to be beyond anything you can imagine . . .'

'You did that?' whispered Alex disbelievingly.

'No, thank God, some other volunteer did it – to Wheen. But the point is not who did it, the point is that Five, knowing what Byrne and his nutting squads do, *allowed it to happen*. They had the information and they deliberately failed to act on it.'

'So what happened next?'

'Byrne figured that Wheen was the tough guy and Bledsoe – if he scared him enough – was going to do the talking. Well, he scared him all right. The guy was out of his head with sheer terror. But just to make sure, Byrne had the volunteer do Wheen's other eye. And then – just to make the point that it was Bledsoe who was going to do the talking – he cut Wheen's

299

tongue out. Have you ever heard a man trying to scream when his tongue's been cut out?'

Alex shook his head.

'It sounds like percolating coffee. Anyway, I stood there, my brain fuckin' turning itself inside out at this sight – terror, horror, disbelief, whatever the fuck – and telling myself one thing: *smile, or go the same way yourself.* And everyone else was smiling, but I tell you they were all pretty quiet at that point.'

Alex nodded.

'So then Byrne told me to do Wheen once and for all so I pulled out the Browning ready to give him one. And Byrne says no. Hands me, of all things, a fuckin' lump-hammer and a six-inch nail . . .'

'And you did him with that?'

'It made this kind of . . . plinking sound,' said Meehan reflectively. 'The guy died immediately.'

'And Bledsoe?'

'Bledsoe coughed. Told them everything. Every last thing he knew. It took hours – almost light by the time he was finished.'

'And?'

Meehan nodded expressionlessly. 'Yeah, I did him too. Same way. And as I did so I promised myself that the people responsible would know the pain and the terror that these brave men had known. Whatever it took – *whatever* it fucking took – I would make them understand.'

'Surely the people responsible were Padraig Byrne and his Provos,' suggested Alex quietly.

'Those people were evil,' said Meehan, 'but they knew they were evil. They looked evil in the eye, they embraced evil and they knew themselves for what they were. Fenwick and her people, though, were evil at a distance. They never saw the floor of that PIRA abattoir running with blood and shit, never had to look at brave men like Wheen and Bledsoe dying in indescribable terror and agony and tell themselves: yeah, I did that . . .'

'Wise monkeys,' murmured Alex.

'For every action, there's a reaction,' said Meehan. 'My father

300

taught me that. The universe demands balance. For as long as the lives that I had taken were unavenged, there would be no balance.'

Alex stared at Meehan. Was this insanity? he wondered. Or was it logic? Or both?

'Within the week I had been promoted to the IRA's Army Council and Padraig Byrne to the Executive. I continued to file reports to London, but I no longer had the slightest confidence they would be acted upon. I warned them of two bombs: one in a Shankhill pub, one in a Ballysillan supermarket. Both were made by men I had trained, both were set by Bronagh Quinn. Five dead, in total, and over twenty injured. Women and children mostly, in the supermarket. One little girl was blinded when the lenses of her glasses were blown backwards into her eyes.

'There are seven people on the Provisional IRA's Army Council. At the first meeting I attended I looked round the other six faces and I realised that I had done at least as much for the movement as any of them. I had dicked, trailed, scouted, bugged, planned, organised, designed, strategised and taught. I had brought the movement's bomb-making skills into line with the best in the world. And finally, with my bare hands, I had killed. By ignoring every warning I ever sent, Fenwick and her people had made me part of the thing I had dedicated my life to destroying. Can you imagine – *can you imagine* – what that feels like?'

Alex said nothing. Didn't move. Carried on the buffeting wind – distant at first and then louder – was the pulse of an approaching helicopter. If Meehan heard it he ignored it.

'At that first meeting a former OC of the Armagh and Fermanagh Brigade got up. Nasty bastard, name of Halloran.'

'Dermot Halloran,' said Alex.

'The same,' confirmed Meehan. 'And he didn't fuck about. He told us, "Boys . . . We have a problem. We have a mole." There had been indications for some time, he said, that information concerning upcoming operations was reaching the Crown. Top-level information, not foot-soldier stuff. In recent

301

days, he said, these suspicions had become cast-iron. MI5 had an agent in place – an agent whose minimum possible level of seniority was membership of the GHQ staff. That put every man in the room squarely in the frame. The Executive had men on the case, he went on. It was a process of elimination, and until that process had run its course it had been decided that all operations and meetings should be suspended.'

The rhythmic beat of the helicopter's engine and the slash of its rotors was very close now, filling their ears. The sound seemed to hold its volume for a moment, then died away. Again, Meehan showed no sign of having heard it.

'Presumably,' said Alex, 'they wanted to see who cut and ran.'

'That was my calculation. If they'd been sure they were going to identify the mole they would have just let the wheels turn. Said nothing.'

'So what did you do?'

'I drove back to the city and went home. There was a nutting squad waiting for me and I knew then that Five had sold me out. Well, I'll spare you the details but there was a fuck of a battle. I dropped a couple of them, dived through a window and drove like fuck for Aldersgrove.'

'The airport?'

'Yeah. I was on a flight to the mainland within the hour. From that point I was totally on my own. The next morning I cleared the account MI5 had been paying money into all those years and set about establishing a new identity.'

'Did you contact MI5?'

'Are you joking . . . If I'd contacted them they'd have dropped my co-ordinates to PIRA. Within the week of my leaving Belfast every Provy stiffer in the Command was on my tail as it was. No, Five didn't want me alive and compromised – my story would bury them.'

'But why do you think they ignored all those warnings and let Wheen and Bledsoe and the rest of them die?'

'I thought for a long time that they simply couldn't risk me. That if they'd started acting on my warnings they'd have had to pull me out, whereas as things stood I was their man inside the

IRA, the justification for their budget, their meal ticket from the Treasury. That was what I thought at first.'

'Go on.'

'And then – finally – I figured it out. There had to be another British mole. An agent who had been in place not for years but for decades. A man I'd been set up to take the fall for.'

He fell silent for a moment.

'It was something Barry Fenn had said years earlier about there being suspicion in the senior ranks of PIRA that a British agent was defusing the bombs the organisation was making. At the time, all that I heard were the words that applied to me – i.e. "suspicion", "PIRA" and "British agent". I didn't stop to ask myself the vital question: *how the fuck did Barry Fenn know what the senior ranks of PIRA were thinking? I didn't know, so how did he?*

'They had someone all along. One of the very top men, is my guess. And in case such a man ever came under the faintest suspicion of providing information to the Crown forces, it would be necessary to have a decoy set up. Another agent who could be exposed, proved to be the real source and fed to the wolves.'

Alex shook his head and sank back against the granite. 'Enter the Watchman,' he murmured.

'Congratulations!' said Dawn Harding. 'I do believe you've got there at last.'

She was standing above and to one side of them, and her Walther PPK was levelled straight between Alex's eyes.

TWENTY-NINE

She had brought back-up with her, a blank-faced man in a flying jacket carrying an MP5 Heckler and Koch sub-machine gun.

Had the two of them found Meehan dead, Alex knew, there would have been no problem. Anything that Meehan might have told Alex would have been cancelled out by the fact that Alex had killed him – the SAS officer could hardly broadcast a story that culminated with a murder committed by himself.

But with Meehan alive and Alex in possession of the facts about Watchmen – even just the basic facts – the position was hopeless. A glance at Dawn and the icy flatness of those sea-grey eyes told him that she was prepared to watch him die rather than risk him telling the story. Their one-night stand, and that is all it had been, after all, counted for nothing – less than nothing.

You stupid . . .

She and her back-up man would kill the pair of them, and place their disposal in the hands of a cleaner team. One thing was certain: neither body would ever be found.

Having said that, he was still holding the Glock. Still had Meehan's Browning in his pocket.

'Why isn't this animal dead?' Dawn asked, glancing scornfully at Meehan.

'I wouldn't worry yourself,' said Alex coldly. 'I don't think he's going to grow much older.'

She shook her head sorrowfully. 'You *idiot*,' she spat. 'You arrogant fucking *idiot*, Alex! Why didn't you do as you were asked? Can't you see what you're forcing me to . . .'

304

She continued, but Alex was no longer listening. He was holding his Glock in his right hand; with his left, which was concealed beneath his smock, he was trying to inch Meehan's Browning from his waistband. His only chance of escaping what would effectively be an execution was to trust Meehan. The man was two parts insane to one part brilliant soldier, that much was obvious, but . . . The Browning was clear of the waistband, now, and heavy in his hand. With infinite slowness he lowered it to the ground beneath his smock.

'And this man,' Alex asked Dawn, indicating the expressionless figure of Meehan. 'Can you begin to imagine what your people have forced him to do? To torture and kill British agents? To stand back and watch as bombs that he has designed cut women and children to pieces?'

Alex's question was designed to allow him to turn to the former agent. Catching the other man's eyes, he glanced downwards once, saw from the swift flicker of response that Meehan had understood him, felt the first unmistakable rush of adrenalin.

Prepare. Breathe. Only the target exists. Hear nothing, feel nothing, see nothing. Only the target.

Without warning, Alex propelled himself forward. He rolled once, his wounded back smashing with agonising force into the granite rock face, then the air screamed and ruptured as rounds from the MP5 impacted around him. The back-up man's first shots had been fired from the hip and as Alex tightened on the trigger of the Glock – *foresight, backsight, focus, exhale* – he saw the familiar movement as the weapon was pulled to the shoulder.

The back-up man had just closed his left eye in preparation for the aimed killing shot when both the Glock's 9mm rounds punched through his chin and thence his cerebellum, spraying the rocks behind him with red and ending his life in less than a third of a second.

Dawn's Walther was swinging towards Alex and the back-up man was still falling to the blood-shined granite when Meehan fired. The single round took Dawn in the centre of the chest,

305

dropping her to her knees as if praying. As her Walther fell from her fingers, Meehan instinctively lowered the Browning for the double tap to the head.

Alex signalled for him to hold his fire and scrambled back up the hillside towards her.

'Dawn?' he said quietly, making safe and pocketing the Walther. 'Can you hear me?'

But Dawn Harding was very close to death. Meehan's shot had taken her through the sternum, and oxygenated lung blood was frothing at her mouth.

'Dawn?' he repeated, feeling beneath her T-shirt for the sucking chest wound and sealing it with his thumb. '*Dawn!*'

She raised her head and managed a painful smile, showing reddened teeth. 'Tell Angela . . .' she began. 'Tell her I . . .'

She fell silent, and tears ran down her cheeks. Then the blood came with a rush, pouring from her mouth on to her chest, and her head sank down and she died.

Switching off all feeling, Alex wiped his Glock on his shirt and placed it between Dawn's unresisting fingers. Taking the Browning from Meehan, who handed it over without hesitation, he cleaned it and placed it in the dead back-up man's right hand. The scenario wouldn't hold up for very long, but any investigation would lead the police straight back to MI5, at which point the case would disappear from the register anyway.

He turned to Meehan. 'Thank you,' he said.

'She was going to kill you,' said Meehan quietly. 'Don't go through the rest of your life wondering.'

'I won't,' promised Alex.

The ghost of a smile touched Meehan's pale features. 'We'd have made a good team, you and I,' he said.

Alex looked at the man who had shot Dawn Harding. 'We probably would,' he said emptily. 'How badly are you hurt?'

'Does that make any difference to anything?'

Alex didn't reply. Staring over the valley he watched as sunlight and shadow raced each other across the flank of Fan Fawr. Then, taking the MP5 from where it had fallen beside the dead MI5 agent, he searched the corpse for spare magazines.

Finally he turned back to Meehan. 'Do you think you could ride a motorcycle?' he asked.

THIRTY

The members' writing rooms at the Carlton Club are reached by means of a corridor leading off the Small Library, and overlook St James's Street. There are four of them, and each contains a desk surmounted by a blotter and a sheaf of the club's writing paper. The walls are lined with books, and in reading room number four the majority of these are blue-bound records of the club's minutes and proceedings from the Second World War to the present day.

It was now a fortnight since the events on the western slope of Pen-y-Fan. Walking a half-mile up the road from the wrecked BMW, Alex had stolen a battered Fiesta from outside a hillwalkers' hostel, driven to north London – an area with which he had no connection – booked into a bed-and-breakfast hotel in Tottenham under a false name, and spent the days that followed allowing his wounds to heal and planning his next move. His single trip into Central London had been an underground journey to Oxford Circus to withdraw cash from a dispensing machine and he had been back in Tottenham within the hour. On the tube he had read the *Daily Telegraph*'s elaborate account of the 'Civil Servant love tryst' that had 'ended in tragedy' in the shadow of the Black Mountains.

The shot that had creased Alex's back had been acutely painful for several days and would certainly leave a spectacular scar, but had not required any medical attention that he himself had been unable to administer with the help of Dettol and bandages. The knife cuts, with their stitches finally removed, were now no more than pale and occasionally uncomfortable reminders of the fight outside George Widdowes' house. On his thirteenth day at the bed and breakfast he had rung the offices of MI5.

As Alex entered number four reading room at the Carlton Club, he heard the clock in the library strike 11 a.m. Angela Fenwick rose from the desk facing the window, turned and extended her hand to him. 'Captain Temple,' she said, nodding dismissal to the elderly club servant hovering at the door. 'Right on time.'

Alex inclined his head, shook her hand in silence and seated himself in the proffered armchair, a tautly upholstered object of oak and azure leather. Fenwick herself resumed her place at the desk, angling her chair towards Alex. She looked older, thought Alex. Sharp lines had been incised at the corners of her mouth and her skin had a dry, desiccated quality that had not been apparent at their last meeting.

She steepled her fingers, a gesture that Alex remembered from his first briefing with her. 'Given that you have just killed two well-liked members of my Service, Captain Temple, I thought it advisable that we meet on neutral territory rather than at Thames House. I thought it might be more . . . comfortable for you.'

Neutral territory, thought Alex, glancing around him. Like fuck. 'I have no regrets whatsoever about killing Dawn Harding and that other amateur trigger man of yours,' he said coldly, 'given that they were trying bloody hard to kill me. Presumably on your direct orders. And you might as well know right now . . .'

'Captain Temple . . .'

'. . . that I will do the same to any . . .'

'*Captain Temple*! I have not come here to argue with you. I fully accept that circumstances led you to defend yourself. Reciprocally, I would ask you to accept that agents Harding and Muir acted as they did towards yourself in the belief that it was in the best interests of national security.'

'Trying to murder a serving SAS officer?'

309

'Put it how you like.' Fenwick's gaze was ice and her voice was steel. 'The point is that these events have happened and you and I must now discuss . . . modalities.'

'Does that mean that you want to hammer out some kind of deal?'

'That's exactly what it means, Captain Temple, so let's get right on with it. Be assured that I am enjoying this meeting no more than you are. Firstly, do you wish to continue with your army career?'

Alex shrugged. 'I want to be in the position to choose to, if that's what you mean.'

'Very well. I give you my word that you will be left alone. No complaint will be made about your conduct. All that I require is that you never speak of the events surrounding Meehan and the Watchman operation. Not to your colleagues, not to Bill Leonard, not to anyone.'

'And meanwhile you work out how to get rid of me,' said Alex with an ironic smile. 'What's it going to be, an accident on the firing range? A climbing fall? Some mystery virus?'

'Captain Temple, I . . .'

'Because let me tell you, if anything happens to me – anything fatal, that is – a package will be delivered to the offices of a certain national newspaper. That package will contain an MP5 machine-gun together with various expended cartridge cases – all bearing fingerprints, an affidavit sworn before a solicitor by me and a recording of a conversation I had with Dawn Harding on the drive down to Black Down House, in which she discusses in some detail the trapping and killing of Joseph Meehan. It's not watertight, but it's enough to sink you.'

Fenwick pursed her lips but otherwise remained expressionless.

'I've got a copy of the tape here,' continued Alex, taking a Sony Walkman cassette player from his pocket. He pressed the play button.

'*Negative thought leads to negative action . . .*' came Dawn's distinctive voice. '*Just promise me that if there's any chance of taking Meehan out . . .*'

To Alex's amazement he saw Fenwick's eyes sharpen with tears. She turned away from him instantly and pretended to examine her notes. When she looked up again, steely as ever, it was as if the moment had never been. 'Very well, captain. I take your point and I acknowledge that you have the wherewithal to do us serious damage. Let me respond by saying that if you ever discuss or disclose details of this matter pre-emptively – without provocation from my Service – then we will move to defend ourselves in the most . . . vigorous way. Certain accusations will surface – deeply damaging accusations, both of a criminal and sexual nature. You will lose your pension, your credit rating and your reputation. Serious doubts will be cast upon your state of mind. We will do, in short, whatever is necessary to discredit and ultimately ruin you.'

Alex nodded. He believed her. 'Mutually assured destruction,' he murmured.

'Quite so, Captain Temple. A highly effective deterrent in my experience. Do we have a deal?'

Alex met her unwavering gaze, saw in it an iron determination the equal of his own. 'We have a deal.'

They shook hands and there was a long silence. Fenwick stared down at the traffic.

'Are you in contact with Meehan?' she asked eventually.

Alex shook his head. 'No.'

'Rest assured we will pursue him.'

'I'm sure.'

'And we will find him.'

The ghost of a smile touched Alex's features. 'If you say so.'

Fenwick hesitated. 'Captain, would you like to know the real purpose of the Watchman operation?'

'Meehan worked that one out. He was a fall guy – there to take the drop for some longer-established mole. If the shit ever hit the fan and your senior man was threatened, there had to be someone else who could be revealed as a British agent. Meehan was that man.'

Fenwick nodded. 'That's correct. And the longer he stayed in

311

place, the more believable it would be that he was the only mole if he had to be exposed.'

Alex stood up, closed his eyes in frustrated disbelief and shook his head. 'But you sent . . . how many is it now, must be at least a dozen soldiers and civilians to their deaths? To terrible deaths, mostly. And all for the sake of a single intelligence source? Do you honestly think that's a price worth paying?'

'Look, captain, given what we know about each other I think I can trust you with this. The point is that the man the Watchman was dummying for was not just *a* mole, he was *the* mole. The ultimate intelligence source. Have you heard of an agent code-named Steak Knife?'

Alex's eyes widened. 'I've heard about Steak Knife and read about him in the papers – all that stuff about Brian Nelson and the FRU handing over PIRA players' addresses to the UVF – but I didn't know that he actually existed. I assumed that was all black propaganda.'

'Well, of course it is, in part,' said Fenwick with a pale smile. 'But Steak Knife exists all right. And when the history of espionage finally comes to be written, our running of him as an agent will be seen as the greatest coup of them all. He's the very top man, Temple – an international household name – and he's working for British Intelligence.'

'You mean . . .' Into Alex's mind swam the now statesman-like image of the figure he'd seen a thousand times on magazine covers and on television.

'I do mean,' said Fenwick. 'I'm not prepared to sit here and actually name him to you, but yes. He's ours.'

She looked over at Alex who, still standing, was staring bleakly out of the window over St James's.

'Do you begin to understand the scale of the field of battle now, Temple? Forget the casualties – you always get those. At the end of the day, as you well know, there's always the equivalent of the boy left tied to the tree in the Sierra Leone bush. You have to see the big picture.'

Alex closed his eyes. Felt his fingernails cutting into the flesh of his palms.

'The point to grasp,' continued Fenwick, 'is that having a direct handle on IRA policy has saved hundreds, perhaps thousands . . .'

'I can't,' said Alex flatly.

'Can't what?'

'I can't forget the casualties. I can't forget the Wheens and the Bledsoes, and the women and kids blown to smithereens in the supermarkets. I can't forget the boy tied to the tree. The human level – the level on which that stuff happens – is the only real level as far as I'm concerned. The rest is bollocks.'

'Well, that's hardly a very adult attitude. Your Service career's unlikely to prosper if that's how you think.'

'I'm sure you're right,' said Alex. He pulled a book from the bookcase at random, opened it, stared sightlessly at the page for a moment and returned it. 'You were lovers, weren't you? You and Dawn?'

Fenwick said nothing.

'I always used to tease her. Who's the lucky bloke you wake up next to, I used to say, missing the obvious by a mile.'

Fenwick sat unmoving, as if carved from stone.

'And now she's dead,' Alex continued. 'I watched her drown in her own blood on the side of Pen-y-Fan, and the last thing that she said before she died was your name. And you still – *you still* – think that this whole thing was worth it . . .'

He moved towards the door, glanced back at the motionless figure. 'Have a good life, Fenwick. I'd tell you to go to hell, but I reckon that you're probably already there.'

Marching through the dining room and down the main staircase with an alacrity rarely seen in that august institution, Alex departed the Carlton Club. It was midday and after an unpromising start the sun was making a go of it.

Pausing for a moment at the club portals, Alex took out his phone and scrolled through the numbers stored in its memory. After a moment's hesitation he selected one.

'Yep?'

'It's Alex.'

There was a long silence. In the background he could hear

the sound of female voices, shrieks, laughter. In the foreground, her breathing.

'Sophie?'

'Yes,' she said quietly. 'I'm still here.'

POSTSCRIPT
London

By 4 p.m. it was already dark and the rain-slicked pavements of Mayfair gleamed beneath the streetlights. As the driver nosed the big Jaguar into the electric glare of Piccadilly, Angela Fenwick turned to the HarperCollins publicity girl for a final confirmation that she was looking presentable, that everything was in place. Swivelling her head so that both sides of her face could be assessed, she received the publicity girl's smiling confirmation. Presentation, Angela knew, was everything at these affairs. Photographers would do anything to catch celebrities off guard – even a new-born celebrity like herself, who had only emerged blinking into the flashlight of public regard a week earlier.

The launch at the club last night had gone wonderfully well, she mused, but then it wasn't every day that a senior member of MI5 went public with her memoirs. Everyone had come: Tony and Cherie – Cherie looking *lovely*, as usual – Gordon and Sarah of course, Patrick Mayhew, Mo Mowlam looking like something out of the *Arabian Nights*, Salman Rushdie (and boy, did that man owe her a favour), Tony Parsons . . . And Peter of course – *dear* Peter – with head held high since his vindication in the Hinduja passport business. The evening had been a triumph, with the only sour note struck by a scuffle between the security people and a rather tiresome group of civil rights demonstrators. In a way even that little embarrassment had worked in their favour. A paparazzo had been at hand to photograph the incident and the picture had made the cover of the *Evening Standard*.

The publishers had been marvellous, all in all, pulling out all

315

the stops, footing the not inconsiderable bill without a murmur. 'We can only sell your memoirs once, Angela,' they'd told her. 'So let's go for broke!'

And they had. Naturally she hadn't put in any of the really top-secret stuff; that went completely against the grain. But there had been plenty of colour, plenty of telling detail and plenty of human touches. She'd even managed to include a couple of David Trimble's famous 'knock, knock' jokes, a good Martin McGuinness fishing story and the account of how, on April Fool's day 2000, Jack Straw had officially requested that she tap Ali G's phone.

On a more serious note she'd well and truly stuck it to those bastards over at Vauxhall Cross. That had been the real pleasure – kicking MI6 in the teeth. Without ever saying so directly, she'd managed to paint a picture of smug, pin-striped, public-school, all-male arrogance – an arrogance that spilt over with wearying regularity into reckless freebooting on the inter-national stage. Bosnia, Russia, Serbia, Iraq . . . What the sacked MI6 whistle-blower Richard Tomlinson had started with his exposé of Britain's overseas Intelligence Service, Angela Fenwick had finished.

The career-ending deal had been presented to her shortly after Downing Street had been presented with the facts con-cerning the violent deaths of four Service employees. Her failure to protect her people, she had been told, indicated a dangerously cavalier attitude. Resign, she had been told. Go now, honourably and with a full pension. Jump before you're pushed.

It wasn't just the murders, she'd guessed. The Home Office had wanted one of their own sort at the helm at Thames House – it was as simple as that. A white, heterosexual, privately educated male. Someone who spoke their language. Someone they could do business with. Someone who'd behave in a civilised manner concerning Security Services budget deals rather than fighting tooth and nail for every penny. It wasn't to do with the Watchman murders, ultimately. The murders were just an excuse.

So she'd jumped. They'd won. And she had started collecting

up all the notes she'd made over the years. And *A Career Less Ordinary* had been born.

Annabel, the HarperCollins publicity girl, had been particularly sweet and in the run-up to publication the two of them had become quite close. Not quite close enough to fill the aching void left by Dawn, of course – eighteen months after Dawn's death Angela still thought of her protégée every day – but close enough for Angela to look forward to the upcoming publicity tour, and the nights *à deux* in the big provincial hotels.

The tour itself would start tomorrow; today was the big London signing. They'd decided to do just the one, at Waterstones in Piccadilly. The event had been well advertised and according to Annabel, who'd phoned ahead to the shop, there was a good crowd building.

The driver swung the Jaguar across the traffic in a swash-buckling U-turn, pulled up outside Waterstones, and hurried round to open the passenger door.

Dismounting, Angela noticed a tramp in a grease-shined windcheater lounging by the bookshop's main entrance. As she passed him the stubbled, wild-eyed figure raised a can of Special Brew to her in ironic celebration. To add insult to injury he was sitting immediately beneath a poster of herself and her book. The former civil servant averted her gaze in displeasure. The PM *hated* the sight of derelicts in up-scale shopping areas – he'd told her so himself – and yet one still saw sights like this. Weren't Waterstones responsible for their own stretch of pavement? she wondered irritably. She'd get Annabel to have a word with the manager.

Inside the shop Angela was shown to a staffroom, where she left her coat, shook hands with the Waterstones floor manager, declined a cup of coffee and greeted Dave Holland, the ex-RMP officer responsible for her personal security.

'Your fans look docile enough,' said Holland, who had just returned from a recce of the shop floor. 'I'm happy if you are.'

'OK, David, let's do it,' said Angela, briefly unsnapping her handbag to check that she had a pen. She had – an old MI5-issue Pentel.

The signing desk had been arranged at the centre of the shop floor, facing the Jermyn Street exit. It was flanked on one side by dump bins of *A Career Less Ordinary* and on the other by an array of photo floodlights. Behind a rope barrier a dozen photographers waited with Nikons primed. The big photo opportunity involved a handshake with Judi Dench, who played 'M' in the James Bond films. There was a new picture upcoming, and even though 'M' was actually supposed to be the director of the hated Six, Angela was forced to admit to herself that the showbiz association was a flattering one. There was Judi now, approaching from the opposite side of the shop. They'd met once before, at a small dinner at the Ivy.

As the actress approached the desk, and John Barry's *Goldfinger* theme played over the shop's PA system, Angela's heart quickened. This was *fun*!

The two women greeted each other and sustained a long handshake for the cameras. Angela ritually presented the actress with a signed copy of *A Career Less Ordinary* and told her – truthfully, as it happened – that she'd always been a big James Bond fan.

At the photographers' request there were more posed shots. Then Judi Dench took her leave of the event with an actressy twinkle and a flutter of her fingers, Angela sat down and the signing session began.

Soon she was into the routine of it. *Smile, ask the name, sign, hand the book over. Smile, ask the name, sign, hand the book over. Smile . . .*

Angela was enjoying herself, enjoying the attention and the curiosity of the public. There were old-school types in Royal Artillery ties, purple-haired goths, spook-watching journalists, hygiene-deficient conspiracy theorists, radical feminist academics and a host of other London types. One by one, beneath the watchful gaze of Dave Holland, who stood to one side of the desk, they moved forward with their copies of the book.

At the author's side Annabel beamed proprietorially, keeping an eye on the *Daily Telegraph* profilist who was due to interview

318

Angela after the signing. With the exception of a single freelancer the photographers had departed.

Smile, ask the name, sign, hand the book over. Smile, ask the name . . . A pair of Waterstones assistants kept the pyramids of books around the desk stocked from packing cases.

'Geoffrey!' Angela murmured to a particularly well-connected political commentator. 'How sweet of you. How are Sally and the children?'

The writer replied courteously and moved away. His place was taken by a horsy woman in a Puffa jacket.

'What name?' Angela asked mechanically. In the queue behind the horsy woman she caught sight of the stubbled face of the tramp she had seen outside the shop. To her surprise, despite his wild appearence, he was carrying a copy of the book. The horsy woman's lips moved soundlessly.

'I'm sorry?' said Angela, 'I didn't quite . . .'

The woman repeated a name – her husband's, she explained – and Angela signed and then abruptly stopped. Where the hell did she know that face from? The features were wind-roughened and the clothes dirty but there had been a time, she was sure, when this man had been somebody.

But then so many people had been somebody once.

The horsy woman retired and the man handed Angela his copy of *A Career Less Ordinary*. He was smiling, he smelt of beer and the streets, and there was something both intimate and expectant in his smile.

Am I meant to know him?

'What name?' she ventured.

'You don't remember?' he said quietly. 'Angela, I'm disappointed! It's Joe, Joe Meehan.'

Beyond thought, but not yet connected to terror, she started to take the book, to open it to the title-page. And then, gasping, she saw its starched covers close over her hand. She had lost control of her fingers. It was as if they were frost-bitten. Her whole body was frozen.

It had been she – Angela – who had ordered Dawn to take a foot-soldier and eliminate Temple when he had called in to say that he had captured Meehan on Pen-y-Fan. The chances that the former agent had told the SAS officer the truth about Operation Watchman were just too great.

And then, just hours later, Dawn and her back-up man had been found dead. Of Temple and Meehan there had been no sign. Well, she'd found out Temple's whereabouts soon enough but Meehan . . .

Joseph Meehan was dead and buried.

He had to be.

She'd believed it and not believed it. When she left the Service she'd been stripped of the close protection team that had surrounded her for so many years. And, now − here was the irony − there was no one she could go to and say: this man may be alive. And if he is alive he will try and kill me . . .

The weeks had become months and the months had become a year, and still there had been no sign of Meehan, and finally she had begun to relax. Her official security had been stepped down to just one officer and she had begun to tell herself that the Watchman was indeed dead . . .

Dave Holland, recognising at some unconscious level that things were wrong, that the moment was horribly out of joint, stared at the desk. His eyes narrowed as the bearded man held his principal's gaze. What the fuck was going down?

Angela Fenwick, he belatedly realised, was terrified. Paralysed with terror, like a bird faced by a cobra. She couldn't even move.

At Holland's side the photographer had realised something was up too. The big F3 Nikon was already moving up towards his face. Beside the desk the *Daily Telegraph* writer stared in puzzlement at the motionless tableau. Then Meehan pulled out a Browning automatic and jammed the point of the barrel beneath Angela Fenwick's chin.

Mayhem. Dave Holland was aware of a distorted screaming, of panicked bodies falling in slow motion to the floor, of the languid *chakka-chakka-chakka* of the Nikon's motor-drive.

He dived for the gun, but impeded by the press of bodies around him fell disastrously short. A shot, meanwhile, rang out simultaneously with the Nikon's final exposure. This image, which British newspaper picture desks would suppress but which would be syndicated worldwide, showed Meehan in profile. He looked almost courteous. Angela Fenwick's expression, by contrast, was one of incomprehending terror as a spectral tiara of skull fragments and other matter leapt from her head.

The moment after the shot rang out – although no one would remember this afterwards – Joseph Meehan turned to a man in a battered leather jacket who was standing at the back of the crowd. A long look passed between the two men, a look identical to that which had once passed between them in St Martin's churchyard, Hereford. Then Meehan placed the barrel of the Browning automatic into his mouth, pulled the trigger for a second time and blew his brains into the fiction shelves.

No one noticed the man in the battered leather jacket slip out through the heavy glass exit doors into Jermyn Street. In his hand was the edition of the *Evening Standard* in which the signing session had been detailed. Climbing into the passenger seat of a silver Audi TT convertible which was idling at the kerb, he reached out and, after a moment's hesitation, touched the chestnut-brown hair of the girl behind the wheel. She, in her turn, fractionally inclined her head towards him. A close observer might have detected a certain wariness between the two of them.

But there was no observer. The car pulled quietly away and by the time the first police sirens were audible, the couple had vanished.